CLAIMING MARCUS

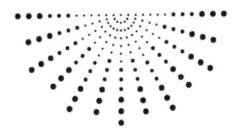

JOCELYNN DRAKE

This book is a work of fiction. Names, characters, places, and incidents are products of the author's imagination or are used factiously and are not to be construed as real. Any resemblance to actual events, locales, or organizations, or persons, living or dead, is entirely coincidental.

CLAIMING MARCUS Copyright ©2019 Jocelynn Drake. All rights reserved under International and Pan-American Copyright Conventions. By payment of the required fees, you have been granted the nonexclusive, nontransferable right to access and read the text of this e-book onscreen. No part of this text may be reproduced, transmitted, introduced into any information storage and retrieval system, in any form or by any means, whether electronic or mechanical, now known or hereinafter invented, without the express written permission of Jocelynn Drake.

Cover art by Stephen Drake of Design by Drake.

Edited and proofed by Flat Earth Editing.

For Mira & Danaus.
You were first.

CHAPTER ONE

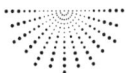

*M*ay 5, 1843

MARCUS LEANED HIS FOREARM ON THE MANTLE, STARING DOWN at the cold, empty grate. From the hall, he could hear the insistent ticking of the grandfather clock as if the damn thing was counting each of the final seconds of his life with a steady determination.

The rest of the house was silent. The few servants he dared to keep around were still asleep in their beds at the top of the house for another couple of hours. His youngest brother, Winter, sat in the dark leather wingback chair close to the window, turning a gold coin over and over again between his fingers. Its shiny surface would catch and toss out flashes of light, but he paid no notice. His gaze was locked on a distant point Marcus knew was not in the room.

One of his other brothers, Beltran, was reading a dusty science tome, seemingly oblivious to the fact that their lives were balanced on a razor's edge. Tonight, everything was changing for them. Very likely ending.

The door to the library opened and Rafe, Beltran's twin, returned, his violin and bow clutched tightly in one hand. The hair at his temples was slick with sweat, and he looked a little pale, but his ever-present smirk twisted his lips. Marcus straightened from the mantle and Beltran closed his book, his quick blue eyes sweeping over his brother.

"Any trouble?" Marcus asked.

"None other than I plan to ram my bow down Bach's throat when I finally meet him in Hell," Rafe muttered. He carelessly dropped his violin and bow in a chair as he marched over to a sideboard. He opened a crystal decanter and splashed some whiskey into a glass. "I'm so bloody sick of Bach."

"Did you ever consider playing some Mendelssohn or maybe Vivaldi for her?" Winter inquired.

Marcus sighed heavily and Beltran shook his head.

"Yes, I've bloody tried Mendelssohn and Vivaldi. Do you take me for an uncultured hack?" Rafe snarled at his little brother.

"Yes," Winter said with glee in his voice.

Marcus pushed away from the fireplace and stepped into Rafe's direct path, toward Winter, his drink forgotten in his clenched hand. He used his bigger frame to block Rafe's view. Rafe's usually elegant appearance was a bit rumpled, with a starched white tie hanging limp and the top of his shirt open, exposing his slender neck and perfect pale skin. His longish dark hair was in wild disarray about his head. The ribbon he used to hold it back now missing. For all his foppish ways and strict adherence to the latest fashion trends, Rafe's body vibrated with hidden power and strength. Rafe was a bit taller than Marcus with a leaner frame, but Marcus could still handle him if necessary. They'd all grown up having one scuffle after another.

Fights were inevitable with four brothers relatively close in age, though bookish Beltran was the least prone to pick one. Winter, on the other hand, seemed to revel in his ability to get under Rafe's skin. But then, Rafe loved to talk down to his baby brother, even though there were barely four years between them. And Marcus remained the perennial peacekeeper whether he wished to be or not.

"This isn't the time," Marcus snapped.

Rafe's lips twisted into a mocking grin, and he lifted his glass in a salute. "Why not? This could be our last chance."

"Is she asleep?" Marcus questioned. He refused to acknowledge Rafe's comment, even if he had been thinking it only moments earlier.

The sneer returned when he lowered his drink. "Yes, Mother is asleep."

"Tonight's hunt?" Beltran asked. Marcus could almost imagine him pulling out a bit of parchment upon which to make a note for his scientific journals.

"Fine." His tone was a little less harsh when talking to his twin. Rafe turned away from Marcus and approached the chair that held his violin and bow. Placing his glass on a table, he picked up the instrument, showing more care now than when he'd entered the room. "The hunt was uneventful. She seemed at ease tonight. Though she's getting faster—there were a couple of times I was hard-pressed to keep up with her."

"Did she draw anyone's notice?"

Rafe sat in the chair, his fingers sliding over the polished surface of the violin in a gentle caress. "Not that I saw. Dinner survived, though they may wake up a little worse for wear come morning."

"Then the timing is right. We must act tonight. This quiet spell will make it easier for her to accept the change," Marcus said.

Rafe snorted. "Except we never know how long her quiet

spells will last. Tomorrow night she could wake in another of her black moods."

"You're also assuming that this will work at all," Winter added.

"We need to decide." There was a soft clinking of a chain and a click as Beltran opened his pocket watch to check the time. "Aiden should be here any minute now."

"I think we should alter our original plan," Marcus announced.

Three sets of blue eyes jumped to him, and he straightened under their scrutiny. He'd been giving this a great deal of thought over the past several years. Their original plan had been full of brotherly love and unity as well as all the rash, impetuousness of youth. But it was flawed and dangerous. He'd made his decision a couple of years ago but had known it was futile to bring it up sooner so they could all argue about it *ad nauseam*. Aiden's imminent arrival forced them to remain brief.

"And how, dear eldest brother, do you think we should alter a plan we all agreed to more than fourteen years ago?" Rafe's words dripped with derision.

"It is foolish for Aiden to change us all at the same time. Not when we're unsure of how it will turn out. I believe he should take me to his home and change me there while you continue to watch over mother. If all goes as planned, I will return and take over her care."

"No!" Winter sat up in his chair, balancing on the edge as if he meant to leap to his feet and launch himself at Marcus.

"And what if all does not go as planned?" Rafe demanded. "Does Aiden kill you on the spot? You just disappear from our lives without so much as a fond farewell?"

"Yes."

"Absolutely not." Rafe crossed his arms tightly over his chest and directed his most mutinous glare at Marcus. "We are sticking with our original plan. We've waited fourteen years for

Winter to reach his twenty-third birthday. We do this together, or we don't do this at all."

"And if something goes wrong with all of us? Do you think it's wise to leave Aiden alone to deal with the mess? What if he can't?" Marcus countered.

"Actually, it's highly unlikely for all of us to have trouble similar to Mother," Beltran chimed in. "Aiden and I have discussed it at length. Mother was troubled before the change. We all saw signs of it prior to her falling ill. I think we should have no problems tonight. I believe our biggest concern will be Mother's reaction when she awakes tomorrow night, but the four of us should be able to manage her just fine."

"Bel, dear," Rafe said with a smile. "We have no idea when our sweet mother started losing her mind. It could have happened later in life, and it could still be waiting for any of us."

Beltran gave a little roll of his eyes at his twin, long used to his brother's somewhat condescending tone. The two brothers didn't look much alike other than the fact that they had similar lean builds. But where there were hints of muscle under Rafe's tailored suit from his hours of boxing at Gentleman Jim's, Beltran was slimmer thanks to his preference for hours spent in his library or laboratory.

"True, but I don't think the odds are great that all four of us will be afflicted," Beltran said.

"I still think it is best if I go alone first," Marcus persisted.

"And then what?" Winter snapped. He rose to his feet and took a couple of steps closer to Marcus. He was several inches shorter than Marcus and smaller in build—the smallest of all of them, but there was a fiery intensity to him that made everyone who knew him learn quickly not to dismiss him. "Let us say that all goes well. Do we follow you one at a time? And how long would we wait to know that all truly is well?"

Marcus's lips pressed into a hard, thin line as he quickly tried to weigh his words, searching for the right thing to say. He should have known this would be asked and prepared a better response.

Rafe chuckled, the sound ugly and almost cruel. "I think our overbearing brother means to go down this dark path alone."

"Marcus?"

Marcus twisted to find Beltran standing as well, a look of pained concern on his face. "You would leave us behind?"

"Only one of us is needed to watch over Mother," Marcus replied, trying to reason with them.

"Ever the martyr," Rafe mocked.

"Yes, willing to sacrifice himself to an eternity of guarding Mother," Winter added.

"You could still have normal lives," Marcus said.

"And we're just supposed to allow you to skip off to damnation alone?"

Marcus wanted to tell Winter that he was already damned. That his life was doomed to be a living hell even before their mother had been transformed, but no matter how close he was with his siblings, he could not bring himself to voice his personal shame. No, this was his only option. If all went well, he'd be dedicating his life to something good for the world. And if not, then at least his miserable existence would be over.

"We're in this together, Marcus," Rafe said. "It was decided fourteen years ago, and we're sticking to the plan."

"Five years," Marcus said. "If all goes well with me, we meet again in five years and Aiden changes another if you still wish it."

"No," Beltran said, surprising Marcus with the hardness of his tone. "We do this together tonight, or we don't do it at all."

Rafe plucked the strings of his violin, sending several discordant notes winging through the room. "Looks like that's three-to-one, old man. You're outvoted."

Marcus shook his head, an odd mix of warmth and sadness stirring in his chest. "It doesn't have to be this way."

He couldn't say he was entirely surprised. Despite their constant bickering, they had always been close and eager to protect one another. No matter who or what they faced, no brother ever stood alone.

A hand landed on his shoulder, and Marcus looked over to see Beltran standing beside him, his expression resolute. "It does."

"It's decided, then."

They all looked up at the new, deeper voice to find Aiden standing in the open doorway. Marcus was sure there had been no sound of him entering the house or walking across the hardwood floor of the entrance. The man moved as silently as a shadow. He was handsome with thick brown hair and rich brown eyes that seemed to catch and reflect the light the same way as Winter's gold coin.

Sadness clung to Aiden like a damp fog. When they'd first met years earlier, he'd been so joyous and quick to laugh when he was around their mother, but with her declining health and then his unfortunate attempt to save her life, the sadness had become a permanent part of Aiden. Marcus knew Aiden blamed himself for their mother's current erratic state, but neither he nor his brothers blamed Aiden. He'd tried to save their mother. That was more than they could say for the dour parade of doctors that had marched in and out of her bedchambers.

Now, fourteen years later, they were finally able to pursue a solution to their problem. And if this didn't work, there was only one option left for their beloved mother and the four brothers.

"We're ready," Marcus said.

Aiden reached behind him, grabbed the doorknob, and pulled the door closed as he stepped fully into the room. He looked up at Marcus, his eyes taking on an eerie copperish glow in the dim light of the library. "I'm sorry," he said, his voice barely over a whisper, "but this is going to hurt."

CHAPTER TWO

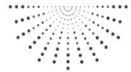

ctober 17, 2003

THE FIRST SCREAM HAD ETHAN JUMPING FROM THE BATHROOM door. That was his mother. He knew his mother's voice. He'd never heard her scream like that, but he knew her voice. Stark terror had him frozen, staring at the back of the bathroom door. He couldn't go out there. But someone had hurt his mother.

It was late. Middle of the night. He'd woken and stumbled from his bed to the bathroom to relieve his bladder. Been just about to shuffle to his room and warm bed again. It was a school day. He had a spelling test.

His father was shouting. Angry, but also in pain. Heartbroken. What had happened to his mother?

And then his father was screaming too.

Oh God, he had to hide.

Ethan turned toward the bathroom, his eyes skimming over old yellow tile and faded white walls. There was nowhere to hide. The shower curtain over the bathtub was clear, and there was no cabinet under the sink like at Kevin's house.

His eyes finally hit on the linen closet. It was tucked behind the bathroom door and was a tiny cupboard, but the back of it was made of boards rather than a regular wall like the rest of the apartment. One of the boards had come loose; his little sister, Macy, had discovered it and tucked herself into that opening when they'd played hide and seek one time. It took them over an hour to find her, and his parents had been so worried they'd almost called the cops.

Ethan silently jerked open the door and started shoving aside their various colored towels. It took a little work, but he managed to crawl into the opening. He forced his mind away from the fact that he was inside the wall. Mice and bugs crawled inside the wall. Never in his life had he ever been so grateful to be the smallest kid in his fifth grade class. It was the only reason he was able to fit in the hole.

Once in place, he pulled the stacks of towels back in front of the hole, further concealing himself. The last thing he did was carefully reach out and grab the edge of the closet door, pulling it closed as much as possible, plunging his little world into darkness.

But he could still hear.

There were sounds of pain from his father and a low gurgling he couldn't quite place. And laughter. Strangers were in his apartment and laughing.

"Mom?"

No! His older sister's voice wavered as she called for their mother. He wanted to shout at her to run, to hide. To grab Macy and get out of the apartment. He couldn't save them. Their father couldn't save their mother. What was he supposed to do? The only thing he could think to do was hide. Lucy and Macy should have been hiding too. Why weren't they hiding?

A startled scream came from Lucy, and Ethan could hear her feet pounding down the hallway, back to their bedroom. Laughter followed his sister. High-pitched evil laughter from a woman.

"*Come out, come out, wherever you are,*" the woman sang in her horrible voice.

There was a loud explosion like someone had kicked in a door, and Lucy screamed. But the scream was cut short. Macy was crying, but that too was silenced quickly.

Ethan grabbed a washcloth and shoved the balled-up mass into his mouth to keep from screaming, but there was no stopping the rush of tears down his face. His family…someone was killing his family. His sisters. They were gone. Why? Why were they doing this? His whole body trembled, and he pulled his legs tighter against his chest.

"Where's the other one?" the woman demanded. She sounded like she was in the hall again.

"What are you talking about?" someone responded. A man with a thick accent. It reminded Ethan of the time they drove hours and hours south to a family reunion in Kentucky. His dad had called it the bluegrass state, but he hadn't seen a darn bit of blue grass. A lot of the people at the reunion had thick, country accents like this man.

"There are three beds back here, but only two brats. Where's the third one?"

"No clue."

"Find him!" she snarled. A second later the bathroom door opened, and Ethan barely managed to stifle his scream. He could hear her moving around the bathroom for a moment, and then the door to the linen closet was jerked open. The woman poked her head into the closet for only a second, but for Ethan, it felt like an eternity. He was sure she could hear his pounding heart.

He got a clear view of the woman through a little opening between the towels, and he knew he'd never forget her. She had long, stringy brown hair and copperish eyes that seemed to glow in the darkness. Her pale face was narrow and streaked with blood. The blood of his family. Her thin lips were parted, revealing a pair of perfect fangs glistening with blood.

Vampire.

She was a vampire.

Oh God. Vampires were real, and they'd killed his family.

She stood at the closet for only a second and then turned to the bathroom. *"Come out, come out, wherever you are,"* she sang again.

She moved into the hall, singing that little refrain over and over again as she walked toward the front of the apartment. Ethan listened to her talking with her companions. He could make out a total of three voices. The woman and two men. They laughed like they were having the best adventure.

Ethan closed his eyes against the darkness and waited, praying for them to finally leave. Praying that he'd wake up to find this was all a horrible nightmare. He'd wake up in his warm bed with his superhero bedsheets and Lucy's soft snores. He'd wake up to his spelling test and his mom making toast as she got dressed for work at the pediatricians' office.

When Ethan opened his eyes again, he wasn't sure how much time had passed. It felt like he'd drifted off to sleep again. The apartment was completely silent. No more laughter or footsteps or unfamiliar voices. The heater kicked on, sending warm air through the apartment.

Hesitantly, Ethan crawled out of his hiding place. He left the towels pulled aside in case he needed to dive back into his secret spot. So very slowly, he peeked out the now-open bathroom door, but there was no one in the hall. Walking on tiptoes, Ethan crept toward the living room. Cold air brushed against his toes. Before reaching the living room, he glanced toward the open kitchen to find it empty.

In the living room, blood was splashed across everything. The walls, pictures, a bookcase with their collection of movies, the TV, and furniture. His mother was sprawled half across the couch, her hand lying limp on the floor. Her pretty green eyes were staring up at the ceiling and her throat had been torn out. Ethan barely managed to turn aside before he threw up on the worn living room carpet. There wasn't much, but his stomach kept spasming over and over again, as if it could purge the image from his body this way.

When he finally stopped, he wiped his mouth with the back of his hand and took another step into the living room. His dad was lying in the middle of the room on the remains of their broken coffee table. His throat was also torn out. One hand was stretched out toward Ethan's mother like he'd died trying to reach for her.

Choking on gasping sobs, Ethan turned toward the front door and was only a little surprised to find it open. He needed to locate an adult. An adult would fix this. Make sense of this. Mr. Pompideaux across the hall was nice. He could help. Call the police.

Ethan darted out the door, no longer caring about the attackers. The concrete floor of the breezeway felt icy to his bare feet, but he didn't care. It was a short distance to that—

Ethan stopped before he reached Mr. Pompideaux's apartment. The front door was standing open, and there were bloody footprints on the pavement leading from his place, just like at Ethan's. Slowly turning, Ethan looked at the other two apartments on his floor. The doors were also standing open.

The vampires had killed everyone on his floor.

Probably the entire apartment building.

Shivering in the cold night air, Ethan slowly trudged back to his apartment. He sat down on the blood-soaked carpet, next to his mother and father, his arms wrapped around his knees. Dropping his head down, he tightened his body into a little ball and cried.

He was alone. The vampires killed everyone.

CHAPTER THREE

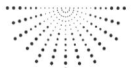

*J*uly 17, 2019

Ethan sat in the uncomfortable chair with his spine as straight as he could possibly get it, his hands pressed together in two tight fists in his lap. The borrowed suit was itchy as hell, making the whole ordeal of sitting perfectly still a nightmare. But he would not give the woman on the other side of the desk any reason to think he didn't have his shit together.

He just kept repeating to himself that in less than an hour, he'd be out of the fancy town house. He would be able to strip out of the suit and climb back into his well-worn jeans and T-shirt. For now, he could suck it up. He needed this job.

Everything hung on him getting this job.

As the woman with the pinched expression reviewed his too-short résumé, Ethan chanced a glance around the austere room. The walls were plain white and the desk, while nice, was somewhat utilitarian and entirely boring. There were no pictures on the walls or on the desk. Just stacks of folders and papers. To one side, he could see a calendar planner that was heavily marked up with notes. The room had zero personality; it was simply a place of work.

"I'll be frank with you, Mr. Cline," the woman said at last. Not a good sign. "Your résumé doesn't exactly show the qualities I am hoping to find for this position."

"I know I've worked a lot of odd jobs, but at each position, I've proved to be resourceful and showed initiative. I am incredibly organized. It's the only way I've managed to juggle three jobs and keep up with my night classes. You can call any of my references. They will confirm that I'm always on time for work and meet my deadlines."

"You understand that this is just a temporary position as Mr. Varik's personal assistant. The bulk of the duties are organizing his home and packing it for the upcoming move. The movers have been arranged for the majority of the household items, but bonded transport will need to be scheduled for some rare and priceless artifacts. In addition, this position may require the person to run various errands at all times of the day and night. This could interfere with your night classes."

"I understand," Ethan said with a quick nod. "I'm taking a semester off to save up money for the last of my schooling."

"You also understand that you will be working mostly in this house."

"Yes."

"Anyone working in the house must keep the window shades and curtains pulled closed during the day. Mr. Varik has a rare skin allergy and cannot be exposed to sunlight."

Ethan nodded, careful to keep his expression solemn while joy zinged around in his chest. That was such a good sign. *He needed this fucking job!*

The woman frowned and looked down at his résumé as if she were trying to think of a new reason to scare him from this position. Ethan wracked his brain, desperate to come up with that one thing he could say to tip the scales in his favor. He was so damn close.

Before either of them could speak, there was a sharp knock on the door followed by a man stepping into the room. Ethan's breath caught in his throat to see his tall form wrapped in a dark suit. The ice-blue tie matched his eyes perfectly, setting them off so that they seemed to glow. His black hair was long, brushing against the tops of his shoulders, and was a little wild as if windblown. Simply, he was stunning.

"Mr. Varik?" the woman said in surprise.

"Janice." His voice was low and rough, almost like two boulders grinding against each other. "What progress has been made on finding me an assistant?"

"I'm working on it, sir. I was just interviewing an applicant—"

Ethan finally broke from his dumbstruck awe and jumped to his feet, extending his hand to the tall man. Even standing, Marcus Varik towered over him by at least five inches. "Ethan Cline, sir," Ethan introduced. His heart pounded in his chest and he prayed that Marcus couldn't hear it. At least his hand didn't shake when Marcus stared at it for a second before taking it.

His hand was warm. Ethan hadn't expected that. He'd thought his skin would be cold and clammy, but he was warm. Ethan curled his fingers when their hands parted, as if he were trying to hold on to that surprising heat to study it later.

"Marcus Varik," Marcus replied. "You've been given the details of this job?"

"I was just starting to, sir," Janice said.

"I've moved several times during my life, sir," Ethan added. "I've gotten quite good at properly wrapping, labeling, and packing things away in a quick and organized fashion. I can get all your property safely moved to your new home."

"And unpacked again," Marcus said. "The job would require

you to briefly relocate to Connecticut. Your living expenses would be covered during that time as well as your travel. You would have to unpack my property and see that it is properly placed around my new home."

"That's not a problem. I love seeing new places."

"You would also be running various errands for me at all times of the day."

"Not a problem."

Marcus narrowed his eyes at Ethan. "Even at two in the morning for violin bow rosin?"

Ethan didn't even let himself blink at the strange request. "I know of an all-night super store that should carry it. I could be at the store and then here inside of an hour."

Marcus's brow furrowed as his frown deepened. "Where do you live?"

Ethan's heart stuttered in his chest, and he fought to keep his smile in place. "In the suburbs. Glenpark. But I can be here by train in about thirty minutes. I'd need to study the schedule for around two a.m., but that's not a problem."

"That's not good enough," Marcus muttered as if talking to himself. He looked around Ethan to Janice. "I want him no more than ten minutes from the town house."

"That would require downtown housing. That could be expensive." She gave a little shake of her head as if realizing at the last second what she was saying. "Of course. It will be handled today."

"Do you drive?" Marcus said.

"I'm sorry..." Ethan replied, his brain struggling to keep up. Had he just been hired? Was he getting put in a swanky new apartment downtown rather than his rat-infested studio?

"Do you drive?" Marcus repeated. From the sharpness of his tone, Ethan could guess that he was a man who did not like to repeat himself.

"Yes. Yes, I've got my license. I don't currently have a car.

Between the gas, insurance, and upkeep, it's just too expensive. But I can drive." Ethan inwardly winced. He was babbling and didn't manage to catch himself until it was too late. Marcus Varik didn't give a damn about his money troubles.

"Fine." Marcus looked at Janice again. "Add him to the insurance and see that he has access to the black Mini Cooper."

"Yes, sir."

"Birds," Marcus said suddenly, turning his attention back to Ethan. "Do you have any problem with or allergy to birds?"

Ethan struggled to keep his face completely blank in the face of that slightly insane question. Definitely not something he'd ever been asked in an interview. "Umm…no. No problems with birds."

Marcus nodded and extended his hand. "Be here promptly at ten a.m. tomorrow. I'll show you around for the first two hours, and then you can get to work. The rest of the time you will start at noon. Tonight, you will research potential places to live while you are working for me. They will need to be within a ten-minute walking distance of the town house. Have them to Janice before you arrive here tomorrow."

"Yes, sir. Thank you, sir," Ethan said, nearly laughing at his good luck.

Marcus paused long enough to acknowledge Janice with a small nod before he was gone again.

Janice sat down in her chair and cleared her throat. "I will also be checking your references. This position will remain contingent upon positive reviews, of course."

Ethan dropped back down in his chair, his knees threatening to give out in his relief. "Yes, of course. I don't think you'll have any problems. Is there any price range I should be looking in for the temporary lodging?"

Janice frowned slightly at him. "Not specifically. Mr. Varik is trusting you to use your best judgment and to not waste his money. That being said, he will not approve of you living in a slum either. There are plenty of furnished executive apartments in the area that offer short-term leases."

Ethan nodded. "I'll email you tonight with a selection of moderately priced places and organize them according to the shortest distance to the town house."

"Very good. I'll meet with you at two p.m. tomorrow so that you have a chance to sign final paperwork and fill out your healthcare benefits." Janice stood and extended her hand to him, but Ethan just sort of blinked at it in shock.

"Really? I'm getting health insurance? I thought this was only a three-month contract position." He slowly pushed to his feet, his brain trying to catch up to what she was telling him.

"This position pays twenty-five dollars an hour on the assumption that you will be working a minimum of forty hours a week. Overtime will be paid as well. You are technically a contract worker, but Mr. Varik demands that all his employees have health insurance."

"That's...that's just amazing. You have to fight most employers for health insurance, and contract workers don't have a prayer."

"Yes, well, thank you for coming in," Janice said, giving him a tiny, stiff smile as if the act of smiling at him was painful.

Ethan hurried out of the office, not wanting to give the dour woman any excuse to steal back the job offer without Mr. Varik's knowledge. He paused at the grand entrance to the four-story town house and looked around. As austere as the office was, the rest of the home appeared to be equally decadent and rich. The gleaming hardwood floors were draped in exquisite Persian rugs. Paintings covered the walls in heavy, ornate frames. There were vases and other ceramic pieces on little shelves and pedestals.

Fuck. This was going to take a long time to pack up. No wonder he was given two months.

But it was very unlikely that he was going to unpack all this stuff again.

Slipping out the front door, he hurried down the quiet residential street, immediately loosening the tie around his neck. He didn't take a full, deep breath until he was several blocks away and surrounded by a crush of people hurrying from one place to another. Safe in the idea that he was lost in a sea of faceless nobodies in the bright summer sun, Ethan pulled his cell phone from his pocket and dialed the number he'd memorized for just this moment.

"Ethan?" a gruff voice demanded after the first ring.

"Yeah."

"Did you get it?"

"I did," he said, nearly laughing with relief.

"Excellent. That's excellent, kid," Carl praised and Ethan had to clench his teeth. He fucking hated being called kid. He was twenty-six. Not some kid. But then, Carl looked like he was in his forties. Probably old enough to be Ethan's dad, not that he was. No one was anymore.

Ethan was willing to put up with Carl's "kid" comments for now if it meant getting one step closer to the fuckers who slaughtered his family.

"When do you start?" Carl asked.

"Tomorrow at ten. I'm being put up in an apartment downtown so I can be close to the town house."

"Great. Give us the address when you get it. We can set it up as a base of operations."

Ethan frowned. "We'll have to be cautious. I don't know if I'm going to be watched. If too many people are seen coming and going from my place when I'm supposed to be working, Varik might become suspicious."

"Smart, kid. We'll save it for staging the final attack."

He didn't know about that either, but he wasn't going to start a new argument with Carl. It wasn't important right now.

"I saw him today. I shook Marcus Varik's hand. Stared him right in the eye and he didn't have a clue," Ethan practically crowed.

Relief and joy were making him lightheaded. He could have danced down the sidewalk. The first step of the great plan was complete. He was inside Varik's lair.

"Good job! Varik has no idea that he's just welcomed his biggest threat right into his home. We'll talk more later."

Carl ended the call and Ethan tucked his phone into his pants. He stood on the busy street corner and tilted his face up to the sky. He blinked away tears of relief. One step closer.

His life had been a lonely, endless nightmare since that horrible night when he was only ten years old. All the love and warmth had been ripped out of his existence. Stolen away.

Killing Marcus Varik would be a start, but he knew he wouldn't feel complete until he found the blood-streaked woman from his darkest memories.

More than sixteen years later, he could still hear her taunting, high-pitched voice.

Come out, come out, wherever you are.

CHAPTER FOUR

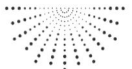

Marcus walked along, his hands shoved into the pockets of his slacks. The evening air still held on to the day's oppressive heat as if it had gotten trapped in the narrow streets of the city. It was already well after midnight, and he had no desire to be out wandering, but he'd put off his task for far too long.

His head was down as if he were oblivious to his surroundings, but he could hear the telltale scrape of worn rubber on the rough concrete. Footsteps followed him. They had started off steady but were picking up speed. He lifted his head slightly and saw the black gaping maw of the alley a few dozen feet away. The perfect place for an ambush.

He maintained his current pace while listening to the approaching person. The wind shifted and he picked up a faint hint of sweat and body odor that had him crinkling his nose in disgust. It would have almost turned his stomach, but he was already so damn hungry. His would-be attacker was not going to be saved by his poor hygiene.

Just a few feet from the alley, the figure finally reached him, shoving the muzzle of a gun deep into his lower back.

"Keep walking into the alley and you won't die," the pungent man instructed.

Marcus took one step toward the alley and quickly spun around, grabbing the wrist of his attacker with his left hand. He squeezed tight enough to feel the bones start to give. The man shouted, and the gun fell to the pavement with a noisy clatter.

Stepping in close, Marcus tried to ignore the smell that grew worse with his increasing panic. "Yes, let's go into the alley, and you might not die tonight," Marcus said calmly.

The mugger placed a hand against Marcus's chest as if to keep some distance between them, but still took one sliding, unsteady step after another until they were cloaked in the thick darkness of the unlit alley.

As soon as they were free from the view of any other midnight pedestrians, Marcus twirled the attacker as if he were a willing dance partner and slammed him face first into the brick wall. The mugger groaned, his free hand pressing against the bricks in front of him.

"Wh-what the fuck, man?"

"Silence, and this will be over quickly," Marcus snapped.

Putting his hand onto the man's shoulder, he pressed him to the wall while he dropped his head back. His fangs slid down, and some of the hunger and desperation that had been gnawing at him for the past several hours receded a tiny bit. He'd waited too long to go hunting. His mind had been too occupied with this damn move, finding a new assistant, and the endless mercurial demands of the Ministry. He'd not wanted to bother with it.

But now that he was walking in the comforting darkness of the night, holding his prey captive, that old need to feed came rushing with a sense of freedom and joy he didn't want to look too closely at. He didn't understand this part of himself, and even after more than one hundred and seventy years, he still kept it under a tight rein. The joy and the freedom felt too delicious and wicked. Too decadent. If he remained in control, there would never be any accidents. Nothing to regret later.

With a tight grip, Marcus pulled his meal a little closer. His fingers dug into the man's shirt, stretching it away from his neck. The smell of sweat and fear was growing thicker, but now that he was so close to him, Marcus could also smell his blood. The sticky sweet scent teased his nose, whispering its dark delights and forbidden promises. God, why did he wait so long to feed?

He struck quickly, digging his fangs deep, hitting veins with unerring precision. His dinner cried out again yet didn't try to escape. Marcus removed his fangs but kept his mouth over the neatly placed holes, allowing the blood to flow down his throat. He sucked hard and captured a delicious mouthful, sending it down his throat. The worst of the hunger pangs eased, and Marcus could finally give a small thought to his donor.

Tapping the swell of magic hiding behind his heart, Marcus sent a feeling of deep pleasure to the mugger. He could hear the man's heart slow from its frantic pace to a steady *thump-thump*.

A low moan escaped from the foul stranger, and Marcus could feel muscles relax in his victim as he continued to feed.

"Oh God, fuck yes," he groaned. It sounded as if he'd reached down and stroked his own hardened cock even though neither of them moved.

Marcus shifted slightly from one foot to the other as if to reassure himself that no part of his body touched his victim besides his mouth and hands. Another needy sound left the man, and it tingled along every nerve ending, sending blood straight to his cock.

Fuck, why? What the hell is wrong with me?

He knew he wouldn't have this problem if he fed off women. He'd heard their cries of pleasure, and they'd not affected him in the least. But with their smaller frames and the risk of them being pregnant, Marcus avoided women for their own safety. At least, that was what he told himself.

But those needy, desperate sounds from men as their cocks thickened and throbbed for release had his dick begging for attention every time. It shouldn't be like this. He'd thought that when he died as a human and was reborn a vampire that maybe his appetites would change as well.

No, he'd been born a gay man, and he'd been reborn a gay vampire.

Of course, times and the social climate had changed. Being a homosexual wasn't the death sentence it had once been in society. His brother Rafe certainly embraced both genders and over the past few decades had suffered no qualms about advertising his love for any and all creatures. Marcus's only problem with Rafe was that he showed no discretion.

But when it came to his own needs and desires, too many old voices rang through his head, shaming him. Life had been hell as a human, and a part of him had hoped that he wouldn't survive the conversion. That he'd finally be free of his shame.

No. Those same desires followed him into his new form, creating an eternal hell as the voices continued to scold him.

The mugger shivered and swore softly as Marcus ran his tongue over the holes he'd placed in the man's neck, wiping up the blood and spreading the healing agent in his saliva. The site of the wound would be tender for a bit, but there was no evidence of the attack.

Turning the attacker again, Marcus released his hold, allowing him to slide down the wall to sit on the dirty ground. He blinked slowly a couple of times and then kept his eyes closed, seeming to drift into a light slumber.

Marcus stared at him as he touched his mouth, checking to make sure there was no smear of blood around his lips. With everything set to rights again, Marcus walked out of the alley and continued down the street with his hands in his pockets.

There was a renewed energy to his step, and the angry hunger in the pit of his stomach was satisfied. With any luck, he wouldn't have to hunt again for another week. Maybe longer, if things stayed quiet.

Those early nights as a vampire had been annoying, with the need to feed each and every night. But then, those nights had been a little less lonely. Those first nights, he and Winter had hunted together as a way of watching out for each other as they learned more about their new selves and their powers. There had also been a feeling of Aiden being close by, as if he were watching over his new children, giving them space but still wanting to see that they were safe.

But after a few years, they started going their separate ways, hunting alone. At first, Marcus had appreciated the distance. He no longer had to worry about his little brother's eagle eyes catching his dick hardening as his victim moaned with pleasure. He was sure his shame stayed private.

As the decades passed, he found he missed those old days and that indescribable closeness. There was even a small thread of jealousy that wove through him when he saw the unshakeable bond between Beltran and Rafe. The twins were always close, from birth and even through their death. Two men couldn't be more different, but that didn't seem to have any impact on them.

At the corner, Marcus paused and looked around, getting his bearings again. Hunting always made him too damn pensive. It was better when he remained home with his books and his work. Spending too much time thinking about the past was dangerous.

With his mind clear and hunger placated, Marcus turned and continued down an older residential street. There was a mix of two-story homes with wood siding and cracked sidewalks. The trees stretched above the roofs and pushed up against the sidewalk, breaking through in spots.

Cars lined either side of the street as there were few private driveways. The houses were mostly dark, but some dim lights glowed in the windows at that late hour.

Glenpark was clearly not the safest area, particularly since his mugger was not the first one to follow him since he'd started walking through the neighborhood. But for some reason, the would-be attacker disappeared after a block. Marcus briefly wondered if maybe they had sensed that Marcus was not the weak and helpless victim he looked to be. The mugger that ended up being his meal either lacked the sense of self-preservation or was simply too desperate to heed it.

As he reached his destination, Marcus knew he was being followed again. But this time there was a familiar itching sensation right between his shoulder blades. It was an annoying, biting sensation that had him fighting the impulse to shift his shoulders, because he knew it would do no good. There was no itch. There was only Rafe.

It was curious that each warning sign associated with his brothers seemed to fit their personalities so well. Beltran was a slight pressure in his temple as if a headache were coming on. Winter brought chilled goose bumps along his forearms. And Rafe was that annoying itch that couldn't quite be reached. He never asked if they got a strange sensation when he was close or what it was. He wondered a bit now.

"My, my, dear brother," Rafe drawled behind him. "This isn't one of your usual hunting grounds."

Marcus turned slightly to his left and narrowed his eyes at Rafe's tall, lean form encased in an exquisitely tailored dark suit. His brother had been a perfectly dressed dandy in his previous life, and that had carried forward untouched into his vampire existence.

"Did you need something? Is it Mother?" he asked, preferring to ignore Rafe's comment.

Rafe gave an irritated sigh before walking the last few steps to stand by his older brother. "I've just come from checking in on Mother and our sweet Bel. Mother is fine. She's calm."

"Thank you," Marcus said simply to annoy Rafe, and it worked.

Everyone knew Rafe didn't check on their mother out of some sense of familial duty. He did it out of worry for his twin. Bel, with his mind always on his research, tended to be the worst of them when it came to watching over Julianna. He too often missed the early warning signs of her mind slipping into a bad episode, which usually ended in bloody consequences that could have been avoided. It was probably best that Marcus would be managing her care once they were all settled in Connecticut.

"Seriously, Marcus, why are you in this part of town? You prefer to hunt closer to your home."

Marcus resumed walking down the street, a frown tugging at his lips. He knew Rafe was going to keep needling him and digging at him until he finally had the truth of it. Rafe was such a nosy bastard.

"I hired a new assistant today. Ethan Cline. He lives in the neighborhood," Marcus admitted.

"Really, now?"

"He's to help prepare my household for the move and run errands as needed."

"It's a shame you couldn't keep that last one. What was her name? Carrie? Cheryl?"

Marcus paused and glared at his brother for a second. "Amy."

Rafe shrugged and they resumed walking down the street. "She was with you for ten years. All broken in."

Marcus couldn't argue with that. Amy had been fantastic, particularly those last six years. She knew his routine, didn't ask unnecessary questions, and generally remained an invisible part of his life. She'd been incredibly well paid and worked well, but the truth was that having an employee around for more than ten years was dangerous. He didn't age, and humans tended to notice things like that after a bit.

"This new assistant? Worried that he's not who he says he is?"

Marcus stopped in front of a plain, square, brick building. The squat two-story looked worn and rundown. The front light flickered, staying off longer than it was on. The apartment building looked as if the owner had simply given up on trying to make repairs, leaving the tenants to live in relative squalor. This was the address Ethan Cline had put on his résumé.

Their meeting had been brief, but there was no denying there had been an instantaneous spark that crackled around Marcus when he met Ethan's eyes. It had taken him a second to remember his own damn name after shaking Ethan's hand. The young man was sharp and eager. His brain had screamed that Ethan was trouble, but he couldn't stop himself from declaring that he was hired within seconds of meeting him. Marcus didn't make snap decisions. He left the hiring to Janice. She dealt with the tedious details of running his financial empire.

But something had demanded that he walk into that office, demanded that he hire Ethan Cline on the spot.

It didn't make a damn bit of sense, and the complete lack of logic bothered him. Not Ethan. Not that the young man would be in his house tomorrow. That they would spend time together as Marcus showed him his duties. Those things simply made his heart speed up and a strange feeling start to shift in his stomach.

"Have you asked Winter to look into him yet?"

Marcus shook his head. That would be the smart thing to do. Winter was the sneaky one of the family. He had a feeling Rafe could easily claim that title if only he would stop running his mouth for more than a couple of seconds.

"Have you spoken to Winter recently?"

"Nope," Rafe said, seeming to pop the "p" with a little extra pleasure.

Of course, Winter was missing. Their brother took pleasure in disappearing for extended periods of time, only to reappear again when he saw fit. Luckily, he seemed to sense when true danger was brewing and managed to be present before things got out of hand.

"I'll speak to Winter about Mr. Cline when he appears again," Marcus muttered. He stood staring up at the apartment building for a couple of seconds more, wondering if the light on in the front left window on the second floor belonged to Ethan. Was he awake still? Excited for his first day of work with Marcus?

Disgusted with himself, Marcus turned back the way he'd walked, stepping around Rafe, who looked at him with a confused expression. He really didn't want Rafe pondering this too much. He didn't want him digging into Ethan. Didn't want him talking to Ethan.

"The Ministry is considering a new vote," Marcus said, mentioning the ruling vampire body for the Americas. The pompous, power-hungry creatures loved thinking of ways to complicate their lives, and their actions were a guaranteed distraction for Rafe.

"When aren't they?" Rafe grumbled.

"They are considering whether to ban vampires from using social media."

"Are you fucking kidding me? I've got more than two million followers on Instagram."

"And you are likely the reason they are considering such a ban."

Rafe tilted his head toward the sky and groaned in disgust. "If only they knew the images I haven't posted. I'm using incredible restraint to keep them happy."

Marcus didn't believe that for a second. Restraint was not something Rafe truly understood. "Try limiting yourself to fashion for the time being. At least until this ban talk blows over."

"Don't attempt to make me boring, dear brother. It will never happen."

"Was there another reason for you to hunt me down?" Marcus asked. He didn't want to think Rafe had come looking for him simply because he was in an unexpected part of town.

He didn't question Rafe's ability to sense the locations of his brothers. Rafe admitted that Bel was the easiest of them to pinpoint, followed by Marcus. Winter was more nebulous, and Marcus had little doubt that it greatly annoyed Rafe. If he tried, he could probably find Winter within a few hundred square miles, but that wasn't incredibly useful.

Of course, they all had ways of keeping track of each other. It was a struggle not to look around for Ozzie. But if Bel's enormous black raven wanted to hide, Marcus wasn't going to see him.

What was surprising was that Rafe could easily trace their sire, Aiden. Unlike his brothers, Marcus couldn't sense their sire when he was close. But then, vampirism had manifested itself in strange and unique ways for each of them.

"Aiden has returned from Rio," Rafe announced.

Marcus stopped and turned to look at his brother. "He's here?"

Rafe shook his head. "Miami."

Marcus grunted and continued to walk to where he'd parked his car. Rio de Janeiro, Brazil, made sense for Aiden. It was a distracting enough place with just enough crime that a hunting vampire could move unnoticed. It was a place where he could forget about his beloved Julianna and the knowledge that he could never be close to her again.

But Miami was less than seven hundred miles from their current location. He had to have returned to the United States because of the upcoming move. He wanted to be close in case there was a problem. Even from afar, after more than a century, Aiden would do anything to protect Julianna, as well as her children. Even if it meant protecting her children from their mother.

Marcus sighed, shoving his hands deeper into his pockets. "I do not think we were meant for love."

Rafe's bright, carefree laugh rose up and echoed through the night above the distant rush of cars. "Nonsense! I fall in love with a new beautiful face and sweetly curved ass each night."

"That is not love, brother," Marcus grumbled.

Rafe purposefully bumped into him with his shoulder, and Marcus looked over to see his brother's wild smile. "You'll forgive me if I don't trust your sense of love."

Marcus couldn't blame him. He'd never been in love. Never known a lover's touch. The soft, tender words whispered from a lover's lips. Maybe Rafe did know more about love than he, but Marcus didn't want to believe that the hedonistic love that his brother had found was all there was.

But he also didn't welcome the endless torture that Aiden suffered for his love of Julianna.

No, their kind was not made for love.

CHAPTER FIVE

*E*than arrived on the Varik doorstep at five minutes before ten the next morning with a heavy duffle bag slung over his shoulder. He felt a little awkward in his jeans and plain black T-shirt after seeing how sharply Marcus was dressed, but Janice had reassured him that casual attire was appropriate, considering the kind of work he was going to be doing.

He'd actually arrived downtown more than an hour ago but hung out in a coffee shop waiting until it was closer to his assigned start time. No reason to be obnoxiously early on his first day.

He lifted his hand to ring the doorbell when his eye caught on a small piece of notepaper taped just above eye level.

Mr. Cline,
    Come inside. Lock the door.
    Meet me in the front blue parlor.
    ~M

. . .

Ethan pulled the note off the door and stared at it for a moment, taking in Marcus's bold handwriting. The instructions were concise and gruff, easily matching the manner of the man he'd met the day before. They also made sense since Ethan was sure that Marcus Varik was a vampire. He couldn't risk answering the door and exposing himself to the sunlight.

Slipping the note into his pocket, Ethan took a deep breath and wrapped his fingers around the cool brass door handle. He was willingly walking into the vampire's lair. He was going to work for this vampire. Uncover his secrets. And when he had all the information he needed, he planned to hand Marcus and the rest of his murderous family over to the Humans Protecting Humans League so that they could be exterminated like the dangerous predators they were.

With his carefree mask in place, Ethan stepped inside the massive town house and locked the door behind him. Turning toward the main foyer, he blinked several times, willing his eyes to adjust to the dimmer lighting. His heart sped up during his temporary blindness as his imagination took over, conjuring up blood-coated vampires with fangs exposed bearing down on him.

But when his vision finally cleared, Ethan found that he was alone in the foyer with his back pressed to the front door. Everything looked the same as the day before. Priceless rugs, vases, and paintings in massive frames covered nearly every surface. Yet, he was alone.

Adjusting his bag on his shoulder, Ethan strolled down the hall, poking his head into one doorway and then another until he came to a large room with a delicate couch that Ethan was somewhat sure was called a settee and an equally delicate-looking coffee table. The walls were painted a pale blue and lacy white curtains hung over tall windows. But it was the heavy blinds over the windows that blocked out the sun.

He paused just past the threshold, looking over the room in wonder. From the paintings to the little ceramic figures on the white mantle to the flowered area rugs on the thick white carpet, nothing in this room looked as if it fit Marcus Varik. But it did look like it had been ripped out of another time period. Like he'd stepped into a museum or fallen through a hole in time and woken in Victorian London.

But then, maybe Marcus felt at home here. Maybe he was so old that this decor was something he was familiar with.

And what was it like for him to exist now, in a time of flat-screen TVs, internet, digital personal assistants, and streaming entertainment? Everything was sleek, liquid crystal, touch-screen, and interactive.

Standing in the middle of the room, Ethan slowly turned, taking in his surprising surroundings as his vision finally adjusted to a shadowy corner where he spotted Marcus sitting perfectly still in a chair, a newspaper clutched in both hands as if he'd just lowered it.

"Holy shit!" Ethan exclaimed before he could stop himself. He jumped back and clapped a hand over his mouth.

Marcus rose quickly, one hand extended toward Ethan as Ethan lowered the one covering his lips to apologize.

"I'm sorry," Marcus said, beating Ethan to the punch. "I didn't mean to scare you."

"Surprised me," Ethan corrected. "I didn't see you there." He forced a smile while trying to get his heart rate to slow to normal.

"When you walked in, you appeared...engrossed. I didn't want to disturb your..." Marcus waved his hand at their surroundings, "your perusal of the room."

"Oh, yeah. It's amazing. It was like stepping back in time or into a museum," Ethan said. "I guess I wasn't expecting something like this."

Marcus nodded stiffly and turned his attention to the newspaper still clutched tightly in one hand. He made a great deal of noise folding the paper up, and Ethan could feel a smile tugging at his lips. Not only was he standing in a room lost to time, but he was facing a man who still read a physical newspaper. He couldn't remember the last time he'd seen that besides at the corner table meeting of old men at the nearby McDonald's. Ethan had seen them there several times, with their coffee, newspapers, and gossip.

If he wasn't sure Marcus was somehow involved in the murder of his family, the man might actually be adorable.

"This is the only room in the house like this. My mother describes it as inviting." Marcus paused, a frown deepening the lines on his face. "The other rooms are...normal." Marcus cleared his throat and tossed his paper down on the chair he'd just vacated. His shoulders straightened and it was like watching him fit himself into a character or a role. "Thank you for showing up on time. After today, you will be here promptly at noon and leave at exactly eight p.m. Is that understood?" The no-nonsense boss was in charge again.

Ethan nodded. "Yes."

"Janice will be here at two. She will have paperwork for you as well as a key to the house and other things you'll need to fulfill your duties."

Marcus started to lead the way out of the "inviting" room but stopped suddenly and looked at Ethan, his brow heavily lined. Ethan's heart skipped a beat and he took a step backward, his hands tightening on the strap on his shoulder.

"Why do you have a bag?" Marcus asked, pointing toward the large duffel.

"Oh," Ethan replied on a relieved sigh. He gave a little chuckle while mentally chastising himself that he needed to pull his shit together if he was going to get through this job. "Janice said that she'd have a key for my new apartment this afternoon. I thought I'd just bring all the stuff I needed now and move in after work."

Confusion still carved lines in Marcus's face as he continued to look at the bag on Ethan's shoulder as if the thing didn't make sense.

"Should I have not brought it? I thought I could just shove it in a closet until the end of the day," Ethan said.

Marcus shook his head as if he was trying to clear his thoughts. "No, it's fine. I was just wondering if it was magic. How do you fit all your possessions in that bag?"

A loud bubble of laughter broke free from Ethan, and he rocked back half a step. "It's not quite everything I own. The temporary apartment is furnished, so I mostly just need clothes and toiletries."

"Yes, that makes sense," Marcus murmured. He looked a bit confused still and a little flustered, but he continued to walk toward the hall.

Ethan hid a smile as he followed Marcus to the same office he'd been interviewed in the day before. He dropped his bag off there and was handed a thick folder that contained all the information regarding the move that had been completed so far. He was also given a brand-new tablet and electronic pen he could use to take his notes.

For the next hour, Marcus led him on an abbreviated tour of the house, giving Ethan instructions on where to find things, what rooms he was allowed to pack, and in what order. Some of the rooms were locked and would remain that way until it was closer to the move. Ethan could only guess those were Marcus's more private quarters such as his bedroom. But if that was where Marcus slept during the day, why was he up on the third floor? Wouldn't it be safer for him down in the basement where there was no chance of sunlight reaching him?

Was Marcus not really a vampire?

Just the fact that Marcus was up and walking around now confounded Ethan. He'd thought vampires were locked in their coffins during the day. Not only to protect them from the sun, but that they were just rendered unconscious during the daylight hours. This didn't make any sense.

Except before he entered each room, he slowly opened the door, peering inside just through a crack. Ethan was pretty sure that he was checking that the room was properly guarded against the sun before taking a step inside.

Once on the second floor, he paused in what looked to be a portrait gallery. The long, heavy curtains over one window were half-parted, allowing in a wide shaft of brilliant golden sunlight. Marcus had stared at it for a moment, seeming to watch as the dust particles danced through the light. And then he was looking uncomfortably at Ethan, asking him to go inside and close the curtain.

The strange thing was that even after the darkness had been restored, Marcus didn't enter the room. He called Ethan back and they continued on to the next room, as if the sunlight had contaminated the area somehow. Marcus seemed to even draw into himself a little more, his words growing clipped.

Marcus was very clear about the ground rules. Ethan started work each day at noon and was gone by eight p.m. He was never to stay later in the house unless he first received approval from Marcus. He was not to seek out or otherwise disturb Marcus unless it was absolutely necessary. Any questions regarding moving could be directed to Janice.

No one was to be permitted into the house unless it was Janice. Arrangements would be made for the movers, but no one else was allowed inside.

All the curtains were to remain shut at all times.

All doors were to remain shut at all times.

And he was not to attempt to enter any room that was locked.

The tour of the house ended in the kitchen just before noon.

"You may eat anything in the fridge or pantry that you like," Marcus said, waving a hand toward the fridge. "I have housekeepers who come once a week to clean and restock the fridge. If there's anything you'd like, please leave a note on the fridge. They will add it to the shopping list."

"Wow. That's surprising," Ethan murmured before he could catch himself.

"What's so surprising about that?" Marcus asked. He cocked his head to the side as he looked at Ethan.

Ethan swallowed hard and he could feel the blood rushing to his face. *Holy shit!* He'd said that out loud. It was on the tip of his tongue to comment that Marcus wasn't supposed to eat food or drink anything at all. He was a vampire! Vampires drank only blood!

"Oh…um…just that you cook for yourself. With this big, fancy house, I thought you'd have a personal chef to handle all that," Ethan said, feeling awkward as hell.

"I don't like having people in my personal space." Marcus stared at the marble counter that was between them. "I don't cook much. I tried to learn once but discovered that I didn't have much patience for it."

"Me neither," Ethan said quickly. "Kind of a grilled cheese and tomato soup guy."

Marcus gave a little nod. Silence settled over the kitchen, and then Marcus seemed to pull himself together. His shoulders straightened and his spine stiffened. Cold blue eyes settled on Ethan and he tried not to shrink under that gaze.

"Do you have any questions?"

Ethan pressed his lips together hard to hold back the barrage of vampire-related questions that were bouncing on the tip of his tongue.

"Umm…is there anyone else in the house with us?"

Marcus's brow furrowed again, but his surprise made his ever-present frown disappear. "Excuse me?"

"Well, we went through most of the house, but there are a lot of rooms I didn't see. I guess I was just wondering if I should expect to run across anyone else. I don't want to accidentally stumble over your old great-aunt Gertrude as she shuffles to the bathroom and we both freak out, giving me a heart attack while she beats me with her house slipper."

Marcus's lips pressed together, but Ethan could still see them moving as if he were trying his hardest not to smile or maybe even laugh. Ethan grinned broadly at Marcus, and he was stunned to find that he really wanted to hear Marcus laugh. The man had a deep, rumbly voice that sort of stroked along his spine in the most amazing way, leaving him feeling like a cat receiving affection. He couldn't imagine how his laugh would sound.

"No, I don't have a great-aunt Gertrude hidden in the house, and there will be no one else besides us. The only person who stops in occasionally is Janice, and that's just long enough to drop off contracts for me to sign."

"Got it."

"Well, there's also Ozzie, but you won't be meeting him today."

"Ozzie?"

"A large black raven. He belongs to my brother, but he likes to spend time at my home as well. I believe he elected to spend today at my brother's."

Ethan nodded. "No great-aunt named Gertrude, but there is Ozzie the raven. Got it. Makes sense."

Marcus stared at him for a moment longer, and Ethan wished he could decipher what was crossing his mind. He didn't think he was sizing him up for a meal. If anything, he seemed confused by Ethan and pretty much everything that came out of his mouth. Not that Ethan could claim to be talking much sense. But he wasn't alone. Marcus apparently shared a raven with his brother and its name was Ozzie. Naturally.

Taking the hand Marcus extended to him across the counter, Ethan shook it, proud that his fingers didn't noticeably tremble.

"Thank you for your help, Mr. Cline," Marcus said formally.

"Thank you for this opportunity, Mr. Varik."

Marcus released his hand quickly and hurried from the room. He moved silently for such a large man.

Ethan counted to ten before he released a heavy sigh and leaned against the counter. Tension and adrenaline buzzed through his body. He felt lightheaded as he gulped in big gasps of air.

He was alone in a house with a vampire.

Maybe.

The Humans Protecting Humans League was so positive that Marcus Varik was a vampire. They were positive that he and his family were the culprits behind the murder of his family and all the other people living in his apartment building sixteen years ago.

When he'd taken the assignment to gather intel on Marcus and his family, he'd been sure he'd find proof of his vampireness, but other than the sunlight issue, there was nothing to prove that Marcus was an immortal bloodsucker.

So far, he appeared to be a slightly eccentric rich guy who didn't like people.

No, that didn't feel right. Ethan was sure it wasn't that Marcus didn't like people. It seemed more likely that he felt awkward and out of place around people. Before he'd slipped into his "boss" tone of voice, he'd been adorably awkward and nervous. As if he didn't know what to say to Ethan.

And of course, gruff on the exterior and squishy on the interior pushed all his fucking buttons. Hell, he was in trouble even if Marcus didn't turn out to be a vampire.

The one thing Ethan felt sure of was that Marcus hadn't been one of the people in his apartment that horrible night. He would have remembered Marcus's voice. The voices of the two men and the woman were permanently etched into his brain like grooves on a record.

So…if Marcus was a vampire, he wasn't one of the killers on his list that needed to be exterminated.

But if Marcus was a vampire, didn't that mean he needed to be exterminated anyway? Hadn't he killed other humans to feed his need for blood? Didn't those murdered people deserve justice too?

Except for the fact that Marcus didn't strike him as a bloodthirsty killer.

Marcus had been quiet and reserved during their tour of his house. Ethan had watched him closely as they walked, noticing the way he would touch little artifacts around the house—a book here and a little porcelain figure there—as if they were precious to him. He would steal quick glances at Ethan when he thought Ethan wasn't paying attention. When he did, his expression would soften, and there was only what looked to be curiosity in his gaze and maybe confusion, but never hunger or malice.

He seemed to be an awkward rich guy who might also be a little lonely.

Not that Ethan thought he was necessarily harmless. The guy was clearly powerful on a physical level. Tall with broad shoulders and a thick chest. He could probably bench-press a car without being a vampire. His suit did nothing to hide his strength.

And then of course he had those piercing blue eyes and longish black hair. Today it had been tamed. Neatly combed back and styled, but Ethan had to wonder if maybe as the day wore on and Marcus ran his fingers through his hair those locks grew wilder.

Ethan could imagine climbing into his lap and shoving the fingers of both hands through those thick waves, plunging into the softness only to hold his head captive as he leaned down—

A low groan escaped him, and he didn't give a shit if Marcus could hear him. Why did he have to be so hot with those beautiful eyes, chiseled jaw, and perfect cock-sucking lips?

Leaning down, Ethan banged his head against the counter and winced as pain shot through his forehead. He should never have agreed to this assignment. This was an enormous mistake. He wasn't some highly trained super spy. He didn't know what the fuck he was doing.

They'd made it sound so easy. The perfect way he could do something valuable to give his family justice. Get this job, gather a little intel, and get out again. The professionals with experience killing vampires would handle all the real dirty work.

Except Ethan didn't want innocent people to get hurt.

And if Marcus wasn't involved in the death of his family, he didn't deserve to be targeted. He definitely didn't deserve to die.

Pressing his hands to the cool marble, Ethan pushed himself upright and glared at the stove directly across from him. He could do this. There was still time. He needed to find actual proof that Marcus was a vampire and a killer. Then he could justify giving information over to Carl and the League.

And if the League was wrong about Marcus, he'd tell them and they could look elsewhere. Plus, Ethan had the added bonus of a damn good paying job for a few months. He'd get to live in a nice place that didn't have mice, and he didn't have to worry about getting mugged when he walked to and from the train station.

Closing his eyes, Ethan fought down the swell of uselessness that seemed to swamp him along with the memories of his older sister Lucy and little sister Macy. Lucy would have been out of college and possibly married now if she'd lived. Macy would just be starting college. They deserved to live, to have long and happy lives. But that chance had been stolen.

As their brother, he needed to do something about their stolen lives. He should have done something about it already.

God, why do I have to be so useless?

CHAPTER SIX

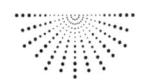

Marcus glared at the book in his hands. He'd started reading it because that latest announcement from the Ministry left him wanting to storm out of the house, but the sun was still up, making such an act suicide. New fucking taxes thanks to the ruling vampires deciding they needed a "cost of living" pay raise. Utter nonsense.

So he walked away from the computer rather than destroying it and picked up a book. But he'd read the same damn paragraph four times, and he still couldn't remember what he'd read. This was his favorite author and one of his favorite books. He could practically recite the damn thing by heart, he'd read it so many times. Why couldn't he concentrate?

Ethan.

It was the same excuse for his lack of concentration all week.

He'd get a few hours of work done and find himself staring off into space, wondering where Ethan was in the house, what he was working on, if he had any questions. And then he'd find himself standing, his hand gripping the doorknob, thinking he'd just go check on Ethan to see if he needed anything.

But this was running counter to the entire reason he hired

Ethan in the first place. He didn't want to deal with the move. He didn't want to worry about the logistics of getting all his accumulated possessions from South Carolina to Connecticut. That was Ethan's job.

As far as he could tell, Ethan was doing fine on his own. Two minutes after eight each day, Marcus would wander out of his self-imposed isolation to look over the room or rooms Ethan had been working in. He'd find towers of stacked boxes, taped and labeled with Ethan's neat letters made with a black marker. Sometimes he'd find a scrap of paper with a few hastily scribbled notes Ethan had left for himself. The air would carry with it a hint of Ethan's sweat and lingering touch of soap. Something minty and soft that made Marcus wonder if it was his shampoo.

Otherwise the young man was a ghost who flew in and out of his house with little sound or evidence of his presence. Marcus had even started checking the fridge and pantry to see if he ate anything. He briefly thought that if he noticed Ethan liking something in particular, he could have his housekeepers bring more of it.

Marcus snapped his book shut and sighed. This was ridiculous. When Amy had been his assistant, he'd not been distracted by her presence in his house. He'd promptly forgotten about her existence, leaving her to handle all his daily needs with Janice.

But Ethan was different, with his shiny blond hair and crooked smile and his talk of Marcus's great-aunt Gertrude. He was never quite sure what was going to come out of Ethan's mouth with his pink lips parted, and Marcus found himself looking forward to those unexpected words.

Chiming from the grandfather clock in the hall whispered through the door. It was five o'clock. Ethan had only a few more hours of work, and then he'd slip quietly out of the house and not return again until Monday. Marcus didn't want Ethan to leave without at least speaking to him once more.

Dinner was eaten by some people at five o'clock. He could order food to be delivered. And he could see if Ethan wanted anything to eat. They could share a meal. That wasn't strange. Since it was Ethan's first week of work, it would also be a way of welcoming him. He could check to see if Ethan was having any problems or had any questions.

Yes, that was a responsible employer thing to do.

So what if it meant that he could secretly enjoy the sweetness of Ethan's voice? Or hear his bubbling laughter?

It didn't matter if he'd never done this with any of his past assistants.

Ethan was...

To hell with it. He didn't need excuses to speak to Ethan or go where he wanted in his own house. No one else would ever know. Especially not his nosy brothers.

Setting the book down on the small table at his elbow, Marcus rose smoothly to his feet and left his private library on the third floor.

Ethan had been working on some of the storage rooms on the fourth floor. Most things were still boxed up there, but there had been a few items placed on shelves that needed to be reboxed and labeled. Marcus quickly passed through the rooms to find them empty. Ethan had completed his work there. Everything was neatly organized and stacked for the moving company that would arrive in a little more than a month to haul it all out of his house.

He returned to the third floor, but Ethan wasn't anywhere to be found. Of course, most of the rooms on the third floor were Marcus's private rooms and locked against Ethan's entry.

His heart sped up a little as he descended to the second floor, trying to find evidence of where Ethan was working, if not the man himself. He tried to remind himself that Ethan could have run out for some supplies or was on the ground floor in the kitchen, grabbing food already. Which would be his luck. He'd miss his chance to share a meal with Ethan because he'd not told him earlier of his intention.

Pausing with his hand on the railing, he tried to decide whether to head straight to the first floor or check the second when he heard Ethan's voice at the end of the hall. He...he sounded like he was singing. Marcus turned toward the sound, the first hint of a smile lifting one corner of his mouth. Ethan was singing, though he couldn't yet identify the song.

It took Marcus only a minute to locate Ethan in a rarely used spare bedroom. A pair of white earbuds were visible in his ears as he danced around the room to music that Marcus couldn't hear. His singing wasn't great. Okay, it was pretty bad, but he looked so damn happy as he danced over to a tape dispenser and picked it up off the bed.

Marcus crossed his arms over his chest and leaned against the open doorway, his smile growing as he watched the man work. While he was smaller than Marcus, there was an intoxicating, lithe energy to Ethan. A vibrancy that Marcus couldn't look away from.

His jeans clung to his legs a little tighter than the first day of work and perfectly hugged his adorable ass. His T-shirt held a cartoon graphic of a squirrel with a flamethrower, admonishing him to "Protect Your Nutz." Probably not the most work-appropriate thing, but then Ethan had been completely alone the past four days. He obviously wasn't expecting to see his boss.

Ethan turned toward the box he was in the process of sealing and that put him facing the open doorway...and Marcus. A startled yelp escaped him, and he jumped back so violently that he landed on his ass. Marcus winced at the loud thud. He hadn't meant to scare Ethan so horribly.

Dropping the tape dispenser, Ethan ripped the earbuds from his ears. "Oh, God! Mr. Varik! I didn't see you there."

"I noticed," Marcus said, trying so damn hard not to sound like he was laughing.

"I-I wasn't disturbing you, was I? Sometimes I get into a song, and I don't realize how loud I am. I'm sor—"

He started to apologize, but Marcus straightened and raised a hand, stopping his words. He'd not come looking for Ethan so he could scare him or make him feel badly for singing while he worked.

"No, I apologize for startling you. You weren't disturbing me."

"Oh good," Ethan said on a sigh. He shoved one hand through his sweaty blond hair, pushing it back from where it threatened to fall into his eyes and leaving some of it standing up.

An uneasy silence settled over the room, and Marcus folded his hands together in front of him, looking down at the carpet. Why did he have to be so damn awkward around Ethan?

"Was there something I could help you with?" Ethan asked after a couple of seconds. "Do you need me to run an errand?"

"No," Marcus said sharply. His head popped up to look at Ethan for a heartbeat, and then he frowned and looked down again. "I...I was thinking of ordering something to eat. From one of those food delivery apps." He lifted his head again to gaze at Ethan. He tried a small smile. "I've gotten quite good at using those." He inwardly winced, regretting his words. He'd thought it would make him sound more normal, but he was sure it just made him sound old. Well, older than the thirty years he appeared to be.

Ethan sort of groaned and chuckled at the same time. The odd noise stirred something in Marcus's stomach and quickened his heart. He wanted to hear Ethan make that sound again. Wanted to be standing close enough to feel the rumble up his chest.

"Me too. It's the only way I've learned to survive after a long day of work and classes," Ethan said.

Something in Marcus relaxed a little. He could feel the

tension unwind from his shoulders and it was just a tiny bit easier to breathe. "Would you care to join me?"

"Um, sure. If you don't mind the company. Where are you ordering from?"

"I haven't figured out that part yet." Marcus reached into his pocket and pulled out his cell phone as he stepped farther into the room. He thumbed through it, going to a familiar app. He kneeled down beside Ethan so that the other man could clearly see his screen. "This is the one I've been using the most. It seems to have the biggest selection. The drivers appear to be quite fast as well."

"Oh wow," Ethan whispered as he watched Marcus scroll through the list of restaurants. "You've got more choices here in the downtown area than I had in Glenpark. What are you in the mood for? Any favorites?"

Ethan had inched a little closer and the minty scent he'd caught earlier in the other rooms was stronger now. Marcus ached to lean forward and press his nose to Ethan's hair, inhale him along with the strong smell of sweat and something musky that had to simply be Ethan. Underlying it was always the alluring hint of blood, but he wasn't hungry. This draw to Ethan had nothing to do with hunger. He didn't want to feed from Ethan ever.

But something within him wanted to bite Ethan. Wanted to pin him down and sink his teeth deep as Ethan moaned and rubbed his body against Marcus's, begging for more.

Clearing his throat, Marcus violently shoved that line of thought away. He was not touching Ethan. Never touching in any way beyond shaking his hand. There was nothing. He was simply making his employee feel welcome and safe as he worked.

Marcus was going to tap the image of his favorite Mediterranean restaurant, but just as his fingertip hit the screen, a text notification from Rafe popped up. The screen went black for a second as the phone changed from the food delivery app to the messaging program.

Rafe had sent a quick message of:

The ONLY way to start the day.

And attached was a picture of him naked in bed. Only he wasn't alone. Of course Rafe wasn't alone. On his left was a naked woman on her side, lying pressed against his brother. And on his right was an equally naked man stretched out on his stomach. One ass cheek even looked like it had a bite mark—without fangs. Rafe, in the center, was looking thoroughly debauched and smug, as if the bastard could sense that he was sending the image at just the worst moment.

"Whoa," Ethan breathed softly, snapping Marcus from his frozen horror.

"Fuck," Marcus snarled, trying like hell to get the image off his phone and return to the damn ordering app. He tried tapping away from it, but as soon as he'd make progress, one of his other brothers would respond and Marcus would hit it, sending him right to the message program and that picture.

Ethan wrapped his fingers around Marcus's wrist and Marcus froze. "Look. No judgment. I swear."

"No, this isn't me," Marcus said quickly. "This is my damn brother."

"Really? Which one?"

For a moment, he thought Ethan was asking which brother had sent the text, but Ethan didn't know about his brothers. Marcus looked over to see that Ethan's head was cocked slightly to the side as he stared at Marcus's phone. Marcus glanced down again to find that the fucking picture was once again on the screen followed by a couple of texts going back and forth between Winter and Rafe. Naturally, Winter was egging Rafe on.

"Totally the one in the middle. I can see the family resemblance," Ethan continued.

Marcus's mouth fell opened and he watched as Ethan's face turned bright red. He could actually see the moment when Ethan realized what he was saying.

"Oh God," Ethan whispered in a pained voice.

Marcus laughed so hard he dropped on his ass. Ethan snorted once and started laughing as well, falling onto his back and rolling to his side so that he was nearly in the fetal position.

It took more than a minute for them to catch their breaths. Marcus looked over at Ethan to find him reclining on his hip while propping himself on his elbow. He grinned broadly at Marcus, a beautiful flush painting his cheeks. His hair was a little wild and disheveled, but his vibrant glow threatened to steal Marcus's breath away.

Deep down, he knew he should never have come looking for Ethan. Should never have stepped into the room. Nothing good waited in a future that included Ethan, but he still couldn't force himself to climb to his feet and walk away. He was happy. Happy for the first time in too long.

An impish smile rose on Ethan's lips and Marcus had to ask.

"What are you thinking?"

"I'm suddenly wondering if you or your brother is the serious one."

Marcus snorted and slowly pushed to his feet. "I am. Though Bel comes in a very close second most of the time." Standing over Ethan, he held out his hand, offering to help Ethan to his feet. "I think we both need a drink before we try again to order food."

Ethan placed his hand in his, and Marcus tried not to react to the tingle of electricity that sizzled along his palm at his touch. It happened whenever he clasped Ethan's hand. It was like a circuit was suddenly being connected, and the energy flowed freely between them.

"Are you sure my boss won't mind?" Ethan teased as soon as he released Marcus's hand.

"I think your boss is praying you don't sue him right now."

Ethan chuckled. "I don't think either of us would come out smelling like a rose in that lawsuit, so let's just call it even."

Marcus led the way to the library, where he had several bottles of very good whiskey, scotch, and other liquors to help smooth over the memory of Rafe's ill-timed text. With a couple of shots in them, they managed to pull up the food delivery app again and decide on some food without any more unfortunate texts popping up.

"How many brothers do you have?" Ethan asked as they moved into the kitchen to get what they'd need before the food arrived. "You mentioned someone called Belle, but I'm assuming you didn't mean the person in the photo."

"Three. Rafe and Beltran are twins. We call him Bel for short. The one in the photo was Rafe. He's the more reckless of us. And then there's Winter. The baby of the family."

Ethan paused as he dug through the silverware drawer and smiled at Marcus. "Are you the oldest?"

Marcus nodded.

"I can't imagine growing up with three younger brothers." Ethan grabbed what they needed and turned to Marcus with a little shake of his head. "That had to be utter chaos."

"Do you have siblings?"

Ethan's open and warm expression closed up in a heartbeat, his fingers tightening around the pair of forks still clutched in his left hand. "I did. I was the middle child. I had an older and a younger sister. Lucy and Macy."

"I'm very sorry for your loss," Marcus said softly. He wanted to ask more questions, to find out why his sisters were stolen from him, but Marcus bit back the words. Ethan's tense frame and deepening frown did not speak of a person who wanted to talk about that horrible moment of their loss.

The silence stretched, twisted and painful between them. Marcus knew the anguish he felt. He'd already suffered a lifetime of loss. People he'd once counted as family and friends had died one by one over the last century. Some due to horrible accidents and unfortunate events, while others simply grew old while he remained perpetually thirty. He counted himself lucky that he still had his brothers, no matter how annoying and reckless they could be.

His mother, Julianna, was another story.

She had good nights and bad nights, but the bad always seemed to overshadow the good. She was little more than a ghost of her former self. Marcus had lost her the night that Aiden tried to save her from the illness ravaging her thin, weak body.

"What was the music you were singing earlier?" Marcus asked, trying to think of a topic that might return the smile to Ethan's face.

It worked. The light started to peek out again, and he shook his head slightly. "And there's where that snowball of embarrassment started," he murmured. Marcus almost apologized again, but Ethan flashed him such a smile that the words became caught in his throat. "That was Tori Amos."

"I don't think I've heard of her."

Ethan groaned and released the utensils he was still holding to grab the phone from his back pocket. "Oh God, you've got to know Tori. I know people call Beyoncé 'The Queen,' but Tori, she's a fucking goddess." He sidled closer to Marcus while tapping away on the screen, searching for what he could only guess was the perfect Tori Amos song.

A second later the first notes of a song tiptoed from Ethan's phone and his entire demeanor changed. His shoulders slumped and his eyes closed. A look of bliss settled over his features, and he started to sway just a little as more notes trickled out. Marcus noticed that he heard only a piano…and then a haunting female voice.

"She's a pianist," Marcus said in a surprise.

"Yes. She's a complete goddess behind the piano. She can make that instrument laugh or weep or rage for her. There's no one like her."

Marcus closed his eyes, letting the piano notes reach into his soul followed by the breathy, lilting voice of the songstress as she wove her magic. She was like a siren stroking her fingers along his soul. For more years than he could count, Marcus had been attached to the piano. There were times that he hated it, sure it was a prison, but there were too many moments in his long life that he sat down behind those black and ivory keys to find solace when he could find it nowhere else.

And it felt like there was a little bit of that reflected in this woman's spiraling words and dancing notes.

"I discovered Tori a few years after my family was stolen." Ethan's words started softly, barely over a whisper. He was staring down at the phone resting on the counter between them. "Listening to her, it was like I could breathe again. And then later with the gay thing, she had a way of empowering me. Providing the shield and shoulder I needed."

Marcus could feel the furrows digging deep in his brow. "I'm sorry. I don't understand. 'The gay thing'?"

Ethan smiled up at him. "I'm gay and Tori is a big-time ally." His eyes narrowed and his smile slipped a little. "I assumed you wouldn't care since your brother is so very bi."

The words coming from Ethan required a few extra seconds to decipher. Everything was getting caught up in his brain. Ethan was gay. He liked men. Not women. And everything about his demeanor and words said that he was entirely comfortable with that. He felt no horror or shame or disappointment in himself.

For his entire life, Marcus had been sure that Rafe's love of both men and women came from his need to assert his individuality over the rules of the world. To show everyone that no one could make him play by their demands. It was all an act of rebellion.

But maybe Rafe truly was attracted to both genders and he was okay with it.

Looking down at Ethan, he knew he didn't think less of the man.

Yet, when he turned that same light of inspection inward, the shame and horror were still there for himself. He couldn't forgive himself…and it hurt.

"Mr. Varik?" Ethan prodded when Marcus had been quiet for too long. He hated how Ethan's expression closed a little, his face growing pale.

"I think after today's adventure, you can call me Marcus," he said firmly. A little part of him hated how Ethan gave a deep sigh of relief. "And no, I don't care that you are gay. The truth is that I've never given much thought to Rafe's…exploits simply because if I did, I would never accomplish anything else."

Ethan's grin returned. "Rafe the rebel, huh?"

"Rafe believes in living life according to his terms, and if it happens to upset other people, then all the better."

Ethan started to reply, but the front doorbell chimed through the house and they both straightened, seeming to take a step back from each other. Marcus couldn't recall how they came to be standing so close.

"I'll go get the food," Ethan offered and quickly hurried from the kitchen.

Marcus grabbed their drinks and utensils before heading into the dining room. Ethan returned a few minutes later holding a large bag with the most delicious smells rising from it.

Ethan chuckled. "I think we ordered way too much food."

"I have faith that we can make some headway in it."

They set out the food on the table and piled their plates full. Conversation settled into lighter topics, and Marcus was surprised at how easy it was to simply talk to Ethan. He was smart and funny. He spoke of various jobs he'd taken over the years and how he'd decided to start going to an online college to learn about coding. He dreamed of travel.

And the most wonderful part was that he didn't press Marcus to share. There was so much in his life that Marcus couldn't discuss, from his family to many of the things he'd seen in life. But sitting there next to Ethan, he found that he wanted to. He wanted to tell Ethan about all the amazing places he'd traveled during his long life. He wanted to talk more about his brothers.

But it wasn't safe.

A loud crack of thunder followed by the long, rumbling growl stopped their conversation and had them both looking toward the window.

"Whoa," Ethan murmured. "I noticed clouds rolling in when I grabbed the food, but that storm got here fast."

Marcus glanced down at his watch to find that it was only a little after six in the evening. The sun wouldn't set for another couple of hours, but a storm could change that.

"Was the sun covered? Is it dark out?"

"I think so."

Marcus's heart skipped a beat. This could be bad. He'd set Ethan's work schedule by the fact that the sun would be up and shining during the hours he was in Marcus's home. No threats could reach him. But an unexpected storm that covered the sky could change that.

"Would you mind checking?" Marcus asked softly.

Ethan stared at him for a second before he finally nodded and pushed from his chair. Before Ethan could touch the heavy curtains to pull them apart, Marcus was already standing by the open doorway that led into the kitchen. He couldn't take a chance. The windows of the house were all covered with a protective UV film, but it only helped so much. He had to stay out of the direct light as much as possible.

Blinking in surprise to find Marcus at the other side of the room, Ethan gripped the curtains and flashed him a tentative smile. "Ready?"

"Yes."

Ethan pulled the curtains open only a little, while making sure to keep them closed toward Marcus. The vampire winced a little as the pale new light washed over Ethan. It certainly wasn't as bright as it should have been.

"There are some really dark clouds overhead. You'd think the sun had already set," Ethan said.

Marcus carefully crossed the room and took the edge of the curtain from Ethan. He pulled it open a little more and peered out the window. The sunlight burned his eyes a little, but he could see that heavy clouds had covered the sky while lightning arced between them. An early night.

"Have you always been allergic to the sunlight?" Ethan asked quietly.

"No, it's something that grew worse as I became older." It wasn't exactly a lie. It did become worse when he was older. It just hadn't been a gradual thing. He simply woke up after Aiden put him through the change and he could no longer go out in the sun without risking a painful death.

"Do you miss it? Going out in the sun?"

Marcus turned his head and found himself smiling down at Ethan's worried expression. "Not as much as you might think."

"Really?"

"You may find this hard to believe, but I'm not very good with people."

"Noooo," Ethan said in mock surprise.

"And I've found I'm more comfortable moving around at night when most people are at home. There's a peace to the night. My brother would argue that there is more freedom in night's embrace."

"We know how much your brother loves his freedom."

Marcus smiled at Ethan's teasing, enjoying that he felt comfortable enough to do it. Of course, that wasn't too hard after laughing over a naked picture of Rafe. He started to reply when someone knocked loudly on the front door.

Another vampire was at his house. He'd been so distracted by Ethan that he'd not noticed its approach. Now that he was paying attention, he could feel the power crawling along his flesh. It was someone older than him, stronger than him. This could be very bad.

"I'll get it," Ethan said easily. He released the curtains and started to walk past Marcus toward the door.

Marcus jumped in front of him, roughly grabbing both of his shoulders to hold him in place. There was no missing the way Ethan flinched at his touch, his entire body stiffening. As if he were afraid of Marcus. But there wasn't time for that line of thought. He tucked it away for later and focused on his current, more pressing problem. Getting Ethan out of the house safely and without being noticed.

"No. I need you to stay in here and remain absolutely silent. Do you understand?"

Ethan nodded, his face becoming pale.

"Do you have everything you need to return to your home?"

"Yes. What—"

The knocking at the front door grew louder and Marcus barely swallowed back a growl of frustration.

"I'm going to take my guest to the second-floor lounge. When you hear the door close, I want you to slip quietly out of the house and go straight home."

Some of the fear clouding Ethan's eyes cleared and he frowned. "What about you? Are you in some kind of trouble?"

"I'll be fine. Just follow my instructions."

Before Ethan could ask any more questions, Marcus left the dining room, shutting the door behind him. The hard soles of his shoes clicked across the wood floor, and his heart hammered in his chest. He had a guess of who was waiting at his door, and her presence was never a good thing.

Taking a last deep, calming breath, Marcus jerked the front door open to reveal a short, slender woman with purple-streaked hair and a knowing grin. Meryl. Behind her stood Cain, a hulking man that made Marcus feel tiny. His dark skin glistened with rainwater as he glared at Marcus.

"Whew! What a storm!" Meryl announced before shoving her way past Marcus into the house. Marcus barely had enough time to move out of the way before Cain plowed through him.

The storm was no coincidence. She'd called it up. From what he could tell, most vampires came with an added gift, though few advertised it like Meryl. The storms gave her the freedom to move about during the daylight hours with reduced fear of exposure to the sun. She loved creating storms during the day so that she could randomly appear on a vampire's doorstep.

Meryl strolled into the house, her heavy combat boots with the thick rubber soles thumping and squeaking on the floor. There was a soft jingle that rose from the bits of metal on her leather jacket and pants. She looked like an escapee from the London punk scene, though her accent was clearly American.

"Why are you here, Meryl?"

"What? I can't stop in for a visit?"

She strolled around the foyer, eyes scanning over everything while Cain stopped next to Marcus as if he wanted him close at hand should he attempt anything against his mistress. Marcus balled his hands into fists at his sides.

"I'm not interrupting, am I?" She flashed him a wide, playful grin as she took a step across the hall, moving away from the parlor and toward the dining room. She took a deep breath and made a dreamy sigh. "Having a light snack?"

Marcus nearly growled. He had a feeling she was referring to the lingering scent of Ethan in the air and not the meal they'd had delivered.

"If you wish to talk, Meryl, then why don't we move somewhere more comfortable?" He took a step toward the other vampire, extending his hand as he tried to direct her toward the stairs.

"That's so kind of you, Marcus, but if you've got another guest in the house, I wouldn't want to steal you away."

Marcus was aware of Cain taking another step closer, positioning his body so that he was nearly between Marcus and Meryl.

"I don't—" he started to say, but it was too late. She darted over to the dining room and threw open the door. Ethan's surprised gasp shot through him and there was no stopping the snarl that slipped past Marcus's curled lips. He rushed to Meryl's side. Cain's heavy hand clamped down on his shoulder and squeezed in warning.

Deep down, Marcus knew he could take Cain in a fight. The vampire was younger and not nearly as strong as Marcus, but he also knew that Meryl wouldn't remain passive in the fight, and he was no match for the older vampire. She didn't need Cain to protect her. She just liked having a flunky shadowing her every move.

"Well, isn't this a delicious-looking meal," Meryl purred.

Marcus growled. He threw off Cain's hand and pushed his way past Meryl to step into the dining room. Ethan had started to move around the table, his hand extended toward the woman with his polite smile in place.

"Hi, I'm Ethan Cline, Mr. Varik's new assistant," he introduced.

Marcus jumped in front of Ethan, blocking his path and Meryl's direct view of him. He didn't care what Ethan thought; he just didn't want Meryl taking an interest in Ethan.

"Oh Marcus, he's so pretty," Meryl cooed. "Please tell me you're going to keep this one."

"This isn't the time or place, Meryl. We can discuss why you're here upstairs in the lounge."

"But we can bring him along." Her bright hazel eyes jumped to Marcus's face and she giggled. "The more, the merrier."

"He was just leaving for the day," Marcus said firmly. She started to open her mouth, but he continued. "Please, Meryl."

She pressed her lips together in a bright smile and nodded at him before spinning on her heel. He didn't move as he listened for the sound of both Meryl and Cain moving up the stairs, and only then did he allow himself to relax a tiny bit.

Ethan's hand landed on his arm and he twisted around, fully expecting to see anger filling his large blue eyes, but he found only concern there.

"Are you going to be okay?" he whispered.

Marcus nodded sharply. "Go directly home. We'll talk tomorrow," he said in a low voice. Not that he could even guess what he'd tell Ethan when he saw the man again. But that was a worry for another day. Right then, he had to figure out what Meryl was up to.

CHAPTER SEVEN

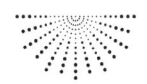

When he entered the lounge, he found Meryl already seated in the leather chair in front of the empty fireplace, while Cain was standing nearby. Fighting to keep his face expressionless, Marcus closed the door behind him and walked over to the chair closest to Meryl.

"It's that time again, isn't it?" Meryl said. The playfulness was gone from her voice, and there was a new seriousness that ran in sharp contrast to her carefree attire. But then, the punk rocker look with the purple hair was all an act. A ruse. Meryl was a cold-blooded killer, and her favorite target was her own kind. "Moving day is nearly upon you."

"We'll be gone in less than two months," Marcus replied carefully.

Vampires were required to move every couple of decades. Otherwise they risked humans catching on that they didn't age, never changed. There were murmurs now among their kind that moving every twenty years wasn't enough. That the rule should be changed to fifteen or ten. With the advent of digital cameras on every cell phone and social media, there was always the risk that someone would notice.

But ten years was a drop in the bucket for a vampire. Marcus was just getting settled in a location, getting a feel for his new hunting grounds in ten years. He hated the idea of constantly packing up and resettling in a new location.

And moving wasn't just a matter of relocating his household. It meant coordinating the move with his three brothers as well, finding new homes for all of them, and seeing that their mother was disturbed by the move as little as possible. The endeavor was exhausting and stressful.

Of course, there was also the problem that his family might be moving into an area already populated by other vampires. Most large cities couldn't be claimed by a single vampire. The hunting grounds were large enough to support several vampires with little difficulty, and in general, everyone could play well together. Complications only cropped up when too many vampires gathered in a smaller town. The risk of someone noticing something rose significantly, increasing the danger for all of their kind.

Their new home in Connecticut was in a somewhat smaller city of fewer than fifty thousand people, but Hartford and New Haven weren't too far away. The only thing that worried him was hunting during the winter when people strayed outside their homes far less. Unfortunately, his family had spent too much time in the south over the past several decades. They needed to head north to escape the risk of being noticed.

"Moving is not enough," Meryl said, and Marcus straightened in his chair.

"What are you talking about?"

Meryl crossed her legs at the knee and lazily bounced her leg as she smiled at him. Her long fingers were folded in her lap. "You know I have no problem with you, Marcus. You're smart. You keep to yourself. And we both know that no matter how cute and tempting that new assistant of yours is, he will never discover the truth about you."

A chill swept down Marcus's spine at the thought of Ethan ever uncovering the fact that he was a vampire. He could clearly see the warmth and laughter dissolving from Ethan's expression to be replaced with one of horror and hatred. He was a monster. A creature to be feared. He didn't kill, but the strength and power to were at his fingertips. He could so easily drain his prey too much or snap a neck. He never wanted to see that fear in Ethan's eyes. No, he could never know the truth.

"Then if I'm not your problem, why are you here?"

"Your family is my problem," she bit out between clenched teeth. Her hands moved to tightly grip the leather-covered arms of the chair. "I would speak with Winter. He's the only other logical, sensible one of your wretched clan, but he's too hard to nail down. But you're the eldest. Everyone knows that you're the only one who can hope to keep that fucking hedonist in line."

"Bel?"

"Rafe!" she snarled, slamming the palm of her right hand on the chair. "We can all do without Beltran's silly experiments, giving vampires the stupid idea that we *need* to be cured. We're not a goddamn disease. We're an evolutionary breakthrough." She sucked in a breath and sat back in her seat. "I'm talking about Rafe. He's too brazen and careless. He's fucking told people that he's a vampire at that stupid nightclub of his. He's admitted it!"

Hell, he needed a drink. Or just to throttle his little brother. But he didn't let his frustration show. This conversation was nothing new. He'd gone before the Ministry time and time again to soothe ruffled feathers over Rafe's newest antic. No one on the Ministry was amused with Rafe's decision to "come out" to the world as a vampire. The only thing that saved Rafe's neck was that no one believed him. Humans thought it was a joke, a publicity stunt to draw more people to his club.

"No one actually believes him. People think it's just part of his act."

"And what if someone starts believing him? What if he does something that removes all doubt that he's a vampire?"

"He won't," Marcus snapped. He paused and clamped down his control over his voice. "He won't. He's having fun. Rafe won't risk revealing our secret. The dangers are too great."

"I think you're giving your brother more brains than he truly has."

Marcus said nothing, just glared at the vampire sitting next to him. If it had been nearly anyone else in that chair, he would have already tossed them out. But it wasn't only that Meryl was older and stronger than him. Meryl also wielded influence. A few whispers in the right ears and the Varik clan could be in serious trouble. This visit was a courtesy. A final warning.

"I'll speak with Rafe. Rein him in if it becomes necessary."

Meryl narrowed her gaze on Marcus and leaned toward him. "We are beyond necessary with Rafe."

"I'll handle it."

Meryl slowly reclined, settling against the leather cushion. Her hands were once again folded in her lap and she stared unblinking at him. "Sadly, this isn't just about Rafe."

A horrible uneasiness twisted in Marcus's stomach, but he kept his face blank. He should have seen this coming. Rafe was the warm-up act. An easy target to get Marcus to agree to her demands. No, what Meryl was truly after was his mother.

"Julianna is insane," Meryl said. There was no more mincing words or pretending that this could be a civil conversation.

"Meryl," Marcus said in warning. He shifted forward in his seat, sliding to the edge, but a heavy hand came down on the back of his neck, squeezing. He'd gotten so wrapped up in the vampire in front of him that he'd forgotten the silent and deadly shadow also lurking in the room.

"Everyone knows it. The bitch should have been put

down the moment she'd been reborn, but Aiden promised he could keep her under control. Why the European Ministry listened to Aiden's request, I will never understand. I truly doubt they would have allowed it if they'd known he planned to turn her four children just to keep her under control."

"Julianna Varik has not caused any problems recently. She *is* under control."

"She's a danger to everyone. Not just to the humans she feeds upon."

Marcus snorted. "I don't believe for a second that you care about humans."

Meryl gave a little roll of her eyes. "No, of course not. But a meal that is killed equals a missing human, and it's much harder for a human to simply go missing now. People start looking into disappearances. Videos are reviewed. Dead humans are bad for vampires."

"She hasn't had an accident with a human in years. Decades even."

"But you can't say the same for other vampires she's randomly attacked."

Marcus nearly growled at her, but he kept his mouth shut. There had been a few instances where other vampires had gotten too close when she'd been out hunting. She'd escaped Beltran as well as Winter when they were escorting her and had attacked the vampires. One had been killed. The other had escaped, but Marcus didn't know if he'd survived through the next morning.

Leaning against the arm of her chair, Meryl reached out and placed her hand over Marcus's wrist. He wanted to rip his arm away from her cool touch, but he didn't move.

"And that's not including the damage that she's done to you and your brothers. How many times over the years has she hurt you or Bel or Winter? Or even reckless Rafe? How many times has she nearly killed them? We all know you're not reporting those attacks to the Ministry."

"Let it go, Meryl."

"You've been given a second chance at life. A better, stronger one than you were born to. Do you really want to spend this eternity patching your brothers together and living in fear that one time you're not going to be able to save them?"

Marcus pulled his arm out from under Meryl's touch and crossed them over his chest. "What goes on behind the closed doors of our homes is a Varik family matter, and that is all. The American Ministry need not be involved."

She smiled sadly at him. "Such loyal, loving sons." The smile disappeared in the blink of an eye and she glared at him. "Julianna Varik is not leaving this city alive. Rafe can be reasoned with. Made to see the wisdom of our ways. Julianna is beyond reason."

"You are not in the American Ministry, Meryl. You do not speak for it," Marcus snarled.

She giggled, the sound disturbingly light and airy. "No, but I'm very good at speaking to it."

Marcus tried to stand, but Cain pressed down on his shoulder. Marcus knew he could break free, and he was sorely tempted to do it. His hands clenched and a low growl rumbled in his throat, but before he could make a move, Meryl was right there, her nose a bare inch from the tip of his own.

"Are you sure you want to do that?" she taunted.

"Get out," Marcus snapped. "Leave my house now."

Meryl reached out and patted his cheek. "Only because you asked so nicely."

She slipped around him, her heavy shoes loudly clomping on the floor as she headed to the hall. Cain released him and followed placidly after her. Cursing her and his own life, he followed after them, if only to reassure himself that they were actually leaving.

Thunder rumbled outside, loud enough to rattle the glass in the window frames. The storm had unleashed its fury on the city. He had little doubt that it looked as if night had settled over the city hours early. Meryl and Cain might be stepping out into a drenching, but they were walking freely while he was still trapped in his house until he could be sure the sun was down. He couldn't risk being out in one of Meryl's storms and not knowing when she was going to end it, sending the clouds on their way. If he was lucky, he'd simply be trapped at another safe location until nightfall. But it could all end very badly if he wasn't so lucky.

Pausing at the open door to the dining room, Meryl peered inside and then she looked back at Marcus who was still descending the stairs. "Ahhh…looks like your assistant has disappeared. I'm sorry to have disturbed your little romantic dinner for two."

"It was time for him to return home," Marcus said evenly while inwardly rejoicing that Ethan had followed his instructions and left. At least that had gone as planned, and he was safely away from Meryl and Cain.

"I can see why you hired him. He's just adorable with that blond hair and big blue fuck-me-daddy eyes."

Marcus stopped on the stairs, tightly clutching the handrail. He didn't trust himself to not launch his body at Meryl. He didn't want her talking about or even looking at Ethan. He hated the idea of her even knowing that he existed. No one should ever talk about Ethan like that. He deserved her respect. Ethan was smart and funny and so damn compassionate.

But he said nothing. Defending Ethan would only make it worse.

Her grin spread as if she could read his thoughts. "Maybe after you move, I'll see if your lovely Ethan Cline needs a new job."

Her wild laughter followed her out of the house and into the raging storm. The door slammed shut and Marcus's legs gave out, leaving him sitting on the stairs. *Oh, hell no.* Meryl was not getting anywhere close to Ethan.

But she had the advantage. He couldn't leave his house for at least another two hours, while she could use that time to try to track Ethan's temporary residence down. He had to warn Ethan. To protect him.

And then he needed to talk to his brothers about Meryl's threat against Julianna.

CHAPTER EIGHT

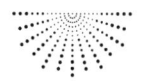

"Having doubts is normal," Carl said with a wide, reassuring grin.

Ethan placed a glass of ice water on the coffee table in front of Carl and forced a quick smile that he really didn't feel.

If he felt anything, it was a tangled mess. There was a little voice in his head screaming that he should never have left Marcus on his own with those two people.

No, two vampires.

Well, at least the woman. There was something about her that made his skin crawl. She had to be a vampire. The silent black man who towered over all of them like some kind of mobile mountain could have been one, but Ethan wasn't completely sure.

Fuck, both of them felt more vampirish than Marcus did.

Leaving Marcus's house when he did had put a sick queasiness in the pit of his stomach. The people who appeared on the doorstep just before the rain started were not welcome guests, but intruders. But for some reason, Marcus couldn't turn them away.

And even with the danger tingling in the air, Ethan was

stunned by how Marcus attempted to protect him. He could see it in the way he positioned his body between Ethan and the two intruders, and the way he'd tried to distract them from Ethan.

His new posh apartment might only be a quick ten-minute walk from Marcus's town house, but he was thoroughly drenched when he squeaked his way through the marble entrance to the elevator. The walk and cooling rain didn't help him clear his head when it came to Marcus.

When he'd agreed to the assignment, his instructions were relatively simple. Gather any and all information on Marcus Varik and any vampires he associated with. They needed addresses, habits, favorite haunts, anything. Considering the way Marcus reacted to the woman, Ethan felt confident she was a vampire, but he had nothing more than a name and a physical description to give about her.

The job didn't require Ethan to try and be friends with Marcus.

But he found himself wanting to be, and he'd been sure that such a thing would never be possible.

This was a mess. He closed his eyes and conjured up the memory of that night. The screams and cries of his family. The smell of the blood. The laughter and the voices of the vampires who slaughtered his family.

He tried to imagine Marcus as one of them, walking through his house. But where Marcus should have been laughing and blood-drenched, he saw only a horrified look on Marcus's handsome face. He could more easily imagine Marcus gathering up young Ethan and tucking him against his chest, carrying him to safety from that nightmare, promising to take care of him.

A fucking mess. This was a fucking mess.

He hadn't thought too much about Marcus during the first few days of the job. On his first day of work, Marcus had been stiff and incredibly reserved as if he didn't quite know what to say or how to act around Ethan. When Ethan didn't see him again over the next few days, he'd been sure such a thing would become the norm. Any information would have to be gained through snooping through his personal belongings. Luckily, it was his job to pack up those items.

But that text from Rafe changed everything. He never expected to be looking at what was essentially porn with his boss. It was only worse because his boss's brother was in the pic. Of course, Ethan had to make the moment more awkward by opening his mouth.

It wasn't like he'd fantasized about the hotness of his boss. Of course, Marcus was a freaking wet dream. Given that his brother looked that mouthwatering, Ethan could only imagine the stunning body hiding under Marcus's suits.

As painfully awkward as it was, that picture broke the ice between them. They'd talked for more than an hour, and Ethan had enjoyed every moment of it except for when he was reminded of his murdered family.

What kind of a person was he to keep forgetting about his family every time Marcus flashed that unsure smile in his direction?

With a heavy sigh, Ethan flopped down in the middle of the couch and rubbed his hands over his face. When he lowered his hands, he inwardly cringed at the way Carl was closely watching him.

The man looked to be in his late forties, maybe early fifties with salt-and-pepper scruff on his chin and jawline. More gray was creeping into his dark hair while lines were digging deep furrows in his narrow face. His dark eyes reminded him of a rodent's, quick and sharp, as they took in every movement. He'd never felt easy around Carl.

When Carl approached him, it had been reassuring that he finally had someone who understood what Ethan had seen so many years ago. There had been no gunshots. No animals tearing at people's throats. There had only been dark voices and a blood-covered woman with fangs. He had talked about getting justice for the dead, and Ethan had been in.

But Carl kept wanting to be this father figure to him, and Ethan wasn't buying it. He'd survived foster homes and boys' group homes. There had been some bad places and some okay places along the way. The key was that he'd learned to get by on his own. He didn't need some pseudo-father coming in when Ethan knew deep down that Carl only wanted him to help take down the vamps. Any vamps.

He had said it more than once. The only good vamp was a staked one.

"You have to remember, Ethan, that vampires are crafty. They want to seduce us and mind-fuck us. They want you to trust them so that you let your guard down," Carl continued.

"Yeah, but what if all that stuff we've seen in movies and books is bullshit? I mean, some of the people in the group think vamps can't walk around while the sun is up. I'm telling you, on my first day I had a meeting with Varik at ten a.m. We had food together today. Real, actual food. I watched him eat it."

"Are you sure? How do you know it wasn't an illusion? It could have been a trick."

Ethan barely stopped himself from rolling his eyes. That was Carl's answer to everything Ethan said that contradicted what he believed. It was a mind-fuck. A hallucination. An illusion.

He was starting to regret a lot of shit when it came to Carl, starting with agreeing to even let him come over to his apartment. It felt like a serious betrayal of Marcus...not like working for the man wasn't a massive betrayal as well. But Carl had called to check on him as he got home, catching him when he was feeling weak and his mind was all fucked up.

Since the first day on the job, he'd been getting calls from Carl demanding to know if he'd seen Marcus's fangs or where he slept during the day or if there were extra coffins in the basement. As more time passed, Carl was starting to seem like a crazed zealot. Probably more dangerous than Marcus could ever be.

But if he left Carl and the League, where did that leave Ethan? He wanted justice for his parents and sisters, but not at the cost of hurting innocent people.

And right now, there was zero proof that Marcus had anything to do with the death of his family.

Marcus's mother...maybe.

What would his own mother say? She was a sweet, compassionate woman. She'd want Ethan to be happy and to move on with his life. To do something positive and bring joy to other people. Not wallow in pain and blood for a memory.

And damn it, did he really have any proof that Marcus was a vampire? Had Marcus done anything to threaten or scare him? His family might be a little crazy and Marcus was a touch eccentric, but that didn't make him a bloodsucker. Just...interesting.

A loud knocking on the front door stopped Ethan's heart for a breath. He jerked his head up and stared in the direction of the noise. Marcus and Janice were the only other people who knew where he lived. And that did not sound like a Janice knock.

Holy shit. Marcus was at his front door and Carl, the crazy vampire hunter, was sitting in his living room.

Jumping to his feet, Ethan pointed at Carl. "Don't move a muscle. He can't see you here," he hissed.

"Is that..." Carl whispered, his voice drifting off as if he was afraid Marcus could hear him through the door. Ethan nodded and Carl practically vibrated in his seat. He had to get Marcus away from the apartment. He didn't trust Carl to keep his butt in the chair.

Ethan jogged through the apartment and paused only long enough to peer through the peephole to confirm that it was Marcus on the other side. His boss had been particularly concerned about a potential threat from Meryl, but Ethan was doubtful that she'd be able to locate him so quickly.

Even through the weird fisheye lens, he could see Marcus's worried expression. His black hair was wild and standing up in different directions as if he'd been endlessly threading his fingers through it or pulling at it. Something in his heart softened and turned a little mushy, leaving Ethan longing to shake himself. If Marcus was a big, bad vampire, he certainly didn't need some little nobody wanting to wrap him up and take care of him. Good God, it was amazing Marcus hired him in the first place.

Pulling open the door, Ethan slipped outside before Marcus could take a step forward and smiled stiffly at him.

"Hey, Boss!" Ethan said a little louder than he meant to as he tried to force cheerfulness in his tone. Luckily, Marcus appeared too distracted to notice. "Do you need me to run an errand?"

"Ethan! Are you all right? Did you have any problems getting home?" Marcus quickly demanded. He put both hands on Ethan's shoulders, holding him in place, but there was a feeling that Marcus wanted to drag him tight against him. And Ethan found he was disappointed that Marcus didn't.

"No. No problem. Just got caught in the storm, but no big deal." Ethan stepped the rest of the way out into the hall and closed the door behind him. That got Marcus's attention. He released Ethan and glared at the door for a moment before looking down at Ethan.

"Who is in your apartment?" he asked quietly.

"Umm...no one...just an old friend. We kind of made a mess and I'd rather you not see it. It'd be kind of awkward."

Marcus's eyes narrowed on him and Ethan's heart sped up even more. He was going to have a fucking heart attack. Marcus could not freaking see Carl. And Carl could not be allowed anywhere near Marcus.

"Are Meryl and Cain in there?"

"What? No! Of course not."

Marcus stunned him by lifting both of his hands to gently cup either side of Ethan's neck. Thumbs pressed under his jaw, carefully tilting his head up so that Ethan had to stare directly into Marcus's stunning blue eyes. His breath caught in his throat as he stared at Marcus as if he were trying to peer straight into his soul. His eyes fluttered closed as those strong fingers stroked down his neck in a tender caress. The most delicious tingles danced along his skin and sent blood rushing down to his cock. He couldn't fucking think.

Before releasing him, Marcus pulled him close, pressing his nose into Ethan's hair and drawing in a deep breath as if he were trying to draw Ethan into his lungs.

Just as quickly as it all started, Marcus was releasing him. Ethan struggled to open his eyes, but when they focused, he was surprised to see Marcus pacing the hall, gripping his hair with both hands. It was only then Ethan realized Marcus had been checking him for bites on his neck and smelling for the scent of Meryl and Cain.

But he didn't believe that Marcus thought he was lying. Not with such a gentle, caring touch. No, he was worried about Ethan's safety. Worried that the two vampires would try to hurt him.

"Marcus?"

"I'm sorry, Ethan," Marcus said softly. "I don't mean to frighten you."

"Right now, I'm more worried about you. Who are they?"

Marcus turned back, his frown in place but there was also sadness in his eyes. "I can't explain. Only that my life sometimes brings me into contact with ruthless and uncaring people. I don't want them to fixate on you. To threaten you to get at me. I'm sorry."

Ethan stepped close to Marcus again, placing his hand on

Marcus's forearm and squeezing. "Don't. You are not responsible for the actions of others."

"Thank you." Marcus gave a little sigh, his frown easing somewhat but there was no touching the sadness that lingered in his gaze. "I am hopeful that Meryl will direct her attention elsewhere and forget about you."

"Well, I am quite forgettable," Ethan joked, but Marcus only shook his head.

Reaching up, Marcus touched a bit of Ethan's blond hair, and Ethan was sure he was going to melt into the floor. "There is nothing forgettable about you. I only hope that Meryl and Cain are too blind to realize it." Marcus's voice was warm and rough, wrapping around him as if he were weaving a spell. But this had nothing do with him being a vampire. This was desire.

Holy fuck....Marcus was gay. There had been little hints earlier in the day when they'd talked over their meal. Marcus had been particularly interested in his dating habits and his life. It had made Ethan wonder, but then their unexpected guests had shoved those thoughts to the back of his mind.

"Marcus..."

As if realizing what he was doing, Marcus released Ethan and took a step away before reaching into his pocket. He pulled out a folded piece of paper and handed it to Ethan.

"What's this?" Ethan asked as he opened the paper. There were four names and phone numbers scrawled on it in Marcus's beautiful handwriting.

"I wasn't sure if Janice gave it to you, but this is my cell phone number, as well as the numbers for all three of my brothers."

Ethan smirked up at Marcus. "Rafe isn't going to start sending me interesting texts, is he?"

"I will strangle him with my bare hands if he does," Marcus growled and gave a quick shake of his head. "No, this is for emergencies. If you are ever out and see either Meryl or Cain, I want you to call me immediately. If you can't reach me, call my brothers. Keep calling all of us until you reach someone."

"Okay."

"Then I want you to stay in an area surrounded by people until we can reach you."

"But what if it's during the day?"

Marcus gave him a weak smile. "We'll figure something out. I promise. You will be safe."

The promise warmed him. Ethan walked Marcus to the elevator and ended up riding it to the lobby, even though they didn't speak again. He didn't want to say good-bye to Marcus, not when he could see the worry weighing so heavily on his shoulders. The truth was that he agreed with Marcus's original assessment—there was no reason for Meryl to come after him. He was just an employee to Marcus. A lowly assistant.

But then, it felt like things had changed since lunch and that silly picture. It was the touch of Marcus's hand and the look in his eyes when he was standing in the hall. He couldn't believe that he meant nothing to Marcus. It wasn't just that Marcus was a good, honorable person. He cared.

The elevator dinged as it reached his floor again. Ethan stepped out and stopped.

Carl was waiting for him in his apartment. Marcus cared about him…and Ethan was plotting with a dangerous group to destroy Marcus and his entire family.

This was wrong. All of it was so fucking wrong, but he didn't know what to do. He had no proof Marcus was a vampire. Well, no really solid proof.

He definitely had no evidence he had anything to do with the murder of his family. If Marcus and his family truly were innocent, he wasn't going to do a damn thing to them. He wasn't going to let Carl and the League hurt the Variks.

But would Carl let him walk away from the Human

Protecting Humans League? Just pretend that none of it happened?

Fuck. He needed to figure things out. Find a way to come clean to Marcus without convincing the man that he'd lost his mind. And he had to figure out the best way to get free of Carl and the League.

CHAPTER NINE

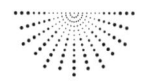

Something was ringing.
       An alarm?
No. Too early.

Ethan scrubbed his hand across his eyes and rolled over in the bed. He blinked at the clock that showed in angry red numbers that it was after three in the morning. As his brain crept toward full consciousness, he realized that his phone was ringing.

Snatching it off the charger, Ethan sat up, glanced at the screen to confirm that it was Marcus calling him, and answered it.

"Marcus?" Ethan said, his voice rough and gravelly with sleep.

"I need you to run an errand as quickly as possible," Marcus replied. "Do you have a pen and paper handy?"

"Umm...just a sec." Throwing off the covers, Ethan jumped out of the bed, the phone still pressed to his ear as he tripped over a pair of shoes as he crossed the room. He could hear muffled shouts in the background and pounding on wood...

maybe footsteps. It was all hard to make out, but there was no missing the desperate urgency in Marcus's voice.

He crossed to the living room, flipping on lights as he moved through the rooms. He winced and blinked, his eyes complaining about the brightness. On the coffee table, he found an old receipt and a pen. He scribbled across it quickly to make sure it worked and sighed with relief. "Okay, I'm ready."

"I need gauze, pads, medical tape—"

"Whiskey. Get some fucking whiskey!" shouted a new angry voice.

"Whiskey and peroxide," Marcus continued.

"She broke my bow. My bow! She broke my bow!" cried another male voice Ethan didn't recognize.

"I know, Bel. We're going to get you a new bow for your cello. I promise." The first angry voice had soothed the other person with such gentleness and care that it nearly broke Ethan's heart. He didn't know what the hell was going on, but someone was seriously hurt.

"Marcus, are you okay?" Ethan demanded.

"I'm fine. Get everything on the list and get to my house in thirty minutes," Marcus snapped and then hung up the phone.

Ethan dropped his phone on the list and ran to his bedroom. He flipped on the light and started grabbing clothes. He wasn't entirely sure if he was even picking up clean clothes or not. Didn't matter. Someone was hurt. Probably one of Marcus's brothers.

But if they were vampires, why would they need all those medical supplies? Vampires were supposed to heal quickly. This didn't make any damn sense.

A week had passed since their interrupted meal and Ethan's visit from both Carl and Marcus. He was avoiding Carl as much as possible as he tried to figure out the best way to tell the man that he wasn't going to do his dirty work anymore. He also hadn't found a good way to come clean to Marcus about why he'd taken the job in the first place. The problem was that if he told Marcus, he'd definitely lose his job as well as any chance of discovering the truth about who killed his family. Fuck, it was all a mess, but at least he had something more pressing to worry about than his own problems.

With his heart pounding, he snatched up the list and his phone from the table on his way out the door. He rode the elevator down to the garage where Janice had stashed Marcus's Mini Cooper in a parking spot for him. Since starting the job two weeks ago, he'd used the car only once to run and get supplies for packing up Marcus's house. The rest of the stuff he ordered and had delivered directly to the town house.

He sped to the nearest all-night superstore, praying that the cops weren't looking as he drove well above the speed limit. Finding the medical supplies wasn't difficult. He grabbed everything Marcus listed and a few items he might not have thought of. Ethan had no idea what was wrong, but he wanted them to be prepared for anything since it was obvious that they weren't going to the hospital.

The store didn't have much selection in the way of whiskey, but he managed to locate a large, cheap bottle. If Marcus's brothers were anything like him, they wouldn't care for the taste, but Ethan knew that they didn't want the alcohol for the taste. They were looking to numb. A trick Ethan had succumbed to more than once on the anniversary of his family's murder.

On his way through the store, Ethan ran across a section that carried musical instruments and other equipment. He glanced at his phone to see that he still had a few minutes before he needed to race to Marcus's town house. Walking briskly down the aisle, he looked over the various instruments, strings, tuning devices, rosin, pics, and reeds until he finally came to a small area displaying bows. There was only one marked for a cello and Ethan snatched it up. He knew that if this was

Marcus's brother, the man likely had something fancy, but this might help ease his pain until he could get something he was more accustomed to using.

He rushed out of the store, putting everything on the corporate credit card Janice had given him on his second day of work. When she'd said he'd need it for planning the move and running random errands for Marcus, he never thought he'd be using the card to pay for medical gauze, whiskey, and a cello bow.

Parking outside the town house with only two minutes to spare, Ethan rushed to the back door and used his key to let himself in. The door led straight into the kitchen. He flipped on the light and his heart stopped to see blood smeared across the black-and-white checkerboard floor. More was smeared across the center island as if someone had slid a blood-covered hand across it, using it for support as they moved through the room.

Swallowing the rising fear and all-too-familiar memories of that horrible night, Ethan forced himself to continue through the kitchen toward the heart of the house. It didn't take him long to hear raised voices. He followed the noise.

At first, it seemed like none of the lights were on in the house, but he finally spotted light spilling across the hall floor from the library.

He picked up his pace, rushing toward the room, but his feet halted at the threshold. A tall, slender man was stretched out on the leather couch, his shirt soaked with blood. There were long scratches across his face, and his dark hair was matted with what looked to be sweat and blood. His skin looked too pale under the yellow light of the lamps.

Another man kneeled at his side, his hands pressing against his chest as he spoke softly to the injured man. From behind, Ethan thought that the kneeling man might be Rafe. Marcus hovered nearby, rubbing his hand through the man's hair. More blood was smeared across his face and coated his hands.

"Marcus," Ethan croaked. His hands shook. He'd not seen

that much blood in years. Not since that night. His entire body seemed to lock up. Air refused to enter his lungs beyond a few tiny sips.

"Ethan." There was no missing the relief in Marcus's tone. The sound helped to snap Ethan's gaze from the wounded figure on the couch to watch Marcus rush to his side.

"What happened?" Ethan whispered. It was as loud as he could get his voice as he forced the words out.

"Thank you for getting this," Marcus said, ignoring his question. "A bow?"

Ethan looked at how Marcus lightly ran his fingers up the bow in a caress that brought tears to Ethan's eyes.

"I thought it might help," Ethan mumbled.

"It will."

"She tried to take my heart!" the man on the couch screamed. "She wanted to rip my heart out. She was trying to kill me!"

Ethan lurched back a step in horror, watching as Rafe shifted one hand to run over his forehead. "It's okay. You're safe now," he murmured over and over again.

"Go home, Ethan." Ethan's eyes snapped over to Marcus, stunned by the cold, hard quality of his voice. Just a moment ago, there had been such kindness and warmth. "I'll call you tomorrow if your services are needed."

Before Ethan could say anything else, the door to the library was slammed in his face. He was officially dismissed.

And yet, Ethan couldn't leave. He didn't know what the hell was going on, but it was clear that one of Marcus's brothers had been brutally attacked and injured. The man on the couch had said "she." Had that woman Meryl attacked Marcus's brother? Was that what Marcus was trying to protect him from?

Backing up, Ethan walked a short distance from the library and sat down on the floor, his back pressed against the wall. The hardwood almost immediately bit into his ass, but he didn't want to move. Not until he was sure that Marcus's brother was okay, and Marcus didn't need him any longer.

He had to wait only a couple of minutes before Ethan heard raised voices through the door. This time, it was Marcus shouting.

"Go, Rafe! You know Winter needs your help, especially if she realizes what she did."

"Bel needs me too!" someone shouted in response. There was such pain in that voice. Ethan thought it was likely Rafe, but there was such a heavy weight of fear and worry in his tone. It was surprising to think this was the same man who sent his brothers a naked picture of himself in bed with two other people. But despite his hedonistic tendencies, he clearly cared for his brother.

"I've got Bel. Winter needs you," Marcus countered.

There was another voice. Softer than the others. Ethan couldn't make out the words through the door, but he guessed it was Bel urging Rafe to leave, because only a few seconds later, the library door was jerked open and the man stormed out.

He stopped sharply when he spotted Ethan. From his impressive height, he glared down at Ethan, his blood-covered hands clenched into fists at his sides. Rafe was a stunningly handsome man in his perfectly tailored slacks and button-down shirt. Blood splashed across him didn't detract from his beauty but added a dangerous edge to him that had Ethan's heart speeding up.

"You're the assistant," Rafe stated and Ethan nodded. "Marcus told you to leave. Why are you still here?"

"I'm staying until I'm sure he doesn't need anything else."

Emotions that Ethan couldn't quite put a name to flitted across Rafe's face for a second before everything was simply washed away to reveal a blank slate. "You brought him the bow," Rafe murmured softly.

Ethan could only nod again. It had seemed like such a silly

thing to pause for when it was clear that someone was seriously injured. But there had been something in the voice shouting about the broken bow that threatened to shatter Ethan's heart. He'd been sure that the broken bow was more important to the person than potentially bleeding out.

"Thank you. It helped." Rafe gave a little wave of his hand as he started for the rear of the house. "Stick around," he called over his shoulder. "Bel might need another donor."

A chill skittered through Ethan and he wrapped his arms around his bent legs. Ethan knew Rafe meant a blood donor. It was clear that Bel had lost a lot of blood. He'd need to have it replaced. Would Bel kill him if he fed off him?

Would Marcus let his brother kill him?

If that was how vampires fed, then Ethan felt pretty damn sure that Marcus wouldn't hesitate to choose the life of his brother over the life of some guy who worked for him. It didn't matter if they were starting to become friends. Family came first, and Marcus very clearly loved his family.

Rafe's words kept replaying in his head. *Another donor.*

How many people had Bel fed from before he reached Marcus's town house?

Was there a long trail of bodies across the city leading back to Marcus's?

That was a lovely image.

And yet, he was still sitting there, waiting for some word or reassurance from Marcus. Why? Because Marcus paid well? Because he treated Ethan with kindness and respect? Because Marcus was some hot guy with the most adorable smile?

Or was it that Marcus was his only real chance at finding out the truth about what happened to his family?

Ethan groaned against his legs. There was a good chance that it was a combination of all those reasons, and that didn't make him feel too great about himself.

He waited another half hour, but there were no more shouts

or cries of pain from the library. Shoving against the wall and floor, Ethan slowly hoisted himself to his feet. His body protested the movement. The hardwood floor had been incredibly uncomfortable, but walking suddenly felt worse. He shuffled toward the kitchen and dug through the cabinets and closets until he finally located the cleaning supplies. There was no going back to sleep anytime soon, and he wasn't leaving. Might as well do something useful, starting with getting rid of all this damn blood on every surface.

And if he was lucky, the physical labor would help him clear his head and maybe find some answer as to why the hell he was so determined to stick close to Marcus when it was obvious the man was the center of violence and danger. Two things Ethan didn't need in his life.

CHAPTER TEN

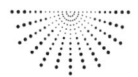

Marcus poured the last of the bagged blood into a glass. He tossed the bag into a nearby trash can, mentally noting that he'd have to empty the garbage before Ethan returned to the house. Bagged blood was a good filler, but for some reason it wouldn't hold a vampire over for an extended period of time. The longer the blood was in the bag rather than running through the human, the less power it contained. Blood straight from the source held the most power when it came to healing and satisfying hunger cravings. There was no surviving strictly off bagged blood.

Luckily Rafe had been with them. They'd managed to get Bel to two donors before they made it to Marcus's house. Rafe was the only one among them who could blur the memories of a human. It seemed to be part of his special gift to charm humans. Bel had fed deeply, but both humans were left alive and unconscious in a safe location before the brothers arrived at Marcus's town house.

The infusion of blood had helped to slow the bleeding, but the wounds on his chest were so extensive, Marcus knew Bel would need a few days to fully heal. At least on a physical level. Emotionally, Marcus wasn't sure if Bel would ever recover.

Earlier in the evening, Bel had sent out a text that Julianna was having a bad night. Rafe had immediately replied, asking if he needed some help, but Bel didn't answer. Marcus waited roughly a half hour. Sometimes Bel got distracted and didn't check his phone right away. Julianna hadn't had a truly bad night in nearly a year. They'd each been able to manage her alone.

Winter sent another text to Bel, and their brother hadn't answered. Something was wrong.

Marcus had raced to Bel's house, knowing Rafe and Winter were doing the same thing. He arrived first, but Rafe was right on his heels. Charging into the old house, they found their mother straddling Bel's chest, both of them covered in his blood. His shirt had been shredded, and there were more cuts on his face as if she'd raked her nails across his cheeks. He was lucky to have not lost an eye.

But the worst, it was like she was trying to dig into his chest and pull out his heart. She was screaming nonsense, claiming that he was evil, that he needed to be destroyed. They all needed to be destroyed.

Marcus had pulled their mother off Bel and subdued her as best he could without hurting her while Rafe worked to stop the bleeding. Bel had only tried to protect himself. They all knew he never raised a hand toward her. None of them would willingly harm their mother. This wasn't her fault. There was something horribly broken in her mind, and no matter what they tried, they could never fix her.

The best they could do was play for her.

For some reason, the music reached the calmer parts of her mind. It soothed her when nothing else could.

Thank God Winter arrived a couple of minutes after Rafe with his guitar in hand. He said nothing, barely even looking over at Bel. He just sat right in front of where Marcus had their mother held and started playing. It was a soft, lilting melody that reminded Marcus of water trickling down from leaf to leaf in a forest before finally slipping into a playfully babbling brook.

Within minutes, Julianna relaxed in Marcus's arms. She hummed along to Winter's playing, swaying from side to side. Her voice was sweet and haunting, calling Marcus back to bittersweet memories of his childhood when life was so wonderfully simple. They'd lived in their mother's fancy town house. There were tutors and instructors filling their days with knowledge. Their mother was almost always around to oversee their education, especially in music. As they learned to play, she would sing along. Even if the song had no words, she'd make up silly songs to match the tune they played.

Now music was the only thing that saved them all.

It took close to an hour to finally get Julianna moved to her own bedchamber with Winter. She had to be away from the blood when they stopped playing. Most of the time, her brain didn't register the carnage and destruction she caused. It was like she couldn't even see it, and she definitely didn't know she'd been the one to create it.

But there had been a few rare instances where she did see the blood and the wounds still healing on her children. She'd remember that she was the one to attack her children. The horror would only throw her right back into a brutal episode. It was just easier for all of them if she was never allowed to see what she did.

Marcus rationalized that it wasn't really her. The sweet, caring woman who had raised them would never be capable of such violence. It wasn't her. Just some darkness in her brain that was only made worse when she was transformed into a vampire.

As children, they all remembered times where they would

catch her talking to herself. Or rather, talking to someone none of them could see. When asked, she'd say that she was just talking to the fairies and laugh like it was nothing. But there were a couple of times she woke them all in the middle of the night, and they all hid in the attic until the servants finally found them and coaxed their mother out.

But it wasn't until she became a vampire that her strange madness turned to violence.

"I don't want to drink more," Bel said wearily when Marcus offered him the glass.

"You've lost a lot of blood. You need to drink," Marcus said stubbornly.

Bel closed his eyes and shook his head. He was propped up on the couch, his long body still hanging off. Marcus hated the sickly paleness of his cheeks. They were all pale after a century of hiding from the sun, but this was more extreme. Marcus needed him to drink just to return the color to his cheeks.

"Rafe? Did Rafe go?" Bel's eyes suddenly blinked open, and he moved like he was trying to rise off the couch.

"He went to check on Winter." Marcus carefully placed his hands on Bel's shoulders, pushing him down onto the cushions. He didn't want to mention their mother. This was the worst attack Bel had ever suffered, and he didn't need to be reminded that she was his assailant.

"Should we go help them? I don't want—"

"They'll be fine. They've got it under control."

"But she's strong. What if Winter and Rafe can't handle her? We can't let anything happen to them."

"They've got it under control. Winter had her calm and in her room before we even left. Rafe is just going to see if Winter needs a break."

Bel relaxed against the cushions, releasing a deep, heavy sigh. His eyes were closed, but it didn't stop the tear that slipped from the corner of his left eye to slide down his temple. Marcus swallowed hard against the lump in his throat as he wiped the tear away with his thumb.

"Why does she hate me, Marcus?" Bel asked. His voice was barely a whisper and shook with a pain that Marcus was sure had nothing to do with the wounds on his chest.

"She doesn't, Bel. You know that. Mother loves you."

"But I can't fix her. I've tried for so long. A century. I can't fix her. Does she know and hate me for it?"

Marcus threaded his fingers through Bel's thick hair, pushing it back from his forehead. "Don't. She loves you. This attack...this isn't her. You know that. These bad episodes aren't her. It's the sickness. She can't control it."

Bel's eyes flicked open, holding Marcus. "Tonight was different."

"What do you mean?"

Bel shook his head and tried to sit up again, but Marcus wouldn't let him. He needed to rest and conserve his energy in order to heal. Bel finally gave up and frowned at Marcus. They were long used to his dominating, dictatorial ways, but that didn't mean they didn't try to push against him every once in a while.

"You sent a text that you thought she was having an episode."

"She seemed off. We went out hunting early. She didn't seem much in the mood for feeding, but it had been two weeks. I knew that if we didn't, she would definitely have an episode by the end of the week."

When Julianna stayed with Bel, he kept a strict log of all her activities in hopes of identifying potential triggers. The one thing they'd discovered was that she couldn't go longer than three weeks without feeding. Hunger would definitely set her off.

Largely, Julianna was indifferent to feeding. Sometimes she was in the mood, but it wasn't often. They'd usually have to coax her into going out.

"Any problems?"

"We both found donors quickly. She fed a little lightly, but she did feed. I figured it would be enough to hold her at least a week, and then we headed home."

"Did she see anyone, or did anything happen?"

Bel shook his head. "No. Nothing. We walked home with her arm in mine, and she was talking about digging out her old sheet music for *Carmen*. That opera has always made her happy. I have no record of it being linked to her bad moods."

"When did you realize she was going to have an episode?"

Bel rubbed the bridge of his nose with thumb and forefinger. Marcus frowned to see his hand was brown with dried blood. They both desperately needed showers, but cleaning up would have to wait.

"As soon as we walked into the house," Bel murmured, "I told her that I'd get my cello. I thought I'd play while she sang. I hadn't played in a while, and I thought it would be nice to play when she was already in a good mood. But she jerked away from me like she was repulsed by me. She said she wanted nothing to do with me and stalked off to the library. The mood change was so sudden, I stood there shocked."

"You sent the text then?"

Bel nodded and swallowed hard. Marcus picked up the glass of blood, pushing it on Bel again. His brother accepted it and drained it, but Marcus didn't think he was aware of what he was doing. His stare was distant, and Marcus was willing to bet he was replaying in his mind what happened.

"After I sent the text, I went to check on her. I'd barely stepped into the room when she attacked me, screaming that I was evil."

Marcus set the empty glass on an end table and resumed running his hand through his brother's hair. "You're not evil. And that's not our mother. She's sick."

"But why? Why can't I fix it? She doesn't deserve to be like this."

"I know, Bel. I know."

Bel closed his eyes, tears slipping down both cheeks now, and Marcus's heart broke for his brother, broke for all of them. "She wouldn't want this, Marcus. It would kill her to know that she's hurting her sons. She wouldn't want to live like this if she knew."

Winter had whispered those same broken words to him, and Marcus couldn't bring himself to disagree. Julianna Varik loved her sons with all her being. She was the soul of kindness and compassion. There wasn't a bit of hatred, anger, or violence within that woman.

But it was not the woman they loved who attacked them. It was the monster that lived within her.

"We don't have much choice," Marcus murmured.

Bel opened his eyes, pain clear there, but also knowledge that they did have one choice, but not one of them had yet voiced those words. Others had. Meryl had stated very clearly that Julianna needed to be killed in order to save them all. And Julianna's death was the only thing that would save them from her attacks.

But she was their mother. Even if she might be the creature that one day ended their immortal existence, they couldn't bring themselves to end her life to save themselves. They were trapped.

"Marcus?"

"Yes, Bel."

Bel licked his lips and closed his eyes for a moment. His little brother seemed so tired, as if exhaustion had seeped down into his bones. "Would you play for me? I just want to forget for a little while and your playing..."

"I know," Marcus murmured. "We'll need to move to the

music room on the third floor. My piano isn't quite as mobile as your cello."

Bel smirked at him. "You could invest in one of those electric keyboards."

"Suggest that again and I'm going to dump you on my doorstep. You know those sound nothing like my baby," Marcus growled, but it was all for show. He felt lighter to see Bel teasing him. Bel wasn't as big of a joker as Rafe, but he did go in for a little playful teasing every once in a while.

"Yes, but your baby weighs a ton…" Bel paused on a hiss as Marcus slid an arm under him and helped him sit upright on the couch. "And she doesn't easily fit through doorways," he continued through clenched teeth.

Marcus carefully got Bel on his feet and his arm around Bel's waist to steady him.

"Wait! My bow!" Bel cried before they could take a step. Marcus bit back a smile as he twisted around and snatched up the cello bow Ethan had gotten. He handed it over to Bel, who gripped it tightly in his fingers like a security blanket. More than anything, he could kiss Ethan for picking up that one item. Music had been so thoroughly ingrained in their upbringing that the instruments calmed them when their world was in chaos around them.

They slowly made it across the room where Marcus jerked open the door. The elevator was a short distance away down the hall. Unfortunately, they didn't get far before the sound of footsteps thundered through the house. Marcus's hand tightened on Bel's waist and he tried to shift his brother so that he was partially behind Marcus's larger frame. No one was supposed to be in the house. They should have been alone.

Fangs slid down and Marcus prepared to launch himself at the intruder to protect his injured brother. No one would touch Bel.

Ethan rushed around the corner and came to a sharp stop at the sight of Marcus, his face going pale.

"What are you doing here?" Marcus snarled, fighting to retract his fangs before Ethan could notice them. "I told you to leave!"

"I thought you could use my help," Ethan replied, his voice wobbling slightly.

"Get out of here or you're fucking fired!" Marcus shouted. He knew he was being irrational, but Marcus was exhausted and at the end of his emotional rope. The only thought running through his head was that Bel was weak and vulnerable. Everyone not family could be a threat to his brother.

To his surprise, Ethan straightened his shoulders and lifted his head, but didn't retreat. "Fine. Fire me."

"What?" He couldn't have possibly heard him correctly.

"Fire me. If you fire me, then I'm here as a friend, and that means I don't have to listen to you anymore."

"What?" Marcus repeated because nothing was making sense.

"Your brother needs help, and I'm not going anywhere."

Bel surprised Marcus by snickering. He twisted carefully so that he could look at his brother, who was giving him a somewhat crooked grin.

"He's as stubborn as Winter. I can't believe you hired him," Bel teased.

"I have a feeling he was desperate," Ethan replied.

Marcus's head whipped back to face Ethan. "No, I wasn't," he said sharply.

"What can I do?" Ethan's voice was even and there was a flush in his cheeks. If Marcus had scared him, he'd moved past it.

"We're moving to the music room on the third floor. I need you to go into the green bedroom beside it and grab the comforter off the bed. Bring it to the music room. I'm going to place Bel on the couch in there."

Ethan frowned. "Those have to be locked rooms. I haven't seen them yet."

Marcus reached into his pocket and pulled out his keys. He shuffled through them with his thumb until he found the right key and then handed it over to Ethan. "Music room is the second door on the right from the stairs. The green room is to the left of the music room."

With the keys in his hand, Ethan darted off, his footsteps pounding up the stairs in his haste.

"He's interesting," Bel said, reminding Marcus that his brother was right there, watching everything.

"Ethan has been a great help for the move," Marcus replied, ignoring the stiffness in his tone.

"And you asked him to get me a bow?"

"No. I think he overheard you when I called him for supplies." Marcus got them moving again down the hall to the elevator. He rarely used the elevator since it wasn't often that he went from the ground floor to the top floor, but it came in handy when one of his brothers was injured.

"Will he move with you to Connecticut?" Bel's question was broken by pants of pained breaths as he leaned against the wall of the elevator.

Marcus pushed the button for the third floor and closed his eyes. "I don't think so. The position is just temporary. For the move."

"But you've always had an assistant."

"He's going to school for computer coding. I don't think he wants to spend the next ten years running my errands, no matter how well I pay."

How would he let Ethan go after spending ten years with him? As it was, he was dreading saying good-bye after just three short months. For the past week, they'd started eating lunch at five each day. They talked about random things, but Marcus had to admit that it was the best hour out of his entire day. He wasn't ready for that to end, to go back to his lonely existence.

But he shoved that selfish thought away as the doors silently slid open again on the third floor. As they were stepping out, Marcus caught sight of Ethan heading into the music room, with a comforter and a couple of pillows in his arms. Inside, only two lamps burned, offering up soft, dim light.

Marcus focused on getting Bel set up on the larger sofa and then carefully tucked the blanket around his brother. He could feel Ethan standing just behind his shoulder as if he were waiting for the chance to jump in.

"Comfortable?" Marcus asked, his eyes skimming over Bel.

"As much as I'm going to be."

"Do you need anything? A glass of water?" Ethan offered.

Marcus stepped back and looked over at Ethan to find his teeth worrying his bottom lip. He looked nervous, as if the confidence he'd shown outside the library had dissolved as he climbed the stairs.

"No, I'm okay. Thank you for my bow." Bel lifted the bow in his right hand and smiled a little.

Ethan nodded before looking over at Marcus again. "I'm going to go downstairs and finish cleaning up the kitchen and hall. Then I can—"

"Stay," Marcus cut him off and not just because he didn't want Ethan going into the library. He wanted him close. "If you're not returning home, then stay. Rest." He motioned to a smaller loveseat that was positioned next to Bel's couch. "I don't mind an audience."

Ethan's smile doubled in size, and Marcus felt an answering skip of his heart. With a nod, Ethan darted over to the sofa and made himself comfortable.

Marcus turned to the gleaming black grand piano. He had three pianos in the house, counting the old upright in the basement and the smaller baby grand in his own bedroom. But the piano in the music room was his favorite. He'd had her the longest, spent the most time with her.

His fingers easily danced over the ivory keys as he mentally shuffled through the mountain of songs that he knew by heart. He played nearly every day and had since he was a boy. It was as much a part of his daily routine as getting dressed or reading the morning paper.

After a moment, he decided against the tried and true concertos written by the old masters and settled on something different, something original. Taking a deep breath, he started on a song that he'd been tinkering with for the past few years. It was a slow, haunting song that always made him think of a fox sniffing its way through the underbrush of the forest, slinking along in the low-lying fog until finally catching the scent of a hare. The chase was on. The notes sped up, nipping on each other's heels, darting here and there. But the hare escaped. The fox looked up, finding himself in a new pasture, the night sky spread wide above him with stars sparkling. The fox felt small and alone, the world pressing down. He slowly slunk back into the safety of the cover of the woods.

Through the song, Marcus never thought about the notes or the melody he was crafting. Just the lonely fox.

When his hands lifted from the keys, Marcus took a deep breath. He was exhausted, but there was a deeper sense of peace that went with the sadness he could never shake. He wasn't sure how long he'd been playing. Longer than a couple of minutes.

His smile returned when he looked over at Bel. Long enough for his brother to drift off into sleep.

Hesitantly, he turned his gaze to find Ethan watching him. His wide eyes were a little glassy, but there was a beautiful smile on his face. Marcus watched as Ethan quietly crossed the room and came to stand next to the piano.

"That was gorgeous, but I didn't recognize it," he admitted, looking a bit sheepish.

"I've never played it for anyone before," Marcus said.

Ethan's brow furrowed and he cocked his head to the side. "You…you wrote that?"

"Yes."

Ethan gave a little shake of his head. "I think the goddess has met her match."

"I don't think so, but I'm flattered. I've listened to more of her work. She's quite amazing."

"And so was that." Ethan surprised Marcus by extending his hand. "But that's enough for tonight. You need some sleep."

Marcus reached for his hand but stopped at the last second when he saw that his were still covered in blood. He started to pull back, but Ethan grabbed his hand, pulling him up to his feet. Marcus didn't know what was happening, but he was willing to follow Ethan wherever he wanted to go.

CHAPTER ELEVEN

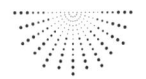

*E*than wanted to feel panic and fear when he stared at Marcus. There really was no doubt in his mind that Marcus and his brothers were vampires. A sane person would have taken his brother to a hospital. Ethan hadn't seen the actual wounds, but just the amount of blood he'd cleaned up meant that Bel had been seriously injured. No one could heal from that without medical assistance.

And yet, just an hour later, Bel's color was starting to improve. He was resting on the couch, his breathing falling in a steady rhythm.

Looking at the aristocratic creature seated on the piano bench, streaked with his brother's blood, Ethan couldn't see anything but a man exhausted and hurting in ways that he couldn't fully understand. He trusted Marcus to not hurt him. He'd already gone out of his way to protect him from Meryl and Cain.

Ethan wanted to take care of Marcus. It was clear that he was the family protector. He was the one who made the hard decisions and directed the others in order to get things done and keep them safe. But who was there to take care of Marcus?

Taking Marcus's bloody hand in his, Ethan pulled him to his feet and led him out of the music room. He paused in the hallway. The third floor held four rooms with locked doors. One of them was Marcus's private bedroom, but he didn't know which one.

"Here," Marcus said, pointing to a pair of double doors farther down the hall.

Ethan nodded and led the way, pulling the keys Marcus had given him out of his pocket. He unlocked the doors and pushed them open. There was only one small lamp on the nightstand burning, but it was enough to illuminate the large room with an enormous four-poster bed and a long bureau made of a dark wood. The walls were a dark blue with white trim. The carpet under their feet was so thick it was almost like walking on a cloud.

"Thank you, Ethan," Marcus murmured. He squeezed Ethan's hand before releasing it. "You can sleep in the green room if you're too tired to return home. And you don't have to come in to work tomorrow…or rather, today. You need your rest."

Ethan turned and smirked up at Marcus. "Work, huh? I thought I was fired."

Marcus gave him a tired little smile. "I don't think I technically fired you. Just threatened to do it."

Taking a step closer, Ethan slowly reached up and touched the top button on his stained shirt. "Well, I think I'm technically here as a friend, because if your employee did this…" Ethan paused and slipped the first button through the hole. "We'd have to deal with a whole lot of HR shit, and we don't want to do that."

Marcus swallowed hard, staring at Ethan. He licked his lips as his breathing picked up, but he didn't say anything to stop Ethan. Yeah, Marcus was attracted to him. Ethan thought he'd caught a few tells over the past couple of weeks but overall,

Marcus was very careful. The guy was stuck so far in the closet, there was little hope of him ever seeing daylight.

But this wasn't about Marcus exploring his sexuality. There was still the issue of him being a vampire and holding knowledge of his mother's killer. This was about Ethan seeing that Marcus got some well-deserved rest.

Still moving slowly, Ethan lowered his hands and unbuttoned the next three buttons before Marcus finally moved, capturing both of his hands in his.

"Ethan?"

"It's okay," he said, giving him a reassuring smile. "I'm just helping you. I'm going to turn on the shower and get the water to warm up. Do you want me to help you finish getting undressed?"

Marcus's mouth dropped open and sort of soundlessly bobbed for a second like he couldn't get the words out.

Ethan chuckled. He was so damn attracted to this man, to this vulnerable side that he was sure his brothers didn't get to see. Ethan pulled his hands free and resumed unbuttoning his shirt. He pulled the shirt from Marcus's pants to get the last couple of buttons. Ethan slowly ran his palms up Marcus's strong chest, reveling in the feel of hard muscle. A low groan rumbled in Marcus's throat, and that sound sent blood rushing to Ethan's cock. Fuck, that was an amazing sound. He smoothed his hands across Marcus's shoulders, pushing the shirt down his arms and to the floor.

"Ethan...I..."

"Shhh," Ethan murmured. "Nothing is going to happen. You're safe." He leaned up on the tips of his toes and pressed a light kiss to Marcus's throat. Strong hands immediately clamped down on his hips, holding him in place. Fingers dug into his ass and Ethan nearly moaned. He'd die to feel those hands all over his body. Just the thought had his cock stiffening.

"Not sure if the promise of nothing has me relieved or disappointed," Marcus admitted in a shaky voice. He looked down and Ethan could feel the slight tremor creeping through Marcus's muscles. "I've...I've never—"

"I know," Ethan interrupted. "That's why nothing is going to happen." Well, one of the reasons, at least. "You need someone to take care of you tonight. Shower and then bed. Once you're tucked in, I'm going to head home, but I'll return later today."

The sadness crept back into Marcus's blue eyes, but there was also relief there. He nodded and released Ethan.

"Finish getting undressed, my sexy friend," Ethan said and sauntered toward the open door across from the bed. He was guessing it was a private bathroom.

He flicked a switch and sucked in a harsh breath as buttery light cascaded over warm marbled and gold fixtures. The bathroom was almost as big as his old apartment. There was a large garden tub that could easily fit three full-grown men, a double sink vanity with a long mirror, and a shower stall that had enough space and heads to cover the same three men who just climbed out of the tub.

There was muffled thump on the floor and Ethan guessed that Marcus had dropped a shoe. "Are you so touchy-feely with all your friends?"

Ethan laughed as he walked over to the shower. "Would you be jealous if I was?"

"Yes," Marcus hissed, and that single word wrapped in a possessive tone warmed Ethan like nothing else could. He'd had more than a few sexual partners in his life, but no one he'd call a boyfriend and no one who ever felt possessive. He was just a warm body, a tight hole, a great mouth to fuck.

But with Marcus, he felt like more.

Opening the door, Ethan turned the handle, starting the shower. He stuck his hand in the spray, checking the temperature. Still cold. He started to turn to make sure that Marcus had a clean towel, but he jumped when he found Marcus standing directly behind him. The man had moved so silently and so fucking quickly. How had he not noticed him?

Because he's a vampire.

Oh, yeah. Ethan's brain kept conveniently forgetting that little fact.

It was even easier to forget when Marcus was standing just a couple of inches away, wearing only a pair of black boxer briefs. He was pale, but it didn't detract from his beautiful body. Every inch of him was hard. Every. Fucking. Inch.

Ethan's mouth watered to see his thick cock pushing against his briefs, the tip of the head poking above the elastic band. Oh God, he wanted to drop to his knees right there and suck Marcus down his throat until he came on a desperate shout. His libido certainly didn't give a shit if Marcus was a vampire. He wanted to taste him so bad.

Marcus placed a finger under his chin and tilted his head so that he was forced to look up at him. "You didn't answer my question."

Ethan grinned at him. "No, I'm not this touchy-feely with my friends. With anyone, ever."

"Then why?"

A low chuckle left Ethan and he let his eyes travel down Marcus's chest and back to his face. "You mean other than the fact that you're incredibly hot and I would really like to run my tongue over every inch of your body?"

Marcus closed his eyes and sucked in a deep breath as if he was trying to regain control of himself. When he opened his eyes and looked at Ethan again, there was such need and raw hunger in those deep blue depths that a soft whimper escaped Ethan's parted lips. No one had ever looked at him like that.

"We can't," Marcus said roughly.

"Definitely not. There are a lot of really good reasons why we can't, not that I can think a damn one of them right now," Ethan muttered.

Marcus huffed a laugh and took a step back. It was like Ethan could suddenly breathe. The bathroom was starting to steam up from the shower, but Ethan was pretty sure all the heat he was feeling was coming from Marcus.

"You get in the shower. I'm going to turn down your bed and peek in on Bel to make sure he doesn't need anything."

Before Marcus could argue, Ethan stepped around him and hurried out of the bathroom, leaving the door open only a crack to allow the steam to escape. He walked over to the bed and pulled down the thick comforter and silky-soft flat sheet. His brain tried to conjure up images of them stretched out naked together in that bed, their bodies wrapped around each other so that they couldn't tell where one started and the other ended, but he banished those thoughts almost as quickly as they appeared.

Once the bed was ready, he turned on his heel and walked to the music room. He didn't need to step past the threshold to see that Bel hadn't moved an inch since they left the room. As quietly as possible, he crossed the room. He checked to make sure that the blinds and curtains were still in place, covering the windows and protecting Bel. He then flipped off the lights on his way out of the room.

In the hall, he paused for a moment. He couldn't return to Marcus's bedroom, but he didn't want to leave without saying good-bye. Turning away from the bedroom, he headed to the small half bath near the music room. He slipped inside and shut the door. With a shaking hand, he turned on the cold water and splashed it on his face.

What the hell was he doing?

Taking care of Marcus was one thing, but every touch had been geared toward seducing the man. No, seducing the *vampire*. None of this made sense. A vampire killed his family. He shouldn't be attracted to a vampire.

But his brain rejected that thought immediately. What if it

had been a gun-wielding human man that mowed down his parents and sisters? Would that mean that he couldn't be attracted to any man ever because a man killed his family? No.

If all men weren't evil because of the actions of one, then couldn't the same be said about vampires?

Maybe.

What facts did he know about Marcus?

1. He was not one of the two men that killed his family. His voice didn't match.
2. Bel and Rafe also weren't those men, based on their voices and accents.
3. Marcus was kind, gentle, and compassionate. He treated Ethan better than anyone he'd ever been with prior.
4. While Marcus was a vampire, Ethan had no proof that he was a cold-blooded killer.

Some of the guilt squeezing his heart eased, and it became a little easier for Ethan to breathe. He splashed some more cold water on his face and turned off the faucet. He looked up at his reflection in the mirror, taking in his flushed face and blown pupils.

There was no denying that he was attracted to Marcus Varik. The man was sexy as hell. He wanted to climb that amazing body and ride his cock until they were both shouting, covered in sweat and cum.

But did vampires date? If Rafe was anything to go by, they definitely liked to fuck. Or at the very least, they could. Yet, it didn't seem like Marcus did.

Wait...was he planning to seduce his boss?

Fuck, this was a mess. He needed to figure his shit out with Carl and the League before anything potentially happened between him and Marcus. He also needed to come clean about his past and why he'd approached Marcus in the first place. Marcus deserved to know the truth.

But...would Marcus push him away if he came clean?

Didn't matter. He had to be honest with him.

He grabbed a hand towel and dried off his face. Taking a deep breath, he told himself he was just going to check on Marcus and go home to jerk off. Then maybe, he could get a few hours of sleep before trying to figure out what the hell he was going to do next.

That plan was really hard to stick to when he found Marcus sitting on the edge of his bed in a pair of burgundy boxer briefs while he rubbed a towel over his wet hair. The muscles in his flat stomach and biceps flexed with each movement.

"Why the hell do you have to be so sexy?" Ethan groaned.

Marcus lowered the towel, a little smile lifting one corner of his mouth. All the blood was gone from his hands and arms, making him look like a normal human again. But there was a sharpness to his eyes in the dim light that made Ethan think there was something more to him.

"I was afraid you left," Marcus confessed.

Ethan shook his head and stepped farther into the room. "Not yet. Wanted to make sure you were tucked into bed before I left."

"Worried I can't do it on my own?"

"Nope. I just think you need someone taking care of you for a change."

Ethan stood in front of Marcus, staring at his handsome face. He looked tired, but there was also a nervous energy about him. There was no missing that his cock was still straining against his underwear. He hadn't taken care of himself in the shower.

Giving in to the urge, Ethan threaded his fingers through Marcus's hair, pushing it from his face. Marcus closed his eyes and tilted his head into Ethan's touch. "When was the last time someone took care of you?" Ethan whispered.

"An eternity," Marcus mumbled.

Marcus shocked him by leaning forward and wrapping his strong hands around the backs of Ethan's thighs. He lifted and pulled him, earning a yelp of surprise a second before he landed in Marcus's lap, his knees on either side of Marcus's hips. He could feel Marcus's hard cock lightly pressed against his own.

"What?" Ethan croaked, his brain still trying to catch up to what was happening. Marcus's hands moved up his thighs to squeeze and massage his ass, scrambling what little thought he could pull together in his brain.

"Kiss me, please. I've never kissed a man before. And I just want one from you. I won't ask you for another—"

Ethan didn't let him finish. He leaned in and captured Marcus's lips in a slow kiss. He nibbled his bottom lip until Marcus moaned and allowed him entrance. He licked into his mouth, sliding his tongue along Marcus's, earning a hungry sound that shot straight to Ethan's dick. Hands slid up his back, pulling him in tight so that Ethan's body was completely flush with Marcus's from his groin to his shoulders. Ethan wrapped his arms around his neck, giving in to the building desire between them. Marcus kissed Ethan as if he meant to devour him.

Shifting on Marcus's lap, Ethan rubbed his cock against Marcus's and they both groaned. The kiss ended on broken pants for air. Marcus dropped one hand to Ethan's ass, holding him pressed to his dick.

"Oh God," Marcus groaned. "That feels…"

"Good?" Ethan said with a grin as he shifted again. Pleasure spiked through his body, setting every nerve ending on fire.

"Fuck yes," Marcus said.

"You gonna give me a raise, boss man, if I make you come like this?" Ethan teased.

Marcus grabbed Ethan's mouth in another rough kiss that had Ethan melting against him. Marcus was getting more comfortable being with a man by the second, and it was frying every brain cell Ethan had. "I thought you were just a friend right now."

"Maybe I just want to call you 'sir' while you spank me and bend me over your desk."

Marcus growled and thrust against Ethan, grinding their dicks against each other. "Oh God, Ethan, you're going to make me come."

Ethan leaned in and kissed Marcus again, but this one was softer, lighter than before. Every time Marcus tried to deepen the kiss, he pulled back, keeping it tender as he slowed them down. As he ended the kiss, Ethan placed his hands on Marcus's shoulders and gave a little push. And just as he expected, Marcus released him. The man was in tune with him. He'd never force himself on Ethan, no matter how badly he wanted him.

Standing on shaky legs, Ethan smiled at Marcus as he adjusted his rock-hard dick in his pants. He fucking hurt, but he'd take care of that later.

"I think it's a good idea if I leave now," Ethan said, wanting to laugh at his own breathless and needy voice. Everything in his body was screaming to crawl onto Marcus and drive them both to a messy but glorious completion.

"Yes. You're right," Marcus said. He nodded, the motion jerky, like he was still trying to get his brain to work correctly.

With a smile, Ethan bent down and picked up the towel Marcus had dropped on the floor. He tossed it onto Marcus's lap. "You're going to need that." Marcus looked at him in confusion. "When I leave, you're going to jerk off to thoughts of bending me over your desk while you fuck my ass."

Marcus's eyes closed and he sucked in a deep breath. "Ethan."

"Or maybe you'll imagine me sucking your cock down my throat while I finger your tight hole."

Marcus's eyes snapped back open, and the heat Ethan saw there nearly melted him into the floor. "Ethan." This time his name was wrapped in a warning. If he pushed any further, he might not be walking out of the town house. And Ethan was truly torn over whether he wanted Marcus to tackle him to the floor and fuck him senseless. He was having a hell of a time remembering why leaving was so damn important.

"Sorry," he murmured, though he really wasn't. "I guess I just want you to blush when I see you this afternoon."

"Not going to be a problem." Marcus's expression cooled a little, and a frown wiped away the hungry look. "We're going to need to talk later."

Ethan sighed and nodded. "I have a feeling we're going to have a lot to talk about. But later. Get some sleep."

Backpedaling, Ethan spun and quickly left the room, his feet clattering down the stairs in his haste. He couldn't linger or he'd crawl into Marcus's bed, and they'd never get their talking done first.

The early morning air was surprisingly crisp and cool. The dark sky had lightened to a pale gray with hints of yellow weaving through it. The sun was rising. He'd been up half the night with Marcus and his family.

This was getting so much more complicated than it was supposed to be. He wasn't supposed to feel anything for them. But his heart broke to see the brothers together, caring for their injured Bel. There was a helplessness in their shared looks. He hadn't caught much of their conversations, but he felt like if Meryl had been the attacker, they would have been angrier. But Ethan hadn't seen much anger. Just pain and bone-deep sorrow.

Who had hurt Bel so badly, appearing to nearly kill him? And why were the brothers so broken over it? Why couldn't they strike back at this person and get their revenge?

Ethan walked briskly to his apartment. Even though the sun was nearly up, he still found himself looking over his shoulder and watching for Meryl and Cain. Just because she didn't attack Bel tonight didn't mean the woman didn't have some grand evil plan.

When he finally stepped into his empty apartment, his body was shaking with fatigue while his mind was wide awake and ready to analyze everything he'd seen and heard. Or better yet, relive every touch he'd experienced under Marcus's strong hands.

Fuck, he wanted Marcus so damn bad. Why did the man have to be so sweet, sexy, vulnerable, and adorable? One perfect package all rolled into one. Except maybe for the fact that he was a vampire.

Was that really such a bad thing? It wasn't like he'd tasted of blood when they kissed, and he didn't get pierced by a set of sharp fangs.

But working for Marcus wasn't supposed to be about finding a hot fuck. He was supposed to be locating and destroying the person who murdered his goddamn family.

Ethan flopped face first down on his bed and groaned. He wished he could hear what his mother or father would say about this mess. He couldn't even be sure they'd accept him for being gay, but he liked to imagine they would have.

When he was alone and on his own, he'd imagined how it could have been to tell them. Sitting nervously on the couch, clutching his hands together to keep them from shaking as he admitted in stumbling words that he liked boys. He pretended that his mother and father would hug him and say that they loved him regardless of who he liked. His mom would kiss him and say she was proud of him. His dad would wink and say that the same rules applied to him as his sisters—no boys in the bedroom. It would have been the perfect moment.

But he never got to have that moment. The only good thing

was that at least he missed out on having the bad one where they disowned him and kicked him out of the house.

What the hell was he supposed to do?

If he came clean, would Marcus understand about him going to Carl and the League? Would he even help him find the vampires who slaughtered everyone in his apartment building?

Everything was a giant damn mess, and it was supposed to be so fucking easy. He would find the killers and take them out. He would get justice for his family and finally be able to move on with a sense of completion. He'd have the knowledge that no one else could be harmed the way he'd been.

With that done, he'd finish getting his degree and he'd find a real job. He'd start living his life. No more vampires. No more death and chaos.

No more Marcus.…

He could easily imagine Marcus telling him to fuck off after he found out that Ethan was with the anti-vampire hate group. They bragged about killing scores of vampires in the name of saving humans. But after spending two weeks with Marcus, Ethan was figuring out that a lot of their information about vampires was utter bullshit. And if their info about vampires was bad, did that mean these lunatics were killing innocent vampires? Hell, they could be murdering people who weren't actually vampires at all.

He needed fucking help and right now—but the only person who could possibly help him was Marcus. Ethan couldn't figure out if it was more or less fucked up for him to turn to the person he'd been setting up to be killed only a few weeks earlier. But he knew deep down in his soul that Marcus wouldn't hurt him. He might very well be the only person he trusted in this world.

CHAPTER TWELVE

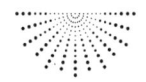

Marcus slid his hands into his pockets as he stood over Bel's sleeping form. The long cuts on his face had healed completely in his sleep, restoring his natural beauty. While Rafe and Beltran weren't identical twins, their looks were very similar. But where Rafe had a devilish and wicked cant to his features, Bel's face held a sweetness to it. As if they were the good angel and wicked devil that stood on a person's shoulders.

For a moment, Marcus debated pulling aside Bel's blanket so he could peel away the bandages over his heart. In the end, he decided against it. His healed face was proof enough that he was on the mend. Bel needed his sleep. If he was lucky, he wouldn't wake until sunset. Then he'd be able to hunt again to regain his strength, and possibly talk about their mother.

It was not a conversation he was looking forward to. The attack on Bel was the worst any of them had suffered in a few decades. Marcus had started to entertain the silly notion that maybe their mother was evening out a little, that her episodes were growing less violent, or they'd gotten better at managing her.

But he'd been wrong.

Marcus had no doubt that Bel could handle Julianna. He'd been handling her well enough for nearly two hundred years. The problem was that they never wanted to hurt her, while she showed no restraint in trying to harm them.

Swallowing a sigh, Marcus silently left the music room and shut the door behind him. He paused in the hallway, straining to hear every sound in the house. He'd slept until nearly four in the afternoon. The worries over Meryl's threats, the coming move, the antics of the Ministry, and then his mother's episode had left him drained.

The worst was that he could feel something building. The Variks were careful to stay out of vampire politics, but that came at a price. They remained largely ignorant of the newest movements and factions that could threaten them. Meryl's threats against Julianna and Rafe were just the tip of the iceberg. She wasn't the normal type to stir up trouble.

In fact, Meryl was a dedicated member of The Hidden faction. They believed that vampires should have no human interaction beyond feeding. Vampires should only associate with other vampires. His brother Winter subscribed to their beliefs and was generally displeased with Rafe's lifestyle, but he'd never go so far as to threaten the life of his own brother.

Marcus was seen as more of a moderate among their people. He thought limited interaction was healthy and necessary to keep a vampire current with the changing world and technology. Otherwise, it was too damn easy to fall into a stagnant frame of thought, and that way led to madness.

He needed to talk to Aiden. His sire was much better at keeping up with what was happening among their people.

A soft thump from farther down the hall had him looking in that direction. He waited and then smiled to hear Ethan's soft singing. Before he reached out to Aiden, he needed to talk to Ethan.

Another conversation he wasn't necessarily looking forward to.

Things last night had gone too far. He'd kissed a man. Hell, he'd nearly devoured Ethan and still wanted more. The kiss had been amazing, better than he could have ever imagined it would be. And to feel Ethan's hard cock against his own, to know that he'd affected the man in such a way was an intoxicating experience. He wanted to wrap himself in all of Ethan's little moans and whimpers, to drag one after another out of him until he wove them all together into a symphony of Ethan's pleasure.

But the sun was up, and they had to face what happened, right? They couldn't do that again. He was Ethan's boss. Last night had been about feeling something other than pain. Forgetting for a short time that his mother had tried to kill his brother.

He was also a vampire, and with that existence came danger. Marcus refused to put Ethan's life in more danger than he already had.

Their time together was almost over. The move was happening in just a few short weeks. Then Ethan would be around for another month to help unpack everything at his new place. Afterward, they would go their separate ways, never seeing each other again.

Yes, that made the most amount of sense. It didn't matter if his loneliness yawned at him like a massive gaping void threatening to swallow him whole. It didn't matter if Ethan had been the first bright spot in his entire existence. They had no future.

Ignoring the ache in his chest, Marcus trudged down the hall to find Ethan finishing up what had been a spare bedroom. Boxes were stacked neatly against one wall. The rugs were rolled up. The pictures had been taken down and carefully covered.

As he finished labeling the box he was working on, Ethan looked up and gave a little start before smiling at Marcus. Just that simple expression of joy sped up Marcus's heart. How was he supposed to return to a life that smile was not a part of?

Marcus started to say something when a loud caw split the room. Ethan winced and they both looked over at the raven perched on one of the stacks of boxes, his long talons scratching on the cardboard.

"Ozzie! How did you get in?" Marcus said. He lifted his hand and the raven spread its wings, launching itself off the box. He glided easily across the room and landed on Marcus's hand, talons digging into his flesh to steady himself.

"Thank God," Ethan breathed as he pulled his earbuds out and stuffed them into his pockets. "I let him in through the window. I heard him pecking and banging against it. I hoped it was Ozzie and not some random bird I was allowing into the house."

Marcus smiled, stroking his index finger across the head and down the back of his neck along his sleek feathers. The bird lifted his beak, pushing his head against Marcus's touch. "This is Ozzie. I have a feeling he was looking for Bel."

"Does your brother have any other pets?"

Marcus stopped rubbing Ozzie's head and looked at Ethan. "Why?"

"Because I stopped two blue jays and three cats hanging out by the kitchen door, acting like they were expecting to be let in."

No, they weren't Bel's, but they were. Where Rafe had his gift of "charm" as he called it, Bel could speak to animals. He didn't keep pets, but animals had a way of flowing in and out of his life. They'd stop by, spend a little time with him, and eventually move on. Ozzie was one of the few that had stuck around.

But Marcus also knew that Bel used Ozzie as a way of keeping an eye on his older brother. Ozzie would fly to Marcus's house, hang out for a night or two, and then fly to Bel. Marcus always knew he'd be back, just never knew exactly when.

"No, those must be strays looking for handouts," Marcus murmured. But he hated saying it. He wanted to tell Ethan the truth. He wanted to tell Ethan about Bel's amazing gift. Wanted to tell him everything, but that just wasn't an option. "Have you been here long?"

Ethan shook his head. "Couple of hours. Just finishing up this room. Also called the piano movers again. Told them you've actually got three pianos in the house, not just one." He paused and lifted one eyebrow at Marcus. "You don't have any more hidden around here, do you?"

"No. Just the three."

Ethan chuckled. "Yes, only three pianos."

"I wanted to thank you for your help last night, as an employee and as a friend. You helped to save my brother's life and we will always be grateful to you for that."

"You're welcome. Did you see Bel? Is he better?"

Marcus nodded. "He's still sleeping, but he's healing well."

Ethan's expression turned grim. "Do you know who attacked him?"

"Yes."

Ethan's frown deepened and Marcus knew he was waiting for him to continue, but this was a difficult thing for him to discuss.

"Would you mind letting Ozzie outside? I'll step into the hallway," he said, then turned his attention to the raven. He stroked him a couple of times more, staring into the all-too-perceptive black eyes. "Go home. He'll be there tonight to see you." The bird cocked his head to the side and cawed at him once before flying to the box he'd been perched on. Marcus didn't question whether the bird understood him. Maybe he really was that smart. Or maybe it was Bel's influence. Either way, he was ready to go.

Marcus stepped into the safety of the hallway. He could hear Ethan shoving aside the heavy curtains and opening up the old window. There were no screens on the upper floors because of Ozzie. It just made it easier for him to come and go. A flapping of wings filled the room for a moment and then a distant cry as the bird hit the air.

"It's safe," Ethan called out when the curtains were closed again, putting the room back into darkness.

Marcus entered the room and found his heart skipping a beat when he realized that he'd walked in without checking first. He trusted Ethan, trusted him to keep him safe. It was a feeling he'd not had with someone for a long time.

"Marcus, I know you've probably got plenty of people who can help you, but if your family is in trouble or if you need some help, I'm there for you. As a friend," he quickly added at the end.

Marcus sighed, the warm feeling giving way to the weight of old worries. He paced the room, walking toward the windows, but he didn't reach out to shove aside the curtains like he wanted. The sun was still up and would be for another few hours. He was trapped inside with Ethan and the nagging fears in his brain.

"It's…complicated, Ethan," he softly said. "I appreciate your concern and your offer, but there isn't anything you can do."

Turning at the sound of movement, he watched as Ethan closed the distance between them. Marcus only had to reach out and he could pull Ethan against him. They hadn't yet talked about what happened in his bedroom, and he hoped that Ethan wouldn't bring it up.

"I can listen," Ethan offered. "Sometimes we just need someone to listen."

Marcus nodded and looked back at the curtains. They were a deep emerald green with gold threads that made the shape of leaves. He opened his mouth to thank Ethan again, but a different set of words came tumbling out.

"My mother attacked Bel. If we hadn't arrived when we did, I think she would have killed him," he confessed.

Ethan's gasp had Marcus wincing. He shouldn't have said that, but he needed to talk to someone. His brothers were too close to the problem. None of them were thinking clearly anymore.

"Why?"

"Because she's ill." Marcus looked over at Ethan and only saw worry and fear in his wide gaze. "She's been ill for a very long time, and she occasionally has these episodes. She's not thinking clearly and doesn't see us. She sees something evil that must be destroyed. And when it's over, she usually doesn't recall anything that happened."

"Oh God, Marcus!" Ethan reached out to place a hand on his arm, but Marcus was quick to pace away from him. He was weak. If Ethan touched him, he would be pulling the slender man into his arms. He'd kiss him and he wouldn't have the strength to stop again.

"My brothers and I have watched over her. We can usually stop her before any of us get severely hurt, but last night was a particularly bad episode. It came on fast, too fast for Bel to reach out for help."

"Has she...has she ever hurt anyone outside of your family?" Ethan's soft voice wavered, sending a slice of pain through Marcus's heart.

"No. Never. One of us is always with her. She's done some property damage, but never harmed anyone outside of the family." Marcus inwardly winced at the partial lie. Ethan would have meant humans. She'd never been allowed to kill a human, but Marcus couldn't say the same for his own kind.

Marcus watched Ethan carefully. The young man chewed on his bottom lip, staring at the ground, as if he were battling some very uncomfortable thoughts. Marcus felt bad for putting this burden of knowledge on his shoulders. Ethan had his own life to live, his own difficulties. He didn't need to worry himself with Marcus's problems.

"Ethan…I'm sorry I bothered you with this—"

Ethan's head quickly snapped up. "No! I'm glad you told me, and I'm so sorry you're dealing with this. I can't imagine the pain this has caused you and your brothers over the years."

Marcus gave Ethan a sad smile. "She's still our mother. We love her. Most of the time, she's laughter and gentleness. We never question that she loves us completely."

"But to have to deal with this other side…"

Marcus could only shrug.

Ethan stunned him by quickly closing the distance between them and wrapping his arms around Marcus's waist. He hugged him tightly, head resting on his chest. Marcus's heart skipped a beat, some of the ache inside him subsiding. His smile became a little less sad as he hugged Ethan back.

"Thank you."

"Have…have you ever thought about getting her some professional help?" Ethan asked, his voice muffled against Marcus's chest. "They might be able to help her more than you and your brothers have been able to. At least, so that you're all safer."

Marcus sighed. Ethan was talking about a psychiatrist and drugs. Unfortunately, human drugs had no effect on vampires and there were no institutes for insane vampires anywhere in the world. They were completely on their own.

"Yes, and unfortunately that is not an option for Julianna," Marcus said gently as he stepped out of Ethan's embrace. "She is the responsibility of the family."

Ethan frowned and Marcus couldn't blame him. It was an imperfect answer to a difficult problem, but there was no other option.

After a moment, Ethan nodded. "If you need anything, please don't hesitate to call me. I'm happy to help you and your family."

Marcus managed a small smile before turning toward the door. "I should leave you so you can get your work done."

"Marcus!" Ethan called, stopping him before he could get more than a few feet away. Marcus looked back to find a faint blush brightening his cheeks. "I...are you okay...with what happened between us last night?"

Dammit.

His hopes of avoiding what happened in his bedroom evaporated and the usual nervous awkwardness he so often felt around Ethan reappeared. What was he supposed to say? That he'd enjoyed the kiss and had wanted so much more, but there was still a little nagging voice in the back of his mind telling him that it was all wrong because Ethan was a man? That there could be no more kisses because he was a vampire?

"I guess I'm just worried that you weren't comfortable with it. Or that maybe I forced you to do more than you wanted. I'm sorry—"

"No!" Marcus crossed the room toward Ethan. He cupped his hands on Ethan's cheeks, tilting his head up so that he could look into his worried blue eyes. "I loved every second of last night, right up until you left me alone."

"Oh," Ethan whispered.

"But I grew up in a place where such things between men weren't allowed. That upbringing still rings in my head. I need more time to adjust. To think about this."

"Okay. I get it," Ethan said quickly with a couple of nods. "If you want to talk about it, I'm here for you."

"Thank you."

Marcus was dying to explain all the confusing thoughts flying through his head. He wanted to tell Ethan that he wanted to kiss him and keep kissing him, but kissing Ethan was really the stupidest thing he could possibly do. That way just led to pain.

Ethan had a chance at a good, normal life when his time with Marcus was up. He could return to Glenpark with money in his bank account. He could finish school, get a good job, and find someone who could offer him a safe and happy life.

Marcus might be able to provide financial security for Ethan, but that was about it. A life with Marcus promised only blood, violence, and pain. Ethan deserved better.

"Marcus, are you…" Ethan started to ask, but he stopped himself, the words seeming to get caught in his throat.

"What?"

Ethan suddenly snapped his mouth shut and shook his head. "I'm just…worried about you and your brothers. That's all."

Marcus smiled at him. "My brothers and I are going to be fine."

"Are we still going to have lunch together…like we have been?"

"I would like that very much."

Ethan breathed a heavy sigh, his smile returning. "So would I."

Marcus nodded. Even if he never got to kiss Ethan again, he would be content with being able to share lunch with him, to sit across the table and share their thoughts with each other. To laugh.

"Do you mind if we push it back to six? I just need to check a few things in my office."

"No problem. I really need to make some more progress today. We could also see if Bel is awake so he could join us."

"I think he would like that," Marcus murmured and then left to go to his office. He was torn by the surge of warmth he felt at Ethan's suggestion to include Bel, but there was also an angry possessive surge that didn't want to share Ethan with anyone, even his brother.

Definitely not Rafe. He didn't want Rafe anywhere near Ethan.

Marcus scrubbed a hand over his face, trying to clear his mind. He was a fucking disaster, and he needed to get his thoughts in order. He needed to find out why the threats against his family were growing and figure out how to protect them. Ethan was only cluttering things up and putting himself in danger by remaining in the Varik household. The sooner this move was done, the better they'd all be.

CHAPTER THIRTEEN

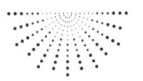

Ethan slammed the door behind him when he arrived at his temporary apartment. This was a fucking nightmare!

Nothing was working out the way it was supposed to. He wasn't supposed to give a shit about these creatures. These people.

And they were people to him. Not animals that needed to be put down. They had lives and family they cared about. They had hopes and dreams and feelings.

Did he have any actual proof that they were vampires?

For Marcus, no. So the guy was allergic to the sun. There was a rare disease called xeroderma pigmentosum that made people extremely sensitive to the UV rays of the sun. Maybe he had that. It certainly didn't make him a vampire.

Bel?

Ethan would stake his life on the fact that Bel was a vampire. No one healed that fast. No one.

Marcus had talked Bel into eating with them and when he appeared in the kitchen, all the long scratches on his face were

CLAIMING MARCUS

completely gone. His movements were a little stiff, but he definitely didn't look like a man who'd lost a few liters of blood across the floor of Marcus's home just the night before.

After talking to Marcus about his mother, Ethan felt pretty sure that she was one as well. If she were a human and ill, he liked to think that Marcus would at least get her some psychological help. Maybe some drugs to calm her a little. She was threatening their lives!

But drugs probably didn't help vampires, and you certainly couldn't lock one up in the psych ward of a hospital. It was the only reason that made sense of why the burden was on Marcus and his brothers to watch over her.

Ethan had no idea if Rafe was a vampire, and he'd never even seen Winter.

He walked into the kitchen, jerked open the refrigerator, and glared at the contents without really seeing them. He had no idea what he was looking for or why he'd even gone in there. He slammed the door shut again, leaned against it, and slid to the floor. What the hell was he supposed to do?

Didn't Macy and Lucy deserve justice? His sisters had been young and innocent. They deserved to have a shot at life too, but it was stolen away by some sick fuckers. He wanted to stop dreaming about them. He wanted to stop dreaming about walking down the blood-soaked hallway and finding their lifeless bodies staring up at the ceiling, their open hands outstretched as if they'd died reaching out to him.

Resting his elbows on his bent knees, Ethan rubbed his eyes roughly. He shouldn't have been the one to survive. Why couldn't the killers have gotten him and spared Lucy? She was smarter and more determined. She would have known exactly what to do. No one would have escaped her.

But he was just useless and weak.

Someone strong would have killed all the vamps by now.

Didn't matter if they were involved in the murder of his family. A strong person would have exterminated them all so no one else could have ever been hurt.

He couldn't hurt Marcus, though. Marcus with the sad eyes and nervous smile. The man who was fighting to protect his own family and keep them safe even at the cost of his own life if necessary.

Ethan was falling for him. He knew it. With every smile and laugh and worried look, he was falling more and more for Marcus.

He'd never been in love before. Never even dated. No one had ever captured his attention like Marcus. He'd never met anyone who was such a contradiction. Marcus was strong and powerful, but there was also something incredibly vulnerable and soft about him. He was surrounded by family, and yet he felt so very alone to Ethan. So painfully isolated.

Meanwhile, Ethan had lost his family and had been floating alone for so long. He had few friends. When he met Carl and was introduced to the Humans Protecting Humans League, he thought he'd found a group of people that would give him a sense of belonging. But it was like they'd watched every vampire movie ever churned out and taken notes from that. Their personal accounts of encounters were vague—and worse, clearly embellished. He truly doubted they'd recognize a vampire if they were really faced with one.

And their agenda held only one goal: kill them all.

A few years ago, such an idea was fine with Ethan. He'd been full of anger and loneliness. He'd told himself that he was on a noble mission to get rid of all the creatures that had murdered his family and probably thousands of other families just like them.

But after spending time with the League, he realized that so much of what they did was hate speech and talk. There were few real plans that he saw.

What bothered him was that he'd never met the true leaders of the group. They remained away from the monthly meetings. Carl had said that they were members of powerful families or politicians who had to protect their images. That the rest of the world wasn't ready to deal with the truth that vampires really existed.

Of course, those same shadowy figures had no problem handing down assassination orders. He'd heard whispers of an elite team of former military League members who gathered and took out vampires when the timing was right.

But who decided which vampires had to die and when? Were they sure they were killing vampires and not humans?

Ethan knew one of those hit squads was waiting on the final information from him. They wanted to know the address where Marcus was moving to. They wanted the addresses of the rest of his family. Ethan had lied to Carl on several occasions, telling him that Marcus hadn't trusted him with that information yet, but the truth was that Ethan had been handed that info on his first damn day of work so that he could coordinate with the movers on getting Marcus's stuff to the right location on time.

He couldn't hand it over.

Marcus wasn't a killer. Ethan knew it down in his bones.

Bel wasn't a killer either. When sitting around the small table in the kitchen, the man talked almost nonstop about science and these interesting experiments that he was running. Ethan hadn't understood most of what he said, but his enthusiasm was so damn endearing. Marcus had smiled at his brother, looking at him with an expression of love. Ethan had a feeling that Marcus was relieved his brother was focused on his work rather than what had happened to him.

Ethan didn't know much about Rafe, but if the texted image was anything to go by, the vampire was a lover, a playboy, and a perpetual partier. He wasn't a killer. He wasn't serious enough for that. Rafe was all about his next good time.

Winter worried Ethan. Marcus spoke very little about his youngest brother. He was a complete enigma, but if he was anything like his other brothers, then Ethan was skeptical that Winter would easily kill.

That left only Marcus's mother, Julianna.

An insane vampire.

Lovely.

Ethan's heart broke for Marcus. He couldn't imagine what he was going through. It sounded like most days she was the loving, caring woman that he grew up with. But in the blink of an eye, she became someone determined to kill her sons. And was that rage just limited to her sons?

What if she escaped Marcus and his brothers? Would she kill innocent people while lost in her fractured mind?

Ethan hated to admit that he didn't entirely believe Marcus when he said that she'd never hurt anyone else. How could he be sure? What if she'd escaped just once and murdered an entire apartment building of people before they could get her back? What if there was someone else goading Julianna on before her sons could capture her again?

Sighing heavily, Ethan rested his head against his hands and closed his eyes. He knew his decision was made. He would not hand any information over to Carl about Marcus and his brothers. But he needed to see Julianna, to speak with her. He knew if he saw her, heard her voice, he'd know if she was the vampire from his nightmares.

And if she was…then he'd have to figure out if he had it in him to kill her despite his growing affection for Marcus. But he prayed that he wouldn't have to choose between his dead family and Marcus.

A loud knock on the door had Ethan jerking upright. His heart sped up and he sat frozen on the floor for a moment. He had a dark feeling he knew exactly who was standing at his door.

Slowly, Ethan pushed to his feet. He steadied himself, fingers pressed into the cool metal surface of the fridge door, before he walked to the small foyer. He took a deep breath and worked hard to wipe all expression from his face.

Opening the door, he found Carl standing on the other side, shifting from one foot to the other as if he couldn't contain his nervous energy.

"Carl, what are you doing here? I told you it wasn't safe for you to stop by," Ethan said.

"Yeah, well, you haven't been returning my calls or messages the past week, so I thought it was a good idea if I stopped in and checked on you." Carl shoved his way past Ethan and strode confidently into the living room like he was entitled free passage to Ethan's apartment.

Grinding his teeth together, Ethan closed the door and silently followed behind him. He was getting sick of Carl and his holier-than-thou attitude. The man wasn't his father, and Ethan was pretty sure he didn't know shit about vampires. Ethan was a little disgusted at how he'd looked up to him when they first met a few years ago. At least he'd finally come to his senses about Carl and the League.

"What's going on with you, Ethan?" Carl said as he flopped down in the big comfortable chair in the living room.

Ethan remained standing, his arms folded over his chest. "I don't know what you're talking about."

"You! You're not calling or reporting in any useful information. You've been happy to tell us what he ate, even though we all know he's not really eating food, and that he's up walking around the house during the daylight hours."

"Something you said he'd never be able to do," Ethan quickly countered.

Carl gave a shrug. "So we were wrong about that one little thing. It's good information to have. The point is that you were hired to be his moving coordinator. That means you've got to have the information on where he's moving to and when. Why the hell haven't you told us yet?"

"I don't have it!" Ethan shouted, hoping that it made the lie more convincing. "He's got another assistant. She's handling the actual movers. I box things up, close up rooms. I give her details on what needs to be moved and she tells the movers."

"And you don't know the moving date?"

"Nope," Ethan said, shaking his head. "I have just been given a deadline for when I need to have my work done. He could be moving the next day or a month after that. I don't know."

"And the rest of his family?"

Ethan shrugged. "I'm not involved in any of that stuff. He has me working on his house."

Carl narrowed his eyes on Ethan as he scooted to the edge of his seat. "And yet he takes the time to eat lunch with you every damn day." His voice was low and soft, making the hair on the back of Ethan's neck stand up. "What do you talk about?"

"Not much. The weather. What I'm studying in school. Different things happening in the news. Nothing personal."

Swearing softly, Carl shook his head and stood up. "This is fucking unbelievable. You were supposed to be our big break in getting full details on an entire family of vamps, and you've been completely useless."

Carl's words stung, but Ethan bit his tongue, hating the burning embarrassment he could feel in his cheeks. He didn't like the idea of being a failure at anything, but if it kept Marcus and his family safe, then it was worth a little humiliation.

"The job turned out to be different than we all thought. He's careful. He doesn't trust me with his personal information," Ethan said.

"Or you're not trying hard enough. You've clearly got several hours out of the day when he's not awake and roaming the house. You should be spending that time going through his papers. He got a private office?"

"Yes."

"Why haven't you gone through the papers in there?"

"He keeps it locked at all times along with his bedroom. I told you. He's careful."

With his hands on his hips, Carl swore again and started pacing the room. "I should have known better than to give you this job. I thought you'd be an easy hire since you've got that innocent face, but I didn't realize that you've got zero brains in your damn head."

"Fuck you! You guys are convinced that vampires are these dead zombies existing purely on blood. If Varik is a vampire, then he breaks every one of your goddamn rules. I'm not entirely convinced he even is a vampire. You guys are going to fucking rush in and kill an innocent human being! That's not what this is about. I joined you to get justice for my family. If you're killing humans, you're just a bunch of deranged murderers."

Ethan wanted to say that they were a bunch of fucking murderers for even wanting to kill vampires. If there were more vamps out there like the Variks, then Ethan was sure they were innocent of murdering anyone. He wanted to kick himself for ever getting involved with these people. He should have fucking known better.

He got so wrapped up in his dark thoughts that it took him a moment to notice that Carl had gone completely silent. Ethan looked up at the man who was staring at him from across the room, his face pale and lips parted.

"They got to you," Carl whispered.

"What?" He couldn't begin to fathom what he was muttering about now. This whole endeavor had been a giant mistake. The only good thing that came out of it was that he was able to meet Marcus. Sure, he was going to be fired and lose Marcus forever when he confessed everything, but at least he'd have the happy memories of Marcus's smile and the sound of his laughter.

"They got to you," Carl repeated. "They got in your head and made you one of their little minions. You've probably been reporting back to them what we've been doing."

"You've fucking lost your mind!" Ethan shouted. Panic slammed into him, speeding up his heart and making it hard to draw in a deep breath. He didn't doubt that Carl was armed in some way. He always bragged about having some wicked blade or gun hidden on his person. "There's no getting to me. I'm just an employee. I pack up shit in his house."

"And you share a meal with him almost every damn day. He's gotten in your head!"

"Carl, you're being an idiot. No one is in my head. I just came to my senses that you and all those idiots at the League have watched too many damn vampire movies. My family was attacked and murdered. I let you get in my head. I let you convince me that I could get justice, but I've realized that all you're talking about is fucking murder of innocent people."

"We're protecting people!"

"You're lying to yourselves, and you know it."

Carl charged Ethan before he could move. Balling up his hand, Ethan swung his right fist. Carl ducked and Ethan managed to only clip the edge of his jaw. It didn't even slow Carl down. The older man slammed his fist into Ethan's face. Pain exploded across his cheek and the world exploded in a wall of white before he was hit again. He staggered, crumpling to his knees as he tried to suck in a jagged breath. But it was knocked out again as Carl kicked him in the stomach.

Ethan was thrown backward. He rolled on the ground in the fetal position, trying to protect his soft organs while fighting to get air in his lungs. Pain radiated through his gut and across his face. He hadn't been in a damn fight since he was in middle school, but apparently he was more than a little rusty when it came to protecting himself.

Fingers grabbed his hair and twisted before pulling so that he was forced to lift his head. Carl leaned down close so that Ethan could see his face mottled red with rage.

"Stay the fuck away from us and Varik. If you warn him that we're coming, we'll kill you along with his entire family," Carl snarled at him, sending spittle across Ethan's cheek. He shoved Ethan's head down to hammer against the wood floor before he stalked out of the apartment. Ethan managed a shuddering breath when the door slammed behind him.

Moaning softly, Ethan curled up on his side, pressing his uninjured cheek to the cold floor. Everything fucking hurt. It hurt to breathe, to even think. He knew he needed to get up, grab some ice and painkillers, but he didn't want to move.

For the past couple of weeks, he'd been afraid of telling Carl that he thought the League was a group of nutjobs. He knew the man wasn't going to just let him quietly walk away. Ethan might know some things about the organization, but he was sure none of it was particularly important or vital. But he didn't doubt that Carl or some of the other lunatics would hunt him down if they were convinced that he warned Marcus or his family.

Ethan didn't have a death wish, but he certainly wasn't going to let these assholes hurt Marcus or Bel or anyone else. He had to find a way to quickly warn Marcus, and then he needed to get the hell out of town. He'd made some good money working for Marcus, but not nearly enough to easily disappear.

Lying on the floor, he wracked his brain, trying to think if he had anything that he could sell for some quick cash. His one luxury item was a laptop, but he knew he couldn't get much for it since it was already two years old. His cell phone was the most basic of smartphones and definitely wasn't worth much.

Fuck. What the hell was he going to do?

He needed to tell Marcus the truth. He had to come clean so Marcus could take steps to protect himself and his family. After that, Ethan could worry about his own ass. He had enough money for a bus ticket. Once he got to a new city far from here, he could maybe worry about things like where he was going to sleep and how he was going to eat.

He'd screwed up, but he still had a chance to make it right.

To hell with Carl and the League.

CHAPTER FOURTEEN

Marcus tugged at the cuff of his black button-down shirt and smoothed his hand over his deep blue tie. Matched with a pair of black slacks, his entire outfit was what Rafe would have called boring.

But Marcus wanted to be boring. He wanted to sink into the shadows and not be noticed by the roving eyes within the nightclub, but there was no chance of that. Marcus rarely made appearances at The Bank, and when he did, the others always seemed to take notice.

The Bank was an exclusive bar that catered only to vampires. But that didn't mean only vampires were roaming the club. Humans worked as servers and entertainment.

There were more than a few personal pets wandering around, their flashy collars reflecting the dancing lights. The idea of pets was something Marcus had always struggled with. The human was well aware their owner was a vampire, and they just willingly served as an in-house source of food, sex, and other entertainment. The pets even had their own society of cliques and rules. The most expensive and extravagant collars proved that the pet was highly valued by the master.

But what they were all seeming to ignore was that pets didn't last long. Humans weren't meant for that much constant blood donation, and vampires tended to play too rough. The idea that the master would turn the pet into a vampire was an absolute fairy tale. There was no happy ending. After a while, pets disappeared and no one talked about it. It ruined the fun, endless party image.

It made Marcus glad that he and his brothers never indulged in such things. Rafe liked to dress up his playthings and one-night stands in fancy collars, but those weren't true pets. Those people didn't know what they were playing at, and they were shuffled out his door the next morning with no clear memory of what had happened.

The few humans moving around him tonight either worked at the club or belonged to someone else, but they all had the same job: to be a source of fresh blood. And every last one of them within the club was a willing donor. At least, that was what the law said. Marcus wasn't entirely convinced, but he had bigger problems to worry about besides whether some of the humans had been coerced into their servitude.

Colored lights flashed around him and bodies writhed in time to the throbbing bass of the music pumped from the speakers at the far end of the large room. Marcus wove his way through the crowd, his eyes constantly skimming for familiar faces. Particularly, threatening faces. There was no sign of Meryl or Cain so far, but there were others who were not fans of the Variks, and there were more than a few who were not fans of Aiden, which naturally made them enemies of the Variks.

When they'd decided to follow their mother and become vampires, not one of them had contemplated the notion that they would have to find a way to maneuver through an entirely new society with new rules and new politics. It wasn't too different from human life, but it definitely had the potential to be bloodier.

At the back of the long room, he climbed a set of old wooden stairs that creaked under his feet. There was a set of double doors that were opened by a pair of men in tuxedos.

"Good evening, Mr. Varik," they intoned at the same time. Marcus gave a small nod as he walked through.

A soothing hush fell over everything as the doors were closed behind him, blocking out the noise from the first floor. Where the nightclub was loud and garish, this club on the second floor was polished and ordered. The floors were covered in a thick burgundy rug that seemed to soak up the noise while cushioning feet. The walls and doorways were all covered in rich mahogany wood. The club reminded him of the exclusive clubs that he was a member of while he lived in London nearly two centuries ago. Back when he'd still been human.

The key difference here was that nearly everyone was a vampire. Humans still worked there, offering up refreshments of one form or another. There were a handful of pets, but they sat quietly on little cushioned stools beside their masters. Their faces were all composed but bored as they waited on their master's desire. It all had a slightly civilized air to it versus the chaos that reigned on the first floor.

Of course, that civilized pretense was all an act. Everything could fall apart in a heartbeat if someone said the wrong thing to the wrong person. Or maybe simply snacked where they shouldn't have.

Wandering through the wood-paneled rooms with painted portraits of unknown people, Marcus finally spotted Aiden in a shadowy corner, seated in a high-back leather chair. His dark eyes were sweeping the room slowly, taking in all the occupants. When those eyes landed on Marcus, he gave a small nod and returned to his perusal.

Marcus was surprised by Aiden when meeting him among

the vampires for the first time. With their own kind, Aiden was quiet and reserved. He rarely spoke and never showed emotion. It was so different from the laughing, loving man he'd met when he'd first started dating Julianna so many years ago.

Aiden had swept his mother off her feet, which was no easy feat considering she'd already been burned by their biological father. But then, Marcus could see why Julianna had fallen in love with him. His soul was filled with love and kindness that he not only showered on Julianna but on her sons as well.

When they finally met, Aiden treated them as if they were his flesh and blood. He cared for them and did everything he could to teach them and show them the love they stopped receiving from their biological father.

In his own way, Marcus saw Aiden as his father before he became his sire. He respected his quiet strength and dignity. He had a strict code of honor, which became even more important when he learned Aiden was a vampire.

Neither he nor his brothers blamed Aiden for what happened to their mother. They were grateful that he tried to save her life. She had been at death's door, and the doctors had failed at every turn. There had been no other choice. But the vampirism had driven her from subtle madness to brutal hostility when triggered.

Violence that was made ten times worse anytime she saw Aiden.

Marcus fought back the swell of sadness that hit him every time he saw Aiden. The man had risked everything to save the woman he loved and when he succeeded, the cost was that they could never be together. It wasn't fair.

But regardless of the pain it caused him, he remained as close as he possibly could be to help her sons and keep his family safe.

Stopping a server in a sharp black uniform as he passed, Marcus ordered a dark whiskey, which was simply half whiskey and half blood. He then paused next to the open seat beside Aiden.

"May I?" he asked out of habit.

A small smile formed on Aiden's lips and he nodded. It was an old ritual for them. Aiden made it clear that they were all welcome to visit with him at any time, but Marcus clung to old manners and rules of society. It gave him a sense of comfort in a constantly changing world.

"It's good to see you again," Aiden murmured as Marcus sat.

"And you. Rafe mentioned that you were in Rio briefly."

Aiden's smile shifted to a smirk. "Rafe usually isn't the one with the intel. I'm assuming Winter has been keeping an eye on me."

"Always." Winter was a sneaky bastard. He made it his business to keep an eye on everyone who interested him, and that included his own family.

"I went to Rio because I thought the *Carnival* season would be a nice distraction and I ended up staying for a few months."

"It sounds like you found your distraction," Marcus murmured, but Aiden didn't answer, not that Marcus was really expecting him to. Aiden didn't reveal much about himself when he was out among the other vampires. He didn't trust them, and neither did Marcus.

"How is Julianna?" Aiden asked and Marcus could only answer with a frown. Aiden needed to know, but he hated causing his sire any kind of pain.

Aiden shifted in his seat, moving toward the edge while positioning himself so that he was turned toward Marcus. "What has happened?" Aiden surprised him by placing his hand over Marcus's wrist. "Who was hurt?"

"Bel," Marcus admitted softly.

Aiden's hand tightened on his wrist, and he shifted again as if preparing to launch to his feet. "When? Has he recovered? Does he need me?"

"Last night and he has fully recovered." Marcus placed his hand over Aiden's and met his gaze. "He's fine. So is Mother."

Aiden sighed and sat back in his chair, releasing Marcus. "What happened?"

Marcus shook his head a little. He waited until the server dropped off drinks for both of them and left. He picked his up and sipped the alcohol and blood mix. When he'd chosen to become a vampire, he never thought he'd become accustomed to the taste of blood, let alone long for it, but his new hunger soon had him craving the coppery taste far more than any food. He knew that he didn't need to eat food, but the action gave him a little bit of normalcy to cling to. It gave a rhythm and predictability to his day that would otherwise be missing.

And now, it gave him a chance to spend at least one hour with Ethan. He wouldn't trade that short time with Ethan for anything.

"We don't know. Bel was alone with her and said that she'd been having a fine evening. He is unsure of what set her off, but it was fast and extremely violent." Marcus hated to ask, but it was the one thing that he could think of that couldn't be accounted for. "Were you near Bel's last night?"

Aiden frowned. "No. I was within the city limits, but not particularly close to his home."

"It must be the move, then."

Aiden sipped his drink. It was a dark red that left Marcus thinking that it was probably all blood. He could definitely have used some alcohol, though the liquor's effect on their body was incredibly short-lived. "I'm sorry it's that time again."

"So am I. Twenty years has passed far too quickly."

"I've heard some crazy talk of wanting to establish a town where only vampires are permitted inside. A place where we never have to move, never have to hide."

Marcus snorted. "Yes, sounds like Eden, but how will we survive? Are we just going to swarm out each night and prey on the nearest town, draining it dry? Our secret would be protected for all of one night, and then we could count on the local government bombing us into extinction."

Aiden smirked at Marcus before taking another drink. "That sounds about right, but I fear they have another solution for feeding the masses."

"What?"

"Live-in slaves. Humans would be captured and raised in warehouses like cattle until they were sold to their new vampire masters to feed from."

"That's barbaric! Whoever is suggesting this can't be serious."

"The Hidden are very serious about this scheme. They've even managed to locate three or four potential sites for the plan. Two are in Europe and they've brought it up for the European Ministry's approval."

"I can't believe they are actually considering this. Humans can't simply disappear without people noticing."

"Sadly...they can." Aiden stared at his glass, turning it around and around with the tips of his fingers so that the soft lighting glinted off the fine crystal. "There are plenty of cities around the world who would be happy to be rid of their homeless population. Same with the countless refugee camps. If a cunning vampire came in and offered to just fly those people to another city where they would have jobs and a place to live, who would argue?"

"No. It can't be allowed."

Aiden sighed. "You're right, but I do not have enough faith in the European Ministry to believe they will actually put a halt to this madness."

"Has a similar proposal been put before the American Ministry?"

"Not that I'm aware of."

Marcus tapped his fingers on the table. It would have explained why Meryl was so eager to get rid of Julianna and

Rafe. The Hidden would prefer if the Ministry had no distractions or disturbances to deal with if it was considering such a proposal. Or maybe not. Sometimes there was no understanding Meryl's behavior.

"Meryl stopped by my house a week ago. She threatened both Rafe's and Julianna's lives, though she seemed most intent on seeing Mother killed. Rafe, she seemed deluded enough to believe that he could be reformed."

A hint of a smile lightened Aiden's features for a moment. "No one is going to change Rafe but Rafe, and I am glad for that."

"But Mother?"

"There's no changing her either," he murmured. "But for entirely different reasons."

"True, but Meryl is an ardent member of The Hidden and if they've got some plan…"

"That group isn't the only one who wants Julianna dead."

Marcus fought the urge to shove to his feet and demand to know who else was threatening his family. He'd had enough of his nonsense. The Variks kept to themselves. They avoided all political maneuvering and power struggles. There was no reason to go after their mother.

"What the hell is going on, Aiden?"

"I'm still trying to discover the root of it all, but I was approached while in Rio by a vampire called Camille. She is not a member of The Hidden."

"And yet, she wanted Mother dead as well," Marcus irritably filled in.

"No."

Marcus frowned at Aiden, waiting for him to continue.

"She is a Predator, and they are very much opposed to the new city plans of The Hidden. They would very much like for us to set Julianna loose during one of her episodes on some place like…Times Square."

"What?" Marcus gasped. "They can't be serious."

"She was very serious. Julianna's destruction would not only announce to the world that we exist, but it would prove to humans that we are the dominant species of the world. Their natural masters."

"I'm assuming that she didn't take your rejection well."

Aiden surprised him by chuckling. He picked up his glass and smiled at Marcus. "She did not. She attempted to follow me back to my temporary home while in Rio."

"Insane," Marcus whispered.

Coming to a vampire's resting place uninvited was threatening business. Meryl had gotten away with it in his home only because it was known that he conducted business there as well. His own sleeping chamber was well protected during the daylight hours and he had a prepared escape route if it was necessary. A temporary home for Aiden's travels wouldn't have been nearly as well protected.

"Yes, well, she'll never make that mistake again."

Marcus wasn't surprised that Aiden had killed this Camille. It wasn't that she'd gone to Aiden's daytime resting spot, threatening him. It was that she was a threat against Julianna, who couldn't properly protect herself. Not once in her nearly two hundred years had she been in a fight for her life. Aiden, Marcus, and his brothers had protected her every waking moment. Her mind was already so fragile. They couldn't even begin to guess as to what would happen to her if she suddenly found herself attacked or even just kidnapped. If she survived, there was no telling if she'd recover mentally.

"What's going on, Aiden? Why is she being targeted now?"

"I'm not sure. I'm catching just small whispers."

"I hear nothing, so you have to tell me," Marcus snarled. "I can't be kept in the dark if I'm going to keep my family safe."

Aiden smiled a little at Marcus. It was soft and he imagined it was how a doting father might look on his son. "I think we are standing in the eye of a storm that is twisting around us. I've heard whispers that The Hidden mean to make a play for the American Ministry."

"And by play, you mean The Hidden intend to kill the sitting members and claim their seats."

"Yes. Naturally, The Predators faction won't tolerate it. They plan to make their own attack on the members first. When I arrived in Miami a few weeks ago, I heard that Percival had been found dead. His head torn from his body. Each side is blaming the other for his death."

Marcus swore to himself. Nothing good would come of either side ruling the vampires of North America. The Hidden would be safer for the humans, but they would enact stricter laws that would cut into Marcus's business as well as demand the lives of both Rafe and Julianna.

The Predators, on the other hand, would start a war with humans, which would result in mass casualties on both sides and general chaos.

The American Ministry, like its sister ruling head in Europe, was a mix of the four factions—the Hidden, Predator, Equalists, and the Moderates—and they found a way of balancing their rule through compromise. It also helped that since it took them so long to agree on anything, their rule was a relatively light touch.

Marcus had always considered himself, like Bel, a Moderate. He believed in limited interaction with humans so that they could enjoy the benefits of modern technology and keep up with the changing times rather than stagnate and be blindsided by the developments of man.

Only Rafe was an Equalist. That ragtag bunch supported coming out to the humans and seeking equal status with them. Few took them seriously, convinced that vampires would simply be hunted into extinction before equality could ever be achieved.

"I don't understand why either side has decided to target our family."

"It's not just our family. They are going after all the clans that aren't clearly aligned with either the Hidden or the Predators."

"We're not a clan."

"The Variks are six in number," Aiden calmly pointed out. "That is more than enough to be considered a clan. And with our combined age and experience, the Variks could be a force to be reckoned with if we chose to align ourselves." Marcus scoffed but Aiden leaned in closer, expression intent. "There are just eleven seats on the Ministry, and the Variks claiming them would make a near majority."

Marcus laughed louder this time, reclining in his chair. "I've never heard anything so ridiculous in my life. The Variks claiming the Ministry seats?"

"Lower your voice," Aiden said in a harsh whisper. "And while I know that such a thing has never crossed the minds of this family, others aren't so confident. The Variks are seen as an unknown. We've kept to ourselves far too much over the last century. We do not involve ourselves in politics, and that has left others to fill the silence in with their own speculation."

Marcus frowned. He'd not taken Aiden's suggestion seriously only because he knew his brothers. Rafe thought about nothing besides his nightclubs and sex. Bel couldn't be drawn out of his laboratory. Winter...well, only God knew Winter's plans, but Marcus felt secure in believing his little brother was not after power. And then Marcus wanted only to keep his family safe.

But it didn't matter what the truth was—it was what others believed. He knew he couldn't simply announce to others that the Variks were not chasing power or planned to be involved in the current struggle. Not one person would believe him.

For now, their best option was to strengthen their defenses

and hope to speed up the move. The sooner they were in their new home and hidden from other vampires, the safer they would all be until this latest power struggle was over.

"I'll speak with my brothers. Make sure they are aware of what is happening."

"I'll see what I can do about uncovering potential threats. I may reach out to Winter for help on this."

Marcus smirked. "I think Winter would be happy to help you sneak about. It's what he enjoys the most."

Aiden nodded. "I've always thought you were wrong to believe that Rafe is the biggest troublemaker. Winter enjoys stirring up mischief far more."

"Maybe, but Rafe tends to be the most flamboyant about it, while Winter's methods are far more secretive."

It also went without saying that Rafe's version of trouble tended to have a much lower body count when all was said and done. Winter had no qualms about turning one clan against another if he thought it would protect his family.

Marcus picked up his glass and started to take a drink when he paused just before it touched his lips. His gaze had caught on a familiar face. Meryl was standing at the bar, her glass raised in a mocking toast, but Cain was nowhere to be seen.

Lowering his glass and setting it on the table, Marcus turned his attention back to Aiden. "We need to leave now."

"What—"

Aiden didn't get to finish the thought before muffled screams could be heard from the first floor. Considering the amount of soundproofing that separated the two floors, Marcus could only assume that anarchy had broken out in the nightclub.

Grabbing Aiden's arm, he pulled the older vampire to his feet and started walking through what had been a quiet respite from the world. Other vampires were rising and hurrying toward the door to either investigate the growing sounds of chaos or to escape.

Human servants rushed around, and Marcus could only hope that they had their own hiding spots within the building. Any wounded vampires would be seeking them out before the night was over as a quick and easy meal. The humans were the least likely to survive if things grew worse.

Heart pounding within his chest, Marcus started for the exit with the others, constantly scanning through the panicked throng for signs of Cain. Meryl was a danger all by herself, but Cain's size and strength naturally made him a formidable adversary as well. Marcus would rather not find himself fighting against both of them if he could avoid it, even with Aiden at his side.

Before he could get more than a few steps, Aiden was stopping him and leading him down a dark corridor. He followed without question, praying that it was an alternate exit. At the end of the hall, they pushed through a swinging door and into the bright lights of a kitchen filled with stark white walls and stainless-steel counters and appliances. The scent of cooked meat and vegetables rose up. There were hints of spices and something sweet, maybe chocolate for a decadent dessert. A couple of humans were working on orders and preparing plates. They gasped and shouted at the sudden intrusion. The noise from sizzling food and general shouts from the staff as they worked had drowned out the cries from the first floor.

"Get out!" Aiden bellowed before anyone could argue. "There's an attack on the first floor. Everyone out."

No one lingered to question Aiden. They just flowed through the kitchen, running toward another exit at the back of the room. Marcus started to follow, but Aiden grabbed his arm and motioned with his head toward the chopping block at Marcus's hip. A butcher knife with a black handle was resting among some fresh cuts of beef. Without a word, Marcus snatched up the knife and stepped away from Aiden, giving them both some room to maneuver in the aisles of the kitchen.

The door swung open again and Meryl strolled through, a grin slicing wide across her face. "I knew it was only a matter of time before Aiden rolled into town to join his little clan. The wayward sire has returned."

"Aiden is never far from his family," Marcus snapped.

The elder vampire might be forced to travel great distances to give Julianna a break from his presence, but the brothers always stayed in contact with him, giving him updates on everything. Aiden and Julianna might not have ever married, but Marcus had always seen Aiden as part of their family.

Aiden glanced over his shoulder and flashed him a grateful smile before directing his attention to Meryl. "We want nothing to do with your faction's plans," Aiden growled.

"Doesn't matter."

A cold prickling crept up Marcus's neck. Tightening his grip on the knife, he swung around, raising the knife. Cain lurched out of the reach of the blade, his eyes wide in surprise. He'd been attempting to sneak up on them from the exit at the rear of the kitchen. The massive vampire hadn't made a sound, and yet Marcus had sensed some movement, some growing threat.

He swung the knife again, forcing Cain back another step. Meryl screamed as she launched her attack on Aiden, but Marcus couldn't risk looking over at his sire to see if he needed help. Cain might be large, but he was also fast. He'd undoubtedly take advantage of any distraction.

Cain's fist flew through the air, and Marcus barely managed to get out of the way in time. The breeze ruffled his hair and brushed his jaw. The aisles were too damn narrow for him to place more room between them. He and Aiden were trapped between Cain and Meryl. Marcus needed to take out Cain in some way before he could help Aiden.

Marcus kept slashing at Cain, trying to drive him back,

while cookware crashed to the floor, sending up an awful noise. Meryl screamed again, but the cry seemed more out of frustration than pain.

"Do it, Marcus!" Aiden suddenly shouted.

He didn't know what was happening to Aiden, but he didn't hesitate. With a small grin, he tapped into the one power he'd been granted when he'd been reborn as a vampire. There was a sense of relief in using it. Like he'd been tensing a muscle for too long and was finally able to relax.

In a breath, all light in the room flowed into Marcus's body, plunging the room into total darkness. Vampire eyes operated more like cat eyes. The pupils could expand, sucking in all available light so that they could see on the darkest of nights. But there had to be at least some light in the room. Marcus's power turned the room into a black hole. He drained it of all light, making Cain, Meryl, and even Aiden completely blind.

But Marcus could still see using the light he'd gathered inside of himself.

Both Meryl and Cain cried out in panic. Marcus chanced a quick glance over his shoulder to see that Aiden had gotten a hold of Meryl and was pulling her into him already. Looking at Cain, he found the large vampire's hands out in front of him, fingers trembling, as he searched for Marcus. Dipping under his hands, Marcus soundlessly slid in close and plunged the knife into Cain's heart. Cain shouted in pain, his hands clamping down on Marcus's shoulders, but his hold was weaker than it normally should have been.

"Aiden?" Marcus called out.

"Finish it, Marcus. They mean to kill us and our family."

Meryl screamed out, but the sound was suddenly cut short. Marcus ripped the knife from Cain's chest and plunged it into Cain's throat until he hit bone. Cain's mouth opened on a gurgle and he released Marcus to reach for the knife. Blood poured from his chest and neck, weakening the giant further. Marcus pulled the vampire down, hacking at his throat and pulling at his head, while bracing one foot on his chest. Cain fought as much as he could, but he was growing weaker by the second. At the end, there was only a small gasp of air as Marcus pulled his head from his body.

"Marcus?" Aiden demanded, worry thickening his voice.

Dropping the knife with a clatter to the blood-slick tile floor, Marcus pulled back his power and released the light he'd captured. He looked over to see Aiden blinking and squinting as his eyes tried to adjust to the sudden brightness. Meryl's dead body lay on the floor of the kitchen while Aiden clutched her head by the hair in his hand. Decapitation wasn't the only way to kill a vampire, but it was certainly the quickest and most effective.

Marcus looked down at himself and sighed. His suit was soaked with blood. He could feel it running down his face and dripping from his fingers. He'd been expecting a quiet meeting with Aiden to discuss recent issues. Not a fucking bloodbath.

"This is merely the beginning, Marcus," Aiden said softly.

Marcus could only nod. He needed to speak with his brothers. They needed to come up with a plan to protect themselves. To protect their mother.

※

IT WAS AFTER ONE IN THE MORNING WHEN MARCUS SAT ON THE edge of his bed, holding his phone in his hands. He'd just gotten out of an extremely long shower, scrubbing away Cain's blood from every inch of his body. He might crave blood for his survival, but that didn't mean he longed to bathe in the sticky substance. His lingering human side still demanded that he maintain some semblance of civility.

Luckily, the suit he'd been wearing hadn't been one of his favorites, because the damn thing needed to be incinerated.

He hadn't heard yet how many other vampires had been slaughtered at the club, but he knew he'd be hearing from the American Ministry about the deaths of Meryl and Cain. Aiden had already said that he would handle that matter, and Marcus could only grunt his agreement. He didn't want to worry about standing before the Ministry for an accounting of their deaths. Not that he was overly worried about it. Meryl had gone out of her way to threaten Marcus in his home just days earlier. He and Aiden were protecting themselves. The matter had been concluded outside the view of humans. Nothing needed to be resolved. Case closed.

Before his shower, he'd taken the time to call all three of his brothers to give them an update on his conversation with Aiden and to give them warning that more threats were likely to come their way.

Yet, his family was not on his mind as he sat staring at his phone. He wanted to call Ethan. Since stepping out of the club and climbing into his car, he had an overwhelming need to go to Ethan, to talk to Ethan, to reassure himself that he was safe. At first, he'd argued that he couldn't go to Ethan while he was covered in blood. That would only cause the young man to panic.

Now he was clean, and the world was quiet. Rational thought was kicking in again to battle the feelings trying to command his actions. His heart was demanding that he throw on the first clothes he could find and rush over to Ethan's apartment. It wanted to not only know he was safe, but to gather his small body against his own, to feel his heart beat and soak in his warmth. He wanted to taste his mouth and listen to his needy sounds of pleasure.

But going to Ethan was a mistake. He was bringing danger and potentially death into Ethan's world. His family had already been stolen from him. Somehow Ethan had managed to escape such a horrible fate and deserved a chance to live a long, productive life doing whatever his heart desired.

Marcus refused to risk Ethan's life.

There was no tomorrow for them. There would be no more kisses. No more lingering looks and little touches that sped up his heart. And if he was smart, no more lunches filled with Ethan's laughter and brilliant mind.

His world was slipping back into the pale gray it had been before he met Ethan. As it should be.

What he'd told Rafe so many nights ago was true. Vampires were not meant to find love.

CHAPTER FIFTEEN

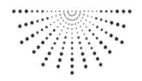

*E*than pushed up to his feet slowly after sealing the last box. Everything fucking hurt—his face, his ribs, his guts. He hadn't wanted to crawl out of bed this morning, and he'd winced at his reflection in the mirror as he was getting ready. His face was swollen, and he could barely see out of one eye. He moved like a fucking old man. Packing up Marcus's stuff and stacking it was proving to be miserable work.

It was no less than what he deserved for hooking up with Carl and his band of nutjobs. At least he put a stop to it before anyone got hurt. He'd never be able to live with himself if his actions harmed Marcus or any of his family.

Pulling out his phone, he checked on the time. It was a little after two in the afternoon. Marcus was usually up and moving around by now. Since Marcus had kept the third floor mostly locked up until recently, Ethan had worked around him, completing the fourth and second. He was now ready to start making some serious headway on the third floor. Luckily, it looked like that floor had fewer rooms. He was praying it meant less stuff as well.

Of course, working on the third floor mean there was an

increased chance of seeing Marcus, and Ethan was considering hiding out on the first floor until some of the swelling went down. He didn't want Marcus seeing him like this. Not that he'd be able to hide it when they had lunch together.

Marcus was going to ask what happened, and Ethan would have to come clean. A soft sigh fell from his lips. At least with the injuries, there was a chance that Marcus might believe him that he left the group.

With his mind too full of muddled thoughts, Ethan found himself wandering into the music room. The blood-smeared blanket had been cleared away, cleaned, and put back on the spare bed since Bel's departure.

The morning after Bel's attack, Ethan had gone into the library to clean up for Marcus. He knew the man had a cleaning crew, but he wasn't too sure what they were accustomed to seeing. In a small trash can, he found three empty bags of donated blood and a blood-stained glass. It was more than a little obvious that Bel hadn't gotten the typical infusion of blood. No, Marcus had poured it into a glass, and Bel drank it down like he would a protein drink.

Ethan put the empty bags in with the rest of the trash as well as some bloody gauze and cleaned out the glass in the kitchen. There was no evidence that anything had happened. There was no reason to bring it up to Marcus. Ethan knew what he was looking at. Bel was a freaking vampire, but there was some reassurance that he'd drank bagged blood rather than lining up a bunch of poor schmucks for involuntary blood donation to save Bel's life.

Would Ethan have given blood to Bel to save his life?

Would it have cost him his own life? Ethan would have liked to help Bel just to make Marcus happy, to relieve his worry, but he couldn't believe that Marcus would ask him to trade his life for Bel's.

But then, the belief that vampires killed every time they fed came from the League group, and Ethan had proved several times that they didn't know their shit.

In the music room, Ethan found himself drawn over to the massive black piano, gleaming in the light from the hall. He didn't bother to flip on the light as he crossed the room and slowly ran his fingertips along the smooth surface. The instrument was gorgeous and so damn elegant. It reminded him of Marcus. There was something regal and authoritative about the man. Maybe a little stiff and unmovable without the help of a few people. Ethan had a feeling Marcus was the type to dig his feet in whenever he set his mind to something, and it took all three brothers to change it.

Sitting down on the bench, he looked at the keys to find small smears of blood across the pristine white surfaces. He grabbed the bottom of his T-shirt and carefully rubbed one key after another to remove the blood. A soft note played as he pressed down each key and moved along the scale, wiping away the blood. He hated the idea of a beautiful instrument being sullied in such a way.

Listening to Marcus play was like being lifted by angels and carried into the clouds. He loved the music created by the goddess, but there was something different in listening to Marcus play. Maybe it was because he knew the man and was finally getting a glimpse of his soul. He'd suspected it was beautiful, but he hadn't expected to hear such pain there as well. Marcus had old, deep wounds that he hid from the world, probably from his brothers, but there was no hiding them in his music.

When he was first directed toward Marcus, Ethan was sure that he was hunting a monster. The vampire linked to the deaths of his family would be a cold, evil creature who didn't care about anyone or anything but himself.

What he found was a wounded soul, trapped by love and duty. Was he at all happy in his life? Considering that Ethan was the first man Marcus had ever kissed, it was unlikely he'd ever known love.

Fuck. Was Marcus incredibly old? Vampires could live forever, right? Was Marcus centuries old and a virgin?

The thought stopped Ethan cold, his shirt tightly clenched in his fist. Ethan suddenly felt bad about complaining about his six-month dry spell. He would have gone insane if he'd never had the chance to feel the pleasure of another's touch. Sure, all his hookups were emotionless things. They were about both people getting off, but it was better than nothing, right? For a brief moment, he felt alive and connected to another human being.

Where did that lack of contact leave Marcus? Was that dark loneliness swallowing him whole?

The sound of a hard-soled shoe stepping onto the wood floor almost had Ethan jerking around to look at Marcus. It had to be Marcus. He was the only other one in the house. But he remained facing the piano with his back to the doorway. His aching face was a clear reminder that he wasn't in a rush for Marcus to see him. His boss would demand to know what happened, and that would upset the delicate dance they'd been doing the past couple of weeks. He didn't want Marcus to look at him with disappointment or hatred.

"Teaching yourself one of your goddess's songs?" Marcus asked.

Ethan smiled at the keys. They'd talked about Tori Amos and her music over dinner on more than one occasion. Marcus was quickly working his way through all her albums.

"I think Tori is a little advanced for me," Ethan said with a smile. He winced as pain throbbed through his cheek. Yeah, smiling was bad.

"Well, I think you—" Marcus stopped midsentence as he came to stand beside the piano and got a clear view of Ethan's face. Reluctantly, Ethan looked up at Marcus, and it was like watching a violent storm coalesce above his head, preparing to throw a barrage of thunder and hail down on him. "What happened?" Marcus finally bit out.

Ethan shook his head, lowering his gaze down to the keys. "It's nothing. No big deal."

He didn't see Marcus's hand approach, but fingertips like the touch of butterfly wings pressed against his chin, directing him to look back up at Marcus. There was still anger in his expression, but also worry. So much worry and fear that it caused a lump to form in Ethan's throat.

"Please tell me."

"This doesn't have to do with Meryl or that Cain guy," Ethan quickly said. Some of the tension relaxed from Marcus's shoulders, but not nearly enough.

Marcus moved his hand away from Ethan's chin and motioned toward the bench. "May I?"

Ethan nodded and slid down enough that Marcus could sit next to him. It was a fight not to take a deep breath to draw that wonderful spicy scent of Marcus's cologne into his lungs. He loved the heat that radiated from him as if it were trying to wrap around Ethan and hold him tight.

Marcus placed his hands between his legs, threading his fingers together tightly. "You don't have to tell me anything. I just…I want to be there for you. If you need anything, either as an employee or as a friend, I am here for you. You know that, right?"

"I do." Ethan licked his lips, his eyes back on the black and white keys. "I guess I fell in with the wrong group. At the time, what they were saying, it made sense. Or at least, it helped me to not feel so powerless. But after a while, I woke up and realized that they weren't the people I thought they were. I had to get out."

"And this was their response to you leaving?"

Ethan sighed. "Yeah. I probably didn't handle it as calmly as I should have, but I had to get out. Before something bad happened."

Marcus leaned closer and brushed his lips against Ethan's temple. "I'm sorry this was the result."

"I keep thinking that my mom would have been disappointed in me if she'd known."

"I think she'd be proud that you were brave enough to walk away. You're a good person."

Ethan shook his head. He squeezed his eyes shut, and the tears that had been burning there slipped out. He wasn't a good person. If Marcus found out the truth, he'd never forgive him. "If I was such a good person, I wouldn't have joined up with those people in the first place."

Marcus cupped his face again. His thumb gently caressed his cheek, wiping away a tear. "I said you were a good person, not a perfect one. Good people still make bad choices sometimes. They just try to make it right later."

Turning his head, Ethan rubbed his uninjured cheek against the palm of Marcus's hand, wanting to revel in his touch for as long as he possibly could. "I think you're pretty damn perfect."

Huffing a laugh, Marcus leaned close so that his breath brushed against Ethan's ear. "If I was so damn perfect, I wouldn't be sitting here thinking how I want to find the person or persons who touched you and rip them to bloody, fleshy shreds with my bare hands." The low growl in Marcus's voice had a wonderful shiver running through Ethan's body. Yeah, he definitely wasn't a good person, because he was sorely tempted to hand over Carl's name and set Marcus loose on him.

But he wouldn't.

"But you won't," Ethan murmured.

"I still want to." Marcus lightly kissed Ethan's jaw. "Tell me a name. Let me protect you. Defend you. Set me free, Ethan." He kissed up along his jaw to his ear. "They'll never touch another person again." The tip of his tongue touched his earlobe and

Ethan nearly groaned. Goose bumps rushed down his arms and blood filled his dick.

"But if you go after this asshole, you won't be here kissing me, and I really don't want you to stop."

Marcus chuckled darkly. "I wouldn't stop. I'd wait until tonight when you're snuggled in your bed asleep alone. I would hunt this man down and tear him apart for you."

"Or…"

Marcus lifted his head a little so that he could look into Ethan's eyes. "Or?"

"I don't have to be sleeping alone. Then you couldn't go after this person. You wouldn't dare leave my bed, would you?"

It felt like the air was knocked out of his lungs as he watched Marcus's pupils dilate, his bright blue eyes becoming nearly black with desire.

"My choice is being wrapped around your body all night in bed or getting vengeance?"

"Yes."

"Would I be able to feel your bare skin against mine?"

Ethan smiled slowly at Marcus, and he couldn't feel the pain. There was only Marcus. "Are you asking if I would be completely naked and stretched out next to you?"

"Next to me. Beneath me. On top of me. Yes."

"I could be if that's what you wanted."

Marcus slowly brushed his lips back and forth over Ethan's parted lips, teasing him. Ethan was practically begging for a kiss. His body was trembling and pressing as close as he possibly could on that tiny bench.

"I think I was wrong about you. You're a very evil person," Marcus murmured. "Teasing me with vengeance and my darkest desire."

"And which would you choose?"

Marcus crushed his lips against Ethan's, plunging his tongue deep into his mouth. The kiss was perfect. Demanding, possessive, and yet so fucking tender. He could feel Marcus's concern and his heartache for Ethan's pain. Ethan kissed him, trying to give all of himself, to show Marcus that he trusted him, that he wanted more than just this kiss or even a quick fuck. He wanted to show Marcus that he wanted everything that came with being involved with a vampire, even if he wasn't ready to actually say those words.

Wrapping his arms around him, Marcus tried to draw him closer. Pain shot through Ethan, forcing him to break off the kiss as he cried out.

Marcus instantly released him and leaned away. "I'm sorry," he quickly said.

Ethan reached up, cupping the side of his neck. "Don't. I'm okay."

"You're not," Marcus snapped. Slowly, he lowered his hands and grabbed the edge of Ethan's shirt. Ethan knew he could stop him, but he sat still as Marcus raised the shirt to reveal the motley of bruises that covered his torso.

A low growl rumbled up Marcus's thick chest, reminding him of an angry bear, but instead of being afraid, he was turned-on by the sound. No one had ever wanted so badly to protect him. No one had cared about his well-being in so damn long, it was intoxicating.

"I'm very attracted to you, Ethan, but my need for vengeance is winning out over my hunger for your body," Marcus grumbled.

Ethan smiled and rose from the bench. When Marcus tried to follow him, Ethan placed a restraining hand on his shoulder, keeping him seated. He walked around the bench so that he was facing the piano with the bench in front of him. With his hands on Marcus's shoulders, he directed the man to spin on the bench until his back was pressed to the keys. Ethan then surprised him by climbing onto his lap so that his knees were on either side of Marcus's hips. Marcus sucked in a harsh breath while holding his hands out to the side.

Grabbing his wrists, Ethan placed Marcus's hands on his hips so that his fingers dug into his ass. "It's safe to hold me here. You won't hurt me."

"Ethan..." Marcus exhaled with longing.

"I know, I'm not a good person," Ethan whispered, pressing a soft kiss to the corner of his mouth. "There's a part of me that wants you to get revenge." He kissed the other corner. "There's a part of me that's so damn turned-on that you want to protect me." He pulled away from Marcus and gave his best sexy smirk despite the pain in his face. "There's another part of me that's dying to have you fuck me on this piano."

Marcus groaned and carefully pulled Ethan in for a draining kiss that had Ethan pressing his hard cock against Marcus's stomach. He finally gave in and thrust both of his hands into Marcus's thick hair, twisting the silky strands around his fingers. It was even more luxurious than he'd dreamed, and now he had Marcus completely captive. He never wanted to stop kissing him. It didn't matter if he was a vampire. Didn't matter if Marcus was going to outlive him by centuries. Ethan had this wonderful moment, and Marcus felt so damn good against him.

He broke off the kiss and ran his tongue along Marcus's swollen bottom lip. His eyes were glazed with passion and they might have glowed a little bit, but it could have been a trick of the light. There was another wicked part of him that wanted Marcus to lose control, for his fangs to finally come out.

"I thought we had a good reason for not doing this anymore," Marcus murmured. "But I can't for the life of me remember what it was any longer."

"You wanted to go slow so you could adjust." Ethan shifted again, grinding his cock against Marcus and wringing a moan out of him. "Feels like you're adjusting fine to me."

"I take it all back. You're evil. So very evil," Marcus said with a choked laugh.

"Only to you, I promise."

Marcus blinked and his face suddenly became very serious. He lifted his hand and his fingers brushed across a part of Ethan's face that wasn't swollen and bruised. "There's no one else in your life…"

Ethan sat still on Marcus's lap, the teasing at an end. "No. I've never really dated, and there's no one in my life that I'm seeing. That I'm physical with."

Marcus drew in a deep breath and held it for a moment before he slowly released it. "You make me want things, Ethan."

"That's not a bad thing."

"No, but for me, it's a complicated thing."

Ethan started to say that complicated didn't bother him, but Marcus was already pushing him to his feet, putting space between them.

"I'm sorry I took you from your work," Marcus mumbled.

"Don't, Marcus. Not to me. Don't block me out." Ethan's voice was sharp, and he stood up straight, closing the distance between them so that Marcus couldn't escape.

Marcus surprised him by chuckling. "I can't, can I? At least not for long."

"I don't want you to." Ethan grabbed his hand, needing to cling to that connection between them for as long as possible. "You want to beat the shit out of the asshole who touched me. I want to help slay your dragons too."

"I would like that, but it may have to wait a little while longer. Things are growing more complicated."

"What are you talking about?"

Marcus glared at the floor. "I can't say. Just that we will need to push up the moving date."

"How soon?"

He shook his head, still not looking at Ethan. "I'm not sure yet. I need to speak with my brothers to finalize plans. Just continue working as you have been until I have more details for you. Then we can look into bringing in more help as necessary."

"Okay. Whatever you need," Ethan murmured, hating the way his voice wavered just a tiny bit. Speeding up the move meant that his time with Marcus was growing even shorter. He didn't know what kind of future they had, if they had a chance at anything at all, even with his horrible secret, but he didn't want to give up any time with him.

Marcus gave him a small smile and pressed a kiss to the top of his head before pulling his hand free. Ethan watched him walk out of the music room, likely heading back to his office where he could call his brothers and make his plans.

Ethan wasn't willing to give up on Marcus yet. He could get the vampire to understand and forgive him. And then maybe they could figure out what a real relationship would look like for them. He wanted to see the smile on Marcus's face, to hear his laughter. The man was far too lonely and his life too empty.

CHAPTER SIXTEEN

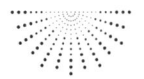

Ethan closed another box and glared up at the shelves. He'd already filled six boxes of books and still not made a dent in Marcus's collection. The boxes were also impossibly heavy now and couldn't be moved without a dolly. It also wasn't helping that he'd paused on several occasions to flip through some of the more interesting books in his collection and read the back covers.

He sighed again. There just wasn't enough time for all the books he wanted to read. Of course, he couldn't remember the last time he'd lain around reading a book. The past few nights he'd worked late packing with Marcus at his side. It really was sinful how sexy the man was in a pair of jeans and a tight black T-shirt. He'd freaking tripped over shit twice crossing the room while staring at Marcus's ass.

Since the encounter at the piano, they'd managed to behave themselves and keep their hands off each other, which Ethan couldn't say he was thrilled about. It probably hadn't been too hard for Marcus since Ethan's face hadn't looked its best. The swelling was gone, and the bruising was starting to fade at last.

Even if they weren't taking little breaks to explore each

other's bodies, they did have the chance to spend the time talking. Marcus told him about all the interesting places he'd lived over the years.

The funny thing was that the longer they talked, the more often Marcus failed to catch himself when he slipped up on the timing of something. Marcus looked as if he was in his early thirties, but if Ethan tallied up all the different places Marcus had been and the time frames, the man had to be at least seventy. But Marcus didn't seem to notice the slipups. Ethan chalked that up to Marcus growing more comfortable around him, and that warmed Ethan in ways he couldn't quite explain.

Ethan even found himself talking about the family he lost, a topic he avoided under almost all circumstances. Marcus felt safe, though.

Just as there had been no more kissing, there had been no more important talking either. Carl had stopped contacting Ethan, for which he was grateful. Each night, he hurried from Marcus's home to his apartment, looking over his shoulder the entire time. He also installed a little more security in his apartment to watch for anyone breaking in while he wasn't there. But the League had been quiet so far.

It didn't change the fact that he needed to tell Marcus about the Humans Protecting Humans League and his assignment at the town house. He'd briefly considered tucking that secret away and not telling him. If the League never did anything, then there was no reason to stir up trouble. But that was a coward's way out. Marcus deserved the truth.

He just didn't know when to tell him. Marcus already seemed extremely stressed about the move as well as something else he wasn't telling Ethan. He could feel it building. It was like looking on the horizon and seeing a wall of dark clouds crawling closer day by day. Ethan didn't want to add to the problems weighing on Marcus.

Right now, he was leaning toward telling Marcus after the

move was completed. He would be more relaxed. One problem would be solved, and he could breathe a little easier.

Or was he still being a coward?

Growling to himself, Ethan turned to fold up another box as he continued to work his way through the library. A high-pitched yelp escaped him when he saw a short but elegant-looking woman watching him from the doorway.

"Oh God, sorry!" Ethan gasped, pressing his hand to his chest as if he were trying to keep it from jumping out of his chest.

She giggled, her smile sweet and kind. "I apologize. I didn't mean to startle you."

Ethan gave a dismissive little wave. "No worries. I tend to get lost in thought while I'm working. Oblivious to the whole world."

"I heard you working in here and I thought you were Amy, but I forgot that she doesn't work for my son any longer."

Ethan's heart ramped up again and he fought the urge to take a step backward when he suddenly realized who he was talking to. There was only one other woman who might appear in Marcus's home and that was Janice. But this wasn't the stern woman who interviewed him. This was a lovely woman with black hair that was graced with a few random strands of gray and too-familiar blue eyes.

This was Julianna, Marcus's mother.

The woman who instilled in Marcus and his brothers a deep love of music.

The woman who had clawed at Bel, trying to rip his heart from his chest with her bare hands.

But…she didn't look like the woman he remembered from his childhood nightmares. This wasn't the blood-stained woman calling for him after murdering his family.

No.

That couldn't be right.

It had made sense after seeing what she'd done to Bel, her own son. Of course this woman had escaped her captors and gone on a blood-soaked rampage that ended in the deaths of more than a dozen people. It had to be her.

"Are you okay?" she asked softly. Ethan hadn't realized he'd gone quiet as he stared at her like she was the angel of death. Well, she was sort of, but not the one he'd been looking for.

"Sorry. Tired, I guess," he chuckled. He wiped his hands on his pants and slowly crossed the room. When he was within a few feet, he extended his hand. "I'm Ethan Cline. Mr. Varik hired me about a month ago to pack up his house for his move and to work as his assistant."

He was proud that his hand didn't tremble. She seemed fine right now. Not murderous in the least. And if she was here, Marcus had to be somewhere in the house as well. Marcus would hear him if he screamed for help, right?

Of course, if she was here, it meant that it was now dark outside. *Fuck.* How late was it? He'd completely lost track of time. He'd promised Marcus that he'd leave on time tonight rather than staying late. Obviously, that was because his family was stopping by for some unknown reason.

"Julianna Varik." She took his hand without hesitation, smiling warmly at him. "I'm Marcus's mother."

"It's a pleasure to meet you, Mrs. Varik. Is there anything I can help you with?"

"Oh, no! I didn't mean to disturb you. I just heard someone moving about and was curious who else was here."

"You're not disturbing me at all. Actually, I just realized how late it was." He pulled out his phone and confirmed that it was well after eight in the evening. So damn late. Marcus was not going to be pleased, but Ethan couldn't bring himself to fully regret his absentmindedness. It meant that he got to meet Julianna. That was the only way he was going to remove the last of the doubt and questions from his mind about her and his past.

"I won't keep you," Julianna said. She started to move toward the door. "It was a pleasure to meet you."

"I was wondering…" Ethan quickly said, stopping her. "Were you the one to teach Marcus how to play the piano?"

Her expression instantly brightened, and it was like she was shining in her joy. "You've heard him play?"

"Yes. It was amazing." Which was the honest truth. Marcus's skill behind the piano was stunning. His nimble fingers flew across the keys, moving like the instrument was simply an extension of his body. He didn't need to mention that the one time he'd heard Marcus play was at the request of his injured brother to soothe him.

"Well, he actually had several tutors growing up that taught him and his brothers to play instruments. I was just there to encourage him and find him new sheet music when he mastered the songs he had. All my boys are just so skilled."

"You must be so proud of them."

She nodded, taking another step into the room. "I am. I am a very lucky mother to have four such amazing and talented sons."

"I think Marcus, I mean, Mr. Varik, is very lucky to have you. He speaks very highly of you."

A rosy blush rose to her cheeks and she gave a little shake of her head. "Your mother must be proud to have raised such a kind child."

"I like to think she would be," Ethan murmured softly.

"Would be?"

"My mother was killed when I was very young."

Julianna gasped softly, her cheeks losing their blush. She took a step toward Ethan with her hand outstretched toward him. "I'm so very sorry. That's just horrible."

"Thank you. If you don't mind me saying so, you remind me

of her a little bit. You're kind like she was. Similar smile too." He paused and looked down at the carpet for a moment, trying to gather together the courage to continue. He felt dirty and underhanded, but he had to know. Had to know the truth. He had his doubts, but he had to finally remove *all* the doubts from his mind.

"We...we used to play hide-n-seek in the house when I was little. Me and my two sisters," he continued. "Did you ever play that with your sons?"

Juliana laughed and Ethan looked up at her. "I did, actually."

"Did you ever sing 'Come out, come out, wherever you are,' as you sought them?"

Her brow furrowed a little in thought. "I...I don't think I did."

"Would you mind saying it now? You just remind me of her, and...I guess I just kind of miss that moment."

Juliana's smile was wide, but there was no missing the sad look in her eyes. "Come out, come out, wherever you are," she sang.

Ethan blinked back tears. Her voice was like that of an angel, sweet and pure. So very perfect. And nothing like the woman who tried to hunt him down in his own apartment.

This wasn't the woman that slaughtered his parents and sisters. She wasn't the one who killed several families in his apartment building. She wasn't the one.

He'd known it from the moment that she walked into the room. Probably known it from the moment he heard Bel and Rafe speak. Known it since Marcus had told him about their dedication to Julianna. She would never have had the chance to escape her sons and go on a blood-soaked rampage.

And he put Marcus and his entire family in danger because he'd been so damn desperate to find his family's killer. It wasn't fair. Not to him. Not to Marcus. He should never have fallen in with Carl and the stupid League. He was never going to find the vampire that destroyed his life. And if it meant that he didn't potentially destroy another innocent family in his search, he'd just learn to accept it.

"Ethan?" Julianna said.

Ethan's head popped up and he was surprised to find her standing only a couple of feet away. She slowly reached out and placed her small hand on his arm, her touch so gentle and cautious. For a moment, his brain rejected all the things that Marcus had told him about her. This couldn't be the same woman who hurt Bel. She was warm and loving. She'd never hurt one of her sons. It would kill her to harm her boys. Ethan could see that.

But then maybe Marcus was right. It wasn't her attacking her sons. The illness twisted and warped her mind, stealing her consciousness away and replacing it with that of a monster.

"Are you okay?" she asked, pulling him from his swirling thoughts.

"Yes. Sorry. You have an amazing voice," he murmured.

"Like your mother's?"

Ethan barked out a harsh laugh. He pressed the heel of his palms to his eyes, wiping away unshed tears. "Oh God, no! I loved my mother, but she had a horrible singing voice. She loved to sing along to the radio while she cleaned. Dogs would howl, but she didn't care. She just loved music and singing."

Julianna laughed again, and for a moment, Ethan felt lighter. Maybe he didn't have his mother or the rest of his family, but it felt so good to just talk about them, to remember the good parts of his childhood. It had all been overshadowed by the dark, bloody memories for so long, but there had been good parts. Fun parts.

"Ethan!" Marcus's loud voice was like a thunderclap breaking over his head. He winced and even Julianna gave a little jump. They both looked over at the open doorway to find Marcus standing there, flanked on either side by Bel and Rafe.

"What are you still doing here? You should have been gone hours ago!"

"I'm sorry—" he started to say but Julianna interrupted him.

"Marcus! I raised you better than that. Ethan has been working very hard for you. We were just talking. It's my fault that he's stayed so late. Now apologize to this lovely young man."

"I'm sorry, Ethan, but you need to leave now," Marcus said firmly, his eyes narrowed in nearly a glare.

"Really, Marcus. You can do better than that. Ethan is such a nice young man."

Behind Marcus, Rafe was laughing like a hyena, while Bel's expression had turned more speculative and curious, as if Ethan had suddenly become a very interesting specimen that needed studying. Ethan did not want to find himself under Bel's microscope. Marcus still didn't look pleased, but the glare had been replaced with more of a look of resignation.

"Ethan is well aware that I appreciate his hard work," Marcus grumbled.

Ethan opened his mouth to make a playful, snarky comment, but a single, sharp shake of Marcus's head had him biting his tongue. The comment would have given away that there was more going on between them than a little packing, and Ethan didn't need to force Marcus to admit anything to his family that he wasn't ready to. Marcus deserved the right to figure things out at his own pace.

"Thank you, Mr. Varik. But you're right. I need to leave. It's past my dinnertime."

"Oh! Then you must join us!" Julianna cried, clapping her hands together.

A fresh peal of laughter from Rafe echoed through the hall, and even Bel snickered. Marcus only groaned. His every attempt to bring things under control had them slipping further from his grasp. Ethan decided to have pity on him. It was smarter. It also increased his chances of getting another kiss from the man sometime soon.

"Thank you, but I can't tonight. Can I have a rain check?" Ethan asked, placing his hand over Julianna's.

"Of course. I understand. We would love—"

Whatever Julianna was going to say was stopped by a loud explosion in the front foyer that seemed to rock the entire house. Ethan stumbled to the side, trying to keep his balance. Julianna was thrown into him and he instinctively caught her, cradling her against his slightly larger frame, protecting her as best he could.

There was a loud ringing in his ears, and he blinked several times. The world didn't make sense for a moment. He looked at the doorway and the cloud of smoke that was rolling through the hall. Marcus and his brothers had been thrown forward and were in the process of picking themselves up off the floor.

The front door had exploded.

But…that would mean someone was attacking Marcus's town house.

Marcus met Ethan's eyes, fear twisting up his features. "Run!"

CHAPTER SEVENTEEN

*P*anic slammed into Marcus as he picked himself off the ground. He quickly looked around to see Bel and Rafe rising as well. Ethan was holding his mother steady on her feet. Someone had set an explosion off against his fucking front door. There were deep voices shouting directions. Their attackers were coming. He needed to get Ethan and Julianna to safety.

Looking at Ethan, he could think of only one thing.

"Run!" he bellowed.

Ethan's terrified gaze held his for a moment before he gave a sharp nod and started pulling Julianna toward the other door out of the library. It would lead him to the rear parlor, which had a door onto the hallway farther into the town house. They could escape through the kitchen and out the back door, assuming they weren't already surrounded.

A different swell of fear threatened to consume Marcus. These attackers weren't the only threat to Ethan's life. If this attack triggered another episode in Julianna, Ethan would be defenseless. He had no way of protecting himself against her.

"Bel, go with them!"

Bel wordlessly ran after Ethan and Julianna as they disappeared into the dark room. His heart went out to his brother, who was still anxious around their mother following her latest attack. He wasn't comfortable being around her alone yet, and it would likely take several more months before that occurred, but Bel knew that of him and his twin, Rafe was the stronger fighter.

Marcus had no idea who was attacking his home, but he had a few guesses. Unfortunately, he had no weapons tucked away in the library. Hell, the closest on hand were in his office and bedroom on the third floor. With Ethan packing up the house, he'd moved all the weapons he kept hidden about his home because he didn't want his assistant stumbling over them and asking awkward questions. At the time, he didn't think Ethan would understand that he was always at risk of being attacked by another vampire.

Now it wouldn't be quite so hard to explain.

As Rafe and Marcus turned toward the hall, they watched as the first few men entered wearing what looked to be body armor while wielding automatic weapons. These weren't vampires. They preferred knives for hacking off limbs and heads. Bullets didn't always slow down vampires.

Marcus glanced over at Rafe, who tossed him a jaunty smile and a little shrug.

"Can you grab the lights, dear brother?" Rafe asked.

Marcus relaxed the little part of him that seemed to hold back the power. Tension flooded from his body while all the light in the hallway rushed into his body. Pitch blackness crashed over the area and shouts rose in the darkness. The intruders floundered a bit, waving the nose of their guns wildly from one side to the next, blind to everything. Night vision goggles didn't even work in his version of a magical night.

He'd asked Rafe how he managed to fight in that complete

blackness and his brother said that he relied on sound to take down his prey. Marcus watched his brother easily slide through the room without making a sound, his eyes closed against the darkness. He'd pause here and there, his head cocked to the side as he listened. The attackers breathed heavily, their clothing and armor rustling as they shifted. So very easy to find.

A scream pierced the relative silence as Rafe took down one man, his body thudding loudly on the hardwood floor. The other attackers jumped backward, moving away from the sound while turning toward it. Marcus launched himself into the thicket of men, grabbing two of them. He slammed one hard to the ground, attempting to knock the air from his lungs while grabbed the other by the throat. Fingers dug deep, tearing through flesh and sinew. Blood spurted hot across his hand and the ever-present hunger pushed back, demanding to be sated. The second man's scream was immediately cut off in a wet gurgle. Marcus pulled his hand free as he tossed the man to the ground and turned his attention to the first man.

Shouts from the rear of the house echoed to the front and Marcus's heart jumped. They were surrounded. He heard Ethan shouting instructions and then Bel answered, but he couldn't quite make out their words. He could only assume that Ethan was directing them to take the servants' staircase to the upper floors as a means of escape. He wanted to go to them, save them, but he couldn't leave Rafe alone. They were outnumbered.

Before he could grab the intruder at his feet, pain seared through his arm followed by another near his collarbone. He'd been fucking shot. He lost his hold on the power and light flooded into the room. People shouted in pain. Marcus dove at the bastard who shot him, ripping the gun from his hands and potentially breaking fingers in the process. With a snarl, he snapped the man's neck and dropped his corpse to the floor.

He looked up to do a quick count of attackers, hoping that Rafe might be able to handle them on his own so he could check on Ethan and their mother, but it proved to be wishful thinking. Behind the men already standing in the open hallway, four vampires strolled into the house, wicked grins on their pale faces. They wore no body armor and carried no guns. Each had a long blade in their hands. Marcus recognized only two of the faces of vampires who liked to associate with Meryl. Fellow members of The Hidden looking to take out the people who would be most likely to cause problems for their master plans.

"Rafe! Watch out!" Marcus cried. The humans were a nuisance. The vampires were the true threat.

Marcus leaned down and pulled a knife from the dead man's sheath. The newest intruders hung back, waiting for Marcus and Rafe to finish dealing with the humans before they fell on them in a flurry of steel and fangs. Marcus fought them as best he could. Fists pummeled him as he sank his blade deep into a gut. The grip grew slick with blood and he tightened his hold. He couldn't risk looking over at Rafe, couldn't think about Bel alone at the rear of the house against an unknown number of assailants. He could only keep moving, keep fighting.

One vampire went down, but Marcus was bleeding heavily already from his earlier wounds as well as the new one on his neck. He didn't know if they were winning. It certainly didn't feel like it. Adrenaline and fear were the only things keeping the pain at bay, but he felt like he was slowing down. Each movement growing more sluggish.

A new roar made his tired heart skip. He glanced up to see Aiden and Winter standing in the open doorway. They jumped into the fray, taking on the last of their attackers. Marcus stumbled away from the fight, his feet sliding in the blood and gore that covered the hardwood. He ran as fast as he could to the kitchen where he saw Bel kick away the corpse of a shredded vampire. His brother was covered in blood and his breathing was heavy. There were fresh cuts across his chest and a bullet wound in his thigh.

"Mother? Ethan?" Marcus shouted.

Bel pointed toward the half-hidden staircase as he leaned heavily against the center island. "Two vamps followed. I...I couldn't stop them all," Bel panted.

"No!" Aiden gasped from behind Marcus. He hadn't even realized that his sire had followed him. "Julianna!" he roared, his deep voice echoing through the house a second before he charged up the stairs.

Marcus inwardly cringed. The sound of Aiden's voice was likely to send her straight into an episode, putting Ethan's life in even more danger. Or it would do nothing because she was already dead.

Clenching his teeth, Marcus pulled together the last of his strength and rushed after Aiden. He prayed there was a third option he wasn't thinking of.

～

ETHAN GRIPPED THE NARROW WOODEN HANDRAIL WITH SWEATY palms and pulled himself up the stairs as fast as he could, following on Julianna's heels. The woman had tightly held his hand as she guided him easily through Marcus's house to the kitchen. But as they reached it, the back door was kicked open. Without hesitation, she pivoted and turned them up the back stairs.

Voices shouted and among them, Ethan thought he heard Bel's strong, angry voice. Ethan shouted at him to watch out before disappearing up the stairs. They had just reached the second floor when a new set of feet pounded up the wooden stairs, chasing after them. He prayed that Bel was okay as he and Julianna rushed hand in hand to the next set of stairs, continuing up to the third and now the final narrow stairs to the attic. There was nowhere else to go. His only hope was for them to barricade themselves in the attic and call 9-1-1 on his cell phone.

His heart pounded in his chest and his legs burned from climbing so many stairs so quickly. He didn't know what the hell was going on, but he needed to get back to Marcus. Ethan didn't have a weapon, and he was pretty sure he didn't stand a damn chance against a bunch of assholes with machine guns, but he was not leaving Marcus. He'd find a way to help him, but first he had to get Julianna somewhere she'd be safe.

At the top of the stairs, Julianna threw open the door and held it back for Ethan to run through. As he stepped into the attic, he turned around in time to see her flash him a sad smile before she stepped out of the room, pulling the door closed behind her.

"No!" Ethan screamed, lunging for the door. It took him a couple of steps to reach it, but he was already too late. Grasping the doorknob, he pulled but the door wouldn't budge. He didn't know if she jammed something in the door or what, but he couldn't get out.

"No! Julianna! No! You can't do this! You have to let me help you!" he shouted desperately at her.

"It's too dangerous for you," Julianna said, her voice muffled through the door. "You have to stay safe for my Marcus. He needs you."

"No!" Tears streamed down his face. "He needs you too. Julianna!" He clamped his teeth together and tried to hold his breath, straining to hear her through the door. After a moment, he heard a thump and then another of her footsteps on the bottom stairs. He banged his hand against the door and paced away from it, eyes desperately searching the room for something he could use to break out.

The attic had been completely boxed up, and most of the boxes had been moved down to the third floor where they were placed in a bedroom close to the elevator. His hope had been that it would speed up the move, but it had left him without a damn thing to use.

Fuck! She couldn't leave him alone like this. Marcus needed him to keep his mother safe. He couldn't let Marcus lose his mother the same way he lost his own. She wouldn't be stolen away.

Marching back to the door, Ethan braced his foot against the doorjamb and wrapped both hands around the doorknob, pulling with all the weight he could behind it. The door wouldn't move.

Voices could be heard through the door and Ethan froze. There was someone else in the hallway with Julianna. He didn't know who it was, but there was no sound of gunfire. Was it Winter? Something in his gut said no.

Ethan released the doorknob and banged loudly on the door with both fists, trying to draw the person away from Julianna. He had no weapon. No way of effectively defending himself, but if he could just buy Julianna a few minutes, maybe they'd be able to last until Marcus or his brothers could reach them.

A scream pierced the air and then was cut short. Ethan cried out, backing away from the door. There were more sounds, deeper male voices. Voices in pain and angry. Ethan's knees gave out and he found himself sitting on the floor in the center of the room.

Something heavy banged against the door and Ethan's heart jumped. With a trembling hand, he pushed against the floor and climbed to his feet. He would face Julianna's killer standing. The heavy weight pounded against the door one more time before exploding inward.

Marcus stumbled inside, his shirt soaked in blood. His face was pale, and tears filled his eyes. "Ethan," he said on a relieved sigh.

"Oh God, Marcus," Ethan gasped. He rushed across the room, wanting to launch himself at Marcus but at the same time he was afraid of hurting him. Marcus solved the problem by wrapping his arm around Ethan's shoulders and pulling him in against his chest. "Julianna?"

Marcus shook his head before pressing his face into Ethan's hair. "No. We didn't reach her in time."

"I'm sorry. She locked me inside. I couldn't—"

"I know. She was trying to protect you."

Ethan helped Marcus down the stairs and along the hall to where the other three brothers were standing around a man kneeling on the ground as he held Julianna's body in his arms. There were three other dead bodies on the floor, but only one of them wore the body armor he saw on the men as they were coming through the back door. The other two appeared to be in regular street clothes, but wielding knives instead of guns.

"I'm taking her out of here. I have…I have a place for her," the man murmured against Julianna's hair.

"Go, Aiden. We'll say our final good-byes later," Bel said. He shoved one hand through his hair, pushing it from his face and smearing blood on his forehead in the process. "We'll stay and arrange for the cleaner. Secure Marcus's place for the day."

Ethan watched as Aiden gently cradled Julianna against his chest as he rose to his feet. They watched him slowly walk away before their attention was turned to the other dead bodies littering Marcus's floor.

"I don't understand," Rafe murmured. "Who did this? And why?"

"The humans were a part of the Humans Protecting Humans League," Winter replied. He lifted his gaze from the floor, pinning Ethan with eyes so pale blue they almost looked white. "As for the why, I suggest we ask one of their members."

Ethan's heart lurched in his chest and started racing. He tried to retreat, but Marcus's hand grabbed his and tightened, holding him in place. He looked over at Marcus, seeing the pleading there and he could barely breathe. "I can explain. I swear. I didn't know about this."

But with each word he spoke, the hope died in Marcus's eyes and was replaced with rage. He wouldn't be surprised if Marcus killed him that night, and he couldn't blame him. It was what he deserved, but he wanted a chance to try to make it right.

CHAPTER EIGHTEEN

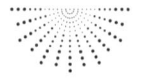

*E*than found himself quickly hustled to the library, where he spent the better part of an hour tied to a chair with a rag stuffed in his mouth while the others handled getting what they called "cleaners" in the house to get rid of the dead bodies. Bullets were removed and other wounds were covered with gauze and tape. Supplies were also found to secure the front and back doors for the day.

He could hear them arguing with Marcus to go feed, but his boss refused to leave the house until he had the truth of what the fuck was going on. Ethan had a feeling that he was going to end up being Marcus's meal when he didn't supply them with the answers they wanted. Unfortunately, he was pretty sure they weren't going to believe what he had to say.

Closing his eyes, Ethan dropped his head forward. He should have told Marcus weeks ago. Come clean. Maybe they would have been better prepared. Maybe they could have attacked the League instead of the other way around. He didn't know, but his mind kept circling back to Julianna. If he'd done things differently, she'd be alive now.

Footsteps echoed across the floor, the sound growing closer.

Ethan's head popped up and he opened his eyes to see the four brothers file into the library. Although the others had more than their fair share of cuts and gunshot wounds, Marcus looked as if he was in the worst condition.

Marcus slowly made his way over to the leather sofa and dropped onto it with a hiss of pain. Bel sat next to him, a look of worry on his face while Rafe hovered behind his twin.

Winter approached Ethan and stared at him for a moment before reaching for the tail of the cloth in his mouth. He was smaller than his siblings, possibly even the same height as Ethan, but there was a dangerous kind of energy that vibrated around him. His hair was longer than his brothers and the black strands were liberally threaded with stark white, as if he'd just barely escaped winter's icy hold.

"Tell the truth. I'll know if you're lying." He leaned down and smiled coldly as he stared into Ethan's eyes. "I already know more than you might suspect," Winter warned before pulling the cloth from Ethan's mouth.

Ethan coughed and moved his tongue around his dry mouth, trying to get some saliva back in it before he tried to speak.

"Why?" Marcus demanded in a low, rough voice.

He stared at Marcus for a moment, willing him to understand, but he was afraid to hope that it was possible. "Vampires killed my family."

Marcus immediately shook his head and Ethan leaned forward against the ropes holding him in place.

"It's true! Sixteen years ago, just outside of Indianapolis. I was ten years old, living in an apartment building with my parents and two sisters. I woke up in the middle of the night and went to the bathroom. I heard a loud bang against the front door, and then my mother screamed. I hid in the linen closet. There was a hole in the wall. I curled up in the hole behind some towels and bedsheets. I could hear everyone screaming and people laughing. I saw her through a crack in the door. She had long brown hair and a pale, blood-covered face. And fangs."

"Fuck," Rafe swore softly. He paced away from the sofa, rubbing his eyes.

Ethan swallowed past the lump in his throat, hating the old pain that rose with talking about the memory. "I should have helped them instead of hiding. I kept thinking I was just a little kid. What could I do? But I should have tried to help them." He paused and cleared his throat. "When I crawled out of the closet, my entire family was dead. I ran across the hall to the neighbor. His door was open and I found him dead. All the apartment doors were open with bloody tracks leading from them. After that, I went back to my apartment and sat next to my mom's dead body until the cops came. All three floors. Twelve apartments. I was the only survivor."

"So, you wanted revenge," Winter supplied.

Ethan turned his head toward the cold voice to find Winter sitting in a chair turned toward him. He looked relaxed, as if they were talking about plans for the weekend and not deciding Ethan's fate.

"I did. My sisters didn't deserve to die like that. Neither did my parents. They all deserved a normal, happy life. I should have grown up in a home!" Ethan shouted, tugging against his ropes. "Not alone."

"You planned to kill us because we're vampires?" Bel asked.

"No! I just want the woman who killed my family. When I moved to Glenpark about two years ago, I ran into this man. Carl. Apparently he tracked me down from the news story about the apartment building murders. He started talking about this group who believed in vampires. He was the first person to ever confirm they were real. He promised to help me get justice for my family. I…I was alone and I missed my family. If I couldn't save them, I could at least get justice."

Taking another deep breath, he put as must steel as he could muster in his voice and looked over at Marcus. "I told them about the woman, and they told me about a clan all centered around a woman that matched my description. When the job listing came up, it was like fate was handing me exactly what I wanted. They already knew Marcus's home address. My task was to get the job and feed them back any information I could."

"What did you tell them about my family?" Marcus growled.

"Nothing."

"I don't believe you!"

"It's true. I told them nothing of importance. I had to have proof that this was the same woman. Two years with the group had made it clear they were just a bunch of murder-happy lunatics. I wasn't going to sic them on innocent people! I didn't tell them where you were moving or anything about your brothers other than that you have three, which they already knew. I told them that you loved Italian and Greek food, which they didn't believe. They're convinced you only drink blood. I told them that you played the piano. I never told them about your mother, even after I saw what she did to Bel," he said, ending on a whisper.

"No!" Marcus tried to shove to his feet, but both Bel and Rafe were there to keep him seated.

"It's the truth! I swear!" Ethan cried back at him.

"He's telling the truth," Winter confirmed, shocking the entire room into silence. Winter crossed the room, pulling a knife out of his pocket.

"What?" Marcus demanded.

Winter paused and smirked at his older brother. "You asked me to look into your new hire, so I did. I found the ties to the League immediately and I wanted to watch them. I bugged his apartment and cloned his cell phone," he casually admitted.

"Holy shit," Ethan muttered.

Rafe snorted. "Sneaky bastard."

Winter gave a little bow of his head to Rafe before turning to

Ethan. He cut the ropes tying him to the chair. "He didn't tell this Carl or anyone else from the group anything of value." A strange expression crossed Winter's face, sort of like pride, when he said, "He actually gave a pretty impassioned defense of our family right before getting the shit beat out of him. He also didn't know about the attack that happened tonight."

"But I don't understand," Bel interjected. "The Humans Protecting Humans League is an anti-vampire group. They've been attempting to hunt us for decades. But there were also vampires that attacked here tonight. How could they be working together?"

"I don't know," Winter admitted. He wandered back to his chair while folding up the knife in his hands. He flopped down, looking for the first time like the little brother he was. "My guess is that the vamps were using the humans. Maybe feeding them info about their enemies."

"They were fucking cannon fodder," Rafe growled. "They came through the door first. It was only when they were nearly wiped out that the vamps followed."

"Probably hoping to weaken us," Bel added. "But who would do this?"

"I saw known associates of Meryl among them," Marcus said. His voice was like a low rumble of thunder, and it felt like it was a warning of worse still to come. "This could be a retaliation for the nightclub incident. Or just the Hidden striking at us again. Or even a larger political move. Aiden thinks they are aiming to take control of the Ministry. Did you see anyone you recognized among the dead?"

Winter sneered at his older brother. "No, and this kind of blatant attack isn't our way. It's not a good way of staying secret and hidden. This screams Predators. They're sloppy and prefer to use bold attacks to scare the humans."

"I don't understand. Are we getting pulled into the middle of a political war? Why?" Rafe demanded.

"Someone is making a play for the American Ministry. Both the Hidden and the Predators," Marcus said. He relaxed against the sofa and released a heavy breath. Ethan watched him, taking in the signs of discomfort clear on his face. But when Marcus turned his gaze back to Ethan, rage still burned bright in his eyes. "Aiden seems to think that the same person is trying to take out clans that might challenge them or cause problems in the power shift. For some reason, the Variks have been listed among the possible troublemakers."

"This is fucking bullshit!" Rafe snapped. He paced across the room and kicked a box of books before turning back. "What the hell do we care about the fucking Ministry and all that nonsense?"

"Some of us do happen to care about which maniacs are in charge," Bel said primly.

Rafe lifted an eyebrow and turned a skeptical eye on his brother. "Really? You're going to climb out of your lab and books long enough to voice an opinion on the rule makers?"

"I care," Marcus declared, stopping the bickering between siblings. "I've heard about some of the recent insanity coming through both the American and European Ministry from Aiden. It can't be allowed to continue. It doesn't matter why we've been targeted. The important thing is that we have been, and that isn't going to change. There will be another attack. We all know that."

"But what can we do?" Bel asked. Rafe walked to his brother and placed a reassuring hand on his shoulder.

Ethan marveled out how Rafe was always the first with the snarky, cutting comment, but he was also always the first to be right there to reassure Bel. Marcus had commented on Rafe and Bel's closeness, but it was another thing to see it in action.

But then, it was clear that all the brothers were close in their own way. Winter might have physically separated himself from his brothers, but he was right there, watching over them and protecting them.

"Tonight, I say we feed and rest," Winter suggested. He stood and shoved his blood-smeared hands into his pockets as he stared at Ethan. "They won't attack again tonight. They'll need to regroup."

"And what about tomorrow? Are we supposed to wait around for the next attack?" Rafe grumbled.

"No, but we need time to think and gather information. We need to talk to Aiden, if possible," Marcus said.

Winter nodded. "I'll go check on him."

"You know where he's at?"

"I've got a few guesses. I'll talk to you tomorrow about next steps." Winter crossed the room and placed a hand on Marcus's shoulder with the smallest amount of blood soaked into his shirt. "Rest and feed, dear brother. You will need your strength," Winter said in a near whisper before leaving the room.

"As much as I hate to say this, Winter is right. Let us help you hunt tonight—" Rafe started.

"No, I've already got what I need here," Marcus said.

All three sets of eyes fell on Ethan and he tried not to squirm in his chair. Yeah, he had a feeling that he might end up a blood donor for Marcus. There had always been a part of him that wanted to know what it was like to feed Marcus, to know if it was as sensual and sexy as they made it in the movies, but he didn't want to do it like this. Not when Marcus looked at him with such anger and betrayal in his eyes. But it didn't look like Marcus was going to give him much of a choice.

Sadly, he really couldn't blame Marcus for it either.

"Don't, Marcus. You're going to regret it," Bel said.

"Fuck it. Drain him dry," Rafe countered with a cold bark of laughter.

"Just leave. I'll take care of Ethan. We still have things to discuss…in private. We'll meet tomorrow night to talk more."

Ethan watched as Rafe and Bel looked at each other for a moment in silent communication. Rafe gave a little shrug, and Bel sighed before getting to his feet. They both filed out of the room without another word.

Tension crawled across Ethan's skin, leaving behind tight little pinpricks. He wanted to say something, but he didn't know what words would make things better. Maybe there was no making it better. There was no way he could get Marcus to forgive him. He'd made a choice, and it was a bad one. There was no going back, and there was no getting Marcus to give him a second chance.

"Marcus—"

"Don't!" Marcus's voice was like the crack of a whip. "Don't talk. You talk only when I ask you a question." He tried to push to his feet, but he struggled and fell to the couch again. Ethan instantly leaped to his feet and hurried to Marcus's side, grabbing his arm to try to steady him.

Marcus jerked his arm out of Ethan's grasp. "Don't touch me!"

"Look! Be angry with me. Go ahead and rip my throat out if that's what you want to do, but don't expect me to just stand by and watch you hurt yourself!" Ethan shouted at him.

Marcus's hand shot out and wrapped around his throat before slamming Ethan down on the couch beside him. Ethan tried to gasp, but it was difficult to breathe with Marcus's tight grip pressing against his windpipe. He instinctively grabbed Marcus's wrist, but didn't struggle, didn't fight back no matter how much terror clawed at him.

"You're going to wish you had," Marcus said. He opened his mouth and Ethan could see a pair of sharp, white fangs slide down behind his teeth. If there had been any doubt in his mind before, it was erased. Marcus Varik was most definitely a vampire.

CHAPTER NINETEEN

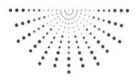

Rage burned through Marcus as he stared Ethan. He felt so fucking betrayed. He'd trusted Ethan, let him get so damn close. He'd spent weeks agonizing over if and how to tell Ethan that he was a vampire, but he'd always known. He'd known and gotten close to Marcus with the sole purpose of destroying his family.

He wanted to make Ethan pay for his treachery.

But there was a small voice in the back of his mind reminding him that Ethan had already paid. He'd lost his family. They'd been murdered by a vampire. He'd been left alone in the world with no one to watch over him, protect him, hold him tight. Even when the world was at its bleakest, Marcus always had his brothers. Ethan had no one.

Marcus stomped down on the voice. Ethan had plotted to steal away his family.

Yet, Winter said Ethan hadn't given any information to the League. He'd had ample chances. He could have unlocked the doors during the day and allowed them to walk right into his house. He could have given them the address of his new home and even the addresses of his brothers. Access to that information was given on his very first day at work. But he didn't. He'd protected Marcus as much as he could.

"You've known all along," Marcus snarled.

"Yes," Ethan whispered, his voice sounding pained and choked. Marcus loosened his hold on Ethan's throat a little, and Ethan sucked in great gulps of air, coughing a little.

"Why? Why didn't you tell me?"

"Because I was afraid."

"What? You were afraid that I'd kill you. That I'd rip your throat out." Marcus barely managed to keep from tightening his hand on Ethan's throat again.

"No. I was afraid you'd send me away. That I wouldn't see you again."

Marcus lurched back, releasing Ethan's throat so quickly it was like he'd been scorched by his touch. "What?"

"I was stupid and scared," Ethan admitted. Ethan blinked and two fat tears rolled down the sides of his face. "I was afraid if I told you the truth, you'd fire me and send me away. I couldn't let you go. Not yet." Very slowly, he lifted his trembling fingers to Marcus's face, lightly touching his cheek as if he was afraid Marcus would move away from him. "I think I'm falling in love with you, and I'm not ready to lose you."

Marcus shoved away from Ethan, his mind spinning. Of all the things he'd expected Ethan to say, that was not it. He shook his head, trying to clear it, trying to think through the chaos, but his brain kept repeating the same joyous phrase, *Ethan loves me. Ethan loves me.*

Ethan sat up beside him, carefully placing both hands on his body. "Marcus? Are you okay?"

"Light-headed," Marcus murmured, though it was the least of his problems.

"You've lost too much blood. You need to feed."

Marcus couldn't argue with that, but he needed to get out of the house to do that. As they sat there, he was far too aware of the enticing smell of Ethan's blood wafting to him, tantalizing him. A ready, warm blood supply was only inches away. No need to haul his pain-riddled body into the streets in search of a victim. Ethan was right there.

Yes, it had been his original plan to feed from Ethan. He'd been angry and felt betrayed, but in just a couple of seconds, his world had been turned upside down. Ethan had protected him because he was a good person. He'd lied to the League, because…he loved Marcus. He couldn't feed from Ethan now. Couldn't risk taking too much. Marcus needed to get away, find someone else. Once he started to heal and some of the pain eased, he'd be able to think more clearly.

"I need to go." Marcus shifted on the couch, gathering his strength to try to rise again.

"No. I'm right here. You're too weak to go out." Ethan jumped up from the couch and whipped his shirt over his head. He stood before Marcus, bare-chested, smelling so damn delicious. Marcus reached out, fingers skimming over bruises that were still healing from the attack he'd suffered just days ago. An attack that happened because he was protecting Marcus and his family.

"This is going to happen. Just tell me where you want me, to make this easiest on you," Ethan said.

Marcus grabbed Ethan's arm and pulled him into his lap so that he was straddling him. He'd dreamed of doing this when Ethan had sat on his lap against the piano and now he was going to fucking have it. For the first time in his life, he was holding his victim flush against his body, reveling in the feel and pleasure of the person. And it was going to be that much sweeter because it was Ethan.

He closed his eyes against the fresh wave of pain that rocketed through him as Ethan pressed against him. He buried his face in Ethan's neck and breathed deep. The scent of sweat and blood and Ethan filled his nostrils. God, he'd wanted this, wanted Ethan for so damn long. He wanted to savor every second of it, draw it out, but he was so fucking hungry he could barely think. Opening his mouth, he carefully scraped his fangs across his tender flesh.

"Marcus?" Ethan said on a whimper.

"Shhh…I've got you."

"I know. I trust you."

Those three words helped Marcus tighten his control over his hunger. He was not going to take more than he needed.

"I'm sorry. This is going to hurt at first, but I promise I'll make you feel better."

Ethan took a breath and Marcus was sure he was going to say something else, but he didn't give him the chance. He struck quickly, plunging his fangs deep into Ethan's neck, piercing arteries with expert skill. Ethan jerked and stiffened in shock. A little cry of pain escaped him before he could catch it.

Marcus removed his fangs and sucked hard, pulling that first mouthful of blood into his system. The relief was exquisite, and the pain almost immediately receded to the back of his mind. On the second swallow, he reached deep and sent a wave of ecstasy crashing through Ethan. With each drink, he washed Ethan's body in physical pleasure. He could feel Ethan's cock swelling against his stomach. Ethan shifted his hips, moaning softly. One hand slid down his spine to cup his tight ass, holding him against his body.

"Oh, God! Marcus!" he cried out, lost to the bliss Marcus was weaving. "Please! I need to come."

Reluctantly, Marcus swiped his tongue across the two holes he'd created, using his saliva to heal the wounds. Ethan shivered, his body still thrusting against his. Marcus's cock was swelling, begging for attention, but he ignored it. His focus was on Ethan and giving him the release he needed.

Marcus removed his mouth from Ethan's shoulder and leaned against the cushions, putting enough room between them so he could open up Ethan's jeans. "Grab your dick," Marcus commanded. Ethan nodded, his eyes glazed over and still lost to the building need. He thrust his hand inside his pants and pulled his straining cock free of his jeans and underwear. Marcus sucked in a breath to see the slick member flushed dark red and glistening with pre-cum. Ethan wrapped his hand around his dick and roughly stroked himself.

Grabbing a handful of Ethan's hair, Marcus forced him to meet his gaze. "Tell me what you want, Ethan."

"You. Want you. Want to feed you and then I want…want you to fuck me. Want to be yours always," Ethan panted. "Please, Marcus."

"Then come for me. Be mine."

Ethan moaned, his entire body jerking and tensing as he came hard. Marcus could feel the ropes of cum landing on his shirt, and he wished he'd been naked so he could feel the warm liquid branding his skin. Ethan was his, but what Ethan didn't realize was that Marcus now belonged to Ethan.

∽

Ethan lay against Marcus's chest; his entire body felt so fucking relaxed and warm. Everything was right in the world when he was snuggled against Marcus, his arms wrapped tight around him like he never wanted to let go. He wanted to cling to that feeling of rightness forever, but conscious thought was starting to creep into his brain, demanding things to make sense. His brain was also demanding that he face the things that were happening around him, particularly that he was putting all his weight on a man who was terribly injured.

Carefully placing his hand on the back of the couch, Ethan pushed, trying to climb off Marcus. The arms around him loosened a little to allow some space between them, but Marcus didn't fully release him.

"What's wrong? Did I hurt you?" Marcus murmured against his hair.

"No, but you are hurt. I need to get up," Ethan said.

"No." Marcus tightened his arms again, pulling Ethan down against him. "I don't want you to move yet."

Ethan gave a little huff and settled in his lap. He hadn't really wanted to move. He was just trying to be considerate of Marcus's injuries. "I don't want to hurt you more."

"You're not. I'm already healing."

Of course, that brought a new whirlwind of thoughts to his brain. Marcus was a vampire and they could finally talk about all the things that had been rattling around in his mind. Ethan's head popped up and he gazed at Marcus.

"I'm alive."

Marcus frowned, lines crisscrossing his brow. "Yes. You sound surprised."

"I thought…I didn't know if you had to kill the person when you fed."

A look of horror crossed Marcus's face, and he released Ethan so quickly that Ethan nearly fell backward off the couch. "And you willingly offered to feed me, thinking that I'd kill you?"

Ethan placed his hand against Marcus's cheek, trying to soothe away the stunned expression. "I love you. I know I fucked up, but I wanted to fix things. Help you. Even if it meant…"

"No," Marcus said on a gasp. He grabbed Ethan and pulled him tight against his chest, wrapping strong arms around him while tucking his head against his neck. "No. No sacrificing yourself for me. I can't lose you too."

"But—" Ethan managed in a muffled voice.

"No. There are no exceptions to this. I need you. God, I need you so much."

Ethan closed his eyes soaking in his words and the strength

of his embrace. They weren't lovers, but it was close enough for now.

"I'm sorry for not telling you sooner about the League."

Marcus sighed and loosened his hold on Ethan, but Ethan didn't move. It was easier to face these things with his face buried in Marcus's neck.

"I understand why you were drawn to them. You lost everything. I would have wanted revenge as well." Marcus rubbed his hands up and down Ethan's back. "I want you to know that you can tell me anything, and I will try harder to earn your trust."

"I do trust you."

Marcus sighed again. "I feel like you are trusting the wrong things."

Ethan brought his head up, confusion filling him. "What? How?"

A funny look crossed Marcus's face. "You thought I was going to kill you. You climbed into my lap, offering yourself up, thinking I was going to kill you."

One corner of Ethan's mouth quirked up. "Well, the French do call the orgasm *la petite mort*. The little death. It definitely wasn't the kind of death I was expecting, but I'll take it."

The smile that crossed Marcus's face seemed a little sad, but before Ethan could remark on it, Marcus was carefully pushing Ethan to his feet. "Let's get cleaned up. We need to talk."

Ethan climbed off Marcus and the couch. He was a little shaky for a moment, but Marcus was there with his hand on Ethan's elbow, steadying him. Flushing when he looked down at himself, Ethan quickly tucked away his softened cock and closed his pants. Dried cum and blood were smeared across his stomach and chest, while both were encrusted on the remains of Marcus's shirt. It was a harsh reminder of what they'd both gone through only hours earlier.

"Marcus...I'm so sorry about your mother. I spoke to her for a little bit before the attack. I know she wasn't the woman who killed my family. Your mother..." Ethan paused when his voice cracked. Unshed tears burned his eyes, but he held them back. "She was amazing. She was so nice. So determined to protect me. Keep me safe. I tried to get to her."

Marcus's warm hand cupped his cheek, forcing him to look up. "And if you did, you'd both be dead right now. I hate to lose her, but I want to believe that she's truly at peace now. My brothers and I said good-bye to the mother of our childhood a very long time ago. The woman who was reborn a vampire wasn't truly our mother. Our mother would never have hurt one of us."

Ethan wrapped his arms around Marcus's waist and laid his head against his chest. "Then I'm glad she's at peace."

Marcus placed one last kiss against Ethan's temple and released him. "Come. I need to feed more and we both need to shower."

"I can feed you," he offered as they started to walk out of the library. He stumbled, his feet seeming heavier than he'd realized, but Marcus was there to help steady him.

"I've already taken as much blood as you can safely spare. No more donations from you."

"But does that mean you'll have to find some other human?" The thought of Marcus putting his mouth on another person's throat, that intimate contact, the idea of them being turned-on by that touch, all sent a wave of red-hot jealousy surging through Ethan. He didn't want Marcus touching anyone like that. But he had to in order to survive.

Oh, this was bad.

Marcus's low chuckle broke into his dark thoughts. He pressed the button to call for the elevator. "Your face is so expressive. I take it you don't like the idea of me feeding on someone else."

Ethan tried to nonchalantly shrug it off, but he had a feeling he was failing miserably. "It's none of my business. I mean, you need blood to survive, and I certainly can't dictate who you feed from."

The metal doors slid open, and they stepped into the small box. Ethan leaned against the wall while Marcus reached over and pressed the button for the third floor. He then crowded close to Ethan, placing his hands on either side of his head so that he felt trapped in the very best way.

"Your blood has already started the healing process. I can supplement with bagged blood. I won't be biting anyone else tonight," Marcus whispered in his ear.

"Oh," Ethan said, hating how obvious his relief sounded in that single word.

"I don't want to bite anyone else. Don't want to touch anyone but you, Ethan." The tip of his tongue slid along his neck and Ethan groaned. Blood raced to his cock, which probably wasn't a good thing since he definitely didn't have enough in his system to run both his brain and dick at the same time.

"Fuck, Marcus," Ethan groaned. His brain was scrambled. In a short period of time, he'd gone from relief to horror to fear to heartbreak to more fear and then a bone-melting orgasm. He was struggling to wrap his head around things that were all changing so damn fast. And in the eye of the storm was Marcus. Strong, immovable Marcus. Ethan wanted to wrap himself around Marcus and hang on tight until the storm was finally over.

The elevator softly dinged, announcing it had reached the desired floor. The door slid open and Marcus pulled away from him. Ethan's heart picked up as Marcus threaded his fingers through Ethan's and led him to the master bedroom. He never thought he'd be alone with Marcus in this room again. Hadn't realized how badly he wanted it until they were standing there. The moment felt so big that a part of him was afraid to move or breathe. Ethan gave Marcus his best jaunty smile. There was nowhere else he wanted to be.

"Shower," Marcus began, pointing toward the en suite bathroom, "while I grab another pint to drink. Then I want you to climb into my bed. I'll join you after I shower."

"Don't you want to..."

Marcus just smiled and gave him a little push with a pat on the ass. "Go. Trust me."

Ethan threw a skeptical look over his shoulder but went into the bathroom as instructed. He would have preferred to shower with Marcus, but he knew that Marcus needed to get more blood in his system. He couldn't possibly have replaced all that he'd lost already. Marcus might also not be comfortable with Ethan seeing him drink blood. The idea curdled Ethan's stomach a little. While he wanted to know everything about Marcus, maybe it was best if they took things one slow step at a time.

There was no stopping the happy sigh that slipped from his throat when he stepped into Marcus's bathroom. He'd forgotten how amazing it was. Instead of harsh overhead lighting, the lights were soft and warm like a sunset. The walls were a buttery yellow while everything else was white marble and gold fixtures. His eyes stuck on the giant garden tub and he wished he could stretch out in it with Marcus. He started to tuck that idea away for a later date, but he suddenly remembered that Marcus was moving very soon. They likely wouldn't have the chance to use the tub.

And Marcus was moving....What would that mean for them?

Ethan hurried over to the massive shower and turned on the hot water as fresh panic started to set in. He stripped off the rest of his clothes and stepped into the glass-enclosed stall. The hot water pounded down on him from the showerhead, helping to beat back some of the fear that was eating at him. He closed his eyes and tried to think logically when the whole night seemed to defy logic.

Marcus didn't say that he reciprocated his feelings. He might have said that he needed him, but he could have just been talking about Ethan's blood. That was it. They had some fun, but then Marcus would move, and Ethan would stay behind. That was for the best, right?

Marcus's world was filled with danger and death. Ethan wasn't the fighting, killing, chaos type. He liked computers and books and listening to Tori Amos.

But he loved Marcus. He could deal with danger if it meant keeping Marcus safe.

He didn't want one night. He wanted all Marcus's nights.

Even if Marcus was a vampire and would live forever. Ethan wanted as many as he could get. One wasn't enough.

So, he'd just have to convince Marcus to keep him around longer.

Grabbing the shampoo bottle from the shelf, Ethan popped the cap and smelled it, nearly moaning at the familiar fragrance. It smelled woodsy and spicy just like Marcus. He quickly scrubbed his hair and then moved on to a thorough washing of his body, loving that he was wrapping himself in Marcus's scent.

When he finally stepped out of the shower, he was more relaxed and clinging to the notion that he could hold Marcus's interest for a least a little while longer. He grabbed a thick towel and looked up to find Marcus leaning against the counter. His arms were folded over his bare chest and his feet were crossed at the ankles. The long cuts across his chest and neck were much more healed than they should have been. They were largely red and angry, but with no real threat of reopening. His color was much better now. If he wasn't still covered in blood, Ethan would never have believed he was just in a vicious battle.

"You look much better. Not at death's door any longer," Ethan murmured.

"And you look beautiful," Marcus softly said.

He pushed off the sink and took the last couple of steps separating them. He pulled the forgotten towel from Ethan's fingers and started drying off his shoulders, down his arms, and across his chest. Marcus dropped to his knees and took great care in drying off Ethan's dick and balls before sliding down one leg and then the other. Ethan reached back and grabbed the shower door to steady himself. No one had even shown such care in touching him before.

When he was done, Marcus looked up at him from where he kneeled, his hands clenched tightly in the towel. There was such stark need and desire in his eyes, Ethan was fucking drowning.

"You're so beautiful," Marcus said, his voice trembling. "So perfect. I'm afraid I'm in a dream and I'm going to wake up at any second if I keep touching you."

"Not a dream. I don't ever want you to stop touching me." Ethan bent down and kissed Marcus, slowly at first but steadily building until Marcus parted his lips, letting Ethan thrust his tongue inside. He moaned and Ethan swallowed it down.

He broke off the kiss and smiled. "Minty fresh," he teased.

"I had to. I didn't think you'd appreciate the taste of blood."

Ethan huffed a laugh and straightened. "I hadn't even thought of that. I only wanted to kiss you."

Worry bled into Marcus's gaze. "I don't ever want to make you uncomfortable with what I am. I don't want to give you any reason to fear me."

"I don't fear you," Ethan said.

"Good." Marcus leaned forward and pressed a nibbling kiss to Ethan's stomach before rising to his feet. "I put a pair of sleep pants on the bed if you'd prefer them. I'll be out after I wash off this blood."

Ethan gave him his best cocky smile. "I'm staying the night, am I?"

Marcus's expression grew deathly serious. "You are not leaving here tonight. It's not safe. I have other rooms if you'd prefer not to be in my bed, but—"

Ethan stopped him by pressing his fingers to Marcus's lips.

"The only way you're getting me out of your bed is if you pick me up and carry me out. And honestly, I think you'd have to call at least one of your brothers for help. I'm not leaving willingly."

"Good," Marcus growled. He swatted Ethan's ass, getting him moving out of the bathroom.

Ethan dropped the towel on the floor as he walked into the bedroom, putting a little extra sway in his hips since he knew Marcus was staring at his ass. He picked up the folded blue pants at the foot of the bed. The material was the softest he ever felt and would have been a caress against his skin, but he put them back with a smile and climbed naked across the mattress. He distinctly remembered having a conversation with Marcus about sleeping in his bed naked, and Marcus had seemed very interested in the prospect.

Sliding into the silky cool sheets, he sighed as he sank into the bed. He squinted at the small clock on the nightstand, reading that it was just after midnight. Later than he thought, but he usually didn't go to sleep for a few more hours since he didn't start work until noon.

Snuggling down into the blankets, he burrowed into the pillows. This bed was so damn comfortable. He wasn't really tired. He just needed to rest his eyes for a minute while he listened to the shower running. Then when Marcus joined him, he'd give that sexy man the release he so badly needed.

Ethan fell asleep a second later with a smile on his lips.

CHAPTER TWENTY

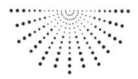

*E*than woke up horny. No, that was wrong. He woke up hard as a fucking length of steel and aching. Oh God, he needed to come. It was a second later that his sleep-addled brain registered strong hands rubbing up and down his legs, across his chest. And then, yes…a hard cock was pressing against his ass, slipping between his cheeks. Marcus's scent wrapped around him, and the ache became that much sharper.

"Oh fuck, please don't let me be dreaming," he moaned.

"Not a dream," Marcus growled. His face was pressed against Ethan's shoulder. He licked and nipped with human teeth, sending a dark thrill through him. "Need you, Ethan."

"Yes. Now. Want you inside me now." Ethan didn't want foreplay. Didn't want a slow buildup of teasing. He wanted to be filled. He wanted to feel Marcus pounding into him, driving him toward the explosive orgasm that was hovering just beyond his reach.

Marcus's hands stopped, tightening on his body. "I want that too, but…I've never…"

Those nervous words were enough to get the rest of Ethan's

brain online and above the fog of desperate need. He rolled in Marcus's arms so that they were pressed chest to chest. The room was cloaked in shadows, with the only light coming from the bathroom, but it was more than enough to see the strain cutting lines of need in Marcus's handsome face.

"Don't worry, lover. I can show you how to get us both there," he purred and he could hear Marcus's breathing catch just a little. "Do you have lube? Condoms?"

Marcus released him and rolled to the other side of the mattress. He dug in the nightstand for a moment and pulled out a brand-new bottle of lube with the plastic wrapper still around the top.

"Condoms aren't necessary," Marcus said. Ethan was about to argue when Marcus gave a little smile. "I can't contract or transmit human diseases."

Ethan could feel a couple of brain cells explode with joy in his head. It meant that Marcus would be bare inside of him, coming deep inside of him. He'd never gone bare with anyone. Fuck, he wasn't going to last long at all.

Shoving back the blankets, Ethan sat up and took the lube from Marcus, quickly ripping off the plastic. "I'm sorry, but we're gonna skip the foreplay this time. I fucking need you."

"Not arguing," Marcus said. His voice was low and rough. Ethan couldn't decide if it was from sleep or desire. Probably a mix of both. "Just tell me what you want. I will please you."

Ethan leaned in and quickly kissed him. "Don't worry. You will. Now hold out your hand." When Marcus did as instructed, he squirted some lube on his fingers and then on his own before tossing the bottle aside. "Put that on your dick and watch me."

He never thought of himself as an exhibitionist, but there was something thrilling about how Marcus's eyes widened at his words. He wrapped his lube-covered fingers around his hard dick and moaned. Ethan could still feel Marcus's eyes on him as he turned to face the wall while balanced on his knees. He grabbed the edge of the wooden headboard with his clean hand and reached behind himself with the other. He slowly circled his hole a couple of times before plunging a finger inside. The burn was sharp, but it had been a damn long time since he'd last had sex.

The sensation faded quickly as he continued to move his finger in and out of his body. He ached for Marcus, to feel him pushing inside, his larger body covering him, pressing him into the mattress. Pressing in another finger, Ethan moaned, stretching himself. Behind him he could hear the slick shuffle of Marcus's hand on his dick. He looked back and smiled, loving how Marcus's entire focus was on him. Marcus released his dick and grabbed Ethan's ass cheeks, spreading Ethan wide so that Marcus could see everything.

"Fuck, Ethan," he breathed.

Ethan tightened the hand holding him upright and closed his eyes, letting himself sink into the moment. Marcus released one cheek and a moment later, he felt a finger pressing against his own. He moaned loudly at the wonderful stretch. He removed his fingers, allowing Marcus time to grow comfortable touching him.

"Ethan," Marcus said, but he barely recognized his name around the growl.

"Oh God, Marcus! Now! I need you now!"

Marcus removed his fingers and the bed shifted under him as the man moved into position. The head of his cock brushed his hole, and Ethan fought the urge to push backward onto his cock, impaling himself. He needed to be patient. This was Marcus's first time. He wanted it to be perfect, but he was also sweating and trembling, desperate to finally come.

Pushing forward, the blunt tip squeezed past tight muscles and Ethan slowly exhaled, willing his body to relax. Marcus swore under his breath and paused for a moment.

"Are you okay?"

"Yes. Please don't stop," Ethan panted. "More. Keep moving."

Marcus pulled back a little and then thrust farther inside. It was like he was teasing him.

"Marcus!" Ethan cried out, and Marcus thrust home. It felt like the air had been sucked from his lungs. He was so damn full. It was as if Marcus had poured himself inside of Ethan, filling in all the empty places that he'd suffered with over the years. Marcus wrapped an arm across his chest and grabbed the opposite shoulder, locking their bodies together.

Lowering his head, Marcus placed his face against Ethan's ear. "You are mine now," he snarled. "Your blood runs in my veins. My cock is in your ass and I'm going to fill you with my cum. No one else can touch you. No one can have you."

"Yes," Ethan said, loving the feel of the little thrusts that kept him balancing so perfectly on the edge of his orgasm. Marcus was wrapped all around him, in him, consuming him. He never wanted this feeling to end. It was like there was no Marcus without Ethan and there was no Ethan without Marcus.

"Do you belong to me?" Marcus demanded. His harsh, dictatorial tone was punching every one of Ethan's fucking buttons so that he was stretched to the absolute limit of his control.

"Yes."

"For how long?"

"As long as you want me."

"For how long?" Marcus repeated and Ethan's brain stumbled. That wasn't the answer Marcus wanted, but everything felt so good. It was so hard to think. He didn't want to think. So he said the first thing that came to mind.

"Forever. I want to be with you forever."

"Forever," Marcus repeated as his free hand closed around Ethan's dick. Ethan cried out as lightning-hot bliss ricocheted through his body. Marcus pounded into Ethan while stroking him. All thought was zapped out as his orgasm exploded across nerve endings. He shouted, his throat becoming raw as he came all over Marcus's hand and pillows.

An answering shout came from Marcus a moment later as warmth flooded Ethan's tight channel. He whimpered, his balls attempting to draw up again at the thought that Marcus's cum was now filling him.

Sweaty and panting, they remained on their knees, their bodies still joined. He didn't want reality and the rest of the world to intrude. Didn't want Marcus to ever stop holding him. But he knew he had to. It felt like everything would be harder now without having Marcus touching him.

Was he becoming addicted to Marcus? Obsessed?

No. This was what it was like to love, to finally belong to someone, to want to be with someone. It was scarier than he'd imagined.

"Did I hurt you?" Marcus mumbled against his skin.

"I feel so damn good right now. I don't ever want it to stop."

Marcus hummed, his arm tightening around him a little bit. "Me too."

But then he sighed and carefully withdrew from Ethan's body. Before Ethan could move, Marcus was rearranging the pillows and gathering him close as he laid Ethan back down on the bed. Marcus stretched out beside him and pulled Ethan against him so that Ethan's head was on his chest.

"Is this okay?"

Ethan managed a little laugh. "I'm beginning to doubt your 'never done this before' claim, because you're pretty damn perfect to me."

"Good. I want you to feel cherished. Loved."

Ethan's head immediately popped up and he looked at Marcus. "Really?"

Marcus's expression turned dark before he cupped Ethan's cheek. "You don't feel it? I love you, Ethan."

His heart skipped over itself in his excitement. "Well, I thought...maybe. But then you didn't say it when I did."

Marcus smiled at him. "I didn't say it because I was afraid that you'd believe I was only saying it because it was expected. I wanted to show you with my actions, with my body, that you own my heart." Marcus rolled him onto his back, covering him as he pressed Ethan down into the mattress. "You are mine, Ethan Cline. You are the first person I have ever loved, and you shall be the last. I will protect you with everything that I am. I never want to be parted from you."

The words sounded like a vow that was chiseled into stone, and Ethan loved it.

"I want all that too."

Marcus grinned, his entire being seeming to glow with his joy. "Good." He kissed Ethan roughly before rolling onto his back again, pulling Ethan on top of him. Ethan relaxed, closing his eyes as he soaked in the feel of Marcus's large hands rubbing up and down his body. After several passes, he felt Marcus's long finger rubbing through the cum leaking from his hole. He held perfectly still, letting Marcus explore, but there was no stopping the groan the rumbled up his chest when Marcus pushed his thick finger inside.

"I can't help myself," Marcus whispered. "I can't stop thinking about it. I just want to keep filling you. Making you mine."

Before Ethan could form a thought, he felt Marcus reach for the lube. His head popped up when he heard the plastic cap snap.

"Wait. Are you hard already?"

Marcus answered by grabbing Ethan's hips and moving him so that he was fully on top of Marcus. With ease, he thrust up into Ethan, filling him. He didn't know if it was a Marcus thing or a vampire thing, but he didn't care. Ethan sat up and pushed Marcus's hands away as he proceeded to ride him hard. The slapping of their bodies and their pants filled the silence of the room. Marcus wrapped his slick hand around Ethan's dick, waking it. Ethan was sure he couldn't come again so soon, but he didn't care. He loved the feel of Marcus inside of him, the sounds they made together.

Marcus shouted and his hand tightened on Ethan's dick as he pumped himself into Ethan. The sensations shoved Ethan off the cliff after him. The orgasm was sharp and almost painful, but it was perfectly balanced with the pleasure surging through every part of his body.

He collapsed on Marcus, sweat and cum mixing together between them.

"I'm dead. You killed me. I'm dead," Ethan panted.

He felt more than heard Marcus's laugh as his chest shook beneath him. "But it was a very good death."

"The best."

Marcus allowed them to lie there for a few more minutes before he started nudging Ethan toward the shower. When it was clear that Marcus wasn't joining him, Ethan crossed his arms and refused to move until Marcus admitted that he was trying to sneak in a quick pint of bagged blood while Ethan was in the shower.

"Why don't you want me to see you drink blood?"

"I don't want to make you uncomfortable."

Ethan reached over and grabbed Marcus's hand in both of his. "We can't have something work between us if you're hiding a really big part of you. I can't ever become comfortable with it if I'm never faced with it."

Marcus gave him a crooked smile. "You're sure?"

"I'm curious, actually."

Still looking a little unsure, Marcus walked over to his dresser and opened a small door to reveal a mini fridge similar to that of a hotel. He pulled out a bag of blood and poured the contents into a large glass.

"You don't mind it cold?"

Marcus wrinkled his nose a little. "It's not my first choice, but I tend to wake up a little peckish in the morning. A glass helps to keep the hunger pains at bay until it's safe to hunt." He lifted the glass to Ethan in a toast before he tipped the drink down his throat. Ethan was a little surprised that he wasn't disgusted by it. It looked sort of like tomato juice, but he knew it wasn't.

When he'd completely drained the glass, Marcus gave a satisfied sigh and wiped his mouth with the back of his hand. Between the two orgasms and the drink. Marcus was looking healthy, rested, and sated. A man on top of the world.

"Do you actually like the taste?" Ethan asked without thinking and then winced. "Sorry. Are you comfortable talking about it? Would you rather I didn't ask questions?"

Marcus smiled. "I would prefer it if you ask questions, but a shower first."

"But—"

Marcus stopped his words by pulling him off the bed and dropping him over his shoulder before carrying him into the shower. He set Ethan to getting the water to the right temperature while Marcus brushed his teeth. As soon as he finished, he kissed Ethan deeply.

There were no questions in the shower because Ethan was completely distracted by Marcus's devotion to making sure that every inch of his body was properly cleaned. Of course, Ethan had to return the favor to Marcus.

It was only when they were standing in front of the open refrigerator, trying to find something for breakfast at two in the afternoon, that Ethan's brain started working again and he remembered what they had been talking about.

"You never answered my question!" Ethan declared out of the blue.

"I was wondering when you'd notice," Marcus said with a chuckle.

Ethan gave him a shove as he grabbed eggs and cheese. There were also some vegetables. Enough for omelets. He set the food on the counter and tossed a green pepper at Marcus. "You can chop that up while you answer my question."

"Yes, sir," Marcus teased, but his smile disappeared and his expression grew serious as he started working on the pepper. "Yes, surprisingly, I like the taste. I wasn't expecting to, but I'm glad I do. Bel thinks that our bodies naturally crave what we need." He lifted his head and looked at Ethan. "When your body needs protein, you crave a steak. When you need carbs, you crave bread. My body needs blood, human blood, so I crave it. As such, it makes me also like the taste."

Ethan cracked a few eggs into a bowl and started whisking them. "If you need blood to live, do you also need regular food?"

"Actually, no."

Ethan stopped whisking and looked at Marcus. "So you don't need this omelet I'm making for you?"

Marcus grinned. "Nope, but I want it." He leaned over and stole a quick kiss from Ethan's parted lips. "I like the taste of food, so I eat it. Rafe does too, but then he likes anything that gives pleasure. Bel sees food as a distraction from his work. He's largely stopped eating it."

"And Winter?"

Marcus gave a little shrug. "I think he eats when it suits his purposes, but I don't think it's about pleasure."

"Damnit!" Ethan suddenly swore.

Marcus froze next to him. "What?"

"I just realized that we missed a chance to send your brother a naked 'best way to start the day' pic like he sent you."

"No," Marcus said fiercely. "I love my brothers, but they are never seeing you naked. You are mine, and I am not sharing you with anyone."

Ethan grinned at him and resumed working on the omelet. "How often do you need to feed? I get the impression that surviving on bagged blood isn't an option."

Marcus pushed the chopped pepper at Ethan and started working on the other items he'd pulled out of the fridge. "It's not. Bagged blood will help stretch between feedings, but whatever it is that's missing from our bodies can only be gotten directly from the source. Bel is actually researching what we're missing and trying to come up with a cure."

"What? So you don't need blood?"

"Maybe. But for now, the goal is to live off bagged blood. To answer your question, if I'm not injured again, I can go comfortably for two weeks between feedings. I have stretched to three, but…"

"What?"

Marcus cringed a little. "My brothers have told me that I can be a bit testy if I wait that long."

Ethan cackled. "Thanks for the warning." They worked in companionable silence for a bit as Ethan cooked the omelet. It was only when he plated a section for both of them and they sat down that a big question suddenly hit him.

"How old are you?"

Marcus smirked a little at him. "I was thirty years old when I was last a human."

"And…?" Ethan prodded, practically bouncing in his seat.

"I have been a vampire for one hundred and seventy-six years."

"Holy shit! That's amazing."

Marcus chuckled and went back to his omelet.

"Wait! How old is Rafe?"

Marcus's smile dimmed a little bit. "One hundred and seventy-six."

Ethan lowered his fork to his plate and straightened in his

chair. Something tightened in his chest, but he still asked. "And Bel?"

"One hundred and seventy-six."

He didn't want to ask, but Marcus nodded, indicating that it was okay. "Winter?"

"One hundred and seventy-six."

"Why?" A lump was growing in his throat because he knew that the answer wasn't going to be a happy one. What could make them all choose at once to become vampires? Unless they'd had no choice.

"To protect our mother and to protect the world from her. We waited until Winter turned twenty-three, and then Aiden changed us all on the same night."

Ethan squeezed his eyes closed, but Marcus was right there, wiping away the tears that slipped out. "Don't, Ethan," he whispered. "My brothers and I have no regrets about our decision. It hasn't always been an easy life, but we've had each other. And if I hadn't, we would have never met."

Blinking back tears, Ethan turned his face and kissed Marcus's palm. "I'm glad we met."

"Me too."

Ethan dug into his omelet, desperately searching his brain for a lighter topic. "Can you turn into a bat?"

Marcus laughed and choked at the same time, spitting the bite he had in his mouth across the room.

Ethan snorted. "I'm gonna take that as a no."

CHAPTER TWENTY-ONE

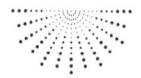

Marcus fought the urge to reach over and take Ethan's hand as they rode the elevator up to Rafe's penthouse. As it was, he couldn't completely dismiss the smile that played on his lips every time he looked over at the young man. He knew he should be heartbroken over the death of his mother, but what he told Ethan was the truth. They'd said good-bye to the woman who had raised them as children nearly two hundred years ago. They mourned her death over the years while caring for the creature that walked around in her body.

Of course, they weren't going to just let her death pass. She was still murdered, and the culprits behind that act had to be dealt with, which was why they were gathering at Rafe's.

But their grim reason for gathering did nothing to diminish his joy.

Ethan knew the truth of what Marcus was, and he still loved him. Ethan still wanted him. They'd spent the majority of the day either talking or wrapped in each other, and he had been the one to drag his feet when it came time to leave for Rafe's. Never in his life had he struggled to get out of bed and put his mind to the task ahead of him. Except this time, he'd wanted to

CLAIMING MARCUS

linger in bed, Ethan's naked body draped around his as they talked or kissed.

And never in his life had he felt so free. He'd largely squashed the voice in the back of his head, but then the little voice cared less about what happened in the secret of his home. It was standing in public where others could see him, judge him. Where others could hurt Ethan for being with a man, not that Ethan gave a shit what others thought about him.

"You know, I don't think I've ever seen you smile so much," Ethan said with a grin of his own.

"I don't think I've ever had such a good reason to smile."

Ethan chuckled. "Yeah, I knew that was totally an 'I got laid' smile."

"That makes sense since I did get laid. Several times, in fact."

"Yes, but I figured you wouldn't want your brothers knowing that," Ethan said, never losing his smile, but Marcus's wilted a little.

"Why would I worry about them knowing?"

"Well, I thought they still blamed me for the attack on your home and the death of Julianna." Ethan's smile seemed more brittle as he looked up at Marcus, and it was becoming much clearer that Ethan was incredibly nervous about going to Rafe's penthouse. He shifted from one foot to the next, and the hands Marcus had thought were tucked behind his back were actually holding the bar around the car in a death grip. "I also wasn't sure how you'd feel about them knowing you're involved with a man."

Marcus stepped closer to Ethan so that their chests were brushing. "I'm not involved with a man," Marcus said with a sneer. "I'm in love with a beautiful, amazing, funny, smart man." He smiled when Ethan's shoulders slumped a little in his relief. "And your only crime from last night is not telling me sooner about the League, but I understand why you didn't and have forgiven you."

"Thank you," Ethan murmured, leaning his forehead against Marcus.

"Last night's attack was not your fault. Julianna's death was not your fault. She wanted to protect you. I will not take her sacrifice for granted. You are precious to me."

Ethan lifted his head and smiled at him, tears glistening in his eyes. He opened his mouth to speak, but the elevator chimed and the doors slid open. On the other side stood Bel, wearing a dark suit with a red bow tie. His hair was standing up a bit as if he'd been pulling at it in frustration, but it was good to see him not covered in blood for once. His brother's eyes moved from Marcus to Ethan to Marcus again before a smug smirk flashed across his face. He turned on his heel and walked across shining black floors, leaving Marcus and Ethan to follow.

"I knew it!" Bel said loudly.

Marcus swallowed back a groan and kept his focus on Ethan as he trailed nervously behind them. Of course, Rafe's place tended to be a lot to take in with its black marble floors and dark woods. But the most stunning thing was the magnificent view of the city in the endless wall of windows. Two walls of windows were visible from almost every spot in the penthouse, which was a damn strange choice for a vampire, but then damn strange was a perfect description of Rafe.

Of course, he was protected. The windows were specially coated to guard against UV rays, and special shades rolled down during the day to block more sunlight. There were also thick metal shields that came down as a final layer of protection if necessary, but Marcus wasn't sure if Rafe had ever used those. For the most part, the penthouse was about Rafe being in the center of all human action and not allowing anything, especially the sun, to stop him from enjoying his extremely long life to the hilt.

What drew Marcus's attention was the forlorn song lifting from a violin, its notes dancing through the various open rooms. He hadn't been sure if he'd ever hear Rafe play again after the death of Julianna. His brother had enjoyed learning the instrument when he'd been younger, but when it had become a tool to control and calm her darker moods, he'd come to resent it. It was a reminder of how they couldn't save her and how they were in constant danger. Marcus could only hope that Rafe found some peace at last with the music and their mother.

As they entered the main living space, they found Rafe's tall, lean form standing just beyond the balcony doors, the violin tucked under his chin. The wind blew his hair partially over his face, but not enough to obscure the look of pain etched into his features. All of his brothers worried Marcus in their own way. Bel tended to get lost in his work. Rafe tended to get lost in his pleasures while trying to run from his personal demons. And Winter just tended to get lost, dropping out of contact for long periods of time.

Bel whistled sharply, and Rafe lifted his bow from the strings. With narrowed eyes, he entered the living room, looking from Marcus to Ethan. Bel snapped his fingers once and held out his hand.

"I can't fucking believe it," Rafe muttered. He moved the bow to the same hand as his violin and reached into his pocket. Crossing the room, he slapped what looked to be a hundred-dollar bill into his twin's outstretched hand.

"What did you bet?" Marcus snapped.

"Whether you'd fuck him or kill him," Rafe grumbled before looking over at a still-smug Bel. "I can't believe you got that right."

"You didn't have a meal with them. They're quite adorable."

Ethan snickered from beside Marcus, and Marcus rolled his eyes. "Is Winter here yet?" he asked wearily.

"No, but soon," Bel replied. "I spoke to him earlier, and he wasn't able to find Aiden. I have a feeling he's gone back to the old estate in England."

Marcus nodded. It made sense. Aiden had owned a large, sprawling estate north of London where they'd all lived for a short time as a family. It would make sense that Aiden would take their mother's body to the last place they'd all been happy together. Before Julianna's illness. Before they were all transformed. Before it all changed.

"I'm guessing in between all the orgasms, you explained things to him," Rafe said, waving his bow in Ethan's direction.

"Well, he explained some things," Ethan said quickly. "There wasn't a lot of time between the orgasms for talking."

Rafe stared silently at Ethan for a moment and then rocked back on his heels with laughter. Marcus looked over to find even Bel shaking his head and smiling, while Marcus could feel his cheeks heating. This was not a topic he'd ever imagined talking about with his brothers.

"You're faster than I expected." Rafe pointed his bow at Marcus. "He's too good for you, I hope you realize that."

"I do."

"Not true," Ethan interjected sharply. "He's just the right amount of good for me, and the perfect amount of bad."

Rafe gave a little shiver. "I didn't think I'd ever say it, but I now know more than enough about Marcus's sex life."

"Agreed," Bel added.

"Like I haven't been saying that about yours for years," Marcus grumbled.

Rafe walked over to a table where a violin case lay open. He carefully placed the violin and bow inside, making sure both were properly secured before closing it. "I just felt that I had to share mine with you since yours was so abysmally nonexistent."

"Well, that has been fixed. Please leave me off your sex picture texts from now on."

Rafe lifted his head and smirked at them. "We'll see."

The argument was interrupted by another soft chime, announcing the arrival of the elevator. They all turned toward the hall and watched Winter stroll in wearing a pair of black slacks and a black button-down shirt. He nodded at his brothers but did a strange double take when looking at Marcus and Ethan. When he looked away, there was a small smirk on his lips as if he could see that things had changed between Marcus and Ethan.

"What?" Marcus barked at his brother and Winter chuckled darkly.

"You've got that 'I got laid' glow. It's about time," Winter said.

"It's true," Bel said. "I wish I had taken more pictures of you before you met Ethan so I could do a comparison study to more precisely identify the differences in your appearance. But you do seem lighter."

"This isn't what's important," Marcus ground out between clenched teeth. He didn't want to be the focus of Bel's latest scientific interest. And while he didn't want Ethan to think that he didn't care for him, their sexual relationship was not the reason they gathered at Rafe's. "Mother is dead, and it is quite clear that someone wants our entire family dead. Now is not the time to discuss my sex life or relationship with Ethan."

Rafe flopped down in a chair, tossing one leg over the arm. "Well, now I'm more interested in talking about you and Ethan since you said relationship instead of nookie monkey."

Ethan made a choking sound and Bel groaned.

Winter dropped into another chair near Rafe. "While I hate agreeing with Marcus, we need to talk about the attack. We can discuss his nookie monkey later."

Marcus knew better than to order them to stop calling Ethan that, because it was the fastest way to make the damn nickname stick.

"We weren't the only ones attacked last night," Winter said, finally leading the conversation in the correct direction.

"Who?" Bel crossed the room and perched on the edge of

one of the couch cushions. His body was drawn together like a little bird preparing to take flight at the first sign of trouble.

"Armand is dead."

"Another American Ministry member?" Bel gasped.

Winter nodded.

"Wait. American Ministry? Like a vampire government?" Ethan demanded.

Marcus reached over and placed a calming hand on Ethan's shoulder, drawing him in close. "Yes. Something like that. There's an American one that oversees the vampires in North America. There's another called the European Ministry that oversees Europe. And so on. There are only eleven vampires on each Ministry."

"How do you get on the Ministry?" Ethan frowned and looked up at Marcus. "I can't imagine vampires stepping into voting booths and electing their favorites to make laws."

Rafe snorted. "Yes, well, some of us thrive in dark little closets."

"Drop it, Rafe," Marcus snapped. He wasn't in the mood for Rafe's little digs. He turned his attention back to Ethan, his expression softening. "There's no voting. It's a position of power that's taken by a display of power. Only the strongest can claim the seats."

"If you can claim it and defend it, then you get to keep it," Bel added.

"Do seats change hands often?"

Marcus shook his head. "Most won't risk their life for it."

"Has someone claimed Percival's seat yet? He's been dead for a few weeks now. Or Armand's?" Bel inquired.

Winter folded his hands on his stomach and glared at the floor. "No. And there aren't any details on who killed Percival and Armand either."

"But you're thinking that the same person or group who ordered their death went after the Variks as well," Marcus said.

Ethan stepped away from Marcus and sat down heavily on the couch. Marcus frowned in worry at Ethan. While he was over the moon at finally finding someone, he did not want to endanger Ethan's life. The young man was too precious to him to risk losing, but he would not turn his back on his brothers either.

"So, what do we do next?" Bel asked.

Marcus shoved his hands into his pockets and strolled over to the wall of windows. The city shimmered against a velvety black blanket dotted with stars nearly washed out by the light. People rushed from one place to another while vampires moved among them. Most humans had no idea that vampires were a part of their world, preying on them, working with them, laughing with them. But that could change very quickly with a war.

"I think we have two options," Marcus started carefully. He turned away from the windows and looked at his brothers one at a time. For now, he avoided Ethan's gaze. He could already guess at his brothers' opinions, and he couldn't yet decide what to do about Ethan. "The first is that we disappear. Instead of moving north, we head very far south into Argentina or Uruguay. We start a new life away from both the European and American Ministries. We let the world forget us."

"I certainly hope that your other suggestion is better, dear brother," Rafe drawled. "Because this one is utter bullshit."

"The other option is to become the power-hungry clan that they claim we are. We set the factions against each other and sow discord among the vampires while dismantling the American Ministry. They brought this on themselves. They killed our mother. This is the same Ministry that would have been in power when Ethan's family was slaughtered. This villain attacked Aiden and me at The Bank, and they attacked my home, putting the entire clan in danger. We can't let that slide."

"I don't understand what you're saying," Bel said, his voice low and anxious. "Are you suggesting that we take down the Ministry? Are you wanting us to claim the seats?"

"There are five of us. We could take it and hold a majority if we rearrange the Ministry to be a count of nine instead of eleven," Winter pointed out.

"Is...is that what we want?"

Rafe gave an elegant shrug. "I would not be opposed to destroying the Ministry altogether. We become rabble-rousers and then use Winter to spread whispers in favor of making Aiden the King of North America."

"Aiden does not want to be king," Bel said sharply.

"No, but he would very much like to punish Julianna's murderers. And I believe he would want to destroy those who attempted to destroy his family."

Marcus nodded. Aiden was extremely protective of all of them and once he was through his mourning for Julianna, Marcus could easily imagine him seeking revenge for the sake of not just Julianna but also his adopted sons. Being king would give him the power to more easily do that as well as make sure that such strikes didn't happen again.

"I know it's none of my business, but when the dust settles from your uprising and discord, what does the world look like?" Ethan stood and walked over to stand in front of Marcus. There was worry etched deep in his handsome face. "I know what it's like to get lost in the need for revenge. How many innocent people are going to be slaughtered? Will humans be forced to finally admit that vampires are among them? I know it's horrible to lose your mother, to have your family attacked, but are you really advocating making the world a worse place than it is now?"

"It doesn't have to be," Bel interjected, and it gave Marcus a little hope because he didn't have a good answer for Ethan. "If we took over the Ministry, we could come up with a system for vampires to settle their grievances that didn't include wiping out entire clans. We could also protect my research. I know there are plenty who would rather see me dead than allow me to work on a cure for our blood issues."

"Ethan, I think we would all prefer to avoid a complete bloodbath," Winter said. "Humans tend to notice these things."

"True," Ethan replied with a smirk.

Rafe shifted in his seat, placing both feet on the ground. "But with the system we have now, there is no avoiding it. Vampires deal in blood and violence. It's who we are."

"It's not all we are." Marcus looked down at Ethan and ran one finger across his cheek. "The world has changed, and we must change with it if we are to survive. I'll not have my family threatened again." He shifted his gaze to his brothers, his voice hardening. "Our first focus is uncovering those who attacked us. Their attack on us will be answered, blood for blood."

"And then stage two is to secure allies," Winter said with a growing smile. He leaned forward, resting his elbows on his knees, rubbing his hands together with a rarely seen glee. "I know we aren't the only ones dissatisfied with the current system."

"Marcus," Rafe said with a note of surprise in his voice. "I never knew you had such aspirations of power. Just over your brothers. Not for the world."

Marcus allowed a small, devilish grin at Rafe. "I will do what I must to keep my family safe." He placed a hand on Ethan's shoulder and pulled him against his chest. Ethan was very much a part of his family now. It didn't matter if he was human. He would do whatever it took to keep Ethan safe.

"I want to help, please," Ethan said quickly.

"No. Absolutely not."

"But I feel like this is at least partially my fault. If I had talked to you sooner, if I hadn't been wrapped up in my own pain—"

"You were used, Ethan," Winter said firmly. "The League used your pain to get information about us. And vampires used the League as fucking cannon fodder in the attack to weaken us."

"Are we being used?" Bel demanded pointedly. "We're in pain over Mother the same way Ethan was in pain over his family. Are we being weaponized to upset the order we do have?"

Rafe laughed loudly and shoved to his feet. He paced over to stand in front of his twin. "Maybe we are. Maybe they want us to do their dirty work. So be it. Whoever it is will regret fucking with the Variks. We will be the new order, and there will be no more personal attacks on clans."

"I still want to help," Ethan said.

"No, it's too dangerous," Marcus growled.

"He's right, Ethan," Bel agreed. "Vampires are much harder to kill. We're a tad bit stronger and faster than most humans. That advantage only grows bigger the older we get. You would constantly be at a great disadvantage."

"Then what? You just wrap me in cotton and tuck me away in the closet until you're done with your war?" Ethan shoved away from Marcus, his face growing flushed with his anger. "Or were you just going to walk away? Leave me behind?"

The thought left Marcus feeling as if his heart was being ripped from his chest. Leave Ethan behind? After just one day of waking wrapped around Ethan's body, he couldn't imagine waking in his cold bed alone. Couldn't go back to that.

"Your pet has some sharp teeth there, dear brother," Rafe teased.

"He's not a pet," Marcus snarled, instantly bristling at the description. Ethan was so much more than a pet.

"Yet another reason to take our place on the Ministry," Winter deftly pointed out.

"What?" Ethan said. Some of the anger slipped from his voice as he turned toward Winter.

"Humans have only two places in our lives—pets and blood slaves," Winter continued.

"I can guess what a blood slave is," Ethan said with distaste. "What's a pet?"

"Not much better than a blood slave, really." Rafe's expression softened a little. "A pet is a plaything and usually a servant of sorts. But mostly a cherished chew toy. No vampire would risk his life over a pet. And ultimately, they are extremely disposable."

"But that's not Ethan," Bel interjected with such sternness that it surprised Marcus. "He means a great deal more to Marcus. He's an equal."

"A part of the family," Winter added, and it was like Marcus could suddenly breathe again.

"And if I'm a part of the family, that means I get to help too."

Marcus groaned and Rafe chuckled.

"Oh, you've got a smart lover there, Marcus."

"You can't, Ethan. It's too dangerous."

"But he could be quite useful. Pets are a wonderful part of a household. They can travel with vampires and are largely overlooked. They hear so many interesting things," Winter said.

"And pets love to gossip," Rafe said with new enthusiasm. "Let's get him a collar!" Rafe hurried through the living room and down a hall that led to his bedroom.

Marcus wanted to shout back at Rafe and the rest of his brothers that Ethan was definitely not a pet. Ethan had become his heart, his happiness. He most certainly wasn't disposable or something to be overlooked. And Marcus would most definitely risk his life over Ethan's safety and happiness.

"So…vampires don't date?" Ethan asked.

Winter groaned softly and closed his eyes. Bel looked a little uncomfortable, but he at least held Ethan's gaze. "No, we don't. We don't form alliances easily for fear of being manipulated or used in power plays. The Variks are unique because we are brothers. We already had a tight familial bond before we were reborn. And I have a feeling it's why others are worried about our intentions."

"But what about with humans?"

"You're food," Winter said shortly. "How many hamburgers have you given your heart to?"

"Winter!" Marcus snapped, but Ethan shrugged.

"He's not wrong," Ethan said. He turned and looked at Marcus. "How many people have you bitten over the years?" Marcus flinched and Ethan smiled softly. "And how many of those people did you care about? Did you know any of their names or dreams?"

"No. Not one."

"It's easier that way. Just a quick transaction. Why should you care about humans so long as our numbers are still growing, and you've got easy access to a source?"

Marcus reached out and placed his hand firmly against Ethan's neck. "You are *not* food to me."

"I know."

Rafe's heavy footsteps echoing off the floor drew their attention back to him as he returned carrying a large box that looked sort of like a trunk. After directing Bel to move his violin, he placed it on the table and flipped open the lid with a flourish.

"I'm sure we can find something suitable for your little pet to wear," Rafe announced.

"Rafe—"

"No, he's right," Ethan interrupted as he stepped closer to the box. "If I pretend to be your pet, then I can more easily blend in. I can talk to other pets. Get gossip and maybe even spread a little."

"Our own little human spy," Rafe said. There was a wicked glee to Rafe's voice that had Marcus shaking his head as he approached the box as well.

"Holy shit! How many pets have you had?" Ethan cried out as he looked in the trunk. Marcus looked in as well and winced. It was filled with collars of all types. "And what happened to them all?"

Rafe glared at Ethan. "Calm yourself, my little piranha. I haven't killed off any pets...yet. In truth, I haven't had what you'd call a real pet."

"My twin likes the idea of a pet, but doesn't like the responsibility of caring for one," Bel teased. "But he does like dressing humans up in collars."

"And little else," Rafe added as he dug through the collars. He picked up a leather one with long, metal spikes and held it up to Ethan. He made a face and dropped it back in the pile before picking up a pink one with a gold tag dangling from it.

"I'm not allowing Ethan to wear something that's already been worn by one of your many sexual partners," Marcus snarled.

Rafe looked up at his older brother with an expression of false surprise. "But they've all been washed."

Several of them snickered, including Ethan, who was also digging through the trunk with Rafe. Something about Ethan's enthusiasm and curiosity was sending the most inappropriate tingling through Marcus's body. He didn't view Ethan as a possession, but the idea of Ethan wearing a collar that marked him as Marcus's property held a dark thrill. All the world would know that Ethan belonged completely to Marcus.

Ethan picked up a collar that sparkled brightly in the light, studded with what looked to be rhinestones and fake gems. Of course, they could all be real gems. Rafe had the wealth for it and really was that careless with valuables. Ethan held it to his neck and grinned up at Marcus as if he knew exactly how he was tempting him.

"If we are going to continue with this farce, then I will order a collar for Ethan myself. Something that is just for him."

Rafe looked up at him as if he'd lost his mind. "It takes time to find a good collar, and you don't want to just buy one off the rack."

Ethan gasped and pressed his hand to his chest. "Do I really mean so little to you that you'd buy off the rack for me?"

Winter laughed and Bel made a noise but tried to muffle it by covering his mouth with his hand.

Marcus just sighed. "You'd rather wear one of Rafe's sex-soaked collars worn by someone that he doesn't even remember than a brand new one because it's off the rack?"

"Maybe. These I'm sure were chosen with love and care."

"And all were special orders," Rafe added.

"Unlike his partners," Marcus grumbled, which only made both Rafe and Ethan cackle.

"Fine. Fine," Rafe finally said. "You want something new and never worn." Rafe leaned over the trunk and dug down to the very bottom. He pulled out a small box and handed it over to Ethan. "I purchased that a long time ago and was saving it for my own pet, but you can have it."

Marcus moved closer to Ethan as he lifted the lid. Inside was a collar made of what looked to be incredibly soft leather. Square sapphires ran through the center along the entire length and were in shining gold casings. There was a solid iron ring near the closure that would serve for a leash and a second smaller ring at the front. From it hung a gold pendant with an elegant V stamped into it. For a collar, it was exquisite.

"Are you sure?" Ethan asked softly, even as one finger strayed across the collar in a light caress. "It's so beautiful."

Rafe shrugged carelessly. "My lovely Bel is right. I'm more enamored with the idea of having a pet than actually possessing one. Too much work. I'd rather just buy pretty things for people who pretend for a short time to be my pet."

"Thank you, Rafe. It is very beautiful," Marcus said, but Rafe was quick to wave off his comments. It stuck with Marcus that Rafe wouldn't meet his gaze. His motions as he placed all the other collars back and closed the trunk seemed rushed and a little nervous. He had a feeling that there was more to Rafe's lack of a pet than just being resistant to caring for someone. It seemed a little hard to believe, but he wondered if Rafe was really looking for something closer to what Marcus had managed to find with Ethan.

They continued to talk for another hour, speculating on which of the factions could have been behind the attack on Marcus's town house as well as the deaths of Percival and Armand. They even wondered if someone on the Ministry could have orchestrated the attacks to secure their own power in the Ministry. But they could come up with no definitive answers until they had more concrete information.

Sadly, Marcus had to admit that his mind was no longer entirely on the conversation. His eyes kept straying to the small box tightly clutched in Ethan's hands. He was grateful Ethan didn't suggest trying it on at Rafe's. No, he wanted them to wait until Ethan was in his bedroom and the door was locked behind them. He wanted to see it for the first time shining around his neck while Ethan kneeled in the center of his bed completely naked.

Ethan most definitely was *not* a pet, but Marcus still wanted to possess him completely and drape him in riches, to pamper him and care for him. Ethan was his, and tonight he was going to revel in that possession.

CHAPTER TWENTY-TWO

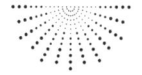

*E*than was a little surprised that they ended up at his apartment after they left Rafe's penthouse. But Marcus instructed him to pack up all his things while he stood guard. Ethan was officially moving into Marcus's town house. It was on the tip of his tongue to ask if this would still be happening if Marcus hadn't already been attacked, but he shoved aside the question and stuffed his clothes into a bag. There was no reason to stir up more trouble. He simply had to appreciate that Marcus wanted him close and wanted to keep him safe.

"Even with everything that is happening, my brothers and I are still moving," Marcus said from the open bedroom doorway. "Connecticut." Marcus paused and winced. Ethan nearly laughed. He obviously knew where since he'd been working on all the logistics of the move.

"Who picked that? You guys missing snow?" Ethan teased to help smooth over the moment.

"It was Bel's turn to pick. There's a small college he wants to be near for his research," Marcus muttered. "Are you fond of living here?"

"Do you mean this apartment?" Ethan paused with a shirt

clutched in one hand. "Oh, you mean Glenpark." He scrunched up his nose a little. "Not particularly. It's a place. I moved south as soon as I hit eighteen. Wanted to be away from where my family died. Besides that, I've never given it much thought."

"I know it's fast, but would you consider moving with me? To Connecticut."

Ethan dropped the shirt on the bed and walked over to Marcus. "Definitely. I was beginning to worry that you were going to leave me behind."

Marcus pulled him into his arms and roughly kissed him. Ethan sighed and relaxed into his wide frame, loving the strength and need vibrating through Marcus. He could lose himself in Marcus's touch and feel so safe and protected by him.

"I don't want to be away from you, but I can't stay here," Marcus said. He dragged his mouth away from Ethan's and up his jaw to suck on his earlobe. Ethan's eyes rolled back in his head, and fire raced through his blood. Marcus was making it damn hard to think.

"Can't stay. Why?" Ethan barely managed to get out.

Marcus pulled away, which wasn't what Ethan wanted at all, but it was for the best. He couldn't finish packing if Marcus was kissing him. "Vampires can't live in the same place for more than two decades. We run the risk of humans noticing that we're not aging."

"Oh, yeah. That makes sense." That was a splash of cold water. Ethan was going to age and Marcus would not. How long until Ethan was too old to hold Marcus's attention? A decade. Maybe two. That would put Ethan in his forties at least.

Or...Ethan could ask Marcus to change him into a vampire.

Ethan's brain shied away from that idea. It was far too early to be thinking about such a mammoth decision.

He walked over to the bed and shoved the last of his clothes into his duffle bag. "Am I going to get my own room in your house?" Ethan asked, partially teasing.

Marcus stepped up behind Ethan and wrapped his arms around his waist, pulling him against his chest. "If that's what you wish, you can have any room in the town house and then any room in my new home, but you should know something."

Ethan tilted his head to the side so that he could look up at Marcus. "What's that?"

"I intend to crawl into your bed each day so that I can fall asleep holding you. After feeling you pressed against me once, I don't think I can live without that feeling every time I rest."

Ethan heaved a very heavy sigh. "Well, then. I guess I should just move into your room to save you the trouble of going to my room."

"That would be very generous and thoughtful of you."

Ethan rolled his eyes. "Come on, sexy. You need to feed me and tell me more about this pet thing."

There was a low rumble in Marcus's chest as his hands slid down from Ethan's waist so that one cupped his ass while the other rubbed against his quickly hardening dick. "I was thinking that I might show you some important things about pets."

A soft whimper edged up his throat and Ethan's body trembled, unable to decide if it wanted to press backward into the hand on his ass or thrust himself into the one against his front.

"Food later. We need to go now," Ethan said breathlessly.

Marcus released him and grabbed his bag off the bed before taking his hand. They briskly strolled out of the apartment and to the elevator. The apartment was only a ten-minute walk to Marcus's town house and only a fraction of that by car, but Ethan swore it took twice as long. His mind was already conjuring up the most wonderful images that included that damn collar and Marcus's magnificent cock. Fuck, if he was lucky, he'd barely be able to walk the next day.

In Marcus's home, they went straight to the master bedroom, but when Ethan tried to press against the sexy vampire, he held him away from his tense frame.

"I want you to shower. When you're done, I want you to come out wearing only the collar."

Ethan sucked in a harsh breath and nodded. He grabbed his bag from Marcus and dug through it until he came up with the box from Rafe. He flashed Marcus a smile and darted for the bathroom. He wanted to make it the world's quickest shower, but he forced himself to slow down so that he could do a thorough job. He tried to get his brain to sink into what he thought of as a pet's headspace. A pet would want to make its master happy. If his master wanted him to shower, then Ethan would come out squeaky clean and smelling of Marcus's personal soap.

Some of this seemed to run so very counter to his own thinking, but he could see how turned-on Marcus was. This was just a little bit of role-playing. Some fun. He could have some fun with Marcus, and he trusted Marcus to always take care of him.

Several minutes later he stepped out of the bathroom. His skin had a slightly rosy glow from the heat and scrubbing. The collar sparkled around his neck, and the little gold pendant was cold against his sternum. There was no hiding his excitement. His cock was already hard, the damp head rubbing against his stomach. Nerves made him a little hesitant to step into the bedroom, but Marcus's hungry gaze wiped away his reticence.

Marcus had stripped off everything but his briefs and was sitting on the edge of the bed, but he got to his feet at the sight of Ethan.

Ethan closed the distance between them, and Marcus looked like he was about to pounce on him at any second. His hard body was tensed, muscles bunched under pale skin. That wonderful cock was tenting his briefs as if it were desperate to reach Ethan.

"You look beautiful," Marcus breathed. His voice was so rough Ethan could barely understand him. "Several lifetimes aren't enough time to spend worshiping your body."

"I'm your pet. Do you want me on my knees licking your cock?" Ethan teased.

Marcus brushed his thumb across Ethan's lower lip before shoving it inside. "If you need something in your mouth, then you must make do with this until you earn my cock."

A low moan pushed out of Ethan as he focused on working his tongue around Marcus's thumb, sucking it just like he would his leaking dick.

"Good boy," Marcus purred. After a moment, Marcus pulled his thumb out, spreading that dampness across his lips. "Listen to me, Ethan. This is all play tonight. You are *not* my pet. You are my equal. My lover. My everything. Do you understand?" Marcus's voice shook with sincerity as he stared into Ethan's eyes.

Ethan blinked against the first prick of tears. "I understand."

"If there is anything you're not comfortable with, you must tell me. I promise I will stop. I will always do whatever you need me to."

"I trust you. I love you. Love you so much, Marcus." Ethan leaned in the last few inches and kissed Marcus. But Marcus allowed only a couple of desperate, hungry kisses before he pulled away.

"Would you like to earn your master's love?"

A tiny thrill ran through Ethan. The game was on, and he loved this playful side of Marcus. "Yes. Very much."

"Get on your knees in the middle of the bed. Lean back and put your hands on the mattress to support yourself."

Ethan scrambled to follow his instructions. He hadn't realized it at the time, but it stretched his body out, thrusting his cock in front of him. Marcus hummed his pleasure as he slowly drew off his briefs and climbed onto the bed with Ethan.

"So perfect." He fingered the collar for a moment. "These gems are beautiful, but they aren't worth a tenth of you. Just pretty baubles trying to match your perfection, and failing." His hand slid down Ethan's chest, lingering for a moment to pluck at his nipples before grazing over his stomach and carefully missing his cock altogether before running over one of his thighs.

Ethan wanted to moan in a mix of pleasure and pain. He needed Marcus to grab his cock and stroke him, but the damn man was teasing him. No one from his past had ever taken such care. It was always a quick blowjob, a quick fuck. Chasing that orgasm and then out the door. He'd never been with anyone who touched him with the reverence Marcus did.

"I have the most beautiful pet."

"P-please..." Ethan stammered, not quite sure what he was begging for.

Marcus chuckled. "I could spend all night looking at you and stroking you like this. Would you like that, my pet?"

"Marcus!"

The damn vampire just answered with a chuckle. He stopped touching Ethan and moved back on the bed to lie against the pillows with his legs spread in front of him. "Suck my dick, pet. If you do a good job, I may fuck you."

Ethan instantly straightened and crawled between Marcus's legs, loving the bristling feel of the hairs on his calves rubbing against his arms. He didn't hesitate but buried his face in Marcus's groin, breathing in his scent deep before swiping his tongue up his hard shaft. Marcus's dick wasn't long, but it was so deliciously thick that it made Ethan's eyes roll into his head just thinking about how it stretched and filled him. He wanted to be fucked senseless, but he'd be happy with Marcus coming down his throat.

Swirling his tongue around the dark red head, Ethan lapped up the pre-cum leaking from Marcus. He loved that he was the first for Marcus in so many ways. The first man he'd ever kissed. The first man he'd ever fucked. The first man he'd ever held while sleeping. And now, the first man to suck his cock.

Oh yeah, Marcus was going to lose his mind.

Ethan slowly took Marcus down his throat, running his tongue over his turgid length. He followed the thick vein, teasing it. Relaxing his throat, he forced himself to take more and more of Marcus, craving each soft sound that he couldn't hold back. His eyes watered and his jaw ached, but he didn't care. He wanted to make Marcus lose control. It had to be the best experience of his life.

Marcus threaded his fingers through Ethan's hair and tightened until his scalp stung with little pinpoints of pain, but Ethan didn't release Marcus's dick. He just moaned, letting the vibrations of his throat add to the sensations.

Snarling a curse, Marcus pulled Ethan off his cock and up his chest, taking his sore and swollen lips in a brutal kiss. One hand snaked down his body and along his crack. Ethan shifted against Marcus, rubbing his cock against his stomach as one of Marcus's fingers circled his hole. Oh God, he couldn't remember ever being so turned-on in his life. He felt like he was about to come, and Marcus had yet to touch his dick.

Ethan whimpered when Marcus broke off the kiss but relaxed into his hold again when his lips moved along his jaw to settle against his throat. Ethan instinctively tilted his head to the side, offering him better access.

"Will you feed your master, pet?"

"Yes," Ethan moaned.

"And if I wanted to drain you dry? Steal your life away…"

"Yes." Ethan grabbed handfuls of Marcus's hair and held him trapped against his throat. "All that I am belongs to you. My heart, my body…my life."

"What if…"

Whatever Marcus was about to say, the words drifted off. Ethan's heart demanded that Marcus ask to make him into a vampire so that they could have forever, but the words never came.

"I am yours, Marcus. Always. Forever."

"Then I want what is mine."

The entire world seemed to shift violently, and Ethan found himself lying on the mattress, on his stomach. Marcus was pressed against him from behind, his fat cock sliding between Ethan's ass cheeks. Ethan moaned and pressed backward, his fists clenching the sheets, twisting them. There wasn't a damn clear thought in his head. All the blissful feelings were coming in so fast and so fucking sharp.

Somewhere in all the feverish chaos, Marcus found the lube. He pressed two slick fingers into his body and Ethan howled before starting to move on those thick digits. He wanted the stretching and the prep done. They needed to get to the fucking.

"Now, Marcus! Now!"

A hand landed on one ass cheek with a loud crack. The pain was sharp but brief, dulling into a low heat. "Pets don't make demands."

"Not demanding. Please. Begging. I beg you. Need you."

A gentle touch smoothed over the abused cheek, soothing away the heat and replacing it with a gnawing need. He wasn't going to make it. All the touching and teasing, Marcus's strength and command, were shredding his willpower.

The fingers in his ass disappeared, but before he could react, the head of Marcus's cock was pressing forward, breaching him. Ethan fought the urge to push backward, taking him all at once. He was afraid if he tried, Marcus would pull out of him completely. A good pet obeyed and tonight, he was Marcus's good pet.

"Fuck. So tight," Marcus growled. Fingers bit into Ethan's hips, holding him perfectly still. He loved Marcus's tight control but also the trembling in his touch as if he were barely hanging on to that control.

"And you're so fucking big," Ethan groaned. "Fill me, please, Marcus. Make me yours."

Those whispered words seemed to have snapped Marcus's control, because he surged forward in one smooth thrust. Ethan cried out, his entire body in shock at the invasion. He was so full again. Marcus leaned over him with his larger body, one arm sliding across his chest so that his hand could clamp down on his shoulder, locking him to Marcus.

"You are mine. Always mine," Marcus vowed. He punched his hips forward in little thrusts. The angle had Marcus pushing relentlessly against his prostate, sending wave after mind-scrambling wave of pleasure through his body. Ethan didn't want to come yet. He wanted to feel Marcus stretching him and filling him for much longer, but his orgasm was so close he could barely pull in a breath.

"Marcus! I need to come!"

"What do you wish?"

"Fuck me. Fuck me hard," Ethan sobbed.

"Anything for you." They were the only words of warning he got before Marcus pulled his cock nearly completely from his body and thrust back in hard. The pounding was brutal, but all Ethan's brain registered was relief for a moment. Marcus felt so damn good.

His orgasm exploded without warning a second later. He never got to touch his cock as it was crushed against the mattress, rubbing against the silken sheets. The world went white and his muscles clenched up. It was like his entire being shattered into millions of sharp splinters and sped through the room. Marcus moaned and continued to thrust into his tightened channel.

As he started to slowly float back down to earth, Ethan heard Marcus roar his release. Heat flooded his ass and then the sharp, piercing pain of fangs digging into his shoulder ripped through his body. Before he could cry out in pain, ecstasy slammed into him like a fucking Mack Truck. A second orgasm obliterated Ethan's mind. It was like he was feeling Marcus's orgasm, and it stole his breath away.

His hips jerked and thrust on their own. He could feel his cock sliding through the cum-soaked sheets beneath him while electric bliss tingled with each slide of Marcus's cock in his cum-slicked ass. He couldn't stop moving. Didn't want to stop. Nothing had ever felt so good.

But exhaustion finally won, and he flattened under Marcus, struggling to catch his breath. Marcus licked along the wound he'd created, and a hum of pleasure rumbled from his throat. He pressed a couple of kisses to the place he just drank from, and Ethan shivered as the last tendrils of joy slithered along his nerve endings.

"Are you okay?" Marcus asked.

Ethan nodded. Everything felt too raw and sharp. He needed the world to mellow and for his brain to get a little more blood and oxygen.

"Ethan," he said sharply, his worry thick in that single word. He started to move, but Ethan's hand shot back with blinding speed, clamping down on Marcus's thigh.

"Don't," Ethan said, and Marcus immediately froze. "Please."

Marcus didn't move, keeping his cock nestled inside of Ethan. With their bodies still intimately connected and pressed so close, Ethan felt like it was easier to take that next breath, to pull together his scattered thoughts, because he wasn't alone. Marcus was there, in him, wrapped around him. They were still a part of each other.

"I'm okay," he said after a couple of deep breaths. "I promise. It was just a little…intense." A wobbly laugh escaped him, and he released Marcus's thigh to grab the hand still holding his shoulder. "That second orgasm…fuck, I didn't know I could have a second orgasm…but it was like I could feel mine and then yours at the same time. I think it fried my poor little human brain."

Ethan could feel Marcus's entire body relax against him. Very carefully, Marcus wrapped his other arm around Ethan's stomach and turned them on their side without losing their connection. Marcus nuzzled Ethan's hair, kissing him on the tender flesh behind the ear.

"Good to know. I'll refrain from biting you during sex," Marcus murmured.

"Don't you dare stop!" Ethan twisted his head and upper body enough to look Marcus in the eyes. "That was…holy fuck…that was insane, and I definitely want to do it again. Maybe…just…not every time."

With a smile, Marcus gently kissed him. "And everything else?"

"Perfect. I know I am treasured and loved."

"And you are mine."

Ethan hummed happily, snuggling against Marcus before dropping his head on the pillow. "And you are mine."

He didn't know how long they lay wrapped in each other. They didn't talk, but they didn't need to. Ethan soaked in all the little touches as Marcus ran one hand up and down his body over and over again. Ethan hadn't done a lot of dating in his life, but he had to admit he'd never thought he'd find something like this with someone. He never expected to find someone he enjoyed talking to, someone who made him laugh and think, someone who treasured him even with his quick temper and impulsive nature.

Ethan definitely hadn't expected to find the perfect person in the form of a vampire, especially after what happened to his family. God, what would they think of him? Lying in bed, his ass stuffed and covered in cum, with a fucking vampire?

"What are you thinking?" Marcus said.

"Can you read minds?" Ethan asked, half joking.

"No, but I felt your body stiffen suddenly."

"Oh."

Marcus kissed his shoulder and his arms tightened around him. "Talk to me, please."

Ethan closed his eyes and swallowed. He tried to sink back into Marcus's warmth, letting it protect him from the dark thoughts running through his head. "I was just wondering... what my family would think if they knew...I'd fallen for you."

"Is your worry that I'm a man?"

Ethan shook his head.

"It's that I'm a vampire." Marcus started to loosen his hold and Ethan grabbed his hand, keeping them tightly pressed together. Marcus tightened his grip again and Ethan relaxed. "Well, since I don't know your family, I'm going to assume that they are as smart as you and as kindhearted as you. Probably well-adjusted and a bit sassy as well."

"I like to think all that is accurate," Ethan said with a smile.

"Then I'd say they would understand that I had nothing to do with their deaths and would accept my vow to help you find the true culprit."

"Thank you."

"And they would believe me when I say that I will do everything within my power to keep you safe and make sure that you always feel loved."

"I love you."

"I love you, Ethan. I've never loved anyone before. Never let myself dream I would have even one night of such happiness. But if I get only one night, I'll take it and cherish it for the rest of my very long existence." Marcus paused, his arms tightening. "I worry too. A war is coming. I don't want to think about you being in danger."

Ethan could sense where this was building to. He roughly pushed Marcus's arms off him and rolled so that he was now facing Marcus. Ethan pushed up onto his knees, allowing the silken blankets to slide down his quickly cooling flesh. With a smirk, he threw one leg over Marcus's hip and straddled him, returning to the warmth he'd found just moments ago in his embrace. The vampire broke all the Hollywood rules. He wasn't some cold, shambling corpse with perfectly persevered youth. He was a living creature…who just didn't age. It was easy to understand why Bel was convinced vampirism was a disease that could be cured. His heart beat, breath whooshed in and out of his lungs, he ate food, and he fucked like a goddamn dream.

With his hands pressed against Marcus's wide chest, he ran his fingers up through the sprinkling of dark hairs that swirled around his brown nipples and the sexy trail down from his belly button. And despite the strength he could feel in every flex and ripple of muscle in that six-foot frame, Ethan knew he was safe. But that didn't mean Marcus was safe.

"I'm not excited about you being in danger either," Ethan said, glaring down at his lover. "But we're stronger together. You need your sneaky pet spy watching out for you."

Marcus smiled, some of the tension leaving his face. "I do."

"Smart man." Ethan leaned forward and pressed a playful kiss to the tip of Marcus's nose. He might not be a vampire, but he would find a way to keep his man safe. He was not losing Marcus.

CHAPTER TWENTY-THREE

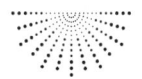

Marcus pushed the doorbell and took a step backward so that he was standing next to Ethan again. He looked down at his lover and smiled. His blond hair was artfully styled off his face and he wore just a deep sapphire blue vest, leaving his muscular arms bare and perfectly accenting the gems in his collar. The black leather pants looked as if they'd been painted onto his body the way they were molded to his every curve and hollow. It was hard to keep his hands off Ethan's ass.

"If you grab me, there's going to be no hiding my erection," Ethan warned in a low voice.

Marcus smirked. "Then everyone will be envious of me. They will know that I have the most beautiful pet who has the most beautiful cock."

Ethan tilted his head, looking up at Marcus with a knowing smirk. "And if you're a good boy tonight, you might get fucked by that beautiful cock."

Marcus fought hard not to adjust himself at that thought. He had to admit that he'd wondered what it would be like to feel Ethan moving in him, his balls slapping against his ass.

But now was not the time for such thoughts. They had come to see Winslow, a member of the American Ministry and the only one who lived within easy driving distance of Marcus. The excuse for the visit was an easy one—there had been an unprovoked attack on Marcus's home that resulted in the death of a clan member. The Ministry was supposed to be keeping the peace.

But Marcus was also hoping to get the latest gossip and maybe spread a little of his own.

In preparation for the night, Rafe and Winter had come over to his town house to give Ethan some lessons on how to act as a pet. It was probably for the best since he and Ethan hadn't gotten much further than how a pet should act in bed. That they had down to perfection, but it wouldn't help them at Winslow's.

After a couple of hours of instruction, Ethan was acting like the perfect, attentive, yet somewhat spoiled pet. God help him if Ethan actually started acting like that. He was both alluring and annoying, leaving Marcus unsure if he wanted to strangle him or fuck him.

The front door swung open, and a butler in a severe black uniform greeted them. The man recognized Marcus, though Marcus couldn't remember his name. Marcus had been called before Winslow once as representative of his family to be reprimanded for some reckless adventure of Rafe's. Winslow was the only Ministry member to live within his city.

"Good evening, Marcus. I was unaware you had an appointment with Master Winslow," the butler said, waving for them to enter the grand foyer. The butler didn't acknowledge Ethan, but that was to be expected. He was an accessory. While it rankled Marcus, he reminded himself that this would work to their advantage later.

"Unfortunately, there wasn't time for scheduling an appointment. My clan has been attacked. Winslow needs to deal with this *immediately*," Marcus demanded, raising his voice. Rafe would undoubtedly be disappointed by his lack of extravagant temper tantrum, but such a display would have been out of character for him.

"I'm so sorry to hear that, sir. If you would follow me to the lounge, I will inform Master Winslow that you are here."

Marcus gave a stiff nod, and they walked across the foyer to a pair of open double doors. The room was larger than the typical lounge, with two leather sofas and matching chairs. The curtains over the floor-to-ceiling windows had been pulled back to reveal a clear black sky glittering with stars. An ornate chandelier shone overhead, casting warm light over the richness of the room.

"Can I get you anything while you wait, sir?"

"Refreshment for my pet. A white wine would be nice and maybe something to nibble." Marcus paused and smiled down at Ethan. "He needs to keep up his strength." Ethan blushed and looked up at Marcus with an expression of pure adoration.

The butler gave a bow and left. Marcus watched Ethan turn around in the center of the room, taking in its richness, before looking at Marcus with a wink. Shoving down his fears, Marcus smiled at Ethan. Anxiety crawled over his skin, and there was a little voice demanding that he pull Ethan into his arms and carry him out of that house. It was one thing for Ethan to be in Rafe's home. Ethan would always be safe around his family.

The home of another vampire was an entirely different story. One of the most effective ways to attack a vampire was to strike through his pet. Too often he'd witnessed "unfortunate accidents" where a pet was maimed or killed because a vampire played too rough. No one played with his Ethan. No one touched his Ethan, ever.

"Get that footstool there," Marcus said, pointing to a leather cushion on intricately carved wooden legs. "Pull it over to my chair." He then selected a chair and sat. Ethan hurried to follow his instructions, though he might have been careful to position himself so that Marcus got a very clear view of his ass when he bent over to pick up the footstool.

Marcus could only smirk at his antics, not quite sure if Ethan was trying to tempt him or if he was merely playing the part of the attentive and sexual pet. It was likely a little of column A and a little of column B in this case.

Ethan carried the footstool over and placed it directly beside Marcus's chair but a little in front of him. Once he took his place, Marcus ran his hand through Ethan's hair in a slow caress before wrapping his fingers around the back of his neck.

"Perfect."

"Fuck, Marcus," Ethan whispered. "It's like my body can't decide whether to be scared or aroused."

Marcus tightened his hand on Ethan's neck a tiny bit. "Be a good boy, and I'll make you come on the drive home."

"Yep. Gonna go with aroused."

Footsteps echoed through the hall for a couple of seconds before a tall man with blond hair so pale it was nearly white appeared. His sharp dark eyes paused for only a second on Ethan before continuing on to Marcus. Pushing to his feet, Marcus kept one hand on Ethan, holding him down on the footstool.

"Marcus, Slate brings me news of an attack," Winslow said as he drew closer. "Is your clan well and safe?"

"If it was, would I be here?" Marcus snapped. He waited until Winslow chose a seat across from him before returning to his own. The butler, Slate, placed a tray on the table in front of Ethan with a glass of white wine and a charcuterie board with a selection of cheeses, crackers, nuts, and meats.

"Very true," Winslow said with a weary sigh as he dropped in his chair. "Can you tell me what happened?"

"My house was invaded by humans with weapons and body armor. Two of my brothers were visiting at the time. We had just dispatched the humans when they were followed by vampires. Vampires and humans working together to attack me and my family!" Marcus didn't have to fake his anger and outrage. The fact that someone had weaponized the humans and turned them into a battering ram was disturbing. It meant that everyone needed to increase their daytime security. There was always the threat of the random, rogue assassin infiltrating a vampire's lair during the daylight hours, but the chance of an entire army hitting a house and killing everyone within was a terrifying thought.

Deep lines of concern dug into Winslow's face and he sat back in his chair, glaring at the floor for a moment. "Was anyone—"

"Julianna. My mother. She's gone."

"Marcus...I'm so very sorry."

Marcus fought to keep the fresh anger from showing on his face. Winslow's comments rang as less than sincere. He knew that most of the vampire community were not fans of Julianna. She was a dangerous loose cannon. She was an unknown entity that could destroy their secret on one very bad night. That didn't mean she deserved to die. Marcus and his brothers had kept the situation under control.

"She died protecting my pet." Marcus stroked Ethan's hair, and Ethan leaned his head against the arm of Marcus's chair, moving that much closer to his touch.

"I can understand why. He's quite lovely. I didn't know you had one. I didn't think you believed in pets."

"I thought they were a nuisance, but then I found Ethan. His skills and beauty were quite convincing that pets could be enjoyable."

Ethan looked up at Marcus and fluttered his eyelashes. "I want to be your perfect pet," he purred.

"Perfect pet? Is someone talking about me?" asked a playful female voice.

Marcus looked up from Ethan's doting gaze to see a slender

young woman stroll into the room, wearing a skirt that was slit straight up to her hip. Long, shapely legs flashed in the red material with every step she took. Her top covered only her breasts, leaving bare a soft, flat stomach. She elegantly lowered herself to Winslow's feet, wrapping one arm and a leg around Winslow's left leg.

"We were talking about Marcus's new pet, dearest," Winslow said, stroking his hand absently through her fire-red hair.

"He's adorable. And such a pretty collar," she gushed, though her eyes were less than welcoming as she carefully watched Ethan.

"The Variks are known for having exquisite taste in expensive things. We shouldn't be surprised that it extends to their pets."

"While this is all fine and good, I want to know what the Ministry plans to do about the attack on my family. About the unprovoked attack and death of Julianna," Marcus snarled.

Winslow lifted both of his empty hands toward Marcus in a motion he could only think of as placating. "The Ministry is sympathetic to your loss, but you've yet to tell me anything concrete about who is behind this attack. If you could give us a name or even a clan, we could look into it. Arrange for appropriate compensation."

Marcus knew that compensation would come in the form of a sacrificial lamb or two trussed up and delivered to the Varik family with well-wishes. He and his brothers would love nothing more than to claim the heads of the vampires who plotted their deaths, but this was beyond just dealing justice to the people who attacked his family and killed their mother. There was the murder of Ethan's family that needed to be dealt with. There were the attacks on the Ministry.

The leaders of their people were ineffective and careless. They cared only about their own comfort and amusement. They'd forgotten about the vampires they were serving and the humans they were supposed to be keeping safe. His brothers were right. It was time for a new order. He hadn't been able to see it before, but sitting opposite Winslow, Marcus couldn't deny that he had no faith in the vampire to bring order to their world.

"If I knew who was doing the attacking, I wouldn't feel compelled to bring it to you. My family would have taken care of the matter," Marcus said stiffly. "I thought with the recent trouble the Ministry has had—including the deaths of both Armand and Percival—the Ministry might know who was on such a murderous streak. Is someone hell-bent on taking out other vampires?"

Winslow shifted in his seat, his eyes dropping down to the head of his pet for a moment. "Victoria, why don't you take Marcus's pet into the kitchen and get him something to eat? If Marcus has an appetite anything like his brother Rafe, his pet could use something with more substance."

Without a word, the woman rose gracefully to her feet and waited for Ethan to stand as well. Ethan looked over at Marcus, not moving until his master gave permission. This was the very thing they'd hoped and planned for, but Marcus found himself hesitating for a heartbeat. He didn't want Ethan out of his sight for a second.

But Ethan could handle himself.

Marcus nodded, hating the way his heart sped up a little bit at the fear that Ethan couldn't quite erase from his wide eyes.

Ethan stood and followed Victoria from the room, leaving Marcus alone with Winslow.

"So, you've heard about them," Winslow murmured.

"Winter is quite good at gathering little bits of news."

Winslow nodded. "Has he heard that Charlotte was also discovered murdered this evening?"

"Three members of the American Ministry dead?"

Winslow nodded again and folded his hands on his stomach.

JOCELYNN DRAKE

"I will admit that the Varik clan crossed my mind at least once when Armand was killed."

"Why's that?" Marcus said. His hands tightened on the arms of his chair and he slid to the edge as if preparing to launch himself at Winslow.

"Because Armand was the most vocally against Julianna being permitted to live," Winslow said with a casual wave of his hand. "If I were the leader of the Varik clan and was making a move to take control of the Ministry, he'd be the first on my list to die."

Marcus froze and stared at Winslow for one tense second before dropping back into his chair in laughter. "You think we're trying to take over the Ministry? That we're behind the deaths of the Ministry members?"

"I did until you brought news of Julianna's murder." Winslow shook his head and it was only then that Marcus noticed that Winslow's hands untensed and he seemed to sink a little more in his chair. He'd been worried that Marcus would attack him. "Seats on the Ministry would be the only way the Variks could permanently protect the life of Julianna."

"The Ministry is not the concern of myself or my brothers. We only want to live our lives in peace."

"Does Aiden feel the same way?"

Marcus made a show of glaring at the floor, his hands tightening into fists. "Aiden is in mourning. He's keeping his feelings to himself right now."

It was true, but Marcus also knew that Winter was checking up on their wayward sire. Aiden would need time to come to terms with his loss, and Marcus couldn't even guess as to how Aiden would feel about their plans. Aiden was the type to keep to himself. Marcus truly doubted Aiden had any interest in getting a seat on the Ministry, let alone becoming king of the vampires. But then, it was much easier for kings to get their revenge.

"Have you heard of anyone with connections to the Humans Protecting Humans League?" Marcus asked.

"The vampire hate group? No," Winslow said, disgust filling his voice.

"I believe they were the humans who attacked my home with the vampires."

"I...I can't believe that." Winslow pushed to his feet and paced over to the empty fireplace, wringing his hands in front of his stomach.

"It's true. And why not? Humans are more numerous than us. Send enough humans in to attack, weakening a target, and then a vampire can stroll in to finish the task."

Winslow shook his head, but Marcus had to wonder. While Winslow sounded disgusted and horrified, he didn't seem particularly surprised. That might have been how Armand, Charlotte, or Percival were killed.

"The Ministry will look into your claims and uncover the truth of the matter. If someone has weaponized the humans in such a way, he or she will be dealt with severely. Humans are to have no proof of our existence beyond pets, and they are definitely not permitted to be involved in our disagreements. Thank you for bringing this to our attention," Winslow said. He firmed up his tone as if he'd gotten control of his growing fears. Three powerful vampires dead in a short time was a frightening thing. Was he going to be a target too?

Winslow returned to his seat and pasted a serene expression on his face that Marcus didn't believe at all.

"Was there anything else you wished to discuss?"

Marcus sat back in his chair and folded his hands in his lap. Time to stir up trouble for the rest of the Ministry.

"I've heard that Robert of the Timber clan is planning to remove Beatrice's head and claim her seat."

JOCELYNN DRAKE

"I can't believe Marcus Varik finally took a pet," Victoria said extravagantly as they entered the kitchen. With one limp hand, she waved for him to take a seat at the center counter while she strolled over to the shiny stainless-steel fridge.

The kitchen was enormous, easily twice the size of Marcus's with a double oven and huge stove with at least eight burners. It was what he assumed a professional kitchen would look like at a five-star restaurant. The counters were dark marble, and everything shone like it was polished within an inch of its life. He was afraid to touch anything for fear of smudging it.

Victoria had no such fear. She moved about the house as if she owned it rather than being a possession herself.

"So, you've met Marcus before?" Ethan asked, even though he already knew the answer. He was curious as to how she'd reply, how reliable she'd be.

"Not personally. But I saw him a couple of times when my master took me to The Bank." She twisted partially around to look at him over her shoulder while still holding the fridge doors open. "Has he taken you to The Bank yet?"

"No. Not yet. I've only been his pet for a week."

"Oh! You must get him to take you soon! Beg him." She smiled slyly at him. "Or use other means to convince him."

"What's The Bank?"

She released the doors and leaned both of her forearms on the counter separating them. "It's this special meeting place only for vampires and their pets. It's the one place they can be out in public and totally be themselves. The first floor is the nightclub, and it's so much fun." She made a little face in displeasure. "The second floor is this stuffy rich man's club, even though women are allowed in. They just sit around drinking, talking, or reading the freaking newspaper. The only music is like harp music. Winslow prefers to hang out there. I've only ever seen Marcus on that floor, but his brother Rafe is at the nightclub occasionally." She gave a dreamy sigh. "Have you met that brother?"

"Yes. I've met all his brothers."

"Rafe's the sexy one. I bet you wish you got that one."

Ethan tried not to sound too pissed when he said, "I adore Marcus. I have no regrets."

Victoria shrugged and turned to the fridge as if his opinion didn't matter. "Is there anything you're in the mood for? I could call the chef to make something for you, but most meetings with my master don't last long. I'd hate for you to leave before it's done. Personally, if I eat one more salad, I might just throw a radish at his head."

"I'd love something sweet."

Victoria giggled and closed the fridge but kept the freezer section open. When she turned back to Ethan, she was holding two gallon containers of ice cream. The fancy, expensive kind too.

"Oh, yes!" Ethan said. He had to admit that this was going to be an expected perk of the job. He hadn't had ice cream in a while.

Victoria put both containers on the counter and grabbed two more out of the freezer. She then quickly snagged two spoons out the drawer and handed one to Ethan.

"Thank you," he said as he pulled the container of triple chocolate fudge closer to him. He broke the plastic seal, stunned no one had opened it yet. If it had been his, he would have cracked that bad boy open the moment he returned home from the grocery.

"This is so much better than listening to them talk politics," Victoria said before shoveling a spoonful of rocky road into her mouth. She moaned around the chocolatey goodness and Ethan couldn't blame her. This was the best ice cream he'd ever tasted.

"Have you been a pet long?"

Victoria straightened, her closed-lipped smile growing as she swallowed another bite. "I've been with Winslow for almost four years. That's three times longer than any of his past pets."

"Is that longer than most pets?"

She shrugged. "It depends. I've heard that most don't last more than a couple of years. But I've heard there are a few out there that have been with their master for over a decade. Those are rare, though."

"What happens to them? Do they just leave?"

Victoria paused, ice cream halfway to her mouth. "There's no leaving. I mean, there's supposedly some vamps that can wipe your mind, but humans can't know about vampires. Most pets die while in service. A few are given away to other vamps as gifts." Victoria lowered her spoon and leaned closer to Ethan. "Winslow has mentioned that he might one day turn me. No vamp ever does that with a pet, but he can't live without me. He wants me this pretty for always." She was practically bouncing with her excitement, and it was a struggle for Ethan to smile at her.

This was not what he was supposed to be talking about with her, but he had to admit that it was good information to have. He'd never given much thought to what his future would look like. He'd just been lost in the glow of their new love and the idea of living with him in Connecticut. But in Marcus's mind, was that only for a year or two? Would Marcus hand him over to another vampire when he lost interest?

Ethan couldn't even fathom such a thought. Marcus would never do that. His lover had been very clear that Ethan wasn't a pet. He was just playing a role. He loved Ethan. But did they mean the same thing when they said those words?

It was only when Victoria's free hand patted his that Ethan realized he'd gotten lost in thought. He looked up to see her sympathetic gaze.

"Don't worry. I'm sure Marcus will take very good care of you. He seems very serious and I'm sure that means he'll be very serious about your care. I didn't mean to upset you."

"Oh, I'm not. I guess I hadn't given much thought to the future. I was just enjoying my time with Marcus so much."

"That's good! Vampires are fun and sexy and their stamina..." She groaned loudly before digging out a scoop of ice cream.

"The best!" Ethan chimed in with a giggle.

"And generous! That is an amazing collar Marcus has given you."

Ethan straightened a little and lifted his chin so that the light could more easily bounce off the sapphires. "This is my first and Marcus has promised me one for every color of the rainbow."

"Ooooh...I'm gonna have to tell my master so he can up his collar game. He's a member of the Ministry. No offense, but he can't let his pet be shown up by anyone."

"Oh no, I totally understand. Marcus has said that the Ministry is very important, not that I understand all of it."

Victoria made a little dismissive noise. "Neither do I. All political nonsense, but it means that other vampires are supposed to respect Winslow and the Ministry members."

"But doesn't it worry you?"

"What?"

Ethan looked over one shoulder and then the other, as if making sure they were completely alone, before he leaned closer to his companion. "The murders," he said in a harsh whisper.

"Is that what your master was talking about before we were sent away?"

Ethan nodded. "Two members of the Ministry were already killed."

Victoria paled, lowering her spoon to the counter with a soft *tink*. "Did they kill each other?"

"No, they were killed days apart, from my understanding."

"Oh, God. Do you think my master is safe?"

Ethan chewed on his bottom lip and gave Victoria a sympathetic look.

"What? What do you know?"

Ethan leaned a little closer to Victoria and she did the same. "I overheard something Winter and Rafe were saying. I don't think they knew I was there. I'd left to run an errand for Marcus but came back because I forgot my keys."

"What did you hear?"

"Winter said that he'd heard that someone named Sebastian was planning to kill Winslow and take his seat on the Ministry since Winslow's only supporter had been killed off. Said he was an easy target now."

Victoria pulled away from Ethan, and he watched the emotions flit across her face. The fear he'd expected, but he was surprised by the look of calculation. Winslow wasn't going to last long. Ethan just wasn't sure if Winslow was going to pick a fight with someone Marcus said he couldn't beat, or if his own pet was going to do him in and then offer herself up to this Sebastian.

Either way, Ethan was ready to leave this house and return to Marcus's home and his embrace.

CHAPTER TWENTY-FOUR

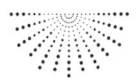

Two nights after the visit to the Ministry member's house, Ethan found himself standing in the foyer of Marcus's new home, directing the movers as they hauled in boxes and furniture. The pianos had arrived a day earlier, and a piano tuner was scheduled to come the next day to retune all three. They'd made the trip in a private jet with Marcus's brothers, which was hands down the most extravagant experience of his life. Ethan had spent the majority of the time talking to Bel as Marcus and Winter whispered about something at the rear of the jet. Rafe was stretched out along a bench, sleeping for most of the flight.

Ethan liked Bel. The vampire was sweet and dedicated to his research. He was also a lot more perceptive about people than his brothers gave him credit for, but Ethan figured it was easier for them to dismiss Bel as an absentminded professor than to accept that their nerdy brother had their number.

"Ethan," Marcus called from the second-floor staircase railing.

Ethan looked up to see his lover leaning over the railing to look down at him. He was wearing his usual dark suit, but his hair was standing wildly about his head. Ethan was quickly learning this was a sign that Marcus was feeling stressed and anxious. His first guess was the sheer number of people running around his house.

"Yes?"

"Has the Wi-Fi been set up yet? Janice needs me to look over some contracts."

"Yes. I wrote down the password and put it in your wallet."

Ethan nearly laughed at the look of surprise on Marcus's face, but he muttered a quick thanks before disappearing again. Ethan's guess was that he'd marched to the temporary office he'd set up next to the master bedroom.

Marcus had tried to fire him, saying that they couldn't work together if they were dating. He wanted to just give Ethan a generous allowance and access to his bank account if he needed anything else. It was a little tempting after living most of his life hand to mouth, but he didn't want to be a "kept man." He wanted to do something useful and earn his own way. And if he'd learned anything in the past month, it was that Marcus needed an assistant helping with all the various tasks of life, whether big or small.

For now, he'd managed to get Marcus to simply extend his contract indefinitely. He figured after they straightened out this political nonsense, he could find a more permanent job within Marcus's companies. Maybe even finish his damn degree.

Yet even with those vague plans, Ethan couldn't completely shake off Victoria's words that no pet ever escaped their vampire. There was no life after Marcus.

Of course, he didn't want to leave Marcus. He loved being with him, loved their talks and dinners together. He loved falling asleep as the sun rose in Marcus's arms and making love to him.

But that damn skeptical voice kept taunting him. What if Marcus got bored? Eternity was a long time, and Ethan was getting older by the day. He wasn't going to stay young and vibrant forever.

Shoving those dark thoughts aside, Ethan focused on getting the last of the truck unpacked, papers signed, and movers generously tipped. He'd just finished ordering pizza when he went to locate his lover.

The vampire had been moody since the last of his things were loaded on a truck. They'd stopped at Ethan's old apartment to grab a few things he didn't want to part with. The rest would be packed up by a service and donated to charity.

After Marcus snapped at the movers the moment they arrived at the house, Ethan sent him off to his room so he could handle the last of the move.

Marcus wasn't in his new office, but he did locate him in the massive closet off the master bedroom. The thing was bigger than most bedrooms and even had its own sofa for lounging, as if Marcus or Ethan were in danger of wearing themselves out trying to choose a pair of shoes.

When he peeked inside, he found Marcus organizing his button-down shirts by color, which was kind of adorable and nerdy. But what had Ethan's heart skipping a beat was seeing his clothes carefully hung up and organized on the shelves and racks opposite Marcus's. He'd never shared a closet with anyone, and he could guess that Marcus was feeling the same eagerness, considering it was the first thing he'd unpacked out of the entire house.

"Have you mellowed?" Ethan asked from where he leaned against the doorframe.

Marcus smiled. He didn't jump, proving that he'd heard Ethan approaching. "Yes. I'm calmer now. The movers gone?"

"Yep. Everything is here. I checked off every box. I've also ordered pizza, which should be here in about twenty minutes."

"Good." Marcus turned from his suits. His eyes darted over to Ethan's clothes and then to Ethan. "I unpacked your things."

"I noticed," Ethan said, unable to keep from teasing his lover. He couldn't help himself. He could feel the power in Marcus, see the way others reacted to him, and yet Marcus treated him like he was the one with all the power. It boggled his mind.

"I know you said that you wanted to share a bedroom, so I assumed it also meant sharing a closet."

"It did." Ethan walked into the room, he moved to his clothes and touched the frayed hem of a pair of jeans before crossing to Marcus's tailor-made suits. He ran his fingers over the silky material of one tie before looking at Marcus. "I think our clothes look good together. Power suits meet lazy Sundays."

"I love how you dress. Don't change if you don't want to."

Ethan moved to the dresser in the center of the room and lifted himself up so that he was seated on the top. Marcus stepped between his legs and wrapped his arms around Ethan's waist. This way, Ethan was only an inch or two shorter than Marcus, giving him much easier access to his lips. They kissed slowly, letting the fire build between them. The hands resting on his hips suddenly slid under his shirt, rubbing against his bare back. And then they were pulling the shirt over his head.

A low laugh turned into a gasp as Marcus started kissing down his chest. Marcus's tongue swept across his nipple, followed by the hint of fang. Jesus fuck, he probably shouldn't be as turned-on as he was by Marcus's fangs, but he couldn't deny the way his cock filled at just the touch.

"We shouldn't," he groaned. "The pizza. It'll be here soon."

"You eat the pizza. I'm hungry for something else." Marcus attacked Ethan's belt and pants.

Ethan leaned back on his hands and smiled at Marcus as he worked on pulling Ethan's jeans down to his thighs. "You can't fool me. I know vampires can't survive on cum."

Marcus leaned down and nuzzled Ethan's cock through his cotton boxer briefs. "That's just an appetizer. I'm craving you tonight. I want to christen our bedroom. Make it ours."

Ethan gave up trying to argue or talk any sense into Marcus when his lover freed his cock from his briefs. "Your fangs better be packed away," Ethan warned.

Marcus looked up, smiling broadly at him. Ethan could clearly see the fangs slide away. Yes, Marcus biting him was a major turn-on, but sadly, that turn-on stopped when it came to fangs in his dick.

Lowering his head again, Marcus licked and lightly sucked the head of his cock, teasing him, before finally taking his dick into his mouth. And then Ethan was in heaven. It was the first time Marcus had sucked him, and Ethan was content to lie there and enjoy every touch. But that relaxation ended too quickly as Marcus found his rhythm, driving Ethan toward an orgasm.

"Marcus," he whimpered, trying to warn him that he was going to come soon. Fingers slipped under his sac, massaging his balls and sliding along his perineum. How Marcus always knew the perfect ways to tease and drive him insane was amazing. It was as if his body were the keys of a piano. Marcus was a master at playing him.

"Oh God, please, baby. So close. Please," he begged. He gripped the edge of the dresser, his head tilted as he lightly thrust into Marcus's mouth. Marcus tightened one hand on his hip and sped up his movement on his dick. He was a fucking goner. Ethan shouted and came hard down Marcus's throat.

Ethan collapsed against the dresser, his body spread out like a damn human sacrifice. He shivered as Marcus sucked and licked his cock clean before letting it slide from his mouth. He blinked and looked up to find Marcus leaning over him with a smug smile.

"Pleased with yourself?" Ethan murmured. He was content to lie there for the rest of the night.

"Very. You?"

"Oh, fuck yeah. At least we've got this room christened."

Marcus glanced around as if assessing Ethan's comment. "It'll do for now. We still need to break in the sofa."

Ethan laughed and then made a lame grab for his underwear. He missed and didn't try again. He was in no rush to get dressed. "As big as this house is, at least I know you're not going to get bored with me soon."

Marcus's expression turned dark as he looked at Ethan. "How could I grow bored with you? I told you I love you. Don't you believe me?"

"Of course I believe you. It's not that." Ethan sat up and started pulling his pants back into place, but it was too difficult still seated on the damn dresser. He hadn't meant for this conversation to get so serious. He hopped to his feet and put his clothes to rights again, but it also gave Marcus a chance to move so that he was standing directly in front of Ethan.

"Then tell me. What is bothering you?"

"It's nothing. Something Victoria mentioned. I'm just being neurotic. We should head downstairs. The pizza guy is gonna be here soon."

"The pizza guy can wait. Please tell me what has you neurotic."

Ethan sighed. He leaned against the dresser and kept his eyes on the line of T-shirts Marcus had hung up. They were organized by color as well, touching some hidden part of his heart. "She was telling me that most pets don't last long. Maybe only a couple of years at most. Sounded like most died or were given away to other vampires. That vampires…sort of got bored. I guess it just got stuck in my head."

Marcus stunned him by grabbing his hips and lifting him so that he was seated on the dresser again. He lowered himself just enough that Ethan was forced to meet his direct gaze.

"You are not a pet, Ethan. If I must tell you this every night for the rest of our lives together, then I will, but you will believe me."

"But—"

"There is no 'but' in this argument. I am not going to grow bored with you. I'm not going to give you to another vampire. I'm definitely never going to harm you in such a way that it ends your life. I. Love. You."

"What about when I'm old? Right now, I'm young and sexy. What about when I'm fifty and you still look twentysomething?"

Marcus cocked his head slightly to the side as he stared at Ethan. "Would you like me to change you to a vampire so that you're always this age?"

"What? No! Maybe. I don't know!" Ethan's heart sped up at the question. He hadn't expected Marcus to ask him that. "I'm just afraid you'll get bored in a year or two. Definitely when I start getting wrinkles."

"I will love you no matter how you look."

"Do…do you want me to be a vampire like you?"

For the first time, Marcus lowered his eyes. "I honestly don't know. I've heard of it affecting people differently, and I am a little scared of losing the man I've fallen in love with."

"Like with your mom?"

Marcus shook his head. "I don't think you'd be changed like my mom, but some people take the new power to a dark place. I don't want that happening to you. But I was also speaking to Winter."

"What does your brother say?"

"Winter says if I want to protect you from the violence that could fill our lives soon, I must change you. Vampires heal faster —we can take more of a beating than humans and keep going. If something were to happen, and I couldn't get to you fast enough…"

"I'd have a better chance of surviving if I was a vamp," Ethan finished.

"Yes, but I don't want durability to be your only reason for changing." Marcus cupped the side of Ethan's face with one hand and stared into his eyes. "Eternity is a long time. What if you get bored with me?"

Ethan leaned his head into Marcus's hand and smiled. "I don't believe that's going to happen, but we don't have to decide this tonight, right? We've got time?"

"Yes."

"Then we keep talking about it until we both feel comfortable with a decision."

Marcus leaned in and kissed him deeply. "Very wise," he murmured against Ethan's lips.

Before Ethan could reply, the doorbell chimed through the house. "Good timing. Let's get me some pizza. I need to keep my strength up if I have to keep feeding you."

Marcus chuckled and stepped back so Ethan could hop down to his feet. "It's your own fault you're so delicious."

Ethan laughed and led the way down to the first floor.

∽

MARCUS LOUNGED ON THE SOFA WHILE ETHAN SAT ON THE FLOOR with a pizza box in front of him. His poor man had inhaled half the pizza on his own after the long day they'd put in with the move. He was finally slowing down, but Marcus didn't know if a full stomach or fatigue was the culprit. It wasn't yet midnight and he'd be up for several more hours putting his house to rights, but he first needed to tuck Ethan into bed. At least he'd had the common sense to put sheets on the bed before tackling the closet.

Tossing a bit of uneaten crust into the box, Ethan groaned and dropped his head against Marcus's thigh.

"Are you sure you're not hungry?" Ethan asked. Marcus just smiled at him and Ethan rolled his eyes. "That's right. I forgot. Vampire." Ethan giggled and shook his head. "And you seem so normal most of the time."

"Don't we all."

"Speaking of normal, I forgot to tell you that Ozzie showed up today, knocking at the kitchen window. He hung out for a while and freaked out some of the movers. I gave him some cheese and he left. Do ravens eat cheese?"

Marcus smiled. He reached out and threaded his fingers through Ethan's hair over and over again in a gentle caress that had Ethan sighing against him. He loved this, the freedom to reach out and touch Ethan whenever he wanted and to know that his touch was welcome, encouraged even. He'd waited a lifetime for this simple joy, but then Ethan was worth waiting several lifetimes for. "I think Ozzie eats whatever he wants. Mostly bugs and lizards, but I'm sure he appreciates it. It was a long flight north. But you don't have to worry about feeding him."

Ethan twisted around to look at him over the edge of the sofa cushion. "You don't feed him?"

Marcus shook his head, placing his hand back on his leg. "No. He's happy to fend for himself. I asked Bel about it, and he said that he and Ozzie don't have that kind of relationship."

Confusion clouded Ethan's face for a moment and he opened his mouth to speak, but the words appeared to be stuck. "You say that like...can Bel actually talk to animals? Can you?"

Something in Marcus relaxed a little as he could actually answer Ethan's question with the truth. No more hiding or lies or distractions. It was all out in the open. "Bel can, yes. I can't."

Ethan dropped back against the sofa, his body still twisted sideways a bit so Marcus could see his smile. "That's pretty cool," Ethan murmured before a comfortable silence settled between them again.

Ethan looked over at Marcus, eyes narrowing. "You've been really quiet tonight. What's on your mind?"

"It's just the usual moving stress," Marcus said with a shrug.

"Really? What were you and Winter whispering so earnestly about? Other than changing me into a vampire."

"We weren't whispering."

Ethan turned so that he could give Marcus more than just side-eye. Yeah, his lover didn't believe him in the least, and Marcus could only sigh. He wanted to keep Ethan out of his plans as much as possible in hopes of protecting him, but Ethan wasn't the type to just sit back and be protected. Ethan wanted to be involved, which both warmed and terrified Marcus.

"I was questioning what our grand scheme was," he admitted.

Ethan closed the pizza box and moved up to the sofa, allowing him to more easily meet Marcus's worried gaze. Marcus sat up and folded his hands together between his legs.

"This is the first time I've not known what my future held, my purpose, since becoming a vampire. Before, my drive, the drive for my brothers, was to protect Mother. But she's gone. Now…we're taking down the American Ministry."

"You think that's a bad idea?"

Marcus quickly shook his head. "No, definitely not. They've all been ineffective for too long. These were the same vampires in power when your family was killed. They've allowed too many attacks on other clans. They've looked the other way when both humans and vampires were tortured in the name of amusement. The Ministry has become corrupt and bloated with power. It's time for it to end."

"I don't see a problem," Ethan said. "As someone who suffered under their incompetence, I say get rid of them. Since you can't vote them out, I don't see how you've got any other option."

Marcus spread his hands in front of him. "So, we sow discord among the vampires. They kill each other and most, if not all, of the Ministry seats are cleared. What then? More vampires with the same mentality assume those seats. We're right back to where we were, but with different vampires. No progress. No change. No safety for the clans or humans."

Ethan laid his head against Marcus's shoulder and yawned. "Why can't you and your brothers claim the seats?"

The suggestion did seem quite obvious. "On a council of eleven, we would need six for a majority vote to pass any new laws. Even with Aiden, we number only five." Ethan opened his mouth to comment and Marcus pushed on. "Plus, I know that neither Rafe nor Bel would claim a seat. Rafe has no stomach for ruling and meetings. Bel can't be away from his work."

"Winter?"

"Convinced that his skills are better saved for spying than ruling. That leaves only me and Aiden. My temperament is better suited for it. I think Aiden is as well. But two against nine can't get much done."

"But you talked about making Aiden king?"

Marcus smiled, feeling a tinge of embarrassment heating his cheeks. "Desperate words from angry and hurt children. We love and trust Aiden. He's more than a sire. He'd been a father for myself and my brothers for centuries. We see him as the one person who could change our lives for the better, but I doubt that most in our world would see that. He created Julianna, though not his fault, and then refused to destroy her. Most see that as weakness, not compassion."

Ethan sighed and Marcus looked over at the human, smiling to see his eyes growing heavier.

"Well, the Variks can't be the only vampires who want change. Can't you form an alliance or something? Recruit other powerful vampires who want a little order and safety."

"Trust isn't something vampires are very big on, particularly outside of our own clan."

Ethan's head popped up and he stared up at Marcus. "But you all learn to do it. Most clans aren't made up of siblings like the Variks. That's outsiders being brought in, right?"

"Yes."

"Then you've got to find some vamps worth trusting."

"Good point."

"Thank you," Ethan murmured, settling his head back on Marcus's shoulder.

Marcus would have been content to sit just like that for the rest of the night, but he knew it couldn't be comfortable for Ethan. "Come on, oh wise one. Time for you to go to bed."

Ethan immediately sat upright, his eyes wide. "No! If I go to sleep now, I won't be on your schedule. I'll be up too early."

Marcus pushed to his feet and grabbed Ethan's hand so he could pull his slender lover up as well. Ethan reminded him more of a dancer than a fighter with his long limbs and narrow waist, a body honed by years of hard labor and desperation. Despite the inches of height difference between them, Marcus knew better than to discount Ethan's wiry strength and sheer determination. He would jump into any fight Marcus faced, but Marcus hoped to avoid that as much as possible. Humans were no match for vampires under most circumstances. But those were worries for another time.

"We'll work on getting you on my schedule later. You're exhausted."

"I'm fine."

"I'll lie with you until you fall asleep."

Ethan looked up at him skeptically, but Marcus could see him weakening. He was truly dead on his feet after all the packing, traveling, and organizing. There was a lot more work ahead of them as well between the house and dealing with the Ministry. Ethan needed to be sharp to get through it all.

"Promise?" Ethan asked petulantly.

Marcus laughed and pulled him toward the stairs. In the bedroom, they stripped down to their boxer briefs and stretched out in bed. Ethan rolled onto his side, and Marcus curled his muscular frame around Ethan, soaking in his warmth and instinctively protecting him. There was a dancer's litheness to Ethan that made Marcus more aware of his own lumbering size. But where he'd felt too large and in the way as a human, with Ethan he became a mountain of strength, an impenetrable barrier that kept all threats at bay.

Marcus had thought he'd understood love when it came to dedicating himself to his family, but Ethan showed him a type of love he hadn't been able to imagine. Ethan was the breath in his lungs and the blood in his veins. He was Marcus's joy and sorrow. His tomorrow.

When their conversation in the closet had drifted to transforming Ethan into a vampire, Marcus couldn't deny that the idea excited him. He'd never have to worry about Ethan growing old, getting sick. Most injuries would be shrugged off and quickly healed. As vampires, they would have centuries together. Not a few short decades, if they were lucky.

But such a decision was not to be taken lightly. Ethan would have to feed on other humans. He'd have to give up walks in the sunlight. Humans would hold a new danger if they discovered the truth about him. Vampires would challenge him, try to kill him, because of the clan he belonged to.

And then there was simply eternity stretching endlessly out before them.

Marcus would say nothing to sway Ethan one way or another. If he elected to remain human, Marcus would cherish the time they had together, no matter how short it was.

A soft snore rose from Ethan and Marcus smiled. He'd managed to fall asleep inside of five minutes. Marcus wasn't tired in the least, but he was content to lie there for a while, listening to Ethan snore and feeling his body pressed against his own. He'd never felt this kind of peace before, and he wanted it to be a permanent part of his life. To have that, Ethan needed to be safe.

Marcus ran his teeth over his bottom lip again and again as

Ethan's suggestion played over in his head. He and his brothers couldn't be the only ones who wanted this kind of peace and safety. There had to be others. Alliances could be formed. Promises made. It would be awkward and uncomfortable at first as they learned to trust each other, but it was worth it if it kept Ethan safe.

Very carefully, Marcus extricated himself from Ethan and tucked the blankets around him before silently walking to his office. Sitting down at his desk, he pulled out a single sheet of blank paper and a pen. It took him only a few moments to make a short list of four clan names.

Montgomery
Arsenault
Wagner
Fernández

To his knowledge, each of them had started with a single strong vampire leader who had eschewed the typical power struggles that had formed the Ministry in the first place. These clans kept to themselves and were never linked to the usual battles that ended in piles of bodies.

Marcus felt that he could trust these clans. Form an alliance with these clans within the Americas. With them, he could feel that he'd be able to get some justice for Julianna and Ethan's family. It wasn't enough to claim the blood of the vampires who slaughtered them. Marcus needed to change the rulers that allowed such a thing to happen. He needed to make sure others would not suffer the same loss they did.

He quickly dipped back into the bedroom and pulled his cell phone off the charger. He texted his brothers the four clan names. They had a starting point for after the dust settled. He had a plan.

CHAPTER TWENTY-FIVE

Marcus glared at the collar shining around Ethan's neck. It wasn't as visible as it had been at Winslow's house. Tonight, he'd asked Ethan to wear a new suit he'd had made for him. It had arrived that morning and fit him perfectly. The dark-navy jacket and slacks against the white button-down shirt only seemed to set off the damn collar rather than make it less noticeable.

Or maybe it was just him. He would have preferred Ethan wear a nice tie with an interesting design.

Yet, the moment he walked into the Montgomery clan house, they would know he wasn't a vampire. It wasn't something that Marcus could clearly explain. When out in the world surrounded by humans, he didn't sense anything at all.

When he was in a house of vampires and one lone human walked in, it was like those predatory instincts slammed into overdrive. Fangs ached and his pulsed kicked up a tiny bit, beckoning him to hunt. To feed.

The collar put common sense back in the driver's seat. Usually. It was a sign that the human belonged to someone. No biting unless invited. And Marcus would be damned if another set of fangs were getting anywhere close to Ethan.

"Don't glare at me like that," Ethan said in a huffy tone. "You're the one that declared we were wearing straitjackets. I do have a pair of jeans without holes and a nice sweater."

Marcus wiped away his dark look. "You look incredibly handsome."

"But...?"

Reaching up, Marcus ran his finger along the collar, the tip bumping along the priceless gems.

"I'm not a pet," Ethan reminded him. There was a sweet patience to his voice that made Marcus wonder how many more times they'd have this conversation in their lives together.

"But others will think—"

Ethan stepped into Marcus, lightly gripping the lapels of his jacket. "I don't care what others think. Let them think I'm a pet. Let them imagine me naked on my hands and knees, eager to fulfill your every wish. Let them be jealous." Ethan paused, his smile so wonderfully dirty. "They don't need to know I'm the center of your universe or that my idea of a perfect night is leaning my head on your shoulder while you play the piano. Even if my butt does go numb on the hard bench."

Marcus brushed a kiss against Ethan's temple, starting to feel a little lighter. "I'll order a padded bench for your poor rear end."

"Good. You need to take care of my rear end."

Before Marcus could reply about how he planned to take very good care of Ethan's sweet ass, a loud crash echoed up from the first floor. Whatever made the noise was powerful enough to rock the house slightly, causing Ethan to reach for the closet doorframe.

"Stay here," Marcus commanded, pointing at Ethan before he ran from the room. He hurried into the hall, which was filling with smoke. Through the gray cloud of smoke, he could make out shapes. People were pouring into his house. Again.

Bastards were attacking his house again!

How could they have found him already?

A soft coughing drew his attention from the hallway to Ethan leaning over the railing next to him, waving the smoke from his face.

Oh God, he had to get Ethan out of the house! Just standing there, he'd counted at least six people. They were horribly outnumbered, and he had no way of getting any of his brothers to his house in time to help. They were completely alone.

Roughly grabbing Ethan's arm, Marcus's pulled him down the hallway toward the back staircase. "You have to get out of here now."

"What? I'm not leaving you."

"You have to. We're outnumbered. You have to head directly to Bel's house. Do you have your phone on you?"

Ethan tried to dig his heels into the carpet to stop their progress, but Marcus was stronger and far more determined. "Yes, but I'm not leaving you alone."

"I can't win against them. We can't." Marcus stopped at the staircase and gripped both of Ethan's shoulders tightly in his hands. "I am going to die tonight trying to keep them from getting their hands on you."

"Marcus, no!"

"If you escape, I'll simply act as a diversion. Stall them. If you get to Bel, you can come up with a plan to rescue me."

Marcus watched Ethan's face for the first sign of him wavering and took it. They couldn't hesitate any longer. Marcus released Ethan and started silently down the stairs.

"Go directly for the Porsche. The keys are in the glove compartment," Marcus instructed in a whisper before reaching the last stair. "If I escape, I'll go to Bel's."

But Marcus didn't plan to escape. The only way to escape

was killing every last bastard in his home and he knew his odds were too slim for that. Besides, capture was the only way to discover who was behind these attempts on his life and the lives of his brothers. He wanted to get to the truth at last.

The kitchen was lit by only a work light over the stove, but it was enough to see that the attackers hadn't reached that room yet. Thank God the house was so damn big. They were likely checking the front rooms and the second floor still.

He looked over his shoulder to see Ethan hesitating, worry filling his eyes. Marcus gave him a confident nod and pointed for the door that led to the garage. Ethan nodded sharply in return and started for the garage.

Clinging to the idea that Ethan would be able to escape in one piece, Marcus paused at the butcher block long enough to pull out a chef's knife. He prayed the damn thing was sharp. Heaven knew he didn't cook much and couldn't remember if he'd ever held the thing before—let alone used it on a side of meat.

Marcus took one step toward the kitchen doorway and stopped when a large vampire stepped into the opening, a broad smile spreading across his face.

"Zale," Marcus growled. That answered his main question far faster than he'd expected. Zale was a loyal foot soldier of the Black Wolf clan. He worshiped its clan head, Minerva, and followed her without question.

Marcus's only question was why the Black Wolf clan had decided to strike against his family. They might not have seen eye to eye over the centuries, but they'd managed to steer clear of each other.

"Marcus," Zale said in an almost taunting tone. "Trying to make a run for it?"

"No, just arming myself. You have no business in my lair. Get out now while you still have your life."

Zale ignored him, looking around the kitchen as he took a

step inside. "Where's that new pet of yours? We were hoping to play with him for a bit before we kill him." His smile widened when his eyes caught on the open door to the garage.

Marcus lunged at him, swinging the knife at his throat. He would not let Zale or any of the others from his clan anywhere near Ethan.

Zale caught his wrist before the blade could kiss his flesh and he laughed. "You're gonna have to be faster than that."

Marcus opened his hand and dropped the knife into the hand waiting at Zale's stomach. Zale couldn't release Marcus's wrist fast enough to back away. Marcus jammed the blade deep into Zale's gut and then ripped it upward, slicing through sinew and organs. He stopped only when he met the breastplate. Zale gasped and choked on blood, his body frozen in what was likely shock and pain. Jerking the blade free, Marcus finished the job by slicing across his throat, severing critical arteries and the windpipe. Zale would not be healing from those wounds tonight or any night.

With a hard shove, Marcus pushed Zale to the floor where he landed in a blood-spewing, twitching heap.

One down, so fucking many to go.

At least he knew his knife was sharp.

Marcus started to bend down and check Zale for other weapons, but the sound of approaching footsteps had him turning away. He needed to get out of the kitchen and help put some more distance between him and Ethan if his lover was to have a shot at escaping.

In the hall, he was met with another vampire. Bullets peppered his wall, throwing up a bit of drywall as they hit. He dove at the shooter, taking two in the shoulder before reaching him. He hissed in pain but focused on driving the knife into the creature's heart.

The damn handle was growing slick with blood and his hand was threatening to slip down to the blade. The kitchen knife wasn't made for this kind of work, but it had saved him twice now, so he couldn't complain.

As the vampire lay bleeding out from the chest and neck, Marcus grabbed up the gun the vampire had been using. There wasn't time to check the magazine. The damn thing could have five bullets, or it could have none. He hadn't been counting when the idiot starting shooting at him.

Pain throbbed in his shoulder, but he was only vaguely aware of it while he tried to figure out how much time had passed since Ethan had disappeared into the garage. Two minutes? Four? He had to be on the road. Bel's house was less than fifteen minutes away in light traffic. He just needed to keep them busy that long. It would be enough to give Ethan and Bel a head start.

Attackers were swarming on him faster now that he'd reached the main foyer. Two vampires were on him in the blink of an eye. He fired the gun, hitting one in the head, throwing him against the wall, while the other jumped on his back, fangs digging deep into his neck. He screamed and threw the woman off him, but she took a chunk of flesh with her as she flew across the room. He could feel the blood pouring down his throat and soaking into his dress shirt.

Pain exploded across the back of his head, and Marcus found himself on his knees. There was a clatter of noise and he looked down. Both the knife and gun had fallen from his hands, but he couldn't remember releasing them. Someone had hit him with something. Maybe a hammer. *Fuck*. His brain felt like it was trying to ooze out of his skull.

He blinked, trying to get his eyes to focus. Another vampire he didn't recognize walked up and kicked him in the stomach. The new pain had Marcus falling forward, barely catching himself as his hand sunk into the blood-soaked Persian rug. *Damn.* He'd always liked that rug and now it was ruined.

"Get the fucking manacles on him!" someone bellowed.

Marcus tried to sit up, but his head was spinning and his stomach ached so badly he was sure he was going to retch, but it would be blood and he couldn't afford to lose more of it than he already had.

Metal chains clinked together, the sounds growing closer and closer. The person behind him grabbed one wrist and jerked it behind his back. Marcus tried to fight, but there was too much pain and his body was starting to feel listless and heavy.

A knife was pressed to his throat as a metal bracelet clamped down around his wrist.

"Behave yourself. We've got to get you home alive for the party." The vampire holding the knife had green hair and was smiling at him like he was the best present she'd ever received.

"Fuck off," Marcus grumbled.

His other arm was pulled behind him, forcing Marcus upright as it was secured as well.

His vision swam, but he forced his eyes to focus on the man walking through the remains of his front door. He had to blink a few times, but his first instinct was right. It was a man. Not a vampire. There was no collar around his neck, but he was working with the Black Wolf clan.

That didn't make sense.

That clan hated humans. They viewed humans as food only. Not pets. Not comrades. Not friends.

The man was older with graying hair sprinkled in his brown buzz cut. Lines crisscrossed his face from what Marcus would guess was a life lived hard. Walking over to Marcus, he stopped a few feet away and leaned down with his hands behind his back. He was at eye level and all Marcus saw was raw hatred.

"I can see what that faggoty bitch saw in you. Guess he never really stood a chance," the intruder muttered before he straightened.

"What? Who?" Marcus barely managed.

He didn't pay him any attention as he looked over at Marcus's captors. "Did you get the boy too?"

"We're still searching the rooms, but it looks like one of the cars is missing. He might have gotten out. Run to one of the other brothers."

The newcomer scowled for a moment and then looked at Marcus, a malicious grin spreading across his face. "That's fine. Let him run. There's only one brother left to capture, and he's going to be the easiest of the four. And I just can't wait to see Ethan again."

Marcus's brain was sluggish, but there were still enough brain cells firing to finally place the man's words with his face. "Carl?" It was the bastard Ethan had told him about. The one who'd hit him.

Carl laughed, the sound harsh and ugly as it grated over Marcus's ears. "Quite the mindfuck, isn't it? I hope Ethan appreciates the surprise. It certainly won't be the last one tonight."

Marcus wanted to threaten this fucker. To threaten all of them to keep their hands off Ethan, but something heavy hit him in the head again. This time unconsciousness swallowed him whole, carrying him at least briefly away from the pain and his worries of whether Ethan made it safely to Bel's house.

Before he drifted completely away, he had at least one secret to cling to. Beltran Varik was far from the easiest of the brothers to capture. These assholes were in for a very serious surprise as well.

CHAPTER TWENTY-SIX

*E*than was shaking when he pulled up to the strangely modern house with lots of fucking windows. It looked like the last place a person would find a vampire. The building struck Ethan as more to Rafe's taste than what he'd expect from Bel. But then Rafe was all about defiance, even of his own nature. He would not be stopped by a severe allergy to the sun.

For Bel, Ethan wondered if it was more about camouflage.

Fuck, he didn't care. As long as he was safely at the house of one of Marcus's brothers. Stumbling out of the car, Ethan ran to the front door and pounded on it. His heart was racing in his chest. He hated leaving Marcus, but he could only hope that he and Bel could get a hold of Winter and Rafe. Maybe even find Aiden. They could form a fucking posse or something to rescue Marcus.

The door was suddenly jerked open, and he was greeted with a frazzled looking Bel on the other side. His blue eyes swept over Ethan and then past him.

"Where—"

"They got him! Those motherfuckers attacked the house and they got him!" Ethan burst out.

Bel grabbed Ethan's arm and roughly pulled him into the house before slamming the door shut again. Bel turned to Ethan, his expression intense. "Who grabbed him?"

"Marcus called one of them Zale. There were so many vampires. They just sort of flooded the house." Ethan shook his head. "He made me run. He kept fighting them and he was screaming for me to run."

"You did the right thing, but you've got to help me." Bel released him and jogged through the house with Ethan following on his heels. Ethan didn't see much of Bel's home. The rooms they passed by seemed to be filled with boxes even though Bel had been in his new place for close to two weeks.

At the back of the house, Bel reached a room and waved for Ethan to quickly follow. When Ethan stepped into what turned out to be a lab, Bel placed his hand against an electronic panel. A thick metal door slid into place. There were the sounds of other metal plates slamming down around the house.

"Holy shit! Did you turn your lab into a panic room?" Ethan said. He turned around, taking in the long table loaded with glassware, microscopes, burners, and equipment he couldn't even begin to name. It looked a hell of a lot like those labs from the CSI shows he would occasionally watch.

"The Ministry has been against my work almost as long as I've been a vampire," Bel grumbled. "They keep perpetuating this myth that we're some kind of magical beings, and it's utter bullshit. They're afraid that if I find a way to treat vampirism like a disease, they'll have to actually act like civilized creatures instead of mini gods. Every time we move, I have to reinforce my house, especially my lab. I've always been sure that one day they'd just attack."

Ethan gave Bel a wobbly smile. "Marcus has had his hands full with his family. Rafe the rebel. Bel the mad scientist."

Bel sighed heavily and nodded. "And then Julianna."

"I'm sorry."

"No, you're right. Marcus has always been the calm, collected go-between for our family and the Ministry, keeping us all from being executed for treason or whatever the hell they wanted to call it." Bel rushed around the large table in the center of the room. He was picking up things and shoving them into his pockets.

"And he ends up with a guy who claims to love him but abandons him."

"Ethan, those were vampires. You were not equipped to deal with them. If you had stayed, you would have put Marcus in even more danger. We both know he'd do anything to save you." Bel held up a matte black handgun and gave Ethan a smile that was wicked to its very core. "I say we equip you better."

Ethan slowly walked around the table and came to stand next to Bel. He watched as the vampire pulled on a pair of latex gloves before he started shoving bullets into a magazine. "What...what are you talking about?"

"I made a discovery quite by accident, not that the Ministry would believe that," he muttered at the end. "I've designed a formula that attacks the blood. Specifically, vampire blood. It spreads very quickly through the blood...and well, the end result is that it turns the blood in the vampire to an acidic goo. Quite disgusting."

"Wow, that's an insane discovery."

He wrinkled his nose as he finished loading the magazine and shoved it into the butt of the gun. "I've coated the bullets with the substance. There are ten in the magazine and one in the chamber already. I've also got a spare magazine. That's twenty-one bullets. The good thing is that I think this would be most effective if you hit center mass." He turned toward Ethan and held out the gun. "You do know how to use this thing, right?"

"Are you just assuming that all humans know how to use a gun?"

"Pretty much."

Ethan groaned and took the gun from Bel. "You're lucky one of my foster fathers was big into guns. Took me to the shooting range when I was a teen. Thought it would keep me out of trouble."

"Never warned you against vampires, did he?"

"Yeah, for some reason, it never seemed to come up." Ethan checked that the safety was in place before snatching up the spare magazine and shoving it into his pocket. He was still in the damn suit when he'd much rather be in jeans and a T-shirt. "So, what's the plan? Do you have any idea who this Zale is? Where he might take Marcus? Do we even know if Marcus is still alive?"

"I know he is," Bel said firmly. He grabbed his cell phone and a set of keys off the table. "I got this text from Rafe just a couple of minutes before you arrived on my doorstep." He held up the phone and Ethan only saw "Williwaw" typed there.

"What the fuck does that mean?"

"It's the name of a cold, stormy wind that blows down through the Alaskan mountains. It means trouble. Run."

"You and Rafe have a secret code?"

"Most of the time he just sends me 'Zephyr,' which is a light and playful breeze. That means he's gone to wander for a bit. Don't worry. But when Williwaw came up, I knew Rafe had been attacked. I'd been pulling my things together when you arrived, so I'm guessing they are going after all of us. Assuming they've got Rafe and Marcus, I believe they will keep them alive until they have me and Winter."

Returning to the electronic panel, Bel typed something in and a panel in the wall across the room slid open. Ethan walked over to it to find a ladder leading downward into total darkness.

"Who the fuck *are* you?" Ethan demanded. "Why doesn't Marcus's house have all this cool shit?"

"Because Marcus didn't spend ten years building his house.

Start going down. Lights will kick in when you reach the bottom, I swear."

Shoving the gun into the pocket of his jacket, Ethan took a fortifying breath and gripped the metal ladder. It was cool to the touch but solid. He kept his eyes straight ahead as he started descending, cursing himself the entire way for ever believing that Bel was the boring one. There was no "boring one" in the Varik clan. Sure, Marcus was the most straitlaced and normal-appearing but get him behind a closed door, and the vampire was sexually insatiable.

And absentminded professor Beltran with his cello and distracted gaze had a secret escape tunnel and blood-destroying bullets. Why not?

As Bel had predicted, lights flickered on near the floor when Ethan reached the bottom two rungs of the ladder. The hard soles of his shoes hit the concrete floor, the resulting sound echoing through the open space. He stepped back and looked up to see Bel climbing down the ladder. He was still wearing his white lab coat, which only made Ethan smile.

"I've got a car this way," Bel said, motioning down what looked to be a long, narrow tunnel. "We have to assume that Winter has already been grabbed. I haven't been able to reach him, and he seems to think that Aiden is in Europe."

"So, we're on our own," Ethan murmured.

"Not quite. We still have Rafe's friends."

Ethan kept his mouth shut. He didn't know what to expect when it came to Rafe's friends. His first thought was that they were a bunch of lazy, fun-seekers who took nothing seriously and certainly wouldn't know how to handle themselves in a fight.

But then, he didn't expect Bel to have a secret tunnel or weapons. It didn't matter to him. If it got Marcus safe and sound and back in his arms, he didn't care if they invited a bunch of Navy SEALs to the party.

An hour after escaping Marcus's house, Ethan found himself pulling up in front of a...yarn store. Ethan rubbed his eyes and blinked a couple of times, but the vision didn't change. It was a large boxy building with the big sign in pink script that read, Knitters' Paradise.

"You're fucking with me," Ethan said, ending the silence that had stretched in the car.

"What?"

"I thought we were meeting with Rafe's friends. The same Rafe who owns nightclubs and spends his evenings drinking and fucking. You just pulled up in front of a craft store."

Bel gave a little shake of his head. "I couldn't go to Rafe's club. It's the first place they'd look for us."

Killing the engine, Bel got out of the car and Ethan had no choice but to follow. God, it was like Marcus had slipped him something with his dinner and he'd fallen down Alice's drug-induced rabbit hole. Bel raised his hand to knock on the glass door, but someone was already there unlocking it. They were both waved inside, and the door was closed behind them.

Ethan glanced at the woman dressed in leather and chains like she'd stepped out of some sub's wet dream. He wasn't sure if she was dressed for a night out or a rescue. Guess it really didn't matter.

"Ethan, this is Lola. An old friend of Rafe's," Bel introduced. "She moves with Rafe and is his partner in the nightclubs."

"You're a Varik, then," Ethan said, extending his hand to her.

Her beautifully arched eyebrows lifted nearly to her hairline and she slowly took Ethan's hand. "If Rafe ever asked me, I would be. You're Marcus's not-pet pet."

"Boyfriend also works," Ethan said with a smirk.

They continued into the dark store past aisles of different types of colored yarns, needles, hooks, pattern books, artificial flowers, and fabric. It definitely looked like a crafters' paradise. At the rear of the store, there was a long table that was probably used to cut fabric. Four other people were standing around, watching them approach.

Introductions were made, though Ethan didn't catch all the names. Including Lola, there were two women and three men prepared to rescue Marcus and his brothers. But he did take notice that one of them had the name Arsenault. Marcus had mentioned them recently as a clan that could help with bringing a more peaceful order to the vampire world. He was hopeful that his assistance meant that they were open to Marcus's initial overtures.

On the table, Ethan found what looked to be blueprints for a very large house and grounds.

"I was just telling them that I saw that useless bitch Roland with the group that dragged out Rafe," Lola spat.

"Ethan said that Marcus called one of them Zale. It confirms that this strike was headed up by the Black Wolf clan," Bel said and then looked over at Ethan. "They've argued for the death of one or more of my family on several occasions over the years. They've accumulated a great deal of wealth over the centuries and seem to believe that it alone is enough to buy their wishes on the Ministry."

"And when it didn't, what? They started killing off members?"

"Quite possibly."

"Have you heard from Winter?" Lola asked.

Bel shook his head. "Nothing. But we can't wait. If Winter is still free, he'll be working his own angle and will possibly join us later."

"Tonight, we get Marcus and Rafe, and we end the Black Wolves," Arsenault snarled. From his bloodthirsty tone, Ethan was willing to guess that the Arsenault clan had suffered their own run-ins with the Black Wolf clan.

Ethan wasn't sure Marcus would approve of the scorched-earth approach this vampire was planning, but Ethan wasn't going to argue with him. They were very likely outnumbered and heading into hostile territory. These bastards had taken the man he loved, and Ethan was willing to do whatever it took to get his lover back in one piece.

CHAPTER TWENTY-SEVEN

Marcus awoke in a large open room with no windows. His hands were still manacled behind his back. Pain throbbed and ached through every part of his body. He was so damn thirsty. He needed to fucking feed. To grab two or three humans and just drain them. He'd lost too much blood. As he shifted, he could feel it crusted on his neck. His shirt was stiff and sticking to his skin from where it had soaked up his blood.

"Marcus! Marcus!" The voice kept repeating his name in a low, harsh whisper. He blinked his sandpaper-coated eyes and tried to look around, but he couldn't see anyone. At least there were no guards in front of him.

"Goddamn it, Marcus! Say something."

Marcus almost smiled. This time he could clearly tell who the grouchy speaker was. Rafe.

"I'm awake," Marcus grumbled. His voice sounded as if his throat had been rubbed raw by the same sandpaper that had left his eyes sore and gritty. Fuck, he felt like hell. "Where are we? How long have we been here?"

"I'm guessing the Black Wolf clan house," Rafe murmured.

"They dropped you off at least an hour ago. They must have hit you damn hard. Your hair is soaked with blood."

"Winter? Have you heard—"

"I'm here, Marcus," Winter said, his voice weary and full of disgust.

"Bel?"

"Not yet," Rafe said in what sounded like a mix of pride and fear.

Groaning softly, Marcus pulled his knees up under his body and pushed against the floor with his uninjured shoulder. It was slow going, but he finally managed to get himself into an upright position. The room swayed for a moment, and Marcus sucked in several deep breaths through clenched teeth while focusing on a clump of dirt on the concrete floor.

When the nausea finally subsided enough that he wasn't in danger of spilling the contents of his stomach, Marcus slowly looked around. Just over his shoulder, he found Rafe manacled to the wall. Blood covered one side of his face in a grisly mask while more blood soaked through his pants on his left thigh. Winter was seated on the floor, his hands bound in front of him with the same thick steel manacles, but his were chained to the floor with what looked to be a heavy steel bolt.

The entire room stank of old blood, urine, and sweat. Lovely. The Black Wolf clan had their own torture chamber.

"Ethan?" Winter asked softly. The one-word question was fearful, as if his baby brother didn't want to cause him more pain.

"Escaped. Sent him to Bel."

"Good," Rafe said. "Now that we've determined who our rescuers are, maybe we should do something about making their job a little bit easier."

"Really, Rafe?" Winter snapped. "You didn't want to hang around and see if they were going to offer room service? Maybe a massage?"

"Fuck you—"

"Enough!" Marcus snarled at his brothers and then groaned as fresh pain washed through his skull. God, he needed to feed to get rid of some of the throbbing in his skull. It was muddling up his thoughts, making it so damn hard to concentrate. For now, he didn't want to think about Ethan and whether he made it safely to Bel's. Didn't want to think about whether they both escaped the bastards that had gone after Bel. He had to cling to the idea that his brother and his lover were safe and plotting to save them.

Before he could say anything else, there was a metal scraping at the far side of the room, like a bolt was being slid back. A door creaked loudly on its hinges, and hard-soled shoes clomped across the cold concrete floor. There were others following behind the leader, but Marcus was focused on the footsteps of the authority figure. It had to be Minerva.

The newcomers appeared from around a corner, and at the head of the little pack was a tall, lanky woman with long brown hair. Her thin-lipped mouth was an ugly gash across her mouth. Even when she was smiling, it looked like it was more of a pained grimace.

"You're finally awake," Minerva announced, throwing her hands out as if she were welcoming him into her parlor rather than her torture chamber.

"What the hell are you doing, Minerva?"

She cackled, the sound bouncing wildly off the stone walls. "I thought that would be obvious." Stopping just a few feet away from Marcus, she bent down. The neck of her blouse gaped, giving him an unnecessarily clear view of her breasts right in front of his face. He gritted his teeth and kept his eyes on her face. Even if he wasn't a gay man, he was sure he wouldn't find a damn thing appealing about her.

Her long, lean face was full of harsh angles, and her skin was pulled tight over her skull. There was something about her that made Marcus think she always looked half-starved. It made him wonder if that had been her unfortunate lot in life as a human before some vampire finally took pity on her. As a vampire, food was always easy to find.

Even now, there was a smear of blood around one corner of her mouth as if she'd fed just before coming down to taunt Marcus and his brothers.

"Haven't you figured it out?" she teased. "I'm taking over."

"Bullshit."

"Really? Isn't that exactly what you and your annoying brothers were planning when you started those rumors with Winslow?"

She straightened and snapped her fingers over his shoulder. One of her little flunkies darted away for a moment and then came running back with a folding chair in hand. He carefully placed it in front of Marcus and Minerva sat.

"I'll give you this—it wasn't a bad plan. Winslow immediately went running, spreading the stories you and your little pet started. Thanks to you both, Winslow and Robert are dead. That's five of the eleven dead now. Only six more to go."

"What? You plan to kill all of the Ministry?"

"I plan to destroy all of the Ministry!" she shouted, shooting straight to her feet to tower over Marcus. "They are a useless waste who value only wealth and privilege. They've done nothing to protect or lead our people. We've floundered for centuries, forced to remain in the shadows when we should be ruling this planet."

Flopping down in the seat, her legs spread wide, Minerva glared at Marcus. She lifted a booted foot and pressed her heel into one of the gunshot wounds in his shoulder. Marcus tried to clamp his mouth shut, but the pain was excruciating, and he was forced to cry out. Only then did Minerva relent, putting her boot on the floor with a heavy thud.

"I don't understand your attack on my family," Marcus said between pants. "If anything, we've helped you."

"Except for the fact that the Variks represent the very worst of our people," Minerva snarled. Leaning forward, she grabbed Marcus's face by his jaw, her long nails digging into his cheeks. "Rafe tells humans that he's a vampire. He makes us into a joke for humans to laugh at as he fucks them and drinks himself into oblivion."

"I celebrate that I'm a vampire. I don't hide who I am!" Rafe said proudly.

Minerva rolled her eyes before she looked over her shoulder at one of her minions. With a little jerk of her head, he walked over and delivered a series of blows. Rafe's pained cries echoed through the room and Marcus strained against his chains, desperate to grab her, to stop the man hurting his brother. But there was no escape.

"And he's just the tip of the iceberg," Minerva continued when the only sounds were Rafe's labored breaths. "His annoying twin seems to think that we need curing. His experiments are going to destroy us."

"Afraid he isn't going to share his discoveries with you?" Rafe taunted and Marcus flinched. Rafe really didn't know when to keep his mouth shut.

Luckily Minerva chose to ignore him this time. "And then that fucking mother of yours. Her madness made us all look bad. Protecting your stupid human. Attacking her own clan. She should have been destroyed centuries ago instead of protected and coddled."

"Julianna's condition was not her fault."

"Too bad. Vampires are the pinnacle of evolution. We are perfection and we should always embrace that perfection. We are not a joke for humans. We are not madness. We are not something to be cured. And we most certainly don't protect and hide those weaknesses." Her glare sharpened on Marcus. "You're the worst of them all. Time and again you've gone before the Ministry, protecting your worthless clan, making excuses for them, making promises that will never be kept. Each of them should have been executed a hundred times over, but you've negotiated, promised, cajoled, and bribed our so-called leaders into looking the other way when it came to the Variks."

Minerva shoved Marcus away from her, forcing him to rock back. Marcus struggled with his balance but managed to stay upright and on his knees. She wiped her hand on her black pants as if he'd somehow tainted her.

"The only one of you that isn't an utter waste of flesh is Winter. The clan's personal spy, collecting secrets on everyone, except for the Black Wolf clan."

"No need," Winter muttered. "We all know that the clan is insane and beneath the notice of others."

Minerva screamed as she launched herself at Winter, her hands wrapping around his throat as they both tumbled to the ground. They struggled for a moment, writhing together, before she shoved away from him and climbed to her feet. Marcus twisted around to find Winter still lying on his side, his breathing heavy. Marcus wasn't sure what his initial injuries were, but there were fresh cuts on his face and neck from Minerva's long nails.

"You talk about weakness of the Ministry and weakness of the Variks, but you're the one who is working with humans to take down your own kind," Marcus snarled, trying to draw her attention to him.

Minerva laughed again and dropped down in the metal folding chair in front of him. "What better spies are there than humans?" she mocked.

Marcus knew that she was referring to Ethan and his initial role as a spy in Marcus's house, but he believed Ethan when he said that he told the League leader nothing about Marcus and his family they didn't already know. Marcus trusted Ethan. Would never doubt him.

"But you're right. Humans are weak. They are needlessly cruel to each other. So petty and vindictive. And so very easily manipulated." Minerva rested her elbows on her knees as she leaned forward. "They outnumber us by more than two thousand to one. Why not use such an army to cull the weak from our own ranks? I would rather waste a hundred human lives than one vampire life on a member of your family."

"Why would they follow you if you're only leading them to slaughter?"

A soft giggle slipped from her and it was more frightening than her rages. "All I need to do is give them some weapons and a little armor. They believe they have a chance at winning. I know they believe that if they assist me, play like they're the good follower, they will get close enough that they will one day be able to kill me." She sat in her chair again and folded her arms over her chest, a smug smile twisting on her lips. "Isn't that right, Carl?"

There was a slow shuffling in the little crowd wrapping around Minerva's back. The vampires parted after a moment and the man Marcus had seen in his own house shambled forward, looking as if he was perfectly balanced on the threshold of life and death. There were several fresh bite marks on his throat. His shirt had been torn at the collar and down the front. There were more bite marks on his chest.

Minerva had handed Carl over to her clan to feed off. When he'd been taken right to the edge of death, he'd been given enough of her blood to hold him in the land of the living but not enough to transform him into a vampire. He was little more than a mindless husk, existing to follow her every instruction regardless of what it was. Movie zombies had more autonomy and drive. If she never spoke to him again, he would remain standing in a room until his body finally decayed into nothingness.

The creation of husks was highly illegal, banned by every vampire ministry for centuries. It was the first one Marcus had ever seen, and he prayed that he never looked on another. It was cruel. He had no idea if any of Carl's consciousness remained in his brain, but his existence had to be the worst kind of torture. The man deserved death, not an eternity of shambling servitude.

If Minerva succeeded in getting rid of the Ministry and claiming power for herself, it was clear that Carl represented a good slice of the world she planned to create.

"Humans are pets. Servants. They are meant to be food for us. Nothing more." Minerva smiled at Marcus. "I will see to it that vampires not only claim their spot at the top of the food chain, but that humans understand that they are at the bottom."

"But you just said they outnumber us—"

"Fear and manipulation are all I need. We will remake the world into a utopia for vampires." Minerva stuck out her bottom lip, giving him a false look of sadness. "But you and your clan won't be around for it. You'll be taken care of as soon as we collect that final brother of yours."

"You're not going to find Bel," Rafe growled. "You'll never find him."

Minerva laughed and stood. She gave a little shake of her head before turning to stroll toward the door she'd entered through. "He's proving to be trickier than we expected, but we'll find him. I'll put a thousand husks on his trail if I have to. I'll get that little pet as well. Turns out he's some unfinished business for me. And I so hate leaving loose ends."

Marcus bit his tongue, wanting to demand what she was talking about with Ethan, but he trapped the question behind his teeth. It was better if he didn't draw her back into the room. He kneeled on the concrete, his knees aching, as he watched all her little minions follow Minerva. Carl brought up the rear, his shoes scraping along the floor with each slow step.

When the door was closed and the bolt slid back into place, Marcus started to count to one hundred. He wanted to give enough time for any of her minions to wander away. Sure as he could be that they were finally alone, Marcus turned as best as he could to look at Winter and Rafe.

"Well, she's a fucking nut job," Rafe muttered.

Marcus couldn't argue that point. Minerva had gone off the deep end, but that wasn't his main concern. "What did she mean by that comment about Ethan? How is he unfinished business?"

Winter sighed. He still lay on his side, his hands pulled down between his bent knees thanks to the short chain bolted to the floor. "Minerva is the one who murdered his family. She and a handful of her clan slaughtered everyone in that apartment building. I'd just uncovered it when she attacked my house."

"Fuck," Marcus whispered. "How was she not brought up before the Ministry? She should have been executed for such a thing. It endangers all of us. Could have led to discovery."

"I would imagine that she got out of execution the same way you've been protecting our family for years," Rafe said with a half smile. "The Black Wolf clan isn't an impoverished clan. Enough money and the Ministry would have looked the other way."

"There is one good thing about crazy people," Winter said. He groaned a little as he pushed himself into an upright position. Sweat glistened on his forehead in the low light despite the coolness of the room. Marcus was willing to wager that it was from pain snaking through his brother's body.

"Really? Because I can't think of any," Rafe mumbled.

"Get them to fly into a fit of rage, and they tend to not notice things going missing. You know…things like keys." There was a soft jingle as Winter opened some of the fingers on his right hand to reveal a ring of keys.

Holy fuck, he'd picked Minerva's pocket while she attacked him!

Marcus and Rafe laughed softly for a moment. They still had an uphill battle ahead of them, but it was at least a little easier if they weren't manacled.

At Winter's instruction, Marcus inched closer to him, presenting his hands to Winter. It was slow going as Winter tried one key after another in the lock, but he finally located the right one, freeing Marcus. Taking the keys from Winter, Marcus freed his brothers as silently as possible.

"What's our next step? If I know Bel, he's already on his way," Rafe asked. He was leaning heavily against the wall, rubbing his wrists, while Winter remained seated on the floor. At the very least, he looked as if he'd found a more comfortable position. They were all in horrible shape. Marcus's legs were trembling where he stood, threatening to collapse before they could even make it to the door. They weren't going to be much use in a fight if they didn't feed soon.

But that wasn't even their first problem. They still had to get out of this torture chamber, and it sounded like Minerva's keys weren't going to do much good against a slide bolt.

"Do you have any idea what Bel's plan might be?" Winter asked.

"Probably grab whatever wicked shit he's cooked up in his lab and storm the house. Well, that's assuming he could even figure out who attacked us." Rafe dropped his head against the wall and swore softly. "Bel," he whispered. "Please, run. Just fucking run."

"He's not," Marcus said.

Rafe blinked back tears and flashed Marcus a crooked smile. "I know." It was a hard thing. They all wanted Bel to escape and be safe, but they knew he wouldn't leave them. It was both touching and terrifying.

Winter pressed his hands to the floor and carefully pushed

to his feet. He swayed for a moment, putting his hand quickly against the wall to steady himself. "Do you think Ethan reached him?"

"Yes." Marcus didn't hesitate. He had to believe that Ethan reached Bel in time. He had to believe that his lover was safely in his brother's hands, or he'd lose all hope. He couldn't think of Ethan injured and dying somewhere. The only reassuring thing was that he was not in Minerva's hands.

"Guess you're wishing you'd listened to me when I told you to change his sexy ass when you had the chance," Rafe grumbled.

Marcus shook his head and was instantly relieved that it didn't make the pounding in his skull worse. "No. It has to be something he wants."

"Yeah, but I'm sure he didn't imagine something like this happening. Bet he'd want it now."

"Don't know. Don't care." He looked over at his brother and smiled. "I love him, Rafe. And I'll always love him, whether he's a human or a vampire. That's never going to change."

"Fantastic. When we get out of this, you can swap out that stupid collar for a wedding ring," Winter grumbled. He pushed off the wall and took what looked like some pained steps toward the door.

"Go to hell. That collar is fucking gorgeous," Rafe said, following Winter.

Marcus couldn't believe it, but he was smiling as he followed Rafe and Winter. His body hurt, and he was moving like an old man. They had little chance of escaping Minerva's house without a lot of help. But he couldn't stop his smile. He had his brothers, his family, with him. And soon, he was sure Bel and Ethan would be with them as well.

"You think Minerva is kind enough to have humans guarding us?" Marcus asked, shoving Minerva's stolen keys into his pocket. "I'm feeling a bit peckish."

Winter snorted and Rafe moaned softly.

"Yes," Rafe said. "I'm famished. I'd kill for a couple of really big ones with strong hearts and slow legs. Let me ride him like a jockey as he pumps that blood straight down my throat. Not going feel guilty about draining them."

Sadly, Marcus had to agree. These humans attacked his family first, and now they were going to feed his family. After that, they could focus on escaping and finding Ethan and Bel. Marcus mentally sighed. And destroying Minerva. She couldn't be allowed to continue on her path of destruction. It was the only way to protect his family and so many other vampires and humans.

But first, food.

Then Bel and Ethan.

Then kill Minerva.

Yeah, that was a sound-ish plan.

Fuck, he needed to feed.

CHAPTER TWENTY-EIGHT

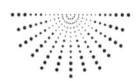

*E*than wiped the sweat threatening to drip into his eyes with the back of his hand. He leaned against the wall and very slowly peeked around the corner. It wasn't even warm out, but between climbing over the huge, strong wall and sneaking past the guards and dogs, he was pretty sure he'd had more of a workout in the past five minutes than he'd gotten in the last three months. And they still had to locate Marcus and Rafe.

Unfortunately, Bel had been unable to reach Winter, and they'd begun to fear the worst. Bel was trying to remain optimistic, claiming that Winter had likely let himself be captured so he could take down the Black Wolf clan from the inside. Ethan could only pray he was right.

Glancing around the corner, Ethan wanted to cry. It was yet another long hallway filled with exquisite rugs and priceless vases. He really wanted to smash each one of those damn things, but he knew the noise would bring people running. They'd been in the house for at least six minutes already and hadn't found a single sign of Marcus or the others. Six vampires had been killed between Ethan's bullets and Bel's formula-coated knives. And those six deaths hadn't been pretty.

Bel's deadly formula did exactly what he predicted. After becoming infected, the vampire had about three seconds before he felt the effects, and then it was only a few more seconds before they were reduced to a hissing and popping puddle of greenish goo. It looked like the blood melted the poor creature's bones into a sticky substance.

Even if it was a relatively quick death, it was not one Ethan would have chosen for himself. But that didn't stop him from using the bullets. They were the only way he was getting through this death house to his man.

For now, he was keeping a close count on them. He'd used five on four vampires while Bel took out the other two with his knives.

"See anything helpful?" Bel whispered.

"More stupid vases and closed doors. Probably bedrooms," Ethan muttered. His palm was sweaty, and it made the gun feel loose in his hand like he was in danger of dropping it. "I feel like we're in going in fucking circles. Where the hell are the prisoners hidden?"

"I've never kept prisoners, so it's hard to say. Away from where anyone might stumble across them."

Bel's calm and sensible tone had Ethan looking over his shoulder at his companion in stunned silence. He said it like it was a complete possibility that everyone at one time kept prisoners and he'd just not gotten around to it yet. Bel was…interesting. Ethan was never quite sure what was going to come out of his mouth. It was a strange similarity he had with his twin. The only difference was that you knew half the things Rafe said were total bullshit. Bel honestly meant the insanity he spewed.

"I'd say we need to find either a door with guards or at the very least, a basement."

"That makes sense."

Ethan bit back a sigh. "Well, that's not this way. I say we turn around and go through the kitchen again. Maybe there's a door off the kitchen that leads to the basement. At least, that's where I'd put it if I was the architect."

"We need to hurry. Lola and the others have got to be drawing a lot of fire."

Ethan grunted as he turned and started jogging down the hall with Bel following behind. Lola and the others were attacking the guards outside the house, drawing everyone's attention away from him and Bel as they conducted their search and rescue. Six minutes was already a damn long time, but even after looking at the rough sketch they had of the Black Wolf clan house, it hadn't prepared him for the sheer size of the place. It was amazing that people were surviving in studio apartments that were only a few hundred square feet when some people felt monstrous structures like this were necessary.

As they neared another corner, the sounds of fighting reached them. Had Lola and her team been chased inside the house? *Fuck.* That couldn't be a good sign. Ethan slowed his pace and was careful as he peeked around the corner to keep from giving their presence away.

The first thing he saw was Marcus's fist slamming into a vampire's face. The vampire staggered but didn't go down. Before he could launch himself at Marcus again, Ethan jumped out and fired his gun at the vamp, hitting him in the back. The impact was enough to spin the vampire around. Fangs bared in a blood-smeared face, he snarled and took one step toward Ethan. That was as far as he got before a look of confusion flashed across his face. A second later it shifted to horror. It never really reached pain before he started to dissolve.

Yeah, Bel was a mad genius. Thank God he was on their side.

"Ethan?"

Ethan looked up to see a blood-covered Marcus staring at him in shock. He was wounded in more than one place, and his skin under the blood was a sickly pale. And he was still the best thing Ethan had ever seen in his life.

"Marcus!" Ethan shouted, joy filling his voice. But it was short-lived. Vampires from the Black Wolf clan were running down the hall, threatening to overwhelm them. It didn't help that Rafe and Winter weren't looking much better than Marcus.

"Take this!" Bel shouted before he tossed the black-bladed machete he'd been carrying in his right hand to Marcus. "Don't touch the blade."

"The poison?"

"Yes. I've got Ethan."

Before Ethan could ask what Bel meant by that, Bel's strong arms wrapped around him from behind, pulling him in tight against his chest. He was trapped, couldn't even lift his arm to fire his gun.

"Bel!" Ethan protested.

Bel lowered his face to Ethan's ear, his arms tightening until Ethan could barely breathe. "Stay still. I've got you."

Ethan wanted to argue that they needed to help Marcus, but the world was suddenly plunged into complete darkness. It was more than someone cutting the power. This darkness was heavy and all-consuming. He blinked again and again, trying to get his eyes to focus, to find some little spark of light to glom onto, but there was nothing.

And then the screaming started.

Ethan sucked in a fractured breath. He could feel the first tendrils of panic wrapping around him, causing his limbs to tremble. His brain kept trying to tell him that he was falling, that he was falling into a bottomless pit and he was never getting out again. Never seeing Marcus or his brothers again. Never seeing light again.

Arms tightened painfully around Ethan and he welcomed it. The pain was better than the pervading sense of hopelessness that was trying to sink into him.

"I've got you. You're safe," Bel repeated over and over again. But even while Ethan could feel his face pressed to the side of his head, his voice sounded so very far away. His words helped ground him, but he couldn't shake the idea that he would only feel better when he could see Marcus again.

A moment later, the lights returned and the darkness receded. Ethan blinked and he swore it looked like the light was actually flowing out of Marcus and back into the lamps, but he was sure his eyes were simply playing tricks on him after being subjected to such complete darkness. Bel released him and Ethan lurched forward, running to Marcus. The hallway was filled with bubbling pools of green goo that had been vampires, while Winter and Rafe leaned against the wall, trying to catch their breaths.

Marcus's strong arms closed around Ethan, and everything felt a little bit better. There was a soft grunt of pain from Marcus, but when Ethan tried to step away, Marcus held him tighter.

"I was so worried about you," Marcus murmured against Ethan's sweaty and dirty hair.

"Found Bel just like you told me to. We also found some of Rafe's friends." Ethan lifted his head and peered around Marcus to smile at an exhausted-looking Rafe. "Lola is a total badass."

Rafe managed a small half smile. "Yes, she is."

"Speaking of, Lola and the others won't be able to keep them distracted for much longer," Bel interjected. "We need to get out of here now."

Marcus nodded and released Ethan. "Agreed, but Minerva needs to be taken care of as well. Get Ethan, Winter, and Rafe out of here. I'll follow as soon as I can."

"Not happening," Winter growled.

"I've got to agree with the wee one," Rafe drawled. He pushed away from the wall, standing on his own. "We're not leaving you, darling brother."

"You're injured—" Marcus started to argue but Winter cut him off.

"We're all injured. Well, except for maybe Bel."

"I did scrape my palm when I climbed over the wall." Ethan snorted when he saw Bel hold up his perfectly healed palm.

"Someone needs to get Ethan out of here," Marcus snarled.

Ethan started to argue, but Rafe beat him to it. "No, he needs to stay, and you know it."

Okay, that was weird and disturbingly ominous, but he wasn't going to counter Rafe. He wanted to stay and try to keep Marcus as protected as possible.

Marcus glared at Rafe for a moment, but the sibling didn't back down. The standoff didn't last more than a second before Marcus nodded. "Let's find Minerva and end this."

They collected a few weapons they found dropped by the attacking vampires and continued through the house on the first floor. They slaughtered several more of the Black Wolf clan, but there still wasn't any sign of this Minerva that Marcus mentioned.

On the second floor, there was no one waiting to stop them, which felt worse than the hordes ready to throw themselves at the invaders. Of course, after the results of some of Ethan's bullets and Bel's knives, the attackers were a little more hesitant to lunge at them. Ethan did what he could to protect Marcus, but his arms and legs were starting to ache from the exertion. He hadn't thought he was in bad shape, but it was clear he needed to work on his endurance the next time he found his way to the interior of a gym.

They moved as quickly as they could, glancing in one room after another until they finally came to a pair of shut double doors. That didn't feel great.

Glancing over his shoulder at Marcus, he threw his lover what he hoped was a reassuring smile before reaching out for the doorknob. The second his skin touched the cold metal a voice rang out from the other side of the door.

"*Come out, come out, wherever you are.*"

Ethan released the door like he'd been burned and jumped away, his shoulders bumping into Marcus's chest. A strong, reassuring hand smoothed down his head and came to rest around the back of his neck. Ethan barely registered the touch, but it was enough to override the flight instinct that was still pushing him.

It was her.

The one who slaughtered his family, who haunted his nightmares.

The reason Ethan had to be there at Marcus's side as he hunted down the vampire behind the attacks, kidnappings, and the deaths.

With teeth clenched, Ethan grabbed both door handles and shoved the doors open. The room looked as if it was a massive ballroom with a shining parquet floor and floor-to-ceiling windows looking out on a black sky. A quick count revealed about a dozen vampires scattered around one side of the room.

And in the center of the waiting group was a woman in a dark-red blouse and black slacks. Her brown hair was long and hung limply down her back. She smiled broadly at him, her mouth smeared with blood and her fangs visible even from a distance. It was the woman who killed everyone he loved, who ruined his life.

"There's my boy. The one that thought he could get away," she said, her words ending in a cackle. "How long has it been?"

Ethan's legs trembled as he walked into the room. Everything within him screamed to run. She was going to kill him, just like she'd murdered sweet Lucy and Macy. She'd rip his throat out just like she'd done to his mother and leave him in a spreading pool of his own blood.

But he didn't run. He didn't beg for Marcus to finish the monster for him. And he knew that Marcus was aching to step forward and rip her fucking head off. This bitch had also threatened his new family. Her fucking soldiers had laid their hands on Marcus and his brothers. They'd broken into his house twice.

Fuck. That. Shit.

"Sixteen years," Ethan said evenly.

"I've let you age like a fine wine. And then I had your friend bring you to me." She raised her hand and Carl shambled over to her side. Ethan's heart gave a little jerk, but he immediately pulled his eyes back to Minerva. She was the target. He didn't give a shit about Carl or whatever mess he got himself into.

"I can't wait to taste you," she continued with a little moan as if she were imagining Ethan as the most delicious dessert.

"Never gonna happen."

She laughed again, the sound going higher and little more hysterical. Minerva definitely wasn't all there. "You really think you can escape. That your little clan has any chance after I've already—"

Ethan swung the hand holding the gun up and started firing, emptying the magazine as quickly as he could. Some of the bullets went wild, but luckily her followers were grouped close enough that any stray bullets hammered them. He watched as her body jerked three times as the bullets hit her, but she remained standing, still smiling at him.

Without taking his eyes off her, he popped the empty magazine from the gun and slapped in the spare. Lifting the gun to eye level, he held it in both hands and waited.

Minerva threw her head back and laughed. "Was that supposed to stop me? I'm not human, little boy. I'm a vampire."

"Yep. That's what I'm counting on."

"Bullets don't…bullets…don't…" Her voice drifted off as the same surprised look crossed her face that he'd seen on the other vampires' all night. She lifted her hand and rubbed at the places where the bullets had hit. Behind her, three other vampires screamed and writhed as the green acidic goo that was now their blood started to bubble through their skin. She tried to jump away from them like the other observers, but she stumbled and fell to her knees.

"Interesting," Bel murmured. "Apparently it takes longer for the formula to work on older vampires. Minerva was what? Three centuries at least?"

"Four hundred and thirty-seven," Winter answered.

Ethan's gaze never wavered as he watched her die before his eyes. Her greenish blood bubbled through her flesh, eating away at it while dissolving her bones. She tried several times to scream, but her vocal chords were already gone. Her mouth simply opened and closed like a landed fish with a soft gurgling sound.

There had been no reason for a long speech about how he wanted her to pay for her crimes or that this was justice for his family. She wouldn't care. Probably wouldn't even understand his hatred. He was just food, and food didn't deserve pretty things like justice and respect.

No, in the end, he simply wanted her dead so she couldn't hurt anyone else, especially his new family.

"We've destroyed Minerva, the head of the Black Wolf clan," Marcus said, lifting his voice so that it echoed in the large room. "As a member of the Varik clan, we declare that the Black Wolf clan is dissolved. We will grant you mercy this one time if you leave peacefully now."

"He's a human. You can't—"

Ethan swung the gun around, pointing it at the chest of the speaker. "You really want to argue that technicality? I'm a Varik. That's all you need to know."

The vamp immediately backpedaled a couple of steps and held up his hands in surrender. No one else spoke as they quickly hurried out the other doors of the massive room, seeking a quick escape. Ethan kept his gun up, pointing at anyone that was relatively close to his family.

After less than a minute, he found only Carl standing beside Minerva's partially dissolved corpse. His face was completely expressionless. He stared at nothing, as if he wasn't really there. Winter took the machete from Marcus and walked over to the human…or sort of human. He reminded Ethan more of a zombie than anything.

Marcus carefully pulled the gun from Ethan's hand and drew him against his chest. Ethan closed his eyes as he rested his head against Marcus's chest, but he could still hear the wet, fleshy sound of the blade going through Carl. There was soft thud followed by a louder one. Ethan flinched, his brain instantly conjuring up the image of Winter cutting the man's head off and it bouncing away from the body.

Strong, familiar arms wrapped around him. "He was already dead. His body just didn't realize it yet."

"Can we go home, please?" Ethan asked, his voice muffled against Marcus's chest.

"Yes, let's get the little Varik home," Bel said.

"Oh, I like that," Rafe chimed in, and Ethan found himself smiling against Marcus despite the stress and fatigue that were causing his body to shake. There was something about the sound of wicked playfulness in Rafe's voice that always made Ethan want to laugh.

"Does that mean you'll stop calling me 'Wee One'?" Winter demanded.

"Definitely not. You'll always be Wee One, and he's Little Varik."

"Home, brothers. We've had a busy night." Marcus sounded tired to Ethan, but also content.

"Food first," Rafe groaned. "I need to feed."

"We'll get drive-thru," Ethan muttered without thinking.

"Most humans won't let you drag them through the little

window," Winter said. Ethan lifted his head from Marcus and found a rare smile on the youngest Varik's lips. Well...the youngest vampire Varik.

Yes, the other kind of feed.

Ethan walked out of the house with his arm wrapped around Marcus. His world had changed over the past couple of months. Feeding now included blood. Explosions and weapons were more common. But so was laughter and playful teasing. And so much amazing sex.

He was only half listening as the four brothers bickered about where to find a quick meal at such a late hour. It might not be the life his parents had expected him to have, but he'd found love and a place to belong.

CHAPTER TWENTY-NINE

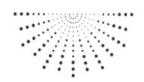

Ethan found Marcus sitting at the piano in the music room, but not playing it. It wasn't the first time he'd caught Marcus staring at the black and white keys, seeming unwilling to touch them but also unable to walk away.

Seventy-two hours had passed since the destruction of the Black Wolf clan, not that Ethan remembered much of it.

The Varik brothers fed. Ethan managed to tolerate Marcus feeding off a stranger only because Ethan knew he couldn't meet all Marcus's needs. Of course, later that night when they were both showered and wrapped around each other, Ethan was more than happy to supply Marcus with a nightcap, hoping to wash the taste of the other man from Marcus's tongue.

For the past two days, Ethan had done little more than eat, sleep, and fuck Marcus. There was almost a desperation to Marcus's touch now, and nothing Ethan said or did could banish whatever thoughts were haunting him.

Whenever Marcus wasn't in bed with him, he was on the phone with the remaining members of the Ministry, explaining what had happened, or he was sitting at the piano. Ethan

CLAIMING MARCUS

wanted to give him time to work it out on his own, but the melancholy seemed to be digging its claws deeper and deeper.

Ethan had to admit that he had expected to feel a bigger sense of relief and accomplishment at finding and destroying his family's killer. He was glad Minerva was gone, unable to torture more humans. But the small, hollow part of his heart where his family resided was still there. He still missed them. Still ached over the lives that Macy and Lucy wouldn't ever live. That would never go away.

But he had a new family. The Varik brothers would never replace his birth family, but they gave him a place where he finally felt like he belonged. It was a home. Something he hadn't had in so damn long.

The old pains were never too far away, but Marcus and his brothers made life a little easier, more tolerable. Definitely more entertaining. His only hope was that he'd be able to help more humans now that he was on the inside of the vampire world, protect them from the pain that he'd suffered.

But right now, his focus was on the pain Marcus was struggling with.

Taking a deep breath, Ethan strolled into the music room and dropped down onto the bench, beside Marcus. The vampire straightened and managed a small, wan smile.

"Did you have a good nap?" Marcus asked.

Ethan shrugged. "The falling asleep part is always the best." Marcus lifted an eyebrow in question and Ethan continued. "Your arms are wrapped around me."

Marcus nodded and looked back at the piano. "I think it's dinnertime. Shall we order something?"

"Later. I want you to talk first."

"About?"

Ethan nudged Marcus with his elbow. "You're not the clichéd, brooding grumpy vampire. You haven't actually touched the piano since that night. You just sit here and stare at it. What's going on in your head?"

"Too much."

"Okay, but you gotta give me something." Reaching over, Ethan slid his hand under Marcus's and threaded his fingers through his. "Is this about your mom?"

"Some. I'm torn on how I should feel about what happened. I'm angry that anyone would hurt her, try to hurt both of you. She was the sweetest, most gentle woman. She loved her sons and music. She dreamed of giving only beauty to the world."

Ethan's hand tightened in Marcus's. "I only knew her for a couple of minutes, but she seemed pretty amazing to me. And looked so much like Rafe and Bel."

Marcus nodded. He blinked and a tear rolled unchecked down his cheek. "But I can't forget that she was also capable of so much pain and torment. She physically hurt all of us. Came so damn close to killing Bel. I don't think he ever forgave her for that last attack."

"It wasn't her."

"No, but it still happened, and we have to live with the memory. The fear of it happening all over again. Of not being able to stop her in time."

"It's over." Releasing Marcus's hand, Ethan twisted on the bench to face Marcus. He reached up and cupped Marcus's cheeks with both hands. "You and Bel and Rafe and Winter, you succeeded. You protected her and each other. You and your brothers are the most amazing people I've ever met. You're loyal and brave and so fucking loving. Even after everything you went through with your mom, you still loved her. After all your fights and frustrations, you still love your brothers and they love you. You guys are there for each other in a heartbeat."

Marcus closed his eyes and nodded. "I feel guilty, because there is a part of me that's also relieved. She tried not to show it, but I think she was unhappy. I think she missed Aiden without

CLAIMING MARCUS

truly realizing he was missing. I think she knew she was hurting us but wasn't sure how. I'm just glad she's not in pain anymore."

Ethan released Marcus's face and wrapped his arms around his lover's neck, pulling him in for a tight hug. Marcus held him back, lowering his face to his shoulder. Silent tears fell on Ethan's bare skin. It was the first time Marcus had really spoken about his mother since her death. Ethan understood the mixed feelings that came with losing family suddenly and violently. For years, the only things he'd been able to feel were anger and hatred. It had probably been what kept him from finding a new home with a foster family.

"I love you, Marcus. So very much," Ethan murmured.

Marcus's arms tightened, and Ethan wished they weren't sitting on a piano bench, but in bed so he could snuggle that much closer. He wanted to be sure that Marcus always felt loved and cherished. The weight of his strange family weighed heavily on his shoulders. He'd protected his brothers and mother for so long, but who did he have to lean on? Ethan wanted Marcus to know he'd never have to carry that weight alone again.

"I love you, Ethan."

Releasing him slowly, Ethan pressed a tender kiss to Marcus's lips and then leaned back, putting his elbow on the top of the piano. "Is that what's been on your mind? Keeping you from playing?"

He wasn't really surprised when Marcus shook his head, his eyes dropping to the keys. "No."

"Is it the fallout from Minerva and the Ministry?"

"In part." Marcus licked his lips, still not looking up at Ethan.

"You haven't changed your mind about the Ministry, have you? You said they were corrupt, and that change was needed to protect people."

"No, I still believe that." He looked up and touched Ethan's cheek. "My worry is that things are going to get a lot worse before they get better. The idea that I could sit on the Ministry along with other members of my family is a silly fantasy. If I'm going to upset things and remove other vampires, how is anyone ever going to trust me? What makes me different than the bastards sitting on the Ministry now?" He paused again and looked at Ethan, fear clear in his blue eyes. It finally hit Ethan what Marcus's final consuming concern was. Him.

"You're worried about the violence. People trying to stop you."

"More importantly, I'm worried about you being in the path of danger."

"Are you worried about your brothers?"

"Yes, of course!"

"But?"

"They're vampires," Marcus admitted softly. His lips thinned as he pressed them together and he stared at Ethan for a second. It was like he was trying to steel himself for the hard truth he wanted to deliver. Ethan smiled at his adorableness. He was making this so much more difficult than it needed to be.

"Ethan," Marcus started again, his voice stern. "You're human. In comparison to vampires, you're weaker and your body frailer. Without Bel's poison, which is a completely different problem for us, you would never have been able to reach me. You and Bel would have been overwhelmed. There will be other attacks. You could be grabbed during the day while running an errand. I'm not the only one with a human assistant. No matter how hard I try, I can't promise to keep you safe."

"No one is asking that you do."

"But I need you safe!" he snapped in desperation. He exhaled and closed his eyes. "I need you safe. I can't lose you."

"Well, you realize there is one very easy solution to this problem."

Marcus frowned at him, his face darkening like a thundercloud. "Don't make light of this. There is no—"

"Change me."

Marcus's mouth hung open for a second. When he finally managed to speak, his voice was barely above a whisper. "What?"

"Make me a vampire. Make me like you."

"Are...are you sure?"

Ethan leaned forward and quickly kissed Marcus again. "Yes. I'm sure."

Marcus grabbed Ethan's hand and squeezed it. "I'm being very serious, Ethan. I know Bel is working on what he thinks of as a cure, but there's no guarantee that he could ever turn you back to a human. This is forever. No more walking in the sun. Dependent on blood to survive. You're fully a part of the vampire world, with all the violent chaos that comes with it."

"This isn't a snap decision for me. I've been thinking about it since we start—well, since the first time we kissed." Ethan looked down at Marcus's hand, feeling the heat steal across his cheeks. "It started as a sort of 'what if?' thought rattling around in my brain. What if we dated? What if something happened to me? Would I want you to change me? Would I want to take a chance on being with you forever even if it meant no more sunlight and a slight diet alteration? The answer always came back yes."

"But the violence and the Ministry?"

Ethan snorted. "Have you taken a good look at human politics recently? We're not doing much better."

Marcus smirked at him. "You do have a point."

"Of course. But I want to be a part of your family."

"You already are. Even if you stay human, you will always be a Varik."

There was no denying the flare of joy and pride that bloomed in Ethan's chest at Marcus's words. His lover would never understand how much that meant to him. He treasured the Variks and he was honored to be counted among them. But with that name came a responsibility he didn't take lightly. He needed to protect his lover and brothers, and Ethan was sure the only way he could hold up his end of the deal was to become a vampire as well. To have all the same strengths and weaknesses. To celebrate and suffer with them.

"I want this, Marcus. If it means you worry just a tiny bit less about me. If it means I get to spend forever with you, then yes, I fucking want this."

Marcus stared at him for a moment before a smile spread across his lips, lighting his eyes and chasing away the worry that had clouded his handsome face for so long. "Really?"

Ethan's heart soared to hear the hope in that single word. "Yes, really. I want you forever. I want us forever."

"W-when? When would you want…?"

"Tonight, if possible." Ethan wrapped his arms around Marcus's neck again and leaned forward. "But first…" He nipped at Marcus's bottom lip. "I want to have sex one last time as a human. I'd like that to be one of my last memories as a human before moving on to the next big stage of my life."

Marcus's grin became a little wicked. "I think that is a brilliant idea. The other will take a little planning, but let's definitely close out your human life like that."

Instead of kissing him like Ethan expected, Marcus slammed the lid down on the piano, covering the keys, and stood. Ethan stood as well, figuring they were moving to the bedroom, but Marcus grabbed him by the waist and lifted him until his butt landed on the smooth surface of the piano. Marcus parted Ethan's legs and stepped between them, his hands burning through the thin material of his sleep pants. Those wonderful hands slid up the inside of his thighs, massaging muscles while drawing so close to his dick.

Marcus leaned down and licked slowly up his neck to his earlobe. Ethan could only moan, fighting the urge to come in his pants. This damn man got him so hot and bothered every time they touched.

"Will you bite me?" Ethan panted.

"Yes, but just a little nibble. We need you to be strong for later," Marcus murmured against his neck. His hot breath danced across the damp skin, sending goose bumps down his arms.

"Will you still bite me after I'm a vampire?"

"If you wish."

Ethan moaned again, losing himself to Marcus's wandering touch. His hands were sliding up his stomach, pushing his T-shirt out of the way. "Yes, please," he choked out. "Never want that to stop."

"Anything you want, my heart."

Ethan grabbed Marcus's head and pulled him in for a rough kiss, his tongue plunging into his mouth. He wanted to taste him. His strength and power were intoxicating. Ethan remembered the way Marcus sucked all the light into him at the Black Wolf clan house and wiped out their attackers. And now he held that powerful creature between his legs. Owned him.

Tightening his fists in Marcus's thick black hair, he pulled back to look into his desire-glazed eyes. "Fuck me hard. Fuck me so hard I'm reborn a vampire still feeling you."

Marcus's voice was little more than a growl when he said, "Anything you want, my heart. Anything for you." A hand closed around Ethan's cock, and he couldn't stop himself from thrusting upward into it. "Lie back."

Ethan wanted to remind him that they didn't have any lube in the music room. They needed to move to the bedroom, but Marcus had shoved his fingers into the waistband of his pants and was pulling, teasing him with the tiniest of touches along his bare cock. *Fuck lube.* He didn't know what Marcus had in mind, but he didn't want Marcus to stop touching him.

The piano was cool against his feverish skin, but he was only vaguely aware of it as Marcus finished removing his pants and tossed them aside. Grabbing him behind his knees, Marcus pushed his legs against his chest while still spreading him wide. He was completely on display before his lover and it felt fucking amazing.

"So sexy. And all mine," Marcus said in a low voice.

"Just yours," Ethan said. His voice sounded drunk, but he didn't care.

Marcus leaned down and ran the flat of his tongue along Ethan's cock. Ethan slapped his hands down on the top of the piano, stretching to grab the edges while arching his back, thrusting his dick toward Marcus as best as he could. Nerve endings sparked and sizzled with each touch of his tongue, licking and swirling around the head.

After what felt like an eternity, Marcus finally took him completely into his mouth, sucking him hard. Nonsense noises poured from Ethan. He wasn't sure what he was saying, just knew that he was begging. Begging for more, harder, faster. It was paradise and he didn't want it to ever end.

Marcus worked his cock, taking him straight to the edge and then backing off again. This happened again and again until Ethan could barely catch his breath. Marcus let his dick fall from his mouth to slap wetly against his stomach. "Grab your knees for me."

Ethan slid his hands under his knees and held them to his chest. Anything if it meant Marcus would return to his dick. But Marcus dug his fingers into the cheeks of his ass, spreading them. Ethan's breath caught in his throat for a second. Marcus wasn't going to…

A long, wet tongue swiped slowly across his hole and Ethan howled. No one had ever rimmed him. He'd heard how amazing it could be, watched it plenty of times on porn, but never dreamed he'd be lucky enough to find someone willing. *Oh, fuck.* He was going to totally lose it before Marcus got inside of him. Marcus slowly licked and sucked on his opening, loosening him until Marcus could poke his tongue inside.

Ethan tried to press against Marcus's wonderful mouth, but he was afraid to move. Couldn't move. He needed to grab his cock to keep from coming, but he couldn't let go of his legs.

"Marcus!" Ethan cried out in frustration. "I'm gonna come. Need to come." He wasn't making sense.

"Yes, my heart." Marcus surprised him by thrusting two fingers inside of him while wrapping his other hand around his dick. He stroked him a couple of times before curling his fingers, expertly applying pressure to his prostate. Ethan's orgasm hit hard, and he shouted, spilling himself across his stomach, chest, and Marcus's hand.

Ethan lay on the piano, trying to get his breathing back under control and his scattered thoughts pulled together. Marcus had such skill at driving him to new heights, each orgasm feeling better than the last. But then, when he said that he belonged to Marcus, he meant it, body and soul. No one knew him better.

He was snapped from his errant thoughts when he felt Marcus's tongue sweep across his too-sensitive dick. He lurched into a partially upright position, cursing softly. From there, he could see Marcus slowly lapping up the cum that streaked across his groin and stomach. When Marcus lifted his eyes to him, there was that faint glow; Ethan could never quite determine if it was a trick of the light or a trait of being a vampire. Either way, it was sexy as hell.

"I wanted to do a taste comparison," Marcus murmured. "I was wondering if you'd taste different when you're reborn."

Ethan gave a breathy chuckle as Marcus's tongue slid along his flesh again. "Sounds like a very important experiment to me."

Marcus continued until he was completely clean, and then he tossed Ethan over his shoulder. There wasn't a huge height difference between them, but Marcus had a way of making him feel as light as a rag doll. Considering they were headed straight for the bedroom, Ethan didn't mind.

The blankets and pillows on the bed softened his drop. Ethan immediately positioned himself in the middle of the bed, watching as Marcus dug the bottle of lube from the nightstand before he tore off his own sleep pants and T-shirt. Just the sight of Marcus's beautiful muscles stretching and moving under all that wonderfully soft skin had his dick trying to spring to life again.

A new idea forming in his head, Ethan jumped up and moved from the center of the bed, directing Marcus to take his place.

"I don't have much control left, Ethan," Marcus warned. His voice was deliciously deep and gravelly, as if the fight for control was shredding his vocal cords. "No teasing."

"No teasing," Ethan agreed, as he grabbed the bottle of lube. "I want you to lie on your back and hold on to the headboard."

Marcus narrowed his eyes on Ethan, but still reached over his head and clamped his hands down on the top of the headboard. His cock was still hard and leaking, standing up as if demanding Ethan's attention. No worries. He wasn't forgetting about that beautiful, thick monster. Squirting lube on his palm, Ethan wrapped his hand around Marcus's dick, coating it. Marcus's hips popped upward, thrusting into his hand as he hissed in what seemed like a mix of pleasure and pain.

Pouring more lube on his fingers, Ethan got to his knees and smiled at Marcus as he shoved the lube inside of himself.

"You can't help yourself," Marcus said in a low voice. "You're always so damn sexy. Like a fucking siren luring me in. I never stood a chance."

Ethan could barely speak. "You were always meant to be mine."

No one had ever made him feel sexy. Not until Marcus. And

then he embraced it. He wanted to drive Marcus wild, make him desperate and lose control.

Removing his fingers, he crawled on top of Marcus, straddling his hips. With one hand braced on his chest, Ethan grabbed Marcus's cock and guided it to his hole. He slowly brushed it back and forth, teasing them both, earning a warning growl from Marcus. His lover was about to give up on holding the headboard and take over if Ethan didn't get to it.

With one last grin, Ethan pushed backward, forcing the slick head past tight muscles. They both groaned, Ethan's head falling to his shoulder. Marcus lay perfectly still except for a small trembling Ethan could feel in his legs. He wanted to thrust into Ethan, burying himself completely, but he was letting Ethan control it. This was his gift to Ethan. One last fuck as a human and Ethan was in the driver's seat.

Resting both of his hands on Marcus's chest, Ethan started to rock on Marcus's cock, taking it in a little bit deeper with each stroke.

"Fuck, you're so big," Ethan groaned. He looked down at Marcus to see that his eyes were glowing a little brighter now. Definitely not a trick of the light. Maybe an indication that he was so turned-on.

"Yeah?"

Ethan's smile felt a little more wicked on his lips. So Marcus was aroused by a little dirty talk. Ethan could give him that. He didn't mind being vocal.

Moaning loudly, he slid down Marcus's cock, taking almost all of him this time. "So fucking big. My hole has never been so stretched. You own my ass."

"*Yesss*," Marcus hissed. He thrust his hips upward and Ethan cried out in pleasure, taking Marcus to the hilt. "Mine. No one but me will ever be inside of you again. No one!"

"No one," Ethan repeated. "No one fucks me like you do."

"Show me. Show me how much you love my cock."

Ethan could only nod. He leaned back, placing both hands behind himself on the bed for balance as he started to ride Marcus's cock. From that angle, Marcus would be able to see the slick slide in and out of his body. The way he stretched Ethan's hole wide.

"Grab yourself. I want to watch you stroke your dick," Marcus commanded.

Ethan wrapped his right hand around his hardening length and started jerking in time to his movement. Marcus increased his thrusts. He wasn't sure which of them had changed the angle, but Marcus was once against pressing against his prostate, sending stars shooting in front of Ethan's eyes as his body tensed with the impending orgasm. He hadn't been sure he'd be able to come again, but now he was sure he wasn't going to be able to stop it.

"Marcus! Marcus, please. Bite me. I'm gonna come. Need—"

Ethan didn't finish the desperate plea. Marcus forced him onto his back, taking control. His cock slammed hard into his ass, adding an edge of pain to the pleasure that sent Ethan careening over the edge. As the first wave of bliss hammered his body, Marcus bit down on his neck. Ethan screamed, his entire body jerking and tensing at the same time against Marcus's. He'd never felt an orgasm so intense, he couldn't breathe.

As the orgasm finally started to fade, Marcus pulled away from his neck. He smiled, Ethan's blood coating his lips and fangs as he thrust hard into Ethan a couple of times more before shouting his own release. Marcus's cock swelled inside of Ethan, followed by an intense rush of heat. Ethan whimpered; his body wanted to leap over the edge again with Marcus, but it just couldn't.

Marcus collapsed on Ethan, arms wrapping tightly around him, their sweaty and cum-covered skin sliding against each other. Marcus licked at his neck, stopping the bleeding and healing the fresh wounds. He barely registered the sweet words Marcus whispered as he nuzzled him.

Ethan wanted to whisper tenderly to him as well, but he was so fucking drained. He'd just close his eyes for a minute. They needed to shower and discuss this whole transformation process, but right now, the world could wait. There was nothing more important than being wrapped in the warmth and strength of Marcus's arms.

CHAPTER THIRTY

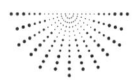

Ethan stretched, a smile spreading across his lips to feel the soreness of his ass. Yes, Marcus had done a wonderful job fucking him senseless. He didn't even remember falling asleep. Just lying there in Marcus's arms…which were now missing. Ethan opened his eyes and was surprised to find that he was in bed alone.

Sitting up, he instantly located Marcus standing at the end of the bed. He looked freshly showered and dressed in a soft, gray sweater and black slacks. There was love shining in his eyes, but also worry.

"You should have woken me," Ethan admonished as he stretched against the sheets. "I would have showered with you."

Marcus shook his head. "You needed your rest, and I needed to make some phone calls. They're here now, if you still want to do this."

Ethan's smile fell away as he turned over Marcus's words. Do what? It took only a moment to recall their conversation in the music room. Ethan's transformation.

"Yes. But who's here?"

"My brothers." Marcus winced a little. "I'm sorry, but I need them here for this. We were together when we were changed, and I want them here for yours."

"As a family tradition."

Marcus nodded, but his frown deepened. "Also, as a precaution." Marcus sat on the edge of the bed and picked up Ethan's hand, holding it tight. "There are risks. I always fear that something could go wrong as it did with my mother, but I know of some cases where people died in the transformation."

The words caused Ethan's heart to skip, but he forced himself to give Marcus a reassuring smile. "There are risks with everything in life. They say you can die when you're put under to have your wisdom teeth removed, and there are few things more boring than that. You're worth the risk. Our future life together is worth that risk."

"I love you," Marcus murmured. Some of the tension eased from his shoulders and they slumped.

"Love you too. But I need to shower if I'm going to see your brothers." Ethan started to climb out of the bed, but Marcus's fingers tightened around his hand, stopping him.

"Just a little. You smell like me, and I don't want you to lose that completely. I want you reborn into this world smelling like you belong to me."

Ethan chuckled and nodded. He could deal with that.

Marcus released his hand and walked out of the room, leaving Ethan to lightly clean off and pull on some clothes.

A few minutes later, he found the four Varik brothers in the library. Marcus was pacing while Winter stood by the window. Rafe was lounging across the sofa, and his twin was perched on the edge of his seat as if he could barely contain his excitement.

"I guess this is a bad time to ask if you've ever done this before," Ethan said, half joking.

Some of the enthusiasm drained from Bel's face.

Rafe snorted. "Definitely late for that question, Little Varik."

"We were all together when Aiden changed us. I went first,"

Marcus said. "I was awake to see my brothers, but still kind of out of it for Rafe's transformation. I helped with Bel and Winter."

Nervous energy zipped through Ethan, and he struggled to sit in the other open chair when he really wanted to pace the room with Marcus.

"Is it hard…to transform someone into a vampire?"

"Nope. Drain them and then get them to drink vampire blood before they die," Winter explained. He turned away from the window and stared at Ethan. "You've got the hard part. Don't die."

"Okay. Yeah. Doesn't sound like rocket science," Ethan said, trying to reassure himself that he was in capable hands. It wasn't like they had to cast some complicated spell or perform some intricate ritual. Marcus and his brothers had drunk a lot of blood over the years, so they had that part down. Ethan drinking their blood, while it sounded disgusting, wasn't a hard thing. He could do this.

Clapping his hands together, Ethan jumped to his feet and moved to the center of the room. "How are we going to do this? Marcus transforms me and you guys stand around as cheerleaders?"

"Ethan," Rafe said and Ethan was stunned to hear him so serious. All the mocking and jokes were gone from his expression. "Is this what you truly want? You must know that you're already a Varik without this step. We'll always protect you. Always count you as one of us."

"It's true, Ethan," Bel added. "You don't have to do this. You're a brother now just as much as Winter or Rafe."

"You're family," Winter said with such steel in his voice that Ethan had no choice but to believe it.

Ethan turned teary eyes on Marcus, who was watching him with a solemn expression. "I will love you the same whether you are human or vampire."

Roughly brushing away tears, Ethan cleared his throat against the lump that had grown there. "My mind is made up. I want to be a vampire."

"Good!" Bel jumped to his feet and whipped out a syringe with a very long needle. "I get to take some blood first."

"Whoa!" Ethan threw up his hand to ward off Bel while backpedaling from the vampire. "I thought you'd be taking my blood the other way, with the fangs and the drinking."

"We are," Bel said, looking undeterred as he continued to chase Ethan around the room.

Rafe laughed loudly. "This has you scared?" he demanded through gasps for air. "We tell you we're going to drain you and kill you, and you freak over a little needle?"

"That's no little needle!" Ethan countered. He grabbed Marcus and positioned his lover between himself and Bel.

"But it's for science!" Bel said.

"My heart," Marcus said calmly, though it sounded like there was a hint of laughter in his voice. But the endearment did its job. It helped Ethan get a hold of his rising panic. "Bel wants some vials of your blood to study. He's never been able to study someone's blood before and after they've been transformed. He thinks it will help him unlock his cure."

"Yeah, well…I don't want to be cured. I want to be a vampire."

"But someone else might," Marcus murmured.

Ethan dropped his forehead against Marcus's back and sighed. Okay, that was a really good point. He wouldn't want to steal that chance from someone else if they were changed into a vampire against their will or were maybe miserable as a vampire.

"All right. That's fine with me," he murmured. He still hated needles. Had hated them since he was a little kid. But with any luck, this would be one of the last times he'd ever have to do this in his life.

Walking over to the couch, he sat down and was pleased to see Marcus force Rafe to get up so he could sit beside Ethan. They held hands as Bel swabbed his arm and drew what had to be close to a pint of blood for his experiments.

"Well, at least Bel gave us a head start," Winter said as he walked over to the couch. Rafe was standing beside him, his arm resting on his younger brother's shoulder. Bel carefully packed away his newly acquired specimens and joined them.

"How are we going to do this?" Ethan asked, hating that fresh nerves were creeping in now that the other distraction was completed. He wasn't a fan of being the center of attention and right then, all eyes were on him.

"It would probably be best if you lose this," Marcus said, plucking at the hem of his shirt.

Ethan pulled his shirt off and clenched it tightly with both hands between his legs. Marcus gently pried it from his grip and set it aside. He placed his palm against his jaw and rubbed his thumb over his cheek. "I'm so proud of you. So brave."

"Nope, getting pretty scared shitless at this point."

"Do you want to stop?"

"No," Ethan said without hesitation and Marcus's smile grew.

"So brave." He pressed a light kiss to Ethan's forehead and dropped his hand. "There's a lot of blood in the human body. I can't take enough from you to take you to the brink, so my brothers are going to drink from you first. They will do what they can to limit any pain you feel. When you're close, I will take from you the last that's needed."

"What do I do?"

"I want you to remain calm and listen to my voice. Trust us to take care of you. When I ask you to be calm, you stay calm. When I ask you to drink, I want you to drink. And when I tell you to open your eyes, you must open your eyes."

Ethan nodded. "Okay. I can do that." He said it over and over in his head. He could do this. He wasn't going to die. He was going to fight for Marcus. He was going to fight for their life together. He was going to fight for himself and the life he wanted. No more being shuffled through a system or following a path someone else directed for him. He wanted to be a vampire. He wanted to build a life with Marcus, one that included a new safety for humans against violent attacks like the one against his family.

Pushing to his feet, he smiled at the men who were his brothers. "I'm ready now."

"Thank God, because I'm starved," Rafe said, stepping forward. But even as Ethan watched the fangs extend, Rafe winked at him in playful reassurance.

Rafe's arms weren't as big as Marcus's but felt as strong. Being held by another man felt so wrong. Ethan tried to make himself relax, but his brain just kept screaming that it wasn't Marcus. Fingers slid along the hand down at his side and Ethan unclenched a little as he took Marcus's hand.

"Just relax," Marcus murmured. "I'm right here. I'm going to be right here the entire time."

Before Ethan could reply, Rafe's fangs sank deep and Ethan couldn't completely hold back his cry of pain. He clenched Marcus's hand, and he could hear his love snap at his brother. Ethan immediately eased his grip, trying to shield Marcus from the pain. He didn't want to give Marcus reason to worry about him. There was enough on his mind already.

After several seconds, the pain subsided to a dull throb in his neck. Ethan closed his eyes and tried to recall every time he heard Marcus play the piano. He concentrated on the way his fingers flew across the keys and the amazing music that drifted up from the instrument.

Ethan didn't know how much time passed before he felt his body being handed off to someone else. Probably Bel. He felt about as tall as Rafe. Ethan didn't bother to open his eyes. He just smiled and kept thinking about Marcus's music. The memory was strong enough that he swore he could hear it.

He was sure no time passed before he was handed off again. This one was definitely Winter. He and Winter were the same height, though Winter was stockier in build. Ethan was struggling to stand on his own. The room felt like it was spinning, and he was just so tired.

That thought had barely formed in his head when he was moved again. But this time, he knew these arms. They were home. Marcus.

"Open your eyes for me, Ethan," Marcus said calmly.

It was a struggle, but Ethan finally managed to look up at Marcus. He was surprised to find that Marcus was seated on the couch and Ethan was lying across his lap.

"Tell me if you still want this."

"Yes, please," Ethan said, wondering why his voice sounded so slurred.

"Yes, my heart," Marcus murmured against Ethan's neck. Ethan let himself sink into that touch, the familiar smell of Marcus, his encompassing warmth. He could no longer remember why he'd been so worried before. Marcus was holding him and he felt so safe, so protected. And all he wanted to do was sleep.

Ethan was sure that thought had barely formed in his head when someone was shaking him awake, but he couldn't open his eyes. Something wet and sticky was being pressed against his mouth. He tried to turn his head away, but it was too heavy, and he was too tired. He just wanted to go back to sleep.

"Ethan, you need to drink." Marcus's harsh voice finally penetrated the fog. He sounded angry, or maybe he was worried. Ethan wasn't sure. He couldn't open his eyes.

"Ethan, you promised me you would drink. You must drink," Marcus said again, his voice growing more desperate.

There were other voices. They sounded farther away, and he

couldn't quite make out what they were saying, but he did hear drink over and over again.

Fine. He could drink a few sips. Then maybe they'd let him sleep again.

He swallowed the liquid that had already begun to coat his tongue and fill his mouth. He winced at the thickness and coppery taste. His brain kept shouting that it was wrong, but Marcus sounded so happy he'd taken that first swallow. He wanted Marcus happy. He wanted the fear and panic gone from his voice, so he swallowed again. The other voices disappeared, but Marcus continued to talk to him. His deep voice was coaxing, reassuring. He sounded so proud of Ethan.

"I think that's enough, Marcus." That voice was clearer. Possibly Bel.

"He can have it all if that's what he wants," Marcus growled. His arm tightened around Ethan, and he just wanted to snuggle into Marcus's warmth.

"Yes, but he doesn't need you weak. You've already given him more than was given to Winter."

"And look at how Winter turned out," Rafe teased.

"You need to stop so he can wake up," Winter said, seeming to ignore his brother's comment.

Whatever had been pressed against Ethan's mouth disappeared and Ethan felt his body relax again. Sleep beckoned. Maybe they were done with him now and he could sleep. Yes, that sounded wonderful. Asleep in Marcus's arms.

"Ethan?" Marcus's voice had returned, but it sounded farther away than before. "Open your eyes."

"I don't understand," Bel murmured. "He should be awake."

"Maybe he's a slow riser like Winter," Rafe said. But he sounded worried. Rafe was never worried. Rafe joked and teased.

"Don't go to sleep, Ethan!" Winter shouted. "You fight it!"

Arms tightened around him, threatened to break bones.

Marcus's voice was strong now, but the panic was clear. "Ethan, come back to me! Don't leave me, my heart. You promised to open your eyes. Please, don't leave me."

Marcus thought he was leaving him. *Never.*

Things didn't make any sense to him, but the idea that he'd ever leave Marcus was absolutely ridiculous. He needed to open his eyes, if only to reassure Marcus that he wasn't going anywhere.

Ethan fought against the cloying darkness trying to pull him into slumber. He was sure he'd never been so tired in his life, but this was more important than sleep. He needed to tell Marcus that he wasn't leaving him, that he was fine.

When he finally blinked his eyes open, his first sight was Marcus's pale, tear-streaked face. Sounds of relief and joy exploded around the room, but his gaze never wavered from Marcus.

"There you are," Marcus said in a choked sob.

"Never leaving you," Ethan said thickly. Now that his eyes were open and he'd spoken, the last tendrils of fatigue were burning away faster. He felt alive and completely rejuvenated. Old aches and pains were gone. He felt…new.

Marcus helped him sit up on the couch, and Ethan looked around at his companions, surprised by their intense relief.

"What happened?"

"You wouldn't wake up," Rafe said. "Lazy just like Winter." But for all his playful words, even Rafe looked exhausted.

"I remember the drinking part, but that stopped just a minute or two ago. I couldn't have been asleep that long."

Marcus touched his cheek, a slight tremble to his fingertips. "Ethan, that was an hour ago. We've been trying to wake you for an hour. You scared me to death."

Ethan lunged at Marcus, wrapping his arms around him tightly. "I'm so sorry. I never meant to scare you."

Marcus held him tightly. "I know, my heart. I know. It's just how it goes sometimes. I have you now. Forever."

Ethan was about to ask him if it had worked, but the most wonderful smell hit his nose. Turning his face into Marcus's neck, Ethan nuzzled him more, trying to get closer to that amazing aroma. He moaned loudly and he didn't care if the others laughed at him.

"You smell amazing," he moaned again. "How have I never noticed that you smell so good?"

"Awww...the baby is hungry," Rafe said, but Ethan couldn't lift his face long enough from Marcus's neck to make a snarky reply.

"Feeding time," Winter chimed in.

Marcus gently lifted Ethan out of his lap and smiled at him. He opened his mouth to say something, but Ethan interrupted him with a cry of pain. There was an intense ripping in his mouth. Ethan cried out again as the pain increased for a second and then faded to a dull ache in his teeth.

"There they are." Bel sounded quite satisfied.

"What?" Ethan asked, looking over at Marcus.

His lover smiled. "Your fangs."

The realization hit suddenly, knocking the air from his lungs. It wasn't just the fangs or the fear that Ethan had come so close to death. It was what had started all this in the first place. The transformation. The rebirth.

He was a vampire.

"It worked," Ethan said, though the statement could have easily been taken as a question.

"Yes."

Ethan shoved off the couch and took a few drunk, stumbling steps before he finally got his balance. He ran to the mirror hanging on the wall. His reflection looked the same, though his hair was sticking up in every direction, and there was a definite red smear around his mouth. He still looked like Ethan Cline, occasional college student.

But then he parted his lips and there were a pair of perfect fangs curved down into a frighteningly sharp point.

"Holy fuck," he breathed. "I'm a vampire."

"My very sexy vampire," Marcus said. Ethan shifted his gaze to find his lover standing behind him, a slightly worried look in his eyes as he watched Ethan.

"Thank you, Marcus. Thank you for this," Ethan whispered. He understood now the risk that Marcus had taken in changing him, and he admired his lover all the more. The gift he'd given Ethan was immense.

"Anything for you."

Ethan turned and hugged Marcus tightly again, but the hug was brief. He shoved out of Marcus's arms, giving a somewhat unsteady chuckle. "You also smell really amazing, and I keep thinking about biting you."

Rafe clapped his hands together and jumped up from his seat. "Well then, let's get this baby fed. I know just the place to try out his new teeth."

Ethan winked at Marcus before turning his attention back to Rafe. "All right old man, let's go do this."

His new brothers laughed, and Ethan felt at peace. He was home.

He was a Varik.

EPILOGUE

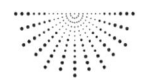

*E*than stopped on his walk up to Marcus's house—well, their house—after their night out with Rafe. Yes, Marcus had made it very clear between the hunting lessons that it was *their* house now. And their money. And their pianos, though Ethan had no desire to learn how to play. He was content to listen to Marcus play.

They had a lot of very long discussions ahead of them about jobs and duties and how Ethan was not going to simply be a mooch for the rest of eternity. But that was the thing; they had plenty of time to discuss things and figure them out. Time stretched out in one long, unending ribbon unfurling out before them.

Instead of the thought being overwhelming and daunting, it was exhilarating. There was no need to feel like every decision was make or break. He could try learning how to paint, and after a hundred years, if he was bored with it, he could spend another hundred years learning how to be a sculptor or wood-carver or a fashion designer or a computer coder. There was finally enough time for everything.

But most of all, there was finally enough time for him and Marcus.

Speaking of, his man leaned against the tree behind Ethan and placed his hand on Ethan's stomach. Rafe had taken them to a nightclub filled with humans. It was noisy and crowded, but the darkness allowed them to more easily conceal their feeding. All four brothers had taken time to show Ethan tricks for hunting, luring, and feeding. He hadn't expected it to be such a bonding experience, but he definitely felt closer to Rafe, Bel, and Winter now.

That wasn't to say that he wasn't looking forward to hunting with Marcus alone. The hunting felt awkward and made him nervous, but the feeding was thrilling. Thrilling enough that Ethan might have dragged Marcus into a bathroom stall for a quick blowjob....Well, once he learned how to retract his damn fangs.

So many things to learn.

It was a little frustrating, but Ethan took a deep breath and reminded himself that there was plenty of time.

The eastern sky was turning lighter now. The velvety black of night was starting to give way to a paler slate gray. There were the barest hints of orange and yellow. The sun was rising. They would have to go inside very soon, protected by the tinted glass and thick curtains.

"I'm sorry," Marcus murmured.

"For?" Ethan asked, though he knew what Marcus was thinking.

"The price we have to pay. No more sunlight."

Ethan turned his head to look at Marcus over his shoulder, his smile clear on his face. "If I have to choose between forever with you and never seeing the sun, it's no contest." Ethan raised his right hand and lifted his middle finger toward the horizon. "Fuck the sun. You win every time. No regrets. No hesitation."

Marcus chuckled. "You'll miss it."

Ethan's hand flopped back down to his side. "So I'll miss it. Big deal. We adapt." Ethan turned so that he was now facing Marcus. "You know what I won't adapt to? Not having you."

"I love you, Ethan Varik," Marcus said, and Ethan couldn't help preening at the name. He wasn't sure if they'd ever do anything as formal as a wedding or even file paperwork. Did vampires have paperwork?

Fuck it.

Didn't matter.

He belonged to Marcus. Marcus knew it. Ethan knew it. His brothers knew it. That was all that mattered.

"I love you, Marcus Varik."

"How would you like to conclude your first night as a vampire?"

Ethan's smile spread as he stepped into Marcus, sliding his arms up around his neck. "I was thinking we could conduct another experiment."

"Do I need to call Bel for assistance?" Marcus teased.

Ethan gave a little shudder. "Definitely not."

"Then what kind of experiment would you like to run?"

"A comparison. I already know what it's like to have an orgasm with you as a human. Now I want to know what it's like as a vampire. Is it different? The same?"

Marcus hummed as he bent down and pressed a kiss to Ethan's jaw. "Those are some very important questions."

"And it might take several tries." Ethan tilted his head up, offering his neck to Marcus. "Need to collect lots of data." Ethan finished the sentence on a groan as Marcus nipped at his neck before moving to his earlobe.

"I am at your service...for the rest of our lives."

Between their plans to take down the Ministry, establish new alliances, and the centuries of love they had ahead of them, Ethan was ready.

Grabbing Marcus's hand, he started dragging his lover

toward the house. Marcus's low chuckle danced on the late-summer breeze.

Fuck the sun. He had Marcus.

AUTHOR'S NOTE

Thank you so much for reading *Claiming Marcus* and taking the time to meet the Variks. They're an interesting clan and they've got many more adventures ahead of them. I'm taking a short break to work on the final Unbreakable Bonds book with Rinda Elliott, which should be out in late 2019, as well as a couple of smaller projects. Then I'll be returning to the Variks to write Rafe's book. With any luck, Rafe's book will be out in February 2020.

If you've enjoyed this story and want to keep up with all my books, please sign up for my newsletter at https://jocelynndrake.com/newsletter/.

Happy reading!
Jocelynn Drake

ABOUT THE AUTHOR

It started with a battered notebook. Jocelynn Drake wrote her first story when she was 12 years old. It was a retelling of Robin Hood that now included a kickass female who could keep up with all the boys and be more than just a sad little love interest. From there, she explored space, talked to dragons, and fell in love again and again and again.

This former Kentucky girl has moved up, down, and across the US with her patient husband. They've settled near the Rockies…for now. She spends the majority of her time lost in the strong embrace of a good book.

When she's not hammering away at her keyboard or curled up with a book, she can usually be found cuddling with her cat Demona, walking her dog Ace, or flinging curses at the TV while playing a video game. Outside of books, furry babies, and video games, she is completely enamored of Bruce Wayne, Ezio Auditore, travel, tattoos, explosions, and fast cars.

She is the author of the urban fantasy series: The Dark Days series and the Asylum Tales. She is also working on a gay romantic suspense series called The Exit Strategy. She has also co-authored with Rinda Elliot the following series: Unbreakable Bonds, Ward Security, and Pineapple Grove. She can be found at JocelynnDrake.com.

ALSO BY JOCELYNN DRAKE

Exit Strategy

Deadly Lover

Lover Calling (a novella)

Vengeful Lover

Final Lover

Ice and Snow Christmas

Walking on Thin Ice

Ice, Snow, & Mistletoe

Snowball's Chance

The Dark Days Series

Bound to Me

The Dead, the Damned and the Forgotten

Nightwalker

Dayhunter

Dawnbreaker

Pray for Dawn

Wait for Dusk

Burn the Night

The Lost Nights Series

Stefan

The Asylum Tales

The Asylum Interviews: Bronx

The Asylum Interviews: Trixie

Angel's Ink

Dead Man's Deal

Demon's Vengeance

By Jocelynn Drake and Rinda Elliott

The Unbreakable Bonds Series

Shiver

Shatter

Torch

Devour

Blaze

Fracture

Ignite

Unbreakable Bonds Short Story Collection

Unbreakable Stories: Lucas

Unbreakable Stories: Snow

Unbreakable Stories: Rowe

Unbreakable Stories: Ian

Ward Security

Psycho Romeo

Dantès Unglued

Deadly Dorian

Jackson (a novella)

Sadistic Sherlock

King of Romance (short story collection)

Killer Bond

Pineapple Grove

Something About Jace

Drew & Mr. Grumpy

All for Wesley

Made in the USA
San Bernardino, CA
30 November 2019